Strange Supes
Odessa Black Book One

Gray Holborn

Cover by Maialen Alonso http://maialenalonso.es/

ISBN: 9781719817585

For my mom, my definition of strength.

ONE

I tipped the pitcher of water over Zeek's head, the cold bath doing nothing to combat the scent of whiskey oozing from his pores.

"What the hell, Odessa?" He stood up, flicked a few ice chips off his shoulder like they were a bad case of dandruff, and proceeded to wring the water from his baggy clothes onto the floor.

I set the empty pitcher down and resumed my efforts at clearing the tables, not bothering to look at him. While he frequently made lewd comments after downing a few fingers of amber liquor, today he took it a step further and grabbed my ass while I was bent over wiping a table. What was it about bars and alcohol that made guys think it was okay to grope any girl within reach?

"You know the rules, Zeek. Being drunk does not get you a free pass on harassment. If you have a problem with it, go talk to Sam. Otherwise sit your ass down, finish your meal, and be on with your night—somewhere else preferably." I paused briefly, my mouth tightening into a parody of a smile. "Unless of course you'd rather I kick you out now and have you banned from coming back to your favorite watering hole?"

He blanched at the threat. To a drunk asshole, nothing was more terrifying than the thought of taking away his steady stream of cheap booze. And in a city like Seattle, cheap alcohol was rare—unicorn-levels of rare. And Zeek was nothing if not an eager regular at The Tavern. He just also happened to be a complete asshat.

"You know very well I can't complain to Sam," he mumbled, shoving a forkful of potatoes into his mouth. I tried not to gag at the

1

way spittle settled into the corners of his mouth while he ate.

I walked back around the bar, refilling the pitcher before setting it down in front of him, just in case he needed a not-so-friendly reminder to behave. Sending him a warning glare, I smiled to myself, imagining what it would be like if he did complain to Sam.

Technically, Sam was my uncle. But he was only ten years older than me and acted a lot more like the protective older brother I never wanted but still loved. There was no chance he would take Zeek's word over mine. In fact, the asshat got lucky. If Sam had witnessed the grope, Zeek would probably have a black eye right now. Maybe two.

We were slow, so I pulled an almost-empty bottle of cheap vodka off the shelf and tried repeating some of the fancy maneuvers Luis was always dazzling the customers with. I was getting better, but where Luis made the tossing-bottles-behind-his-back thing look impressive, I mostly just looked like I was failing out of clown college.

Zeek and I both cringed as the bottle fell on the bar top, soaking us both in the last dregs of vodka.

He smiled at me, and I stared in morbid fascination as strings of milky spit morphed around his words. "I hope you don't think you're getting a tip tonight."

I narrowed my eyes, hating Luis for running late. I didn't usually have to cover the bar, so Zeek wasn't usually my problem. He wasn't exactly setting the mood for a good shift.

Sam walked out of the back room, a small broom and dustpan in his hands. As soon as his shape was discernible, there was an audible sigh from the girls propped up at the other end of the bar, drinking their flamingo-pink cosmos. They were part of Sam's usual fan club hoping to get lucky enough to hitch a ride back to his place. Well, our place since I lived with him. It wasn't always the same girls, but they looked and acted enough alike that they were interchangeable as far as I was concerned. Maybe it was because he was family, but I didn't really get the fascination.

The guy was thirty-one years old and wore the same three dirty band t-shirts over and over again on a predictable rotation with a pair of dark jeans that I was fairly certain he almost never washed. And his shoulder-length black hair was in desperate need of a good brushing. He kind of looked like he should be fronting some nineties grunge band. Of course, the golden hue of his aura gave him a slightly ethereal look, but it wasn't like the chicks at the bar could see his energy—no one could, except for me, so there was no way that was adding to his appeal. Still, I couldn't really complain about his popularity with the female population. I'm pretty sure that most of the bar's revenue was pulled in from women trying to catch his attention for more than thirty seconds. Very few of them ever succeeded.

"Dess, I heard the shatter all the way in the back. If you want to practice tossing bottles around like a lunatic, do it when we don't have customers please," Sam whispered, his dark eyes narrowing at Zeek's laughter. "And Luis called, he'll be here in five."

"Thank the gods." I let out a huge breath. Luis's job was way more difficult than I gave him credit for. Those cosmos the barbies were drinking? Pretty sure I forgot to add in the vodka. There was a reason Luis was behind the bar and I was out jotting orders down on the floor. Not that I'd ever admit it to him. The guy's ego didn't need any more inflating.

"You're telling me. It's a miracle you haven't burned this place down yet," he muttered, more to himself than to me, but I caught the smile in his voice. Sam's dark almond-shaped eyes scanned Zeek's wet hair and clothes. "Zeek, why do you look so guilty?"

"Hey, don't look at me like that," he stuttered, "talk to your niece. I could've been cut by one of those shards. You should've seen her whipping that bottle around at me. In fact," he puffed out his chest, "you'll be lucky if I don't sue."

Sam raised a dark brow, his expression more amused than afraid. "I doubt it'll come to that." Sam turned to me with a quick wink, the corners of his mouth turning up ever so slightly as he focused his gaze back on Zeek's face. "Time to pay your bill. Then go home."

Instantly, Zeek's expression melted into an almost dazed smile. Sam was a persuasion-manipulator, and I bit back a grin when I recognized the usual signs. Generally, he could only manipulate humans and they had to be weak-willed, distracted, or inebriated. Zeek fit the bill for all three. Sam didn't use his ability out in the open very often. For the most part, the existence of energy users was kept secret from humans and it was in everyone's best interest to keep it that way. I didn't think many people would take kindly to being worked over by a supe. And we needed humans to keep spending money at the bar, not boycotting it. I enjoyed not having to pay rent at Sam's place. Luckily, Zeek was a bit of an idiot, so Sam could get away with the whole compulsion thing. And hey, at least he was using his powers for good.

Still, while I was happy for Sam to come to the rescue, I was always a little bit jealous when he used his energy manipulation. Mostly because I didn't inherit it. While he could literally do light mind control, all I could do was recognize the soft gold glow surrounding him and other energy users—a glow that no one else seemed capable of seeing. And after living with Sam for the last six years, I barely even recognized his glow anymore. So I was stuck with a pseudo ability, while Sam was practically a franchise deal away from joining the Avengers.

Without another word, Sam walked to the other side of the bar to serve the girls another round and likely earn himself a fat tip.

Zeek drew my attention away from the glass I was cleaning by waving a twenty at me. "Thanks for the great service, Odessa. I'll see you tomorrow."

Generally, Zeek would only utter a sentence like that if it were laced with irony and the hard slur of Jim Beam, so I knew this was all Sam's doing. Not to mention that the only 'tips' he typically left were loud asides to the female staff encouraging them to wear push-up bras or no bras at all.

He handed me the bill—and lo and behold, there were two—then turned to leave, swaying drunkenly as he made his way to the door. Sam knew I was saving up for a new laptop. I caught his eye and he winked at me without breaking stride as he walked into the backroom on his cell. Did I mention Sam was the best?

After pocketing the twenties, I looked up to find Luis crossing paths with Zeek at the door's threshold. His face pulled in confusion, taking in Zeek's drenched appearance and unusually chipper attitude.

"Odie, so sorry I'm late. Traffic was a bitch." Luis looked at me with his shit-eating grin, knowing full well how much I hated that nickname. There was so much you could do with Odessa: Dessa, Dess, hell even D didn't make me want to hit someone. Odie was what you named a dog, the breeds with smashed in faces and breathing problems.

He hopped over the counter out of breath. Luis was a pretty big guy, so I was always a little bit surprised by how graceful and agile he was—and a lot bit jealous. He smiled and rolled his eyes when he saw the trashcan full of glass. "Why am I not surprised, and why do I have the feeling that had something to do with why Zeek looked like he just got back from a pool party? You're so lucky Sam is your uncle." He laughed and nudged my shoulder, his left dimple on full display. Dark brown hair fell into his face while he helped me clean the last few glasses in the sink.

"Don't I know it." I fiddled with the black pendant on my necklace, a permanent fixture in my wardrobe, before tucking it into my shirt and smiling at him. "Now that you're here to rescue Odessa-the-damsel from the onslaught of killer vodka bottles, I'm going to prep for dinner." I hopped onto the counter, trying to gracefully reproduce his entrance. Somewhere along the way I went wrong though, because two seconds later I was sliding around in the puddle left by Zeek. Karma was a bitch. I ignored Luis's laughter as I walked towards the kitchen, perfectly content to pretend that I'd nailed it.

Four hours later the dinner rush was over, so I was finished with the worst of my shift and finally able to breathe. We were even more slammed than usual and I was kicking Sam for telling Ellie she didn't need to come in tonight. I was too bad at this job to run the floor by myself. Luis was right, if anyone other than Sam owned this place, I would've been out of the job on day one.

I was picking up mashed french fries that were caked into the threading of the carpet (seriously, why didn't parents clean up after their kids?) when the back of my neck started to tingle like someone was staring at me. I turned around and noticed a new customer across the room in the back booth. He must've seated himself, because I didn't hear anyone come in. I could tell from my semi-crouched spot on the floor that he was a supernatural, and from the looks of him, he was a powerful one. Sam's glow seemed dim compared to his—then again, that might be because I was so used to being around his energy that I no longer really noticed it.

His eyes scanned the bar in barely disguised disgust, while I made my way over to take his order. His light blond hair was swept back, revealing eyes that were an unusual mixture of light and dark shades of gray. Something about his rigid posture and unreadable expression made me feel like a mouse in a lion's cage. I suddenly felt self-conscious that my fingers were crusted over with potato mush.

My eyes traveled to the long silvery-white scar running through the tip of his eyebrow when he cleared his throat. I jumped—how long had I been staring?

"Hi. I'm Odessa and I'll be your server tonight, can I get you started with something to drink? Our seasonal draft list is written above the bar if you're interested." Did that always sound so contrived? I tugged nervously on my black shirt and took a deep breath in and out. I wasn't a shy person, but something about seeing someone new with the glow always made me nervous. It didn't happen every day. Hell, it barely happened once a year. Not to mention the fact that all supes seemed to be preternaturally beautiful too, only adding to the anxiety. And it definitely added to the anxiety since, according to Ellie, a supernatural's good looks were nothing more than the tools of a predator. But knowing that didn't stop the butterflies from pounding around in my stomach with a healthy layer of fear.

"I'll take a Jack, neat, and a glass of water." He barely acknowledged my presence as his eyes kept sweeping the bar looking for something. If his perfectly tailored clothes didn't make it clear this wasn't his usual haunt, the curl of his lip did. I turned around and scanned the bar, trying to filter the scene through the supe's pompous eyes. I looked from Sam's grungy Cobain-wannabe look, to the plain bartop that was badly in need of sanding and a fresh coat of paint, to the motley crew of drunk locals and loners that were barely a step above Zeek. My cheeks colored slightly, noticing the mismatched stools, tables, and paint-chipped walls. The Tavern work crew ragged on Sam's love of all things eclectic and dilapidated, and complained discreetly about the rude and often miserly regulars. We earned the right to though, The Tavern was ours.

I swallowed my sudden need to stand up for Sam's bar and kick the pompous ass out—both for making me feel uncomfortable and for judging my second home. "Sure, that'll be right up." I left awkwardly, my limbs tense, and walked over to Luis to get the drink order.

He grabbed a glass and glanced over at the guy in the booth, a small frown tugging down the corner of his mouth. "So what are you and Ellie up to tonight?"

I watched as he flipped the bottle of whiskey behind his back to the appreciation and adoration of a few girls seated in front of him—the crowd at the bar was heavy this time of night. Luis wasn't a supernatural, but I couldn't help but think his coordination was some type of magic. You'd think after six years of friendship, some of that would rub off on me. It didn't.

"Promised El I'd finally go back to that club she's so fond of. I kind of owe it to her since last night I got my way with old movies and beer—" I paused and the air between us filled with awkward silence. Was I supposed to invite him? "You know, girl's night," I added, chewing my bottom lip while he poured the drink without once removing his gaze from my eyes. The trace of amusement that quirked his eyebrow was my only clue that he knew I was uncomfortable and that he was enjoying it. Sadist.

He handed me the glass of Jack and cleared his throat. "Well maybe tomorrow night we can all get pizza or something? Catch a movie or maybe shoot some pool? It's been a while."

He broke the intense eye contact and I let out a quick breath of relief. I smiled and nodded, grabbing the glass from him after I filled up another one with water.

After I set the glasses down on the table, Gray Eyes spared me a quick glance, but no 'thank you.'

"Do you know what you want to order yet?" My words were clipped, terse, but he didn't seem to notice or care.

"Yeah, just bring me a steak I guess. Rare."

I stared at him for a moment, trying to calm the jolt of unease running through my body. Standing this close to him, I could practically feel his energy aura. This guy was powerful, I just couldn't tell if it was in a good way or not. Was he a Glenda or a Wicked Witch of the West? Either way, he had me on edge—part of me wanted to punch him and a much smaller—in fact practically miniscule—part of me wanted to impress him. "Okay. What do you want as your side? We can do salad, fries, or the vegetable of the day. Today it's peas." Peas? There's a way to grab a guy's attention. There's nothing sexy about peas. "They're uh, frozen."

He glanced at the menu briefly, a look of disinterest clear on his face. "Just bring it with some bacon if that's possible."

I started to laugh but bit back my smile after catching the flash of annoyance in his eyes. "Right, steak. With a side of a bacon. Coming

7

right up."

I took his menu and dropped the ticket off for Reggie, our cook.

Since I only had one customer, I started on some side work in the back, hoping I could head out early if I finished soon. And 'soon' was my word of the night. The sooner Ellie and I made it to the club, the sooner we could go home and crash. I was beat. Sam walked by to help me fill up the salt and pepper shakers.

"Sam, did you see that guy in the back booth?"

"Pretentious one that doesn't seem capable of anything but a glare? Yeah, why?"

"He's a supe," I whispered, conscious of the fact that a very human Reggie was only a few feet away. "Golden glow. But it's super bright. Do you know him?"

Sam shook his head.

"Oh, I figured maybe he was looking for you. This doesn't seem like his usual haunt." When my head turned to Sam, my hand went with it knocking the salt to the floor. My nerves were on overdrive tonight. "Damn it. Sorry, I'll clean that up, hold on."

When I turned back, Sam was frowning. "Never seen him, but something about him looks familiar. Maybe he's been here before? Guy looks like he's got a stick up his ass though—don't go out of your way to piss him off Dess. Keep a low profile." He looked up and nodded to the kitchen. "Looks like Reg has your order up. Once your guy cashes out, you can go home. Just text me so I know you got back safely. And you and Ellie be careful tonight." Sam liked to pretend that he was more like my best friend than my uncle-turned-guardian, but the guy worried like a mother hen.

"Thanks." I grabbed the hot plate and made my way back to the front, but not before I straightened my shirt and made sure there was no lipstick on my teeth. I didn't want to give the carnivore any other reason to look down on me or The Tavern.

He glanced at me quickly when I brought his food out. "Actually, I decided I'd rather take it home and eat. Can you just box it up and give me the check?" His eyes moved lower and the look of indifference turned into an icy glare when they reached my chest. I could feel the anger radiating off of him, so much so that his nostrils visibly flared as he clutched his steak knife with just a little bit too much fervor for my liking.

Annoyed and confused, I looked down, feeling my cheeks warm

with embarrassment while my pulse hammered out a tense beat. There was no obvious stain on my shirt. And my boobs? They weren't exactly anything to write home about but still, they usually solicited a different reaction from the opposite sex. And they'd certainly never left someone looking like they wanted to bury steel in my neck.

I stayed in the back while the guy packaged up his own food. By the time I resurfaced, steaming with a mentally-practiced diatribe on rudeness armed and ready, he was gone. And he didn't even leave a tip. My eyes followed the back-and-forth wobble of the unused steak knife, the tip burrowed into the table of my favorite booth. The now-empty plate was cracked into multiple serrated pieces.

TWO

I started the short walk home, sticking to the well-lit side of the street. Seattle was a bike-friendly city but with the way people drove around town, and with my coordination luck (or lack thereof), bicycles started to look a lot like little metal deathtraps. Sam didn't like me walking home alone after sunset, but there was something about wandering around our neighborhood at night I couldn't help but love. We were close to the city but far enough away to have a decent view of the skyline from the right altitude. And then there were back streets covered with trees, views of a lake, and the backdrop of a mountain, giving off the illusion that we weren't in a major city at all. It was the best of both worlds.

"Hey pretty lady, looking for a good time?"

Normally, those were the last words a girl wanted to hear while walking home alone at night, but when they came from the mouth of a 5'2" girl with a blond and pink bob and doll-like blue eyes, the intimidation factor dropped down a notch or two.

"Hey El." I grinned as she pulled up next to me, her short outstretched arm was hanging out the window of her ridiculous hot pink convertible, dangling a large cup.

"I brought you some coffee. I know going to Inferno tonight wasn't your top choice. Especially after a long shift. Hopefully this will help make up for it?" I had a certified addiction to caffeine, as El was well aware. She also knew that I didn't say no to coffee. Ever. Her lips bent into a frowning pout as she batted her lashes at me.

I chuckled. "I'm not your boyfriend, or your girlfriend, or your father El—that face does nothing for me. Except make me laugh at how ridiculous it makes you look."

Her face contorted into an even more exaggerated frown. Ellie was twenty-three, two years older than me, but her large doe-eyes and tiny frame made her look like she was still in high school. The innocent look was made hilarious by the fact that she was a body-manipulator who could shift into a ferocious black panther.

I rolled my eyes before giving up and hopping in the passenger seat. "Fine, fine, I accept your coffee with a side of groveling. To hell we go." Truthfully, I didn't mind going out, as Ellie was well aware. The club scene wasn't normally my thing, but sometimes it was nice to let off some steam with a girls' night out. Especially when my nerves were all jumbled from the mystery supe. I took a sip of coffee before I studied her from the side of my eye. "By the way, I saw a supe at The Tavern tonight. He was kind of an asshole though—" I paused a beat, savoring the taste of late-night caffeine. "Actually, not kind of. Definitely an asshole."

"More of them are assholes than not, so I'm not surprised." Ellie's brows turned down while she drove. She was silent for a while, to the point I wasn't sure she'd say anything more. "What kind, feeder or manipulator?"

Energy users could either feed off of other's energy or manipulate energy in a very specific way. For the most part it was genetic. Since I didn't inherit Sam's persuasion-manipulation and could somehow see energy signatures, I was a bit of an anomaly.

"Golden glow, so I'm assuming manipulator. He seemed really powerful though. Like the most intense aura I've seen. Then again, it could just be relative. Yours and Sam's glows have all but become invisible to me."

"That's odd." She glanced over to me briefly before pulling into our driveway. "And Sam didn't recognize him?" I shook my head. I wasn't surprised though; as far as I was aware, Ellie was the only supe Sam knew. "And he didn't seem interested in you or anything, right? You didn't mention anything about your ability to sense supes?"

I rolled my eyes. "Yes, obviously the first thing I did was tell the rude stranger that I could identify the silver and gold glows of feeders and manipulators." El had only been telling me since the day I met her to keep my ability to myself. No one outside of her and Sam had any idea. Not that I got what the big deal was. Sam's mind-manipulation seemed way more threatening than letting someone know they lit up like Tinkerbell. And Ellie could literally tear someone apart with her bare paws if she wanted to.

"Well, just keep an eye out. If you see him around again, try and get someone else to take your table." Unlike Sam, El grew up on the other side of the Veil so she knew more about supes than she let on. Still, she avoided them like the plague. Well, except for Sam—and even then, it took her a long while to warm up to him and a full three years before she agreed to move in with us. She refused to talk about her past, and denied her aversion to supes anytime I brought it up. I had a feeling she had a bad experience with a seduction-feeder or something—they had a habit of breaking hearts. It was the only topic off the table. And I mean only. The girl could wax lyrical about her bodily fluids like no one I'd ever met, but the second someone brought up supes, she turned mute.

We ran inside for a quick change. If I had it my way, I'd happily spend life in combat boots, jeans, and oversized sweaters. And I was lucky that in Seattle hobo chic was appreciated. But on nights we went out, El put her foot down to some extent.

At least she didn't make me think about it too much. When I walked into my room, she had an outfit already laid out for me: dark pants, a stylish black tank top, and a pair of ankle boots. It was an updated version of my usual style. Simple and comfortable. Especially compared to her dark blue dress and pink stilettos. She'd tried to force me into a pair of those years ago, but gave up. Apparently it wasn't worth my whining. I flipped my necklace onto the outside of my top and she winked at me before flashing her matching black ring. It was the sister to the pendant she'd given me years ago. Who said people outgrow friendship bracelets?

Half an hour later our Lyft pulled up to Inferno and we made the usual run from the car to the line, trying to expose ourselves to the cold air as little as possible. There was a line circling around the building, but El had a way with bouncers. She didn't even need to say anything. She just gave the guy one of her patented stares, mixed with a cheeky grin and wink. Every time I was certain it wouldn't work and every time I was wrong. This was no exception.

Muscles McGee smiled and opened the door, eyes only for El and the deep V of her dress. Who needed persuasion-manipulation when you had boobs? I looked back, smirking at the guy who clearly thought he stood a chance with her—

And then I missed the doorway and banged my head into the window next to it.

The voices that had started to angrily protest El's ability to cut the line quickly morphed into laughter. At least I saved Muscles from having to deal with a tense crowd after we left. That's right, totally did that on purpose. Always the philanthropist.

El stood in front of me, propping herself up with one hand on the wall as she crumbled with laughter. "You left a makeup imprint of your forehead on the window, Dess." Tears swam in her eyes, making them look even bigger than usual.

I rubbed away the milky-brown foundation smudge, begging my body to stop blushing while silently promising myself to go easier on the face makeup next time. Or to at least to pay attention to where I was walking. Turning, I bowed to Muscles McGee and the crowd, then grabbed El's arm and walked through the doorway.

The club was packed. The open-concept room had an industrial-chic vibe to it with exposed beams and natural wood mixed with expensive marbling and metals. It was a sophisticated, more stylized version of The Tavern, slightly better suited for big-city nightlife and Seattle's yuppie population. Where Sam's place often looked like it was falling apart and lived in, Inferno intentionally integrated grunge into its aesthetic. An elevated platform was in the center of the dance floor. During weeknights it was usually used for local bands, but tonight there was a tattooed DJ with blue hair rocking out. His movements were erratic, but he somehow hit every beat with precision. Ellie pulled me across the floor (she was deceptively strong) and managed to weasel her way to the bar. She threw on her classic smile and I counted the seconds until the busty, tattooed bartender made her way over. El was almost always served first at the bar.

I watched as the bartender's eyes immediately swept past me and then drank in El.

"What can I get you, hun?" she asked, her face lit up by a flirtatious grin.

I bit back a laugh as I watched Ellie's blush deepen out of the corner of my eye.

El shoved me lightly, smiling sheepishly at the pretty bartender. "Two bourbons please. Neat."

"And a beer," I added.

El was on a new kick. According to her, bourbon was a classy drink, but an acquired taste. So for the last two months, it's all she would order us at bars, claiming it helped round out our sophisticated style. Personally, I wasn't exactly sure when we were going to 'acquire' the taste or what part of our style could be deemed sophisticated, tonight or any night. Bourbon still made me gag, and there was no way I could drink it gracefully without a chaser. Which I'm pretty sure cancelled out the whole sophistication thing in the first place. El was having more success with the experiment. We grabbed our drinks and made our way to a surprisingly open table; finding one in this place on a Friday night was in and of itself an amazing feat.

"So, no Michael this weekend?" She tried to infuse her voice with nonchalance, but I could feel her fishing for a status update. I'd met Michael a couple of months ago. At first, we hung out a few times just as friends, but the dynamic had been slowly evolving over the last month or so.

"He's at a conference until Sunday I think." I absentmindedly stirred my bourbon with a tiny straw, willing it to transform into almost anything else.

"Still, you've been spending an awful lot of time with him lately. Is he taking you off the market?" She winked, sipping her bourbon with a feigned appreciation.

El was all about romance and seemed to fall in love every other week. My greatest love affair was between myself and mozzarella sticks. She'd met Michael a few times and while she was supportive, I knew she didn't get what I saw in him. Most nights El fell asleep with a trashy novel opened on her bed and she shuffled through love interests quickly enough that I never bothered to learn their names. Michael was a cute med student, but if he wasn't making grand romantic gestures or fighting off a zombie apocalypse, El wasn't going to be impressed.

It didn't take long for El to get swept up by some guy, so I made my way back to the bar for a water. And that's when I saw a bright silvery glow. Was there some weird supernatural convention in town? Two in one night was insane.

He was dancing with a small group of guys and girls, and judging by the pure adoration on their faces I could tell he must be a seduction-feeder. Not that I could blame them for fawning all over him. His skin was a light brown and he had just enough of a five o'clock shadow to make him look rugged but not unkempt. Dark hair made his warm brown eyes stand out. The laughter and arrogance behind his eyes made it clear that he was aware of the effect he had on the three women gyrating around him. To be honest, he probably would have a similar effect even without the seduction-feeding. After a few moments, he caught my eye and grinned.

And if he wasn't confident already, busting me staring at him would certainly help. While I stood there blushing, trying to avoid his eye contact again, he disengaged from the group when the song ended and made his way over to me.

"Jax." He leaned casually against the bar and looked up at me through his ridiculously long lashes. I silently groaned. That was one of the many frustrating things about the world—even though men couldn't care less about them, they always seemed genetically gifted with the longest and thickest camel lashes. It was at least thirty seconds before I realized that I was staring again and hadn't responded to him.

"Sorry, what?" My voice was raspy, like a thirteen-year-old boy.

"My name. It's Jax. What's yours?" He quirked the right side of his mouth up, waiting for me to respond, mirth dancing behind his eyes.

"Odessa. But everyone usually calls me Dess or Desi. Or sometimes Black. That's my last name." Why couldn't I shut up? I knew this guy was basically an incubus, you'd think that would prepare me enough to prevent me from stumbling all over my words like an idiot. It didn't. Also, why did I think it was a good idea to give him my real name?

He started chuckling at me while I babbled, sipping his drink. "You're adorable, Desi-girl, how bout a dance?" I started to shake my head no, but he interrupted the rejection by grabbing my hand and lightly pulling me to the floor. A slight frown pulled his lips down when I resisted.

"I'm good here, but thanks." Jax was cute, but I knew how dangerous feeders were. Even if they seemed incapable of feeding from my energy, El warned me to be constantly vigilant. When I noticed a boredom-feeder in our history class two years ago, she had us drop the class almost immediately, opting for a horribly confusing physics lab instead. Which meant feeders must *really* be on the avoid-at-all-costs list. Personally, I would've been okay with some supe stealing away my boredom—or at least making an attempt—since it wasn't like he could incite any more than my history professor already induced. He seemed harmless. Jax did not.

I turned away from him, scanning the crowd for El. If she knew a supe was here, she'd want to leave ASAP. But Jax didn't let go of my hand and he used his other one to lightly shift my face in his direction. He was wearing dark jeans, a white t-shirt, and a black leather jacket. Somehow he was not sweating like crazy—was that a supernatural thing? And why did he smell so good? Like vanilla and musk. Not that I really knew what musk smelled like, but if I had to guess, it smelled like him. I could feel my heart beating faster, but out of fear, not out of the lust he was probably used to generating. His brown eyes darted to my lips and moved slowly up to my eyes, a cocky smirk spreading across his face—he was completely aware of the effect he was having on me, if not the true nature of it. Were all supernaturals this smug?

The heat in his gaze turned slowly to confusion, and then frustration—an almost constipated look taking over his face.

And that's when I started cracking up.

I used his momentary bewilderment to my advantage, pulled my hand out of his, and crossed my arms. "What's the matter big guy, not used to a little rejection?" I tried to be smooth and badass, but I knew the laughter in my voice wasn't fooling anybody.

He squared his shoulders, focusing all of his attention on me. I could feel the energy he was trying to pull from me filter around the atmosphere, but to no effect. A swarm of people were inching closer and closer to him though, eager to take my spot in the offered dance.

After a moment, he broke his concentration and his face lit up with a perfectly blinding smile. "You know what I am." It wasn't a question. He tried unsuccessfully to hide his amusement, but I could feel the laughter bubbling in his chest. "But what are you? I've never been unable to pull before."

While it was fun goading him, the smarter option would be to leave. And I didn't exactly have an answer for him anyway. The crowd of admirers had paired up and started practically mauling each other as they gyrated in beat to the music. I never understood the whole club thing. I turned around, ready to ditch Jax and earnestly look for El when I found him blocking my path again. I jumped back, startled.

And then I jumped back even more and screamed when a line of fire materialized between us. Jax's eyes lit up in what looked like a combination of fear and intrigue.

"A fire-manipulator, then?" Jax asked.

My mouth dropped open when I looked up from the fire and found Jax studying me. I wasn't doing this. Shrill screams echoed around me.

I turned to the right, following the line of flames as they climbed farther towards the ceiling, until my eyes fell on a bright golden glow emanating from a beautiful, dark-haired and caramel-skinned girl only a few feet away. Her eyes blazed as she glared in Jax's direction. I watched as the glow of embers reflected in the dark black of her eyes and highlighted the gold ring in her nose. She was dressed in a tight black spandex-like outfit. Other than the ferocious stance that set her at odds with the muffled, fearful screams of everyone around us, she fit in perfectly with the young clubbing crowd.

Three supes in one night. Not counting El and Sam, that was more than I'd come across in my whole life. All at once the fire alarm and neighboring screams defeated the blue-haired dj's static beats as water sprinkled from the ceiling. I found myself briefly hoping the water wouldn't ruin his expensive equipment when a stampede of horny twenty-somethings knocked me to the ground as they raced each other for the door.

My head snapped in the direction of a new heat source and I watched as fire engulfed the beautifully-distressed bar. This was so not the way girls' night was supposed to go. And speaking of, where the hell was El?

"Let's go Desi-girl. You might be immune to feeders, but I doubt you're immune to fire." I briefly registered Jax's hands pulling me from the ground and clearing a path for me to get to the door before his heat left my skin and he disappeared in another direction. I looked around the now almost empty club, but the dark-haired fire-manipulator was nowhere to be seen. My eyebrows pulled together briefly while I thought about how ironic it was that I couldn't thank her for saving me from the person who ultimately ended up saving me from her, and then I joined the mass of sweaty bodies until I was outside and reunited with a perfectly dry and singe-free El.

"Dess," she shoved her way past Muscles McGee, and pulled me from the crowd. "Thank gods. Are you okay?"

I could feel her heart pounding fiercely against my stomach as I hugged her back. It helped distract from the heavy ringing in my ears and the dizzying effect of adrenaline that couldn't decide whether to force my body into fight or flight. El was okay and I was okay. I focused on that while I watched as gray tears, tinted by mascara, carved abstract designs down her cheeks, briefly noticing that her hair was tousled and her lipstick smudged.

"Where have you been?" I asked.

She looked sheepishly at Muscles and shrugged, worry and guilt playing across her features.

I covered my fear with a strained laugh. "Oh El, at least this time your hormones actually kept you out of danger, rather than throwing you right in the mess of it."

"Tell me about it," her hands danced across her phone as she ordered a Lyft, "do you know how difficult it would've been to get the smell of smoke out of this fabric." She paused, pulling me with her across the street as she weaved around wide-eyed and drenched bodies.

We looked at each other and I saw my panic mirrored in her eyes. El blinked back tears and smiled. I realized instantly that we were both unsuccessfully trying to lighten the mood for each other.

She breathed in deeply, then let out a shaky breath as her fingers curled around my hand. "For real though, I'm so sorry I wasn't in there with you. When people started screaming and clawing through the door my heart about fell out of my butt. And then you *of course* had to be one of the last ones out." Her brightly-painted fingers waved to a black Subaru and I could see them trembling wildly from either adrenaline or fear or some combination of both. The car stopped and El opened the back door and nodded to the driver before turning back to me. "You're okay? You weren't burnt? Should we stop at the hospital just in case?"

I watched as her eyes combed me over. Since she was a supe, El healed very quickly. But since I wasn't, she was always terrified that I was one breath away from catching the plague or death.

I nodded, my throat clogged with adrenaline. "I'm fine El, really. Let's go home, drink some cheap wine to calm down, and then talk to Sam about this tomorrow. I just need to regroup is all."

"We should talk to him tonight, Dess. As soon as possible. You were in a fire for crying out loud."

I shook my head. "Tomorrow." I hated how shaky my voice sounded, but I knew that if Sam saw us while we were this frazzled, he'd freak out.

THREE

El and I spent the rest of the night drinking cheap wine and watching old reruns of Buffy. She'd tried multiple times to get me to talk about the fire, but I wanted nothing more than to wash the smell of ash out of my skin and process the night on my own.

Like a proper best friend, she let me. However grudgingly.

But the second I woke up the next morning, she demanded that we go talk to Sam about it.

As luck would have it, we walked out of the house at the same time Sam was locking up his basement apartment. He was heading down the driveway with a random girl I recognized from The Tavern's crew of admirers, clearly trying to ditch her without being too big of a douche about it.

"So, I had fun last night." She batted her lashes and pouted her lips. I think she was attempting to flirt, but the effect was minimized by her messy hair and the mascara streaks running down her face. I cringed, overcome with pity. I highly doubted this girl had any idea that her walk-of-shame style was less than glamorous...or that her morning seductress routine was more terrifying than tempting.

"Yeah, yeah me too. Do you want me to call you a Lyft or a cab or something?"

"That's okay, the bus stop is a block away. If you aren't busy, do you want to maybe go out again tonight or next weekend?"

"Uh, well—I mean I thought it was clear after our talk last night that this was a one-time thing? But maybe I'll see you around or talk to you later?" He scratched his chin awkwardly and caught a glance at El and me. A look of mortified embarrassment took over his face. He ran his hand through his hair and started scrubbing his face, as if that would help erase the awkwardness. It didn't.

"I mean, I know you *said* that, but we had fun didn't we? Maybe we could try for a real date next weekend? Here's my number." She slipped what looked like a business card into his front pocket, her hand remaining in the fabric of his jeans far longer than was necessary. I cringed and El was uncharacteristically quiet, a blush growing on her cheeks. We both averted our eyes until the woman turned and started walking away down the street.

"Have a little too much to drink last night, Sammy?" I asked. He usually avoided bringing customers home. Especially since he wasn't exactly a commitment type of guy. It was a lot easier to get repeat customers and tips when you lightly flirted. Not so much when you pulled the whole one-night-stand game with them.

"I hate that name. You girls heading into The Tavern for the typical Saturday brunch and homework binge?"

"Yes...care to bribe Reggie into making us some pancakes?" Ellie asked.

"Reg won't be in for kitchen prep until a little later, but if you both agree to pretend you never witnessed that whole thing, I'll make you the damn pancakes myself."

"Deal," we said in unison, giant grins on our faces.

"Why didn't you just persuade Beetlejuice to lose interest in you?" I asked.

"I don't know. Something feels fundamentally wrong about trying to manipulate a girl who's spent the night." He shrugged.

"Aw, how sweet, I always knew that grungy, rebel-without-a-cause attitude was just for show," I said, rolling my eyes. He was too much a gentleman to use his ability but totally fine with ditching the girl after hooking up with her. Men.

"This is sounding suspiciously like you don't want pancakes, Dess," he said, jogging along in front of us with a smirk.

"Shutting up now!" We caught up with him and made our way quickly to the bar.

When we got to The Tavern, El and I beelined for our typical booth in the back. The same one that the supe sat in last night. Sam went in the back to start on our brunch and put a pot of fresh coffee on.

Sam walked up, hair pulled back into a bun like a true Seattleite, strategically balancing multiple plates along his arms. Seriously? It was one thing to get cheated out of the persuasion-manipulation, but why couldn't I at least inherit good old fashioned human coordination?

"Alright, short stacks for both of you. Two orders of bacon for

El. And a bowl of fruit each, so that we can at least pretend there is some nutritional value to this meal." He shoved me over in the booth, grabbing his own cup of coffee and a piece of toast while he looked over the inventory sheets for the bar.

"We're going to grab a pizza tonight with Luis, you down?" I was already halfway through my pancakes, homework completely forgotten. Reggie was a great cook, but after six years Sam knew how to make my perfect pancake order: extra extra chocolate chips.

"Wish I could, but I'll be here all night. You guys can stop by if you get bored for a drink," he paused, glancing up at us, "speaking of, did you both have a good time last night?"

El's eyes bugged out at me while she tilted her head in Sam's direction. Right, I guess it was time to talk.

"So, um, funny story, there was actually a fire at Inferno last night—er, while I was in the club."

Sam dropped his paperwork, his complexion paling a bit. I watched as his eyes scanned us both, likely looking for injuries or burns.

"Obviously we're both fine Sam, it was just intense is all," I said, trying to placate him.

"Intense my ass, I practically had a heart attack while waiting for you outside," El added.

"But you're both okay?" Sam asked.

We nodded and after a tense moment, Sam made a dumb joke about Inferno and hellfire. The dude was only an uncle, but he had the whole dad-joke thing down to a science.

I chewed a piece of pancake, building enough courage to drop the other bomb. "So," I started, "the thing is, the fire was started by a fire-manipulator. And she wasn't the only supe in Inferno last night. I also saw a seduction-feeder."

El's fork clanked heavily against her plate while she stared at me, open-mouthed and fuming. "Why the hell didn't you mention this last night, Dess? Did anyone else notice how the fire started? Did the supes talk to you? You didn't let them know that you could see their energy did you?" She stood up and began pacing around the room. "Why are there so many in Seattle right now? You don't think the fire-manipulator was trying to hurt you, do you? No humans noticed, right? The last thing we need is for the city to be filled with a bunch of conspiracy theorists—"

21

"El, sit back down and breathe please," I said. "I really don't think anyone noticed that a person started the fire with their mind—they were all too busy trying to leave the burning club while being drenched with sprinklers. The chaos probably covered everything and the two supes didn't seem to know each other at all, so I'm sure it was just a weird territorial sort of coincidence."

Sam was unusually quiet and tense, his eyes traveling back and forth between us.

After half an hour of talking in circles, we didn't land on a solution to the incident. If humans got wind of supernaturals, our life would become insanely complicated. Ultimately, Sam decided that the best option was to just take a wait-and-see approach. We'd carry on like normal, but try to keep an even lower profile until we got more information. That meant no more persuasion-manipulation to dial down Zeek's obnoxious personality for the time being.

By the time Sam and El calmed down, the lunch crowd started filtering in, so El and I decided to leave and let Sam get to work. Zeek entered the bar just as we left and El had to choke down her laughter when he held the door, bowing to us until several greasy locks of his hair brushed the grimy floor. I guess Sam's mind addling was extra strong last night.

Over the last year, we'd made it our tradition to walk to The Tavern on Saturday mornings for breakfast and homework since Sam's place had our favorite two things: wifi and free food. But it was an uncharacteristically sunny day in Seattle, so we decided to arm ourselves with laptops and textbooks (the kind you spent a fortune on and used maybe twice during the semester), and do our work outside.

El and I were finishing our final two months at Walesh College—a small school about a fifteen minute bus ride from our place. I was double majoring in communications and sociology; El was majoring in whatever subject interested her that week. She'd been taking classes two years longer than I had and was probably halfway towards earning a degree in most of the programs Walesh offered. It was like she was trying to cram twenty different lives into her one. I was always kind of envious of her simultaneous ambition and ambivalence. Eventually, she got Sam to persuade the Dean to allow her to build her own major, picking whichever classes suited her fancy each semester—the last couple of years, she'd used that as an excuse to take as many classes with me as she could. Still, even though the end was creeping up, I didn't have any idea what I'd do after school. Most of my peers dreamt of amazing corporate or artistic careers. My most ambitious dream involved finding a diner that served all-you-can-eat grilled cheese for a reasonable price.

"Where to?" El asked. Then, with a coy look in my direction she laughed. "Never mind, stupid question. Usual spot?"

I nodded. Seattle neighborhoods were all either surrounding or surrounded by bodies of water and parks. Those scenic little spots however were also insanely packed on nice days and tended to feel as crowded as downtown during tourist season. We both loved the outdoors, but the company of other people? Not so much. So we hopped in the Barbie-mobile and took a short trip to a trail and pond that had long been abandoned. Maybe it had to do with her panther senses or something, but El had a knack for finding little pockets of isolated heaven in a city that seemed to otherwise be experiencing a population explosion.

The pond itself was small, but it was one of our favorite spots. The trail leading to it was mostly flat and opened to a small empty cabin that seemed to be abandoned, though well maintained. In all the times we wandered here, we never encountered another person. Beyond the trail and clearing around the pond, the area was surrounded by trees which gave the illusion that we were far away from the bustling city.

El walked over to the janky wooden dock and pet the ground lovingly. She did this every time we showed up and I was always impressed that she never got a splinter. Must be a supe thing. "Oh, gods of the little pond, we come bearing thanks for introducing us all these years ago." She curtsied deep and dramatic, her laughter carried gently along on the breeze.

"You should really be thanking me. For not running away and screaming when I stumbled upon a panther." We sat near the pond and pulled the novel we were reading for our English class out; since I'd already taken most of my required courses, and since El's required courses were whatever she wanted them to be, we had a little more fun with registration this semester and both landed spots in a popular class on science fiction. In other words, this was the best homework we were ever going to get.

El's hands ran through the overgrown blades of grass. "You mean I should be thanking your stupidity. What person in their right mind doesn't run screaming from a jungle predator? You were lucky I'd eaten my fill that morning."

I met El almost as soon as I moved to Seattle to live with Sam. The first few months I didn't have many friends and spent my time wandering around the city trying to process all the weird changes turning my life upside down. I'd never met another supe until I met Sam. And I didn't meet Sam until my dad dropped me off on his doorstep and left. After noticing Sam's aura, I booked an eye exam immediately. Eventually Sam realized what I was seeing and gave me a brief rundown on the Veil and supernaturals—and figuring out that a whole other world existed was quite the emotional shitshow, let me tell you. With all of that turmoil, running into a friendly panther seemed almost normal. The rest was history.

"Dess?" El asked, plucking blades of grass out of the ground. "Why didn't you mention the supes last night?"

I flipped through our syllabus for a few minutes, trying to find out how far we had to read. "Honestly, I know how you get about supes and you were already so stressed. I didn't want you spazzing out any more than you already were."

"I wasn't spazzing—" she cut off, catching my arched brow. "Okay okay, fine. I was maybe freaking out a little bit last night."

I cleared my throat.

"And also today. I was also freaking out when you mentioned the supes today. But still, promise me you won't keep things like that from me again, okay? I know I don't like talking about my past or about energy users, but I don't want you to think you can't tell me things. Deal?"

"Deal," I said.

After a few minutes of enjoying the scenery and reading silently, we decided to take advantage of our relative isolation and read the novel out loud to each other. What started off as a normal story-time quickly devolved into a contest over who could read with the most ridiculous flourish. In the middle of describing a war-torn planet Mars the bushes a few feet away started to rustle, turning my best rendition of a Shakespearean Daffy Duck into an embarrassingly girly squeal.

"El, please tell me you saw that."

"Huh? Saw what?" she was facing me, her back to the bushes, buckled over with laughter.

"The bushes moved."

"Quit your screeching. Don't be such a guy, it was probably the wind or an animal or something. Last night just has you extra paranoid." At my skeptical look, she laughed and said, "Well go check it out if it will make you feel better—the faster we get back to that weird Kermit the Frog thing you had going on, the better."

"Daffy Duck. And you're the super kitty, you go check it out. Growl at it or something," I said.

El rolled her eyes and smirked but humored me anyway, like a mother checking under the bed for monsters she knows aren't there. After a moment she shook her head to let me know she didn't see anything, but then stopped for a second to sniff the air. A look of confusion transformed her face, but disappeared just as quickly. "Well, whatever was or wasn't there is gone now. Still, we should head back anyway," she said as she walked back over to me. "It's later than I thought and now I have the heebie-jeebies. Maybe you're not the only one who's extra paranoid today. Not that I'm spazzing out or anything, to be clear. Tonight's hangout with Luis couldn't have been better timed—we both need to relax a bit—" El paused and looked up at me. "Speaking of, you're going to be okay, right? Not telling Luis what really happened last night?"

Shit. I always forgot that Luis didn't know about supes. And I was a rotten liar so I was thankful El's warning gave me enough time to master my 'it was just a freak fire, shit's crazy' explanation.

Luis met us at our favorite pizza joint, around the corner from The Tavern. He was already halfway through a pepperoni pie when we walked through the door.

"Odie, I ordered your plain cheese, it should be out soon." Luis had an ability to speak with his mouth full without being completely gross about it—a rare talent.

"Hey, what about mine?" El sat down across from him, picking off a piece of pepperoni and popping it into her mouth.

"Don't worry, double meat lovers is on the way too." He shoved her hand away before it could steal another piece. It always amazed me how much El could eat, despite being pint-sized and thin. Forget the whole werepanther thing, that was her real superpower.

"Thanks Luis, you spoil us."

"So you guys feel like catching a movie at the theater tonight or should we just watch something at your place?" Luis turned to me, giving El the perfect opportunity to grab a slice before he could protest.

"I vote theater," El said between bites. "There's nothing quite like forking over an hour's worth of pay to hear people talk and obnoxiously chew popcorn while you try and listen to the movie. True American experience, right there."

Most people would think she was being sarcastic, but Luis and I knew better. That was one of my favorite things about El. I didn't know if it had to do with being raised in the Veil or not, but she was always genuinely amused by things that drove everyone else nuts.

"Okay, wow. See you should've left off everything after 'I vote theater' because I'm pretty sure Luis and I are now firmly in the stay-at-home category."

Luis nodded while El scrunched up her nose in protest. A huge smile spread across my face as the smell of just-out-of-the-oven pizza wafted over our table. Bobby, our usual server, automatically set the cheese pie in front of me and the meat lovers in front of El. What could I say, we were creatures of habit.

El picked up a slice before Bobby returned with plates. "You beautiful man, you. I think I'm in love." His lip twitched revealing his dimples, the color in his cheeks reddening a bit. He'd been crushing on El for as long as I could remember, but she was completely oblivious. Bobby was in his late twenties and always wore his long blond hair in a low ponytail. His arms were covered in tattoos, and if it weren't for the layer of grease that always coated him from the kitchen, he could pass as a grungy model or a rockstar. "Fine, fair enough. Are we going with chick flick or horror film tonight?"

"Horror film, obviously," Luis said.

El and I looked at each other and smirked. Luis liked to pretend he hated romances, but the dude got sucked into the Hallmark Channel just as quickly as we did.

"Chick flick it is," El beamed.

"Fine." He rolled his eyes, stretched back in his chair and looked up at the ceiling. "The things I do for friendship."

"What time does Michael get home tomorrow?" El was pulling pieces of pepperoni off of Luis's untouched pizza and adding them to her own heaping slice.

"Good question, I'm not sure."

We boxed up the remaining pizza and El got up to pay. Luis and I grinned from the booth, watching Bobby's cheeks flush pink while El obliviously chattered on, and then we followed her out the door.

Luis fidgeted, pulling down on his sleeves and avoiding eye contact. "Am I gonna get to meet the mystery boy anytime soon or are you just going to keep him all to yourself? Wedding invitation at the very least?"

I laughed nervously. "Yeah of course, so long as you promise to behave yourself." He put a hand to his chest in mock outrage. "That means no embarrassing stories or obscene threats to his manhood," I added.

"Odie, if a guy can't handle one of your best friends making a few threats, he's not worthy. And I would never threaten another dude's junk—that's a total violation of guy code. His life, on the other hand—if he hurt you—now that I would threaten without losing sleep."

Leave it to your friends to give you warm fuzzy feelings by threatening murder. Having Luis and El for friends was more intimidating than having a football team of older brothers.

"Let's stop at the corner store on the way back and grab some snacks for the movie," El said, nodding her head sharply, as if her own approval was all she needed. She then proceeded to walk along the curb as if it were a balance beam. Did I mention she was wearing heels?

Luis ducked his head by my ear, his voice a feigned whisper, "we did just watch her eat almost a whole large pizza by herself, right? Like, I wasn't seeing things, was I?"

I smiled and opened my mouth to reply when I saw a brief flash of a figure turning down the neighboring side street. It was too fast to get a good look, but the golden glow emanating from him, or it, had my heart racing plenty fast.

"That's it Luis, tomorrow we are having a girls' night and you aren't invited. I'll not be mocked or shamed for my love affair with food." El looked back playfully before disappearing into the corner store.

"You coming, Odie?" Luis held the door open.

I nodded and followed him in.

Fifteen minutes, two bags of junk food, and a six pack of beer later and we were home. El shuffled through her bag, trying to find her set of house keys. "Do you have yours on you, Dess? It's like looking for Waldo in here. Except finding my keys is much more difficult. Maybe I need a bigger bag."

"That bag weighs almost as much as you, maybe you just need to clean it out." Pushing her to the side, I opened the door and bowed dramatically. "After you my lady."

Laughing, she walked in, tossed her purse on the ground, and turned on the light. I was in the process of pulling off my shoes, a balancing trick that had me leaning against the wall, while Luis waited patiently outside carrying our haul. I fell forward slightly, slamming into El who was turned to stone. "Dude, move so I can get into the house too. You know, for such a tiny person, you really know how to capitalize on space."

"What are you doing here?" Her tone had gone flat, defensive.

"What do you mean what am I doing here, I live here. What's up with—" I looked up over her shoulder and saw the seduction-feeder from the club sitting at our kitchen table, a giant smile plastered on his face. He looked just as beautiful and lethal as he did last night. Behind him, leaning against the wall with a dark expression was the powerful, gray-eyed supe I waited on at The Tavern.

His cold eyes briefly met mine before focusing back on El. "Nice to see you too, little sis."

FOUR

"Sis? El, what the hell's going on?" I asked. She hadn't moved or made a sound since originally spotting the two supes. I looked back at them, afraid they broke her. El was never silent. "Who are you people and what the fuck are you doing in our house?"

"Aw, come on, are you telling me you didn't miss me, Desi-girl? Have to say though that I did not expect to find you living with Elliana." Jax winked and a giant grin spread across his face, his brown eyes laughing at me. "Not that I'm disappointed. In fact, for the record, this totally qualifies as a good surprise. And who's this handsome dish behind you?" Jax smiled at Luis and I felt him tense slightly at my back.

While that only earned an impatient exhale from Jax's light-haired companion, it got El's attention. She turned to me and tried to blink away her confusion. "You know Jax? How do you know Jax?"

Out of all the questions running through my head, this seemed like the least important thing to focus on. But it was also the only one I could actually answer. "He was at the club last night." My eyes widened and I tilted my head slightly towards Luis. Hopefully she'd figure out Jax was one half of the supe duo responsible for the Inferno shitshow without me having to spell it out for her in front Luis. "We danced when you were outside with Muscles. El, seriously, who are these people?"

"My brother and his stupid friend." Her hands trembled slightly, but she managed to reign in her expression and body language to a semblance of composure. Jax started to rise out of his seat in protest at being called stupid, but was immediately pushed down by Gray Eyes.

El moved forward a bit so that Luis and I could enter the house too, but her body was still angled in front of ours. Every attempt I made to stand next to her was rejected. Was she trying to protect us?

If so, it was kind of hilarious, seeing as I towered over her tiny 5'2" stature by half a foot and Luis by even more. Jax was looking rightfully apprehensive though, so maybe he really did know her. She propped her hands on her hips in a Wonder Woman stance that had me biting back a smirk.

"Why are you here? Is everyone okay?" she asked.

"Everyone's fine. For now." Her brother glanced over at me before covertly adding, "why we are here is...complicated." His head nodded into the next room, a clear signal for El to follow them and leave me stranded in the kitchen.

El rolled her eyes. "Oh please. Whatever you have to say to me, you can say in front of—" she glanced back quickly at Luis and stopped. Then with a loud exhale, I watched as the tension slid out of her small frame. She walked over to the kitchen table, quickly grabbing them both in a tight hug. "I've missed you jerks. A lot more than I will ever admit to your faces," she paused briefly, "except for now, when I am admitting it to your faces." She turned around to look at me, her eyes sending a silent apology for everything that just happened and for whatever explanations would follow. "Dess and Luis, this is my brother, Soren," she nodded briefly in my direction "and you know Jax already, I guess."

Jax walked over with a smile that would make most girls go weak in the knees, picked me up, and swung me around in a monstrous hug. His warm vanilla scent washed over me. Hell, he was two seconds away from making my knees go weak and I was supposedly immune to him. Soren barely acknowledged the introduction. Jax set me down on my feet, careful to catch me when the room started to spin, and then held out a friendly hand to greet Luis.

I leaned against Jax while I recalibrated my relationship to the floor.

Luis gripped Jax's hand and I watched as his eyes hooded briefly at the contact. He quickly dropped his hand and shook his head rapidly. I shoved Jax lightly and mumbled a quick "turn it off," while Luis tried to reign in his confusion. Totally figured. I'd spent almost a full six years keeping everything about supes and the Veil a secret from Luis, and Jax was ready to blow the whole thing in just as many seconds. Guys were the worst.

"Sit down Jax," Soren snapped, his icy stare locked on Luis.

The room was getting smaller from the increasingly awkward

situation, so I asked the first question my mind could actually handle. "Is Ellie really short for Elliana?"

Jax's shoulders shook gently with laughter against me.

"I wouldn't laugh too hard there, Therjax," El shot back. He stiffened instantly and I bit my lip trying to hold in the giggle threatening to escape. "You best swallow that laugh there too, Odessa." She dragged out the 'oooh' sound of my name to make it sound even more ridiculous. Then she smiled, briefly, like the Awkward Name Club gave her a way to start patching up the giant rift that suddenly separated us. "My real name is Elliana. But I've always gone by Ellie."

Not one to let the tension drop, Soren turned his attention back towards El, "in the other room, Ellie. We need to talk." Without another glance at the rest of us, he took off into her bedroom. Though how he knew it was her bedroom was beyond me.

I watched El open her mouth with a retort. She wasn't one to be bossed around. Like ever. But one quick glance at Luis and she nodded in surrender and followed him, the soft click of her door leaving the kitchen in a blanket of stunned silence.

Jax grabbed a beer from the six pack Luis was still cradling, popping the cap off on the metal lip of his belt buckle before he sat back down at the kitchen table and took a giant swig, his eyes dancing with mirth.

Luis took a few careful steps farther into the kitchen before depositing our groceries onto the counter. He studied the distance between Jax and me, as if unsure how much he should say in the unfamiliar man's presence. "Odie, did you—did you know that El wasn't an only child?"

I shook my head, swallowing what felt like an unfamiliar dose of betrayal and hurt. I knew that Ellie didn't like talking about her past, something she made abundantly clear early on, but I couldn't pretend to feel a bit bruised by the fact that she never felt comfortable enough to divulge that she had a freaking sibling. Was Soren the only one or did she have a whole horde of secret family back in the Veil? I'd known El for six years, hell I'd lived with her for three, and I racked my brain trying to piece together all I could about her life before the one she created here. All I was left with was a broken puzzle with more holes than pieces. Hell, I didn't even have the outlining frame or finished picture to go off of.

"Do you know anything about her family? Or where she lived before Seattle?" he asked, pressing me further.

"No, I know as much as you for the most part." The words were more clipped and terse than I'd intended them to be. Luis wasn't to blame for my frustration. And I felt bad enough as it was that the few things I did know about El, he wasn't allowed to be a part of.

Luis scratched the back of his neck, ruffling his hair while he put away the food. "Should I head out? I'm guessing movie night is cancelled and El is probably going to want to catch up with her brother." He turned around, his eyes passing over Jax as briefly as possible. "I can stay though if you want of course."

I shook my head, smirking a little. Jax's feeder surge from a few minutes ago must have had Luis a bit spooked. Especially since Luis was straight. "I'll give you a buzz tomorrow if I don't see you at The Tavern."

After Luis left, Jax stood up and opened another beer for me, and then we both sat in silence while we waited for Ellie and Soren to come back into the kitchen. Part of me wanted to move to the living room which was closer to her bedroom so that I could try and eavesdrop. But I compromised with draining half of my beer and ignoring Jax instead. She needed family time, and I wasn't enough of a stalker to deny her. It made sense now—the glimpses of supernatural energy I spotted earlier, all the increased activity over the last few days. Jax and Soren had been more or less tailing us for days, circling us slowly like predators, only to pounce on us in our own territory, in our home. What if her brother was here to take her home. Would she go?

After fifteen minutes of silence, the light buzz mixed with my impatience and I turned towards Jax, willingly losing the silence battle. "Is the fire-manipulator part of your crew too?"

He shook his head and my eyes narrowed at his smirk. "To be honest, Desi-girl, I thought she was with you. In case you hadn't noticed, she was trying to light my ass on fire, not yours."

My nose scrunched at the stupid nickname. "How did you find us anyway?"

Before he could respond, Ellie's door opened and she followed Soren out into the kitchen. I couldn't help but sneer a bit while he helped himself to a beer. Ignoring him, I turned to her. "El, why didn't you tell me you had a brother?"

She sniped the freshly-opened bottle from her brother's hand. "There's a lot I haven't told you, but I promise that changes tonight. I had no idea anyone from the Veil would be able to find me over here or else I would've been more forthcoming before." She looked at me, eyes pleading, before snapping them back to Soren. "Actually, how did you find me?"

Her fingers tapped threateningly on the kitchen counter while she cocked an eyebrow and looked expectantly at Soren. The typical El, the one that I was used to anyway, was back in control.

Soren shifted slightly before meeting her eyes. "That pendant set I gave you with the protection spell. I didn't tell you at the time, because I knew you'd murder me, but it was also infused with a tracker in case I needed to locate you. I was the only one who knew about it, aside from a trusted acquaintance." His eyes darkened from light gray to a shade closer to black when his gaze travelled towards my direction, homing in on my necklace. "Of course, I had no idea you'd give it away, to a human no less." His lip curled in disgust and I could practically feel his dislike lapping against my skin.

Clearly Jax could sense it too because he gave my shoulders a comforting squeeze and scooched his chair closer to my side. I tried not to relax under the feel of his warmth, while his scent cocooned us. But I failed. For some reason my Stranger Danger Radar was seriously defective tonight.

"Hey, Dess needs the extra boost of protection more than I do by a long shot. You've never seen her try to walk and talk at the same time." El shoved her brother playfully, trying to lighten the mood. "Come to think of it, the protection charm must not be all that effective."

"Soren, don't be an ass. If Desi is a friend of Elliana, she's a friend of ours. I mean, they clearly spend a lot of time together and Ellie's still alive, so she can't be all that dangerous, right?" Jax whipped a bottle cap at Soren who swiftly grabbed it out of midair.

"So okay, you tracked Ellie down. Why wait until now? She's been living in Seattle for six years now," I asked.

"Let's just say that my father is a pretty powerful supe. The human world has all kinds of social and political issues, right? Well, the Veil isn't really different." Ellie tugged at her top, uncharacteristically avoiding my eyes. "And lately, the political tensions have been more...complex than usual. My father is kind of tied into that."

"Ellie, enough." Soren's deep voice was quiet, but it carried a note of disapproval and authority. "The issues of the Veil are not the issues of a human."

Human. He said that word with so much disdain and disgust, even though his sister had been living as one for six years. Did she secretly infuse that much hatred into the word when she thought it, if not when she said it? Was her irreverence for all things to do with the Veil an act?

I let that question settle for a beat. Only a beat.

And then as quickly as the questions came, they left. No, El was not her brother. She was the girl who wasn't bothered by the annoying human sounds in movie theaters. Every class she could fit into her schedule, she took. Every human experience she encountered, she devoured with a fascinated intensity.

El stomped over, pushed Jax's arm off my shoulders and grabbed me to her side. For someone so small, she packed a lot of force. "Dess isn't just a human," she paused muttering softly to me, "not that there's anything wrong with being a human," and then looked back at Soren. "She's my family."

"No." Soren's hand came down loudly on the counter, a startling contradiction to the soft and threatening timbre of his voice. Somehow, his quiet intensity only made him more frightening than if he'd just screamed. A muscle was ticking quickly in his jaw. "I'm family. She's just been a poor substitute for the last few years."

"Soren, of course that's not what I meant. You're obviously my family. It's just that Dess. Well, she is now too." Her hand slid down my arm and squeezed my hand. "Look, Soren, there's some leftover pizza in the fridge from dinner tonight. Why don't you and Jax grab a slice and chill here. I need to talk to Dess for a few minutes." Without another look she stood up and walked towards my bedroom, before coming back to grab a piece of pizza for herself. Then she disappeared back into my room, leaving me with nothing to do but silently follow her.

FIVE

El plopped down on the green and gray blanket on my bed. "Ask your questions, I'll answer everything that I can."

"Okay, let's start with the most obvious. Why is your brother in our house?"

She took a long swig out of her beer, and though she didn't say anything, I could almost sense the relief that it didn't taste like bourbon pass over her face. "It's not really an easy question to answer without talking about why I left the Veil in the first place. You know I came to Seattle after my mom died, right?" I nodded for her to continue. "Well, what I didn't tell you is that my mom was murdered." She made the 'dun dun' Law & Order sound, but it didn't have quite the mood-lifting effect she was likely aiming for.

"Holy shit, El, I'm sorry. That's crazy."

"Crazy yes, but that's just part of the story." She shooed my sympathy away quickly, raining crust flakes across my bedspread. "The thing is, they never caught the person responsible, though it's always been assumed it was orchestrated, if not carried out, by Insurgenti—they're sort of like the Veil's version of anarchist rebels. But Soren and my father were worried that I was in danger in the Veil until her murder could be solved."

My stomach dropped. "What? Why?"

"There was this prophecy years ago that someone in my mom's line would bring great change to the Veil, blah blah blah. Before you ask, swallow your food. Yes, prophecies exist in the Veil but, no, they don't really mean anything. Only crackpot old ladies believe them— and the rebels too, apparently. Most of them never come true anyway, and those that do are so vague that it's hard to tell whether it meant anything in the first place. Not to mention that when they are fulfilled, there's the whole question of did the prophecy come true because it's a prophecy, or did it come true because you found out about the prophecy and made it happen? It's the whole chicken and the egg thing all over again."

"This feels like a really effed up magical philosophy class right now."

"Right? And you know me. Philosophy has always felt like a big clusterfuck of brain power that doesn't actually result in anything useful. So anyway. That's one theory about my mother's murder. The other theory is that people were after her, and by extension me, to get to my dad. He's kind of like a ruler over a very large section of the Veil and has very big, very powerful enemies. I spent a lot of time in the human world with my mom and Soren growing up. I actually preferred it over here. So, my dad and Soren decided it was best to fake my death and send me here instead for a little while, until the political climate calmed down or they got to the bottom of my mother's murder." She paused, absentmindedly pulling gray threads from the blankets piled on the foot of my bed.

I looked up, confused. "Wait, why didn't Soren come with you then? To live here?"

"Soren's actually my half-brother. He's three years older than me, so twenty-six. My dad had him before he married my mom. His mom died giving birth to him and so my mom raised him like her own. But he's not part of her line and it's well known that my father would never give him the throne, so there'd be no reason to go through him to get to my father." Her lips quirked in a small smirk. "Not that many people really stand a chance against Soren."

I felt my mouth drop open stupidly. "Throne? El—are you, like, a princess?" I paused, frowning. "Because come to think of it, that totally makes sense. You act more like a princess than anyone I know. I mean, you've been bossing me around since the day we met."

She smiled and shoved me over with a strength that still managed to catch me off guard after all these years. "I guess you could think of my dad as a king and me as a princess if it makes your freak flag fly. We don't really use those terms though and he doesn't control the entire Veil or anything like that."

"But then why wouldn't Soren be a prince?"

"My father is a bit of an elitist asshole. In the Veil, it's all about merging powers to make sure the next generation is as powerful as possible. My mother was a manipulator, a panther like my dad and me. Soren's mom was not. To be honest, I think the only reason my dad kept him around is because he could sense that Soren was very powerful, even if his lineage was 'impure.'" Her nose crinkled at that last word as if it were a curse. "The Veil's prejudices are just as awful as the prejudices in this world. My mom adopted Soren and treated him like a son, but my father never really acknowledged him as such. He was kept on officially to be my guard." We both stared at the wall for a while, absorbing everything that had been said.

"So Soren being here then, is that good news at least? That the political climate has neutralized or that they captured the asshat who murdered your mom?" I asked.

Her face took on a worried look I wasn't used to seeing. "Not exactly. It seems that someone found out that I'm still alive. In fact, I suspect that's why the supe activity has been so heavy stateside lately. Not just because of me, but my father's rule has been challenged multiple times over the last year and a few of the regions are on the brink of war. Soren came here to bring me back so that my father's guard could protect me."

"What? You're leaving?" I scrunched my nose realizing how selfish that sounded. "I mean, I want you to feel safe, but dude I don't want you to leave." I paused, staring down at my fingers which suddenly seemed super interesting. "And how selfish do I sound right now? Voicing my own pity party when you are potentially in danger right this minute?" I was babbling, we both knew it.

El tackled me into a lopsided hug, spilling drops of beer. "That's the thing, I don't have to leave, but I don't want to put you in danger either. I've convinced Soren that I'm safer here, so long as no one knows exactly where I am. Safer than I would be back in the Veil, most likely."

"Oh. I mean did he buy that?"

"Totally. And it's true. I think regardless of whether or not we stay in Seattle, he'll want to keep me as far away from the Veil as possible. The more supes around, the more difficult it becomes to decipher who we can trust."

"So you might not stay in Seattle?" This conversation, scratch that this whole night, was giving me some serious emotional whiplash.

"This is the part that's up to you. Not only would I be bringing all of my baggage to your front door. Potentially literally. But Soren will only let me stay here if he and Jax act as my guard. And once I mentioned that you can spot supes with that freaky sense you have, he warmed up to the idea more. I told him it's kind of like you're my built in neighborhood watch." Her finger peeled off the bottle wrapper into tiny, uneven strips. "It would be a huge imposition on you and Sam. Knowing Soren, he'll hardly let me out of his sight. And while he isn't the same level of elitist asshole as my father, he's still not a fan of humans. And he's still kind of an asshole."

I picked up the threads from El's label and tied them into little tension-filled knots. "If having them here is the safest way to keep you here, that works for me. What do we tell Sam and Luis though?"

"With Sam, we tell the truth. It's only fair and I trust him like I trust you. Soren won't like letting someone else in on the situation, but this is Sam's house and it's only fair he has a fully informed understanding of the potential danger I'm bringing into it. If he says no, which is totally understandable, then we'll be out of here first thing tomorrow." She bit into a piece of crust, swallowing before she continued. "Luis, we just tell him my brother is coming to stay with me for awhile. It's a complicated situation and I only want people, including you, to know the bare minimum. Truthfully, the more anyone knows, the more it can come around to bite them in the ass. He's better off knowing as little as we can get away with."

I pushed away from the bed and brushed the crumbs off of my shirt and onto the floor. "Let's go."

"Where are we going? Dess, it's after three a.m."

"Sam probably just got home, let's go do this conversation now. The faster he says okay, the faster we can figure out all of the logistics of where to house Jax and Soren."

She laughed, shoving off my bed after me. Her eyes glanced impishly down at my uneven wooden floors for a moment. "I'll go talk to him, why don't you go grab a drink and relax."

I walked back to the kitchen, confident that Sam would make sure El stayed with us, whether we had to house two surly supes or a million. She was family, that was that. Her brother though? I would've been perfectly fine with Sam kicking him to the curb.

The faint drum of water against linoleum carried into the hallway. Either Jax or Soren decided to help themselves to a shower. I leaned back in the kitchen chair, trying to process everything I'd learned in the last hour, when I felt a presence behind me.

"That was fast El, did Sam tell you that you were crazy for even thinking his answer would be n—" I stared down at my chair, noticing two very not-El hands on either side of it. Turning I found myself caged by Soren, his large frame looming over mine. "Uh, do you need shampoo or something?" I bit my lip nervously. He might have been El's brother, but I didn't trust the guy farther than I could throw him. And, well, I couldn't even pick him up so that wouldn't be very far.

"Jax will make do with whatever he finds in your bathroom. He's known for making himself at home almost anywhere. Where's El?" He hadn't moved since pushing my chair in, and I felt my breath pick up as I took in how close he was. His scent washed over me, a mix of rain and something distinctly masculine. His gray eyes pierced mine and I found myself fixated on the scar through his eyebrow. I never thought a scar could make someone look more appealing, but somehow this one did.

"What's the matter? Two minutes on the job of protecting El and you've already lost track of her?" I cocked my eyebrow, secretly pleased to push his buttons.

His nostrils flared slightly. "That's what I'm doing. Right now the biggest threat I see to her is you." My stomach dropped as he pushed off my chair and moved to sit on the other side of the table, his eyes never once leaving mine.

"Me? How am I a threat? I'm human." His accusation was absurd, but the glare he was sending my way was effective enough to push me on the defensive.

"Human-ish. Jax just told me that when he met you at that bar last night, he couldn't feed off of you. Like there was some kind of block. He can always easily feed from humans. Our kind occasionally takes a bit more effort, but he rarely has difficulty. Add that to your supposed ability to visualize energy auras, and it's painfully obvious that you haven't been honest about who you are. El and Jax might trust you. But in case it wasn't clear, I don't." The muscles in his jaw were flexing and I could tell he was trying to hold back some of his anger, albeit unsuccessfully.

"What's your point? It's probably just a random genetic thing I inherited. Sam is a persuasion-manipulator, but he and my dad were half-brothers, so it's totally possible I just have a watered-down trick." I turned back, hoping either El or Jax were back. No such luck.

"Blocking, I could buy. There are people in the Veil who develop that ability to a certain extent. Or they seek energy manipulators who can create blocking spells. The more powerful you are, the less susceptible you are to feeders. From Jax's description that doesn't seem to fit you. You weren't attempting to block him, and he said he felt as if there was some sort of barrier between your energy and his. That's not normal. And your ability to sense supernatural energy isn't connected to manipulation either. I've never even heard of something like that. So, I'll ask again, who are you?" He leaned back into his chair. Though the position looked more casual, it felt intimidating. I could feel him studying me, reading more than just my verbal responses.

"I'm Odessa Black. I don't know what more to tell you. I didn't even know about the sense thing until I moved in with Sam six years ago. We just assumed that his persuasion-manipulation didn't work on me because it was a weaker expression—it doesn't work on El either. Maybe I just have some built up resistance somehow in my family tree. That's all I know."

"What about the other half of your family?"

This was starting to feel like an interrogation and I could feel my anger rising. I knew that Soren was here to protect El, I just hadn't assumed that doing so would require him to see me as the enemy. How could I be blamed for something that I didn't even understand? "My mother? I don't know anything about her. She died shortly after I was born and nobody talked about her. My father wouldn't even tell me her name."

Sam told me a few years ago that my dad met her in the Middle East, which made sense considering my darker complexion. But it was beyond frustrating that the only thing I knew about her was something that I could trace through my own skin—something I could find out by sending my DNA to one of those expensive ancestry readouts. I looked more like Sam than I did my dad, so I figured everything else I got from my mother. It was non-information. I wanted to know the things no one would tell me. What were her favorite things to do? Did she like thunderstorms as much as I did? Did the sound of people chewing drive her as crazy as it did me? What kind of mother would she have been if she survived? I craved the answers to these questions something fierce, but with my dad gone it was as if the last thread connecting me to her was severed. Sam never met her, and my dad never told him anything about her either. They weren't close, and Sam didn't even know I existed until my father left me on his doorstep. He liked to pretend his lack of relationship with my father didn't bother him, but I knew better. Sometimes, the people who pretended not to care were the ones who cared the most.

"And what of your father?" Soren asked.

I looked down, my face scrunched in ambivalence. "He left me here six years ago, I haven't heard from him since." It wasn't something I talked about anymore and Sam never mentioned him. I looked up at Soren, a small crease had formed between his eyebrows. I refused to let him dissect my emotions. Especially after he had been such an asshole. "I don't have anything to tell you, because I don't know anything more about my family than you do. I can promise you though that I would never do anything to hurt Ellie. She's my sister by everything but blood."

"You're naive. There's so much you don't know, can't know, about Ellie and our world. You might not intentionally put her in danger, but seeing as she's strapped you with that necklace, she cares deeply for you. When you let people in like that, they become a vulnerability. She won't leave you behind, won't put herself before you. That makes you a threat. You are dead weight."

My fingers clenched over the sides of my chair, my knuckles growing white. If the cool metal hadn't been protecting my palms, I knew I would have drawn blood already. Don't call him an asshole, don't call him an asshole. If he was going to live with us as a permanent shadow, I needed to make this work.

"Why are you such a dick?" Damn. Well, I held back the asshole part. That should count for something. Points for effort, as Ellie would say. "If I'm dead weight, then teach me how to defend myself and her. You're here to protect her, right? Then teach me how to help and not be a liability. I can't shift into a panther, but I can see threats coming before you probably can." I sat straighter, trying to look as intimidating as possible. Judging by the smirk on his face, I didn't achieve the effect I desired.

He said nothing for over a minute, weighing my words.

"Sam wants us to say," Ellie's cheerful shriek made me jump. I turned back to see her grinning ear-to-ear. "Jax can stay in the extra bedroom downstairs in Sam's apartment tonight and Soren you can take the couch in our living room."

Jax walked out of the bedroom dripping wet and wearing one of Ellie's bright pink towels wrapped around his waist. "You guys have any extra pajamas I could borrow?"

Soren shook his head in amused annoyance and pushed up from the table. "I'll run and grab some of our stuff. I'll be back by morning. Jax take the couch tonight." He left immediately, and I heard the unmistakable thrum of a motorcycle taking off from across the street.

Jax rifled through the bag of junk food from the corner store, settling on a bag of Sour Patch Kids. "So how did you and Ellie meet, Desi-girl?"

I pulled my eyes up from the fluorescent towel that barely closed and the smooth light brown skin of his bare chest. How could someone look so beautiful and so absurd all in one go? "She stalked me in panther-form while I was wallowing by a pond," I answered.

El crossed her arms in feigned frustration. "Hey! I did not stalk you. You were the one who approached me and decided to scratch my ears and name me Bagheera. I was too shocked by your stupidity to do anything but sit there."

The kitchen filled with Jax's laughter. It was a warm and friendly sound and I found myself not hating him quite as much as I wanted to. "Wait. Let me get this straight. Desi, you approached a wild jungle cat that for all intents and purposes was loose in the Pacific Northwest. On purpose?" He looked at me again. I don't know if it was a seduction-feeder thing, but Jax was dangerous. His smile, combined with the dark shadow of facial hair, was doing insane twisty things to my stomach.

I cleared my throat. "Yeah, according to El I don't have the greatest sense of self-preservation. I'm working on it." And considering I'm still alive and functioning at an almost normal capacity, I'd say that my efforts have been paying off.

"Don't forget common sense," El chimed in again, the laughter clear in her voice. "You didn't even bother questioning why a panther of all things was chilling just outside of Seattle."

"You were way more intimidating in human form." I looked back at Jax. "When she was a panther she was as friendly as a kitten. First time I met Ellie in human form, she straight up threatened to eat me if I didn't show her where to get some decent food. I think she was mad I assumed the panther was male."

El and Jax were cracking up. The sound of their laughter filled the room with a feeling of warmth. The sheer power of it forced my smile.

"I like you already, Desi-girl. This is going to be fun." Jax beamed, running his hand roughly over my hair, likely turning it into a bird's nest of knots.

"So since he's your brother, does that mean Soren's a body-manipulating supe too? Does he turn into a super friendly panther that likes to hang out near abandoned ponds while pondering the meaning of life?" I asked, relaxed by the change in atmosphere.

The laughter cut off and after a moment El turned back to me with a small smile on her face. "Oh, um yeah he can shift into a panther." She shared a nervous look with Jax. "But one thing you should know, Dess, is that supes don't tend to respond kindly to being asked about their abilities. It's kind of an intimate thing, especially since your energy ability reveals a lot about your strengths and weaknesses."

"Supe." Jax said the word slowly, like he was tasting it. "I like it. Sounds like superhero. I could get used to being compared to Batman."

I didn't have the heart to tell him that El didn't get the shorthand version of supernatural from DC or Marvel but from an old TV show in which supes were the villains.

SIX

At dawn the next morning, a creeping chill filtered into my room and I felt myself inhaling sharply, relieved the dream I'd been stuck in moments before had ended. Even though my blankets were wrapped around me, my body sought out the purer source of heat to my left. I curled around the warm limbs next to me, snuggling into a hard torso. Long fingers started to trail through my hair, slowly waking me up and simultaneously lulling me back to sleep. I inhaled slowly, the scent of vanilla surrounding me. "You smell good, Michael. I like this cologne," I mumbled, digging my head even further into his chest.

My head began to vibrate as the torso beneath me started to shake with silent laughter. Blinking my eyes opened, I tried to push down the desire to fall peacefully back under—especially now that I was warm and those fingers were tracing a relaxing trail along my scalp and back. And then with a jolt, I remembered that Michael was away at his conference and that he'd never slept over before. When I looked up, instead of being met with Michael's dark gaze, I found myself snuggled close to Jax—a giant, cocky grin plastered across his face. Pushing away the morning haze, I shoved myself off him. "Jax? What the hell are you doing in my room. On my bed. In the middle of the night?"

He laughed as I wrapped my blankets around me. I looked down and exhaled, happy that I'd made sure to dress in my old-man pajama set the night before. But I still felt the need to regain the privacy I lost by cocooning myself in extra layers of fabric.

"Soren asked me to train you this morning. And who is Michael, Desi-girl?"

"Michael is my sort-of-not-really boyfriend," I mumbled. "And you crawled into my bed and let me cuddle with you because? What does that have to do with training?" And why wasn't he wearing a shirt—why was he *never* wearing a shirt?

"You look cute when you sleep and I didn't want to wake you. And for the record, I'm deeply satisfied to know that I smell better than your sort of boyfriend." He moved over, claiming the space that I attempted to place between us.

I groaned and went to push away further but met the edge of my bed. "So what did you do to Soren to earn torture duty?"

The grin slipped slightly on his face. "Soren just got back from picking up some of our things. He heard you screaming through the walls. He woke me up to take you on a run so that he could get some sleep. What sort of demons filter through your nightmares? You're caked in sweat."

I looked down at my hair, feeling the dark strands coated in moisture. What had I been dreaming about? I vaguely recalled Michael being there. And Ellie. But that was it. "Screaming?"

He nodded, pity tipping the corners of his eyes down. "Like a Banshee."

"I don't remember, to be honest. Sorry if I woke you. Feel free to get more sleep and force torture duty on Soren when he wakes up." That asshat deserved my grumbling more than Jax did. Jax was annoyingly flirtatious, but I figured the dude didn't have a choice, what with being a seduction-feeder and all. Soren was just downright unpleasant.

"Don't worry, I'm more than qualified to lead the crusade this morning. Plus my motivations tend to be more effective than Soren's." He winked but at a roll of my eyes continued listing his positive attributes on his fingers. "Or, at the very least, my patience level surpasses his. And just so you know, I'm not wearing cologne. This is all me Desi-girl. Jax-au-naturale." His fingers started trailing down the side of my face, featherlight.

"Out. Not everyone wants to jump your bones, Jax." I shoved him off my bed and waited until he left the room to move.

After slamming back on my bed, I covered my head with my pillow and screamed, trying to erase the morning wakeup from my head. These boys didn't understand the concept of privacy. A girl's sleep was sacred time. And I was most certainly not a morning person. I inhaled deeply, finding that my pillow smelled enough like Jax that he must have been in bed with me for a while. And if I were being honest with myself, I definitely didn't hate that smell. Or the feel of curling up to his warm body in the morning. But almost instantly I realized it wasn't attraction I felt when I was around Jax, it was safe.

I listened to Jax and Soren chatting incoherently outside while I threw on some yoga pants and brushed my teeth. The only thing worse than morning people was morning breath. I opened my door to find Jax's cheerful smile juxtaposed against Soren's tight glare.

"Morning," I said, awkwardly tying my hair back. "You can put whatever stuff you brought in the living room for now."

Without a word to me, Soren turned to Jax and said, "don't go easy on her," before he disappeared into the living room and fell onto the couch, presumably to get some sleep. I guess I wasn't the only one who hated mornings.

Jax was a lot more pleasant during our run than I would've imagined, despite the fact that I had the endurance and grace of a toddler. He frequently slowed his pace to match mine and tried to keep a steady conversation going. Truthfully, I found myself wishing he wouldn't. There was nothing worse than trying to answer questions and hold a conversation when you were busy trying to remind your lungs to keep filling with air. After half an hour of one-word responses that probably didn't even logically match up to his questions, Jax got the message and left the only chatter to his words of encouragement.

We finally reached an isolated hill in a park. Once I was able to ignore the throbbing in my side, I let out a shaky breath of relief. "It's beautiful—"

And it was. The hill overlooked the water and Jax had timed our arrival perfectly so that we were getting a lovely view of the sunrise— the sky streaked with oranges and pinks that mixed with the fresh gray morning dew in the air.

"I thought you'd like it," he said, his voice filled with pride. "I come to the city fairly frequently, so I'm familiar with a lot of the parks and hidden gems. This is one of my favorite spots."

He threw me a water bottle and grabbed a seat. "What now? Do you want me to start on some strength drills or something?" I asked, my fingers crossed behind my back in a silent prayer that the run would be the end of my workout.

"Nah, let's sit and chat for a bit. We've got time and this kind of beauty should be appreciated." He winked at me, making it glaringly obvious that he wasn't talking about the sunrise.

"You're such a cheeseball." Still, I sat down next to him, unable to hide my grin and comforted by the warmth coming from his body that evened out the chill of the morning.

"I prefer shameless flirt. And it's not my fault, I'm a seduction-feeder. Blame genetics. Or magic. Or ephemeral energy."

We sat in a comfortable silence for a few minutes, enjoying the gentle quiet of the morning. "So, you and Soren. How does that work?" I asked.

"What about me and Soren?"

"You just—I don't know, you seem so different from each other. I get that Ellie's related to him, but where do you fit into the equation?"

"Different how?" The grin pulling up one side of his mouth told me he knew exactly what I meant, but he was going to make me say it anyway.

"You know how. Every time I've encountered you, you've had a smile or some sort of arrogant smirk on your face. Whereas Soren seems to fluctuate between completely bored and like he's using every muscle in his body to keep himself from killing somebody."

"And by somebody, you mean you." He knocked his shoulder teasingly into mine. While he meant it to be gentle, the sheer bulk of him left a slight sting that I had to rub out.

"Maybe. And while I definitely seem to be the target of his assholeishness, he doesn't exactly seem the type to be warm and fuzzy around anyone else either."

"Soren's complicated. And really, he and I aren't that different. We both had pretty rough childhoods."

"Yeah but you aren't a total asshat." I paused. "Usually."

"We just have different mechanisms for dealing, that's all. Not to mention that while he had to send his sister away for her own good the last six years, you got to be there for her. I'm sure part of his sourness comes from a weird kind of jealousy there. Or resentment, you know?"

I mulled over the words, filtering my previous encounters with Soren through the lens Jax provided. "Yeah I guess." Though jealousy over my relationship with El didn't really seem to latch on to the Soren freeze-out. "What was it like growing up in the Veil? Ellie seems comparatively normal. Downright chipper, even. Why were their childhoods so different?"

Jax leaned back slowly, staring at the sky for a few minutes. I almost thought he wouldn't respond when he spoke again, much more quietly than before. "Soren's history and life, I can't really tell you those things. Those aren't my stories to tell. He's my best friend but he's also a private guy and it's not my place."

I nodded, realizing that Jax had just earned some of my respect. "That's fair. And you're a good friend for keeping those stories safe, Jax." I turned to him, temporarily ignoring the sunrise. "Tell me something about the Veil then, something that you *can* tell me."

He tipped his head down towards me, amusement playing out on his features. "Like what?"

"I don't know. Anything. El's always hated talking about it. And now it makes sense, she was in hiding and it was probably safest for her to completely disassociate herself from that part of her life. But I can't help but be curious about it. Especially since I'm now living with four other supes. What's your favorite thing to do there?"

"Same as here." The roguish smirk that tugged at his lips left no question as to what that something was.

I rolled my eyes. "You know what I mean," I mumbled.

"Sorry. I should probably tone down the flirting around you. I'm not usually this bad. To be honest, there's something kind of nice about being around someone who isn't affected by my energy pull." He paused for a moment, the space between his eyebrows creasing briefly. "I've always liked spending my time on the human side of the Veil. The Veil though, is somehow both more complex and simpler than life here. There's less technology and consumerism, and at the same time some elements of the society are more advanced, like the Veil embodies both the human world's past as well as its future. They aren't completely different though. The same kinds of prejudices and power plays still haunt life there, just as they do here."

"Yeah, I suppose it would be naive of me to think that any kind of magical power could generate world peace. Though it's a nice thought."

"It can still be a magical place. For the most part, we separate ourselves off into energy manipulators and feeders. And that works for the most part, but it's also much more complicated than that. It's a completely different realm. We have species of animals that don't exist here. The ability to do things there that would be impossible here—with or without our individual powers. And, truthfully, a lot of people in the Veil don't have any energy-using abilities."

We didn't speak for a while, instead I sat soaking in what he shared and lazily appreciating the last of the sunrise. It was peaceful. And when Jax wasn't focused on his double entendres and innuendos, he was easy to talk to. After a while, he patted my knee gently. "Alright, story time is over. Let's start the whole training thing."

I expected Jax to run me through a Rocky montage, but he didn't. He started me off with half an hour of yoga, and that half hour was somehow more intense and strenuous than some of the cardio drills that had left me wheezing in my high school gym classes. Then, Jax had me meditate for a solid twenty minutes, which was way harder than I could have ever imagined. He claimed that it was important to build my breathing skills and focus, to better understand my mind-body connection—whatever that meant. But mostly I found myself daydreaming and thinking about almost anything else. Like super greasy food.

According to him, it would take time to master it, maybe even longer than it would take to master basic fighting techniques. Which he also started to teach me. Nothing super crazy, just basic hand formations when it came to hitting and blocking.

The hour and a half that we were on the hill revealed a completely different side to Jax than the pompous ass I first encountered in Inferno—a more serious and quiet strength that hadn't been obvious to me before. Though Jax told me that he and Soren had a lot in common, seeing him in this light helped prove it—so much so that by the end of the session I was shocked I hadn't seen the similarities before. I started the morning off thinking that Jax's version of training would be as relaxed and chill as he was, but it left me on my ass by the end.

Our jog home was at a slow, even pace. And I was amazed that after such a strenuous training session, a jog could give me the same relaxed feeling as sitting on the couch. Well, almost the same. Jax looked over at me, seeing that I was less winded than during our run to the park and tried again to get me to hold a conversation as we made our ways through the winding streets. "Your breathing will get easier as you practice more yoga and meditation. Pretty soon you'll be running a marathon and chatting easily on the phone."

I doubted that. I'd never been very athletic. But I was already beginning to notice a slight difference. My body was sore, the new muscle aches left me feeling like I was broken and beaten. But still, I was counting it as a win that the light jog which had me whimpering at the start of the workout now felt like a reprieve.

"So, how about a story for a story?" he asked, his head turned back in my direction.

I looked up at him. "What do you mean?"

"I told you a little about the similarities and differences between my home and yours. You tell me something about yourself. Or your life here."

"Like what?"

"Anything. And it will help you take your mind off the fact that you are still training. Never underestimate the power of distraction. Trust me," he added, "seduction-feeders know that trick better than most."

I wasn't sure how effective a story would be at distracting me after already clueing me in to the fact that it was meant to be a distraction. Maybe Jax wasn't as suave as he liked to think. Still, it was worth a shot. I racked my brain, trying to think of something to tell him. It's funny how difficult it is to isolate tiny moments of your life that others might find interesting. Half of the things that meant so much to me probably wouldn't make any sense to someone else.

"Alright, let's see. I'm not much of a storyteller, but I'll give it a go." I paused. "Did you know El loves skydiving? She took me for my nineteenth birthday?"

He shook his head, silently urging me to continue.

"It's something that's always terrified me. Like, seriously one of my biggest fears. It already creeps me out that airplanes fly, that should be physically impossible. The thought of willingly jumping out of one? Insanity. Still, on my nineteenth birthday El dragged me out of bed almost as early as you seem fond of doing." I looked over at him with a playful glare. "She brought me a plate of chocolate ice cream and told me we were going to skip our classes for the day because she had arranged for an activity. At first, I was convinced that by activity she meant something like a random craft project or shopping. But no, for El, jumping out of a plane for fun falls under the umbrella of activity."

"Did you jump or did you chicken out, Desi-girl?" Deep brown hair was bouncing lightly against his forehead as he kept pace with me while jogging backwards so he could maintain eye contact.

"I almost refused. And asked her how something so terrifying could count as a birthday present. She told me that I was so used to falling all of the time." I paused and teasingly looked over at him, thinking back to how he pulled me from the ground while I sat mesmerized by fire the other night. "Maybe you haven't noticed yet, but my coordination isn't the best."

"That might have been the very first thing I noticed about you," he answered.

"So anyway, she told me that since I was so used to falling, it only made sense that I should conquer the biggest, longest fall I possibly could. Like it was my sacred right and duty. And then she may have mentioned something about how now every time I trip, I'll be forced to remember her and that day."

"And?"

"And what? That's it."

"Well, how'd you like it—falling out of a plane? Was it as terrifying as you thought?"

I grinned, recalling the feeling. "I loved it. We go every year now."

The rest of the jog home was peppered with a tennis match of stories, Jax would tell one and I'd repay with one in return. He never revealed too much about the Veil, but told me little things about his life, his likes and dislikes, important moments. When we finally made it home, I found myself grinning ear to ear. I was definitely grateful for the fighting techniques and training strategies he taught me throughout the morning—but I was particularly happy that by the time we ended up at the house, it felt like we were becoming friends.

SEVEN

The kitchen was filled with the smell of bacon when Jax and I pushed through the door. I was clutching my ribs, caked with sweat, while Jax looked like he'd just stepped off a photo shoot, the skin on his chest glistening but not soaked, his breathing steady and even. I probably looked like a drowned rat in comparison. How could I expect to protect El from supes hellbent on kidnapping or hurting her if I couldn't even complete a light morning workout without almost dying?

My face flushed when I realized that Soren was watching me study Jax, his smirk growing at the evidence of my embarrassment. "Jax, put a shirt on and give the defenseless human some breathing room before she joins your fan club. I don't want to chance her following us around like a lost puppy when we go home."

I clenched my teeth and squared my body towards Soren, annoyed that he'd mistaken my jealousy for infatuation. Would El mind terribly if I killed her brother?

I was saved from voicing my retort when Charlotte walked in. She was in her seventies, with long gray hair that was always partially hidden by a strikingly unusual hat. Today, she was wearing a purple sombrero with a stuffed duck hanging off the rim that clashed horribly with her red and green sweater. She could hardly see more than two feet in front of her face, but she refused to wear eyeglasses. Instead, she walked around with a large magnifying glass hanging from her neck that she was constantly holding up to her right eye.

"Odessa, Ellie, I made a fresh batch of cinnamon rolls this morning. Make sure you save some for Luis too, you know they're his favorite." She shoved a large plate of baked goods that smelled heavenly under my nose, and I waited approximately one second before grabbing one and sinking my teeth into it.

"Oh my god Char, you've outdone yourself, these are great," I moaned, passing one over to Ellie as she shoved Jax over to get her hands on the plate.

Charlotte moved into the house next to ours only a few short months after I moved in with Sam, and she almost immediately made it a rule to check on us a few times a week. We were always ecstatic about that because she was always baking, even though she was diabetic and couldn't eat anything she made. If she had children they never came by to visit her, so she had kind of adopted us. Sam and I didn't have any family left of our own, and we were greedy for whatever hodgepodge lineup of warmth we could get. Between Charlotte, Ellie, and Luis we weren't doing too badly.

"Odessa, girl, I haven't seen you in days." She kissed my forehead and pinched my cheek while Sam ran up the stairs from his basement apartment, likely lured by the combination of cinnamon and Charlotte's pungent perfume coating the air. I could feel the soft imprint of her red lipstick even if I couldn't see it, like a third eye. After greeting Ellie and me, she turned around to envelop Sam in a hug. "Good morning Samuel, don't think I can't see those dark circles under your eyes. Don't make me come over and slip you some sleeping pills. You kids these days run yourselves ragged. Never get enough sleep."

I smiled at her motherly tone. "You staying for breakfast Char?" I asked. I looked over at Soren who was quickly making his way through a plate of bacon while he studied Charlotte with an unreadable expression on his face. "There's bacon already made and I'm sure Sam could whip up something else if you'd like." Charlotte learned long ago not to consume anything El and I attempted to cook.

She shook her head. "I already ate, but I'll let Sam cook me something later at The Tavern. I'm going to stop over for lunch—I haven't seen Luis in a few days and want to bring him some food. A growing boy like him needs some homemade cooking every now and then."

El met my eyes and grinned. Charlotte was Luis's was biggest fan. Swallowing his laughter, Jax grabbed a glass of water and sat down at the kitchen, helping himself to the plate of bacon El had abandoned. I grinned while I watched her icy blue eyes shoot him a death glare. El shared many things. She did not share her bacon. And judging by the way Soren huddled protectively over his own plate, that was a family trait they both shared.

Charlotte paused and did a double take, as if just noticing the added bodies at our table. "Who are these good looking young men? Suitors?"

"Charlotte this is my brother, Soren, and his best friend, Jax. They're going to be staying with us for a while." El beamed. Over the last few years, she'd fallen in love with Charlotte just as much as Sam and I had.

Charlotte huffed and waddled closer to Jax and Soren while the rest of us followed. She was quite short, so even though they were sitting, she still had to look up a bit to meet their eyes. Jax tried to hold his laughter in when Charlotte brought her magnifying glass within an inch of his face. She moved over to do the same to Soren, the glass enlarging one of her blue eyes and making her look like an exaggerated fish. Soren studied her with equal fascination. He looked more invested in gaining her approval than he had when he met the rest of us. "Ooh, they are cute. Odessa, if you won't listen to me about marrying Luis already, I like these two better than that stuffy doctor student you've been hanging around lately. Such a bore." She paused, a giant grin sweeping across her face and highlighting her wrinkles. "Yes, if I were young again, I might pass myself back and forth among the whole lot of them!"

El pretended to gag at that behind Char's back. I stifled my laughter when I caught the look of horror on Soren's face coupled with the laughter on Jax's.

Noticing the room's embarrassment, she let out a bark of a laugh. "Trust me, kids. When you're my age you'll learn right quick that subtlety is a waste of time. Honesty is the essence of a life well-lived." Charlotte turned towards the stairs before staring at the dark gray wall, her huge hat bobbing awkwardly on her head. "Well I better get going, want to run to the grocery store before it rains. I have quite a day of errands ahead of me this morning."

Sam's eyes bulged when he realized she thought she was staring out the window. "Here, I'll drive you Charlotte. I need to pick up a few things myself." He guided her down the steps, sparing the rest of us a quick glance. "You three have fun at class today."

Not a moment after the door closed, El turned on her brother. "What does he mean by you three?"

"You're looking at Walesh's soon-to-be-enrolled seduction-feeder.

Sam's persuasion skills are handy. He's talking to the Dean this morning. In fact, that's probably one of the errands he left to tackle." Jax pushed back from the chair, balancing it on two legs. "Which means I'll be in class with you and Desi. Soren will wander the grounds in his usual moody state, scaring away any would-be attackers with his scowl."

El couldn't even be free of her guard while on a crowded campus? "Is that really necessary? Would anyone really harm her in such a public place?" I asked.

"Your own uncle, who has only a fraction of the power persuasion-manipulators are capable of, manipulates human minds with ease." Soren turned to look at me while he passed around a plate of eggs. "You've seen nothing of the power Veil dwellers have. You know nothing of our people. Crowd or no crowd, it won't matter."

True to form, Sam had no problem convincing the Dean to let Jax sign up for all our classes half-way through the quarter. He was even able to wrangle a student pass for Soren so that he could get into all the buildings and wander around the campus without garnering unnecessary suspicion. Normally, I didn't think twice about the amount of power Sam could hold over humans. After Soren's harsh reality check, the thought of what those more powerful and malicious than him could do left me breathless.

It was our last semester of school, so our schedule was light. While we sat down for the lecture in our science fiction class, El and I tried to hold in our laughter. Every few minutes, or however long it took for him to get bored, Jax would start to pull energy. It wasn't a shock to see the girls surrounding him begin to feel the effects of his power, but I wasn't expecting my professor to do the same. Especially since he was a seventy-year-old happily married straight man. The first time Jax began to work his magic, Professor Sadjwick pulled his glasses from his face blinking hard—probably confused to be questioning his sexuality so late in life. Or at the very least, surprised to be feeling aroused in the middle of a lecture explaining a convoluted, intergalactic war metaphor. The second time I could tell Jax was pulling energy, Professor Sadjwick's voice squeaked uncomfortably high while he rushed to stand behind the podium, his eyes casting nervous glances in Jax's direction. Poor guy.

I still didn't totally understand the whole seduction-feeder ability. Jax explained that he very rarely took enough energy to cause any harm to humans. His exact phrasing was something along the lines of never leaving them 'anything but satisfied.' El later explained that it could be used as an energy draining weapon if he wanted it to be one; that powerful energy-feeders not only used the energy to survive, but to heal and increase their strength and senses. In theory, I'd always assumed that energy-feeders were the lesser supes—holding weaker power and utility in their abilities. Watching Jax as he manipulated the entire classroom as if it were his own personal buffet, with a control Sam could never achieve, I knew that wasn't true. It was becoming increasingly clear that Jax used his laughter and flirtations as a mask. That beneath it he was powerful, dangerous even.

In my years at Walesh, I had only seen one other supernatural on campus, the boredom-feeder, years ago. But El and I had never seen him again after that one class. Walking around with what I knew now, with this fear for El that wouldn't quite leave my bones, my eyes were peeled for any slight glimmer or glow. Our classes were uneventful, minus the entertaining show Jax put on, and I was almost happy to head back to the safety and isolation of our home, where we controlled more of the variables.

Still, campus was beautiful this time of year. It was in the early stages of spring and the cherry blossom trees were starting to bloom. The lawns and benches were filled with students soaking up some much-needed sun, and we even walked past an instructor who had brought her class outside for the day's lesson. Even with the larger than usual crowd, Soren stood out. He was leaning against a tree and spotted us just as we spotted him. Like Jax, he seemed to be popular with the college crowd and had already gained a group of admirers camped out on a blanket in the quad, one girl pretending to read an upside-down book while throwing not-so-covert glances his way. Unlike Jax, Soren didn't seem to notice his effect on women—and if he did, he didn't seem to care.

"Any suspicious activity among the coeds, Agent Tesker?" Jax was grinning ear to ear, eyes focused on the group of admirers, their attention now focused on him. "I love college. Should have enrolled ages ago. Nothing quite like the hit of horny humans thrust into the world of sexual experimentation."

Soren ignored him. "You guys done with class? Let me grab my bike and I'll follow you home." Barely sparing us a glance, he scanned the perimeter, alert and cautious.

"How is it that you have a motorcycle in the first place, Soren? Did you bring it from the Veil?" I asked. It never occurred to me how little I knew about the Veil—Sam had never been there, and Ellie never discussed it. Even with all the information thrown at me the last two days, I couldn't help but feel my curiosity about the place rise—I wanted to know more. Did they have the same types of jobs as us? Wear the same clothes? Listen to the same music? How did they even slip from one side to the next? As far as I knew, no human had ever been to the Veil or even knew how to access it. Hell, I only knew about it in the first place because of Sam and El. How did they hide something so huge from humans? And why did they call the other realm the Veil if they also called the seam between our world and theirs the Veil?

Soren glanced at me, but it was Jax who answered. "Nah, he keeps the bike here. Usually parks it at his house." The look Soren shot him would have turned me to ice, but Jax laughed it off. "Dude, not a big deal. Desi is as good as family now." He turned back towards me. "Soren has a cabin a few hours away from here. We spend a lot of our time on this side of the Veil, whenever we can get away from our duties."

"Damnit Soren," El said tightening her grip on her bag. "You've been spying on me this whole time, haven't you?"

Soren, always the cold and collected one in the group, visibly flinched. "Not spying. I've checked up on you a few times over the years. You're my sister, I just needed to know you were okay. Mostly though, I stay at the cabin to get away from everything at home."

Almost as soon as the tension filled El's frame, it left. "Yeah, I can see that. The days mom used to take us out of the Veil were always your favorite."

Picturing a young Soren excited about visiting the human world seemed almost impossible. Maybe it was just strange to believe he enjoyed spending so much time among humans when he'd devoted so much energy critiquing me for being one. Truthfully, it was sounding less and less like Soren had a problem with me because I was a human and more and more likely that he simply had a problem with me.

After picking up some food, we made it home. When we pulled

into the driveway, I had to do a double take. Charlotte was standing in the front yard, now wearing a large yellow and orange fedora, glaring at a figure seated on the porch steps. Before I was even able to unbuckle my seatbelt and open the door, Soren had parked his bike and walked over to her, blocking my vision.

"Who the hell are you?" Soren asked. He squared his shoulders next to Char, like a menacing sidekick, animosity wringing from his voice.

EIGHT

"Umm, I'm Michael, who are you?"

At the sound of his soft, low voice, I exhaled in relief, pushing Soren out of the way so I could see him. Michael was sitting casually on the steps, his dark hair gleaming in the sun. Brown eyes, usually so amiable and unassuming were glaring daggers at Soren. As soon as he saw my face, the tension in his face neutralized a bit. "Dessa, hey. I thought I'd swing by and surprise you after class, see if you wanted to hang out. Didn't realize there would be a welcoming committee, of course."

He walked over to kiss my cheek and pull me into a hug, my head barely coming up to his chin. "Hey Michael, I'm glad you came. You know El and my neighbor Char. This," I motioned to Soren, "is El's brother Soren and," waving behind me, "his friend Jax. They're staying with us for a little while." He nodded to each of them, a crease forming between his brows.

A soft tap on my shoulder had me looking down. Charlotte was shoving a plate of fresh cookies into my stomach, her magnifying glass poised to study Michael's face. "Here, Dessa. I baked these this afternoon."

"Thanks Char, you really didn't need to though. I think we're all still on a sugar high from the cinnamon buns." I felt my lips tug down a little. Char baked for us fairly often, but usually if her oven was going twice in one day it meant she was feeling particularly lonely. I made a mental note to bring her with me to The Tavern sometime this week for lunch, just us girls.

"Nonsense, sugar highs don't last that long. And besides, I've had a very busy day today, and baking helps me unwind and replenish my energy. These old bones aren't quite as resilient as they once were," she brushed me off with a wave of her deeply-lined hand before continuing her appraisal of Michael's smooth skin. "Saw the medical man creeping on your steps so I figured I'd stand guard until you all got back. You never know with young men these days. I say give him the boot for showing up unannounced and without flowers. Manners are important, girl."

El glanced over at me, trying to hold in her laughter. We both knew that the only reason Charlotte disliked Michael was because he wasn't Luis. For as long as she had known him, Char had been pushing me to date Luis. We'd jokingly entertained the idea of trying to be more than friends a year ago, if only to please Charlotte. If she'd known she would've been beyond excited. Or mortified since it didn't actually happen. It could go either way. We'd never see the end of her baking.

The look on Michael's face during Char's inspection and speech was priceless, caught somewhere between fear and amusement. Not that I could blame him. As short as Char was, there was something about her that inspired respect. Power? Charisma? Whatever it was, she had it in spades. I grabbed Michael's hand and offered it a quick squeeze as I looked up at him. "What did you have in mind tonight?"

His body language loosened up a bit when he turned back to me. "Kevin's band is playing. Remember when I mentioned them a few weeks ago? You said you'd be interested in checking them out. I figured we could grab a quick bite to eat and then head over. If you're down that is. We can reschedule for another time if that'd work better for you."

"That sounds great, let me run in to drop off my books and change." I looked over at El. "Keep him company for me, please. And be nice." Then I ran up the steps to hurry the process along; afraid to leave Michael stranded with the wolves for too long. Between Soren and Charlotte, he was on the receiving end of no ordinary amount of nefarious attention.

Unfortunately, with El holding off the troops outside, I'd have to pick something out myself. I loved stylish clothes and makeup, but I wasn't so great at assembling outfits myself—that was a skill I relied heavily on El for. I settled for simple—faux leather leggings and a distressed black top that cut into a V. Just the right amount of revealing for a date. I threw on a fresh coat of mascara and a light pink gloss. My hair had been up in a bun all day, so it fell in nicely tamed waves down my back. Good enough. I stuffed my feet into a pair of cute ankle boots and was out the door before Char would have time to do any real damage.

Still, when I walked outside, Michael gave me a grateful smile. "I brought my bike, so we can take that."

"I didn't know you drove a motorcycle." El looked a combination of shocked and impressed.

"If that's what you call it," Soren said under his breath, the disgust clear on his face as he looked at the black bike pieced together by various parts Michael had found at the junkyard. I thought the Frankensteinian bike was cool. I couldn't even put an Ikea table together, let alone a machine capable of moving people safely from one place to another.

"Don't be ridiculous, girl. You can't seriously be considering getting on that deathtrap." Charlotte waddled up to me, the map of wrinkles across her forehead tight with worry. Underneath her tension, I realized that she was so much paler than I'd ever seen her, her left hand sat trembling by her side while her other looped around the crook of Soren's elbow to keep steady. My stomach sank a bit. I needed to chat with Sam about maybe getting her a caretaker if it was in our budget. I didn't remember my grandparents, but I imagine it would've hurt just as much to watch them age. Life was cruel sometimes.

I reached out and steadied her left hand, palming it between my own. "Don't worry Char, we're only going a few blocks. Besides, Michael drives like a—" I cut myself off at grandma. I'd seen Charlotte drive before. The woman referred to speed limits as 'suggestions for bad drivers and people with nowhere to be.'

"I won't go a notch above the speed limit, ma'am. I'm a very careful driver, especially when transporting special cargo." Michael threw me a helmet before hopping on his bike.

"Ugh, dude, you're never going to get laid with a line like that. Jesus," Jax mumbled, his face contorted in a look of disappointed disgust, while El covered her mouth with laughter.

I rolled my eyes at him but seeing that Char seemed appeased I hopped on after Michael, gripping one arm around his torso and using the other to wave bye to the strange menagerie on my lawn. El and Jax were smiling back and Soren and Char were both sporting identical grimaces on their faces. Char because she didn't like the 'medical man,' Soren most likely because Michael's bike didn't reach his standards.

Over the loud thrum of the engine, I thought I heard Jax yell, "Don't do anything I wouldn't do. Which, in case you're wondering, isn't much."

After the Italian restaurant left us feeling dangerously close to a food coma, Michael and I walked the ten blocks to the bar Kevin's band was playing at. He grabbed my right hand, drawing lazy circles along the inside of my wrist. "So how long are those guys going to be visiting?"

"Jax and Soren? No clue. They just showed up a couple of days ago and it's been a while since El's seen them, so they'll likely be around for a bit." After a few moments of his silence, I glanced up at his face. There was a small frown creased between his eyebrows and I started to chuckle.

"Why are you laughing?"

"You're jealous." I nudged him playfully in the shoulder. "It's cute."

His hand tightened briefly on mine, the rough calluses scraping gently against my skin. "I'm not jealous." When his eyes met my quirked eyebrow he added, "Okay, well I shouldn't be jealous. It's not like we've defined whatever this is," he moved his hand between us, "and I know I have no claims over you, and I'm trying very hard to rein in the caveman thoughts running through my mind. But still, it's a little disarming to find that the girl I really like has just acquired two rather tall, not horrible looking, male roommates."

"Well, as long as you're trying then." I held back a smile. It was strange, when I wasn't around Michael, I forgot how much I liked him. Usually when I was really into a guy, they plagued my thoughts. Not obsessively, but frequently. With Michael, he was kind of an afterthought. It was only when I was with him that I realized how happy I was to be with him. Maybe El wasn't the only one who had to give him more of a chance. "Not that you have anything to worry about. Jax flirts with anything that walks, and I don't think anyone holds his interest beyond thirty seconds. And Soren. Well, he's kind of an asshat."

"Okay good. Not that I'm happy you are living with an asshat. But, you know what I mean," he gestured to himself, "caveman."

"So, the girl you *really* like." I paused. "That is me, right?"

"Wouldn't you like to know? I could be talking about Ellie." He rolled his eyes feigning disinterest, but couldn't hide the answering grin that took over his face.

Michael handed some cash to the bouncer and after shuffling around for my ID, I looked up and realized we were at Inferno. I hadn't even realized it until Muscles reached out his hand to stamp the inside of my wrist. "He's playing here?" I looked between Muscles and Michael, my heartrate accelerating.

Muscles handed back my card and looked up at me with a wide smile. "The klutz. How are you?" He looked behind me, as if to see if I was cloaking somebody with my body. "Didn't bring Ellie with you tonight? I thought I'd have heard from her by now." His hand reached up to awkwardly scratch the back of his head and I watched as a red blush formed along his neck and cheeks.

"You guys are back open already? What about the fire?" I asked.

Muscles frowned at me like he was struggling to understand what I was talking about. "Oh, that. Bartender just got a little too enthusiastic about lighting drinks on fire. The sprinklers did more damage than the flames, but they had everything cleaned up and repaired in a few hours. Boss's brother is a carpenter, so it went pretty smoothly. Have fun tonight. And watch out for the glass window, will ya?" He opened the door with a wink.

"Glass window?" Michael looked at me with a wicked smirk on his face.

"Shut up," I mumbled. "It was a really clean window. I'm sure I wasn't the only one to walk into it."

"Yeah, I mean the birds in those commercials do it all the time." He bit his lip, trying to hold back his laughter and ushered me into the club ahead of him—his hand splayed out against the small of my back. "What was all that about a fire?" he asked, his voice serious as the whisper graced my ear.

I ignored him, stunned both by Muscles' flaming-shots understatement and the fact that the club looked perfectly normal, the bar and floor completely repaired as if nothing had happened here a few days ago.

"You alright, Dessa?" Michael squeezed my hand lightly.

Nodding, I masked my stunned expression and looked up at him with a smile and squeezed his hand back. I'd talk to El about the Inferno crazy later, but for now I needed to play it cool.

It was strange being here on a weeknight, the club had transformed into a completely different venue. Gone were the blue-haired DJ and the scantily clad dancers clogging up the floor. Instead, the room was emptier, filled with people chatting over drinks, throwing casual glances at the instrument-strewn stage to see if the band had started yet. I never understood why people did that—stare at the stage to see if a show was going to begin. As soon as they started playing, you'd be able to hear them. That whole watched pot never boils conundrum all over again, only with drunk people.

Michael snuck up behind me after grabbing our drinks, wrapping a hand lightly around my waist. He timed things well, and we only waited a couple of minutes before his roommate's band started to play. I had only met Kevin once before, but he seemed like a nice guy. They'd only known each other for a few months and were an interesting duo. Michael's preppy sweater covered arms decorated with tattoos, making him an interesting mix of clean and edgy. Kevin, however, was only edgy. His long hair had been spiked up into purple triangles, revealing an ear full of rings that matched the half dozen pierced through the skin on his face. Dark kohl lined his eyes and his pants were even tighter than my leather leggings, which was impressive if only because I didn't think it was possible. Oddly enough, the look worked for him in a way I couldn't imagine it working for anyone else. More remarkable was the fact that the rest of his bandmates were way more conventional looking—dressed in random graphic t-shirts and jeans. They looked like they could've been going into work for one of those yuppie tech firms downtown.

The music was loud and all over the place. Pushing it into any single genre was almost impossible. People in the crowd were trying to figure out how to dance along to the beat; some were headbanging, others were doing an odd mixture of salsa and waltz moves with partners. I tried to focus on the music, but my body was way more in tune with the beat Michael's fingers were tapping against my hip—right at the sliver of skin left bare between my top and my pants.

He whispered something into my ear, but I couldn't hear him over the bass. When I turned around to get him to repeat the question, I noticed a glow in my peripheral. Behind us at the bar, were three supes casually nodding along to the music, beers in their hands. At first, I expected to see the fire-manipulator from the other night, but I realized almost instantly that she wasn't one of them. The first was a girl around my age. Short brown hair framed her innocent, doll-like face; seemingly at odds with the stunning, but revealing, black dress she was wearing with a slit all the way up to her hip. Her head was pressed gently into the chest of a male supe. While she looked like an unusual mix of innocent and dangerous, he looked purely like the latter. His blond hair was clipped short and his eyes were a dark shimmery black—the kind of black that reflects your own image back to you before you could even locate the pupil.

Both of them had a soft silver glow, so I assumed they were feeders. The final man was bathed in gold and his glow was more pronounced than the other two. His looks were unremarkable—quite tall but nothing about his face stood out. I was so used to supes being beautiful that he threw me the most. Still, he was the most eye catching of the trio with his bright purple suit that would have stuck out anywhere.

I stopped my blatant staring when Michael teasingly rubbed a thumb against my back, trying to decipher what held my interest. Smiling up at him, I pulled out my phone to text El and let her know there were three supes at the club. The odds that they had anything to do with whoever was after her were low, but since even Jax was taking the threat seriously it seemed better to be on the safe side. Especially since El loved to spend so much time here. I sent a quick follow up letting her know that Inferno looked completely untouched by the Friday night fireganza.

Having done my watchdog duty, I sunk into the music, swaying gently with Michael while we tried to find a beat to the noise that Kevin's band produced. He had pushed the sleeves of his sweater up and I found myself tracing the tattoos over the arm he splayed across my stomach, which was holding me firmly against his chest. While the supes and being back in Inferno had my heart pounding with fear and curiosity, Michael's grip helped to settle my nerves. Being in his presence felt comfortable, safe. The transition from friends to more had been relatively recent and undefined, but I found myself increasingly pleased by the evolving relationship.

Halfway through the set, he leaned down to my ear to whisper. "I missed you this past weekend."

He spoke so softly that his breath tickled the outer shell of my ear. So soft that I was surprised I could hear him over the music. When I turned back to look at him, his eyes were filled with a vulnerable heat. Smiling slowly, I bit my bottom lip. With all of the chaos this past weekend, I never really had a chance to miss him. Still, I was happy to be with him now.

My stomach flipped when his gaze fell to my mouth. One of his hands remained on my hip, the other reached up to my chin, gently tipping my head back. My eyelids fluttered closed, and I almost immediately felt the whisper of his lips against my own. The kiss started gentle and soft at first, until his tongue slowly parted my lips to deepen it. Fingers dug into my hip as his tongue danced against my own. My hands pressed into his chest and I could feel a low groan reverberating against them, even if I couldn't hear it. Almost as soon as the kiss started, it stopped. Michael pulled back, the heat in his eyes only more intense as he licked his lips, like he was savoring the taste. When he pulled me closer against him, no doubt to start where we left off, his body stiffened against mine.

"Something wrong?" I asked, still in a pleasant daze from the kiss.

He swore softly, scrubbing a hand over his face.

"What? It wasn't that bad was it?" I asked.

"Isn't that your roommate's brother?" His face looked tight, all of the heat that was previously there gone.

"What, where?" He turned me around and nodded his head. My eyes scanned the crowd, which had grown considerably over the course of the band's set, until they met with a pair of familiar gray ones. Soren was leaning against the wall on the opposite side of the venue, one leg propped up against it and his arms crossed over his chest. His face was tight and almost as soon as we made eye contact, he looked away. "Yeah, that's him. Hang on let me check and see what's up."

I reluctantly detached myself from Michael and started to weave in and out of the dancing crowd. When I reached Soren, his jaw was tight, and he was deliberately avoiding acknowledging my presence. Nothing new there. "I take it El told you about the supes?" I asked, looking up at him. "They're at the bar. Why didn't you tell me you were here, instead of creepily eye-stalking my date?"

Silence. When I was convinced he didn't hear me and opened my mouth to repeat the questions, he turned his face towards mine. "Trust me, there are about a million things I'd rather be doing than watching a couple of humans awkwardly maul each other. I just wanted to see if I could find out if they were in the city for El or just their own amusement."

The bitter tone of his voice sent shivers up my spine. It made sense that he would want to check out the club after my text to El, though I had no idea how he'd be able to decipher their intentions. It's not like he could walk up to them and ask if they were there to kidnap or kill his little sister, the fairy princess. I nodded my head towards the trio at the bar, trying to covertly point them out.

"Er, right. They're over there, two feeders and a manipulator if I had to guess. The guy in the ugly suit is the manipulator. I think so anyway; his glow is gold and that seems to be a consistent indicator from my very limited experience with supes. His glow is stronger than the couple, so I'm guessing that means he's more powerful, but it isn't an exact science or anything." I paused, my eyes lingering on Soren's annoyed expression. "Don't give me that look, I kind of make up these interpretations as I go, I don't really understand all the nuances of what exactly I'm seeing, and this sense didn't exactly come with a rule book or instruction manual."

"Clearly." He kicked off the wall, towering over me, his gaze bouncing from me to where I left Michael standing. "I'm going to grab a drink and see if I can overhear anything. Let me know if you sense any others walk in. Otherwise, you should get back to your date."

"I can help, just give me something to do."

"You're human, Black. Not exactly ideal backup material. Besides, I'm not looking for a sidekick."

"Human-ish," I mumbled.

Without a further look or word, Soren pushed his way smoothly through the crowd of dancers. He was leaning against the bar before I had even processed the fact that I was categorically dismissed from whatever midnight operation he was running.

NINE

The rest of the week flew by in an exhausting whirlwind. For the most part, I found myself training with Jax every day, which meant that my body was in a perpetual state of pain. Oddly, I was starting to enjoy the feeling—and not in a masochistic way. After only five days of training, my body felt stronger even though the workouts left me feeling weak; almost as if my body was being broken down to be built back up again—stronger, better. Between grueling morning workouts, class, The Tavern, and another date with Michael, I was spent. Everyone was stumped by Inferno's quick rebound from the fire. Apparently while supes did not, in fact, have their own version of the Men in Black to clean up after them, it would've been possible for the fire-manipulator to control the amount of damage she inflicted to some degree. But that didn't explain Muscles' poor recollection of what actually happened. It was like the reality of the event had been completely erased. According to Jax's pre-workout rambling that meant someone went to extra, unsolicited lengths to make the whole thing blow over so quickly. I also hadn't noticed any new glows at The Tavern, Walesh, or anywhere else which, coupled with the knowledge that the fire-manipulation incident was quelled, sounded to me like things were starting to go back to normal. Jax said Soren was convinced of the exact opposite.

My crazy schedule meant that I didn't see Soren or Sam much, though I was only bothered by the latter. In fact, with training several hours each morning, I ended up spending more time with Jax than I even did with El. Soren was fairly certain that the trio from Inferno wasn't interested in her, but he had been keeping an eye on them anyway. So much so that when he wasn't gracing us with his growly presence, he was stalking the house they were staying in—the one he'd found by unapologetically following them home from the club. Jax was also a calming presence during workouts, so I appreciated his unique blend of support and humor each morning. And surprisingly, I was getting better. I could run for a mile without feeling like my lungs were attacking me, and I could meditate for a full two minutes before my mind started thinking about pizza. I was impressed with my improvements, even if nobody else was.

If only the meditation and balancing techniques Jax was teaching me would transfer over to my serving skills. I was only halfway through my shift on Friday night and I'd already managed to beat my average nightly-plate-drops by two. El was counting. That was loyalty.

"Hey, look at it this way, at least you only dropped Soren's food. It's not like it was a real customer." El was bent over next to Soren's booth, helping to pull the ruined steak bits from the carpet.

Meanwhile, Soren was glaring at me like I'd killed his puppy and smeared its blood on his face.

"I think I'd be safer dropping a rando's food to be honest. Your brother looks like he's about to gut me," I mumbled so that only El could hear me, then looked over at him. "I'll er...be right back with a fresh plate. This one was super well done anyway—Reggie took a smoke break while he was cooking it and forgot about the grill. I don't think he likes you much. So really, when you think about it, I did you a favor. I know all you kittycats like your meat practically still breathing. You're welcome."

His lip twitched briefly in response, but he didn't say anything when I shot up to refill his order in the back. I wiped my greasy hands down the front of my serving apron. Catching a glimpse of my frizzy hair in the metal reflection of a kitchen panel, I frowned. Somehow El always ended her shifts looking just as perfect as when she started them. And not because she was lazy or cutting corners— the girl took more tables than I did and spent half her time cleaning up my messes and running food to my section. Ah well, if I couldn't be perfect I guess the next best thing was to surround myself with people who are.

The Tavern was packed tonight, so by the end of my shift I was practically panting when I took a seat at the bar where El, Soren, Jax, and Luis were already deep in conversation.

"How'd your first Friday night go, Jax?" I rested my head lightly onto my hands, begging myself to stay awake for a little while longer. Soren wasn't interested in letting El work without a babysitter, so Jax volunteered to get a job at The Tavern and work during her shift. Jax was pleased because he had a horde of people to pull energy from, and Sam was pleased because Jax was bringing in a ton of business.

"Not too bad. I got like fourteen numbers." He winked, a proud grin revealing pearly white teeth.

"The best part is that he totally jacked up all of the orders that led to the numbers." Luis shook his head, whether in annoyance or amusement I couldn't tell.

"Well, at least I'm no longer the only one messing up orders around here. Where's Sam at?" I craned my neck trying to find him. We'd just closed up and he usually sat with us for a bit to have a beer when we were all working the weekend closing shift together.

El looked up with a giant smile on her face, practically bouncing on her bar stool. "He's making you coffee."

The mischievous glint in her eye was starting to worry me. "Why would he make me coffee? I'm planning on crashing as soon as I walk into my bedroom. Maybe after scarfing down a grilled cheese."

Jax and Luis were trying to hide their smirks while El started to squirm. Soren simply raised an eyebrow and watched the scene unfold, derisive as always.

"So, um, we were thinking," El started.

Soren cleared his throat loudly.

"Okay okay, *I* was thinking that maybe we could *all* go out to Inferno tonight. You know, since the guys haven't really had a chance to get out and do something fun around town. And you've been going nonstop all week. It might be nice to let loose for a while."

I scanned them all slowly. El looked hesitant but excited, and Jax and Luis were simply amused and resigned to their fate of going to the club. Finally, I turned on Soren. "And even you agreed to this? Clubbing seems way out of your wheelhouse."

His eyes locked onto mine with a hint of mirth, but not enough to cover their usual cool distance. "Oh, it is. She's hard to say no to." He smiled at El, but I watched as his head nodded subtly towards Luis.

I scrunched my face in confusion until El's eyes bulged as she also nodded to Luis, willing me to get the hint. Ah, right. Jax mentioned that he and Soren were planning to scope out Inferno this weekend to try and track evidence of the fire-manipulator, El must've just begged until he agreed to make a night out of it. Because even during fun time, Soren had to find a way to make it business.

Well that was that. If even Soren was on board, there was no way El would let me weasel out of this one tonight. I tried to stifle my groan. And was almost successful. "Fine. You all win, I'm clearly outvoted. Sam better be fixing me up a super Godzilla-sized cup of coffee."

As soon as the words left my mouth, he appeared in the room. I smelled the black liquidy goodness before I saw him. He set a giant glass down in front of me, trying unsuccessfully to stifle his laughter at the worship on my face.

"Seriously, just once I want someone to look at me the way that Dessa looks at coffee," El said.

"No you don't, El," Luis chimed in. "That's borderline obsession. If someone ever looks at you like that, they're probably a stalker or a psychopath."

Sam cleared his throat. "So, has she agreed to go? Taken one for the team?"

My head whipped back and I choked on the liquid I was already greedily inhaling. "What? You're not going." When Sam shook his head, I turned back to El with exasperation. "How come he gets out of it?"

"Because I volunteered to finish closing up here while you were too busy begging Reggie to make you more food. Snooze you lose, Dess." Sam smirked, but squeezed my shoulder in solidarity.
Crap. And Reggie ultimately refused to make me that grilled cheese I begged him for. Double crap. Tonight was not my night.

"Why can't you make your own food, Desi-girl?" Jax asked.

Luis buckled over with laughter, his dimples on full display. "There was an incident with the fryer. Odie has been banned from going within two feet of the kitchen cookware for life."

The glare I directed at Luis did nothing to stop his amusement.

"We should head out then, I need enough time to get both myself and Dessa ready. Dess, you going to invite Michael?" El asked. Soren tensed. I knew he was already annoyed about how frequently Luis was around, especially since we couldn't talk openly about anything supe-involved but seriously, would no one give Michael a chance?

Luis's head lifted at her question. "Yeah Odie, I heard even Soren and Jax have met him. And they've only known you for a second. Hardly seems fair." His voice held a tone of humor, but I knew Luis well enough to recognize the glimmer of hurt on his face.

"Nah, not tonight sorry." And I meant it. Having Michael around would make another Inferno investigative mission slightly less gross. "He mentioned having plans when I talked to him earlier. Study group."

Even though Luis just expressed a desire to meet Michael, I noticed the way his shoulders dropped slightly with relief. Apparently Soren and Jax weren't the only ones uncomfortable with the addition of new people. And on that note, I downed the rest of my coffee, ready to succumb to the night that just inevitably got longer. If Jax was thinking he could drag me out of bed for a workout tomorrow morning, he would have another thing coming.

Luis agreed to meet us at Inferno in an hour as he wanted to head home to shower and change first. Apparently Jax spilled some vodka on his pants at the beginning of the shift. That left El with way less time than she had hoped. Despite her short legs, I had to practically jog to keep up with her pace on our trek home.

The second she threw open the kitchen door, she shoved Soren into the bathroom to shower and went to the boys' room to lay out their clothes, like a mom on a warpath. While she only spent a minute on preparing them for the evening, the way she pulled me into her room made it abundantly clear that I wouldn't be as lucky.

I looked down at my dark skinny jeans and tank top that I comfortably wore all day. It wasn't glamorous, but it was flattering and cute enough to wear on a night out. "El, this outfit is probably good enough as it is, no? Maybe I can just fix my hair and touch up the makeup?"

Without even gracing me with a glance, she yelled a quick "no" before getting swallowed up by her closet. It was worth a shot. "I've been cooped up all week, with Soren hovering over my every move like a drill sergeant. It took hours of bribing and begging to turn tonight into something fun, so we are doing it right."

Two minutes later, she walked out with an armful of bags. Apparently El did more than pick up more groceries when Jax took her shopping the other day. I brushed and curled my hair while she put together her own outfit: a light blue dress that matched her eyes perfectly. She paired it with some black jewelry and stilettos that made me queasy with just the thought of trying to walk in them.

"You can keep the jeans on, but here." In another bag, she pulled out the top she picked out for me and I cringed.
"No way. This is like two pieces of string disguised as a leotard, El. It might as well be a thong for shit's sake."

When I turned to face her, she had that expression on. The expression that made stronger men than me wither in fear and obedience. "Dessa. You are wearing it. If I only have twenty minutes to get us both ready, you do what I say without complaining."

"Yes, Mother." She threw a package at me with a silicone bra contraption in it; and through some impressive sorcery it managed to give my boobs some much needed support, despite the mere scraps. The top fit like a halter, with a V going down almost to my belly button. And the back of the top was pretty much nonexistent. I ducked when she threw my favorite boots at me as a peace offering. It wasn't much, but I'd take it. Though part of me would have preferred for her to bring me a grilled cheese instead.

After getting dressed and finishing our hair, we were left with exactly seven minutes to do our makeup. Surprisingly, that left me with enough time to pull off a decent smoky eye. I was feeling pretty proud of my speed until I turned to look at El and saw that she basically managed to make herself look like an airbrushed model in the blink of an eye.

When we walked out into the living room to grab the boys, they were lounging in front of the television, almost done with a beer. El didn't make them do anything but run under some sudsy water and put on clothes. Guys had it made.

"Damn, ladies," Jax said as soon as he saw us. Followed by a wolf whistle that only he could pull off without sounding creepy. "Too bad I'm banned from sweeping either of you off your feet tonight."

I grinned, recalling the story Jax told me about the one and only time he'd been in a legitimate fight with Soren. It occurred about thirty seconds after the first and last time he ever hit on Ellie when they were younger.

Jax looked good too. El had picked out a dark green button up that brought out interesting flecks of gold and green in his eyes that I never noticed before. The sleeves were rolled up to his elbows, revealing tanned skin and strong forearms. His hair was swept to the side, somehow both messy and neat, complimenting his personality in a way I never knew a hairstyle could.

He watched my appraisal with a cocky smirk, while he returned the inspection with a languid perusal. I rolled my eyes and glanced at Soren, only to find that his eyes were glued to me. The gray looked several shades darker than it normally did, and while the usual boredom was nowhere to be found in their depths, I couldn't read whatever emotion filled them now. The weight of his stare was doing crazy things to my breathing, so I cleared my throat and broke eye contact, briefly inspecting El's outfit choice for him. He was wearing dark jeans and a short sleeve charcoal gray t-shirt that perfectly matched the current shade of his eyes. I latched on almost immediately to the interesting pattern of tattoos he had going down his left arm—I had only ever seen him in long sleeves, so this was the first time I noticed them. The swirls and symbols were complex and interesting, but I couldn't make out a recognizable pattern or image. But they were infused with a golden-white glow. Were all supe tattoos like that?

"We should leave now if we don't want Luis waiting by himself." El's voice snapped me back to reality, and I closed my mouth, annoyed that it had opened slightly without my permission.

When we walked up to Inferno, Luis was leaning against the wall with his back turned to us. He turned around as we approached, and I was surprised to find one of the bar's frequent regulars standing in front of him, drinking his presence in with equal parts glee and adoration.

El walked up to them while I awkwardly followed behind her, wrestling with a sudden tightness in my stomach. "Hey Kay, Luis didn't mention you'd be here tonight," she said, giving her a quick hug.

"El! It's good to see you again." She glanced at me standing slightly to the side and sent a shy smile in my direction. "Odessa, good to see you too, you look great!" She turned back towards El, the earnest smile never leaving her face. "I just texted Luis half an hour ago to see if he wanted to hang out, he mentioned that you were all coming up here and said I could tag along. Since I was already dressed for a night out, I figured why not!"

Luis moved over towards the rest of us. "Sorry, I probably

shouldn't have invited her since our group is already uncomfortably large these days, but I suck at saying no," he mumbled into my ear. "Also, what the hell are you wearing Odie?" His nervous voice was laced with laughter.

"Don't be silly, it's fine Luis. And this monstrosity of a shirt is courtesy of Ellie so if you mock again, I'm telling on you." I'd meant to tease him, but when his eyes met mine I knew we were both thinking the same thing: neither of us enjoyed being on her bad side.

As we moved towards the door, I tripped on a piece of upturned sidewalk. Sensing my fall almost immediately, Luis turned back to catch me, his hands hot against the bare skin of my back. His eyes deepened as they travelled down from my face. When they made their way back up my body, his stare lingered an extra second at the generously revealing dip of the top. Unable to hold it in, I burst into laughter at the awkward moment.

"Shit, sorry." Luis's cheeks reddened while he averted his eyes, and he turned back to the rest of the group so quickly that he ended up accidentally knocking me into a steeper fall than he had rescued me from.

Luckily, Soren's hand reached out to steady me, the touch of his skin against mine sending tingles down my arm. As soon as I was out of danger of face-planting, he ripped his hand away as if I'd burned him.

When I looked back towards the club, I caught Kay's eye. She smiled softly at me, but the slight downward turn of her mouth wasn't there a moment ago. I was pulled from the awkwardness of the moment by Muscles McGee's booming voice at the front of the line.

"Ellie, Klutz—I had no idea you guys were coming out tonight." He paused, looking down conspiratorially at El. "And you, pixie, never penciled me in for a date this week."

Soren growled, and while Muscles looked temporarily taken aback, El placed a small hand on his arm. "Ignore my brother, Ronnie. He's a bit of an overprotective tool sometimes."

That eased Muscles back into his usual easygoing smile. "Hey, can't blame him. I have a little sister too."

"Don't give him any encouragement, Ronnie," El continued. "He's enough of an alpha douche as it is. Anyway, this is my brother Soren and his best friend, Jax. They just popped in this week for a visit. We haven't seen each other in a while, so we've spent the week catching up. Hopefully you can forgive me enough to take me out sometime next week?"

"You got it," he beamed.

"Excellent. Oh, and these are my friends Luis and Kay," she nodded over in my direction, "and I'm sure you haven't forgotten Odessa." After glancing quickly at the window I'd claimed last week, she added, "though it looks like someone has cleaned up her calling card."

Ronnie and El started laughing, with everyone else in our party looking confused by their exchange. I crossed my fingers, trying to mimic their confusion in hopes that El and Muscles would end their reminiscing without detailing the events.

Thankfully they did, and Muscles let me pass him with nothing more than a wink and a whispered "be careful" as I entered the club. If it was possible, the place was even more packed than when El and I were here last week. The same blue-haired DJ was headbanging to the bass on his elevated platform, girls thrashing around all four sides.

I latched onto El, and she pulled our group through the mix as if we were a conga line until we made our way to the bar. There was a cute new dude working as bartender who seemed immune to El's smile and wink. After four minutes of trying to signal for his attention, I shoved Jax to the front in order to try a different tactic.

And it worked, almost instantly. Not only did Jax immediately get served, but the bartender who was an interesting mix of pretty and masculine, with dark creamy skin and better shaped eyebrows than I could ever hope for, gave our entire group drinks on the house in exchange for his number. Secretly, I was hoping that between Jax and El I wouldn't have to pay for a drink in a long while. There were benefits to rolling around with a pretty entourage—and I was more than willing to exploit those benefits. And Jax was an equal opportunity feeder, leaving the bartender with his number, a fat tip, and a playful smile.

El dragged Luis and Kay onto the floor almost immediately, while Jax, Soren, and I stayed behind to nurse our drinks for a few moments. When Soren leaned towards me with a question in his eyes, I realized immediately why Ellie had elegantly divided the group. I shook my head at him after glancing around the club, confirming no glow in sight, while Jax stared at the floor and bar in amazement, no doubt because there wasn't a single clue that a fire broke out here only a week ago.

"Alright, Black, keep an eye out." Soren nudged Jax, "you and I will make a sweep, see if we see anything unusual."

Left alone at the side of the bar, my brain was firing off all kinds of crazy while I watched Kay latch onto Luis, swaying seductively against him. I tried to dissect whatever the uncomfortable feeling in my gut was, but I was always bad at understanding my own emotions. That's what I had El for. While my first guess was jealousy, I couldn't help but sense that wasn't quite it; it was more like a realization that some part of my world was shifting or coming into focus.

Whatever that feeling was, I threw back my drink in an attempt to drown it out, and turned back towards the bar for another helping. Unfortunately, no matter how much I winked and made pouty faces at the beautiful bartender, I didn't hold the same appeal for him as Jax did. Still, he laughed off my abysmal attempts at flirtation and charged me for a single, even though he gave me a double. I'd put that in the win column.

Pushing over my boozy new drink, he leaned towards me with a smile. "I'll give you cheap drinks all night if you talk me up to your delicious friend. Deal?" He paused, laughter clear on his stunning face. There was something about him that just made you fall instantly in like. "And if you promise to never do that winky thing again. It looked like a bug flew in your eye." Yup, he was practically a backup El or Luis already.

"Fair enough." I smiled back at him, taking a sip of his concoction, my body already starting to loosen up from the alcohol.
Too tired to dance, I people watched for a while, chatting with the bartender whenever he had a split second—until the sensitive skin on my neck started to tingle from the feel of warm breath skirting against it.

"Do you see anyone glowing or the fire-manipulator?"

And the deep timbre of Soren's voice was making other parts tingle.

Swallowing quickly to throw off the momentary attraction—seriously, supernaturals were going to be the death of me—I whipped around, only to find myself caged by his imposing frame, impossibly close. Even over the smell of alcohol and sweaty bodies, his fresh scent washed over me.

My eyes locked onto his, acutely aware of how very close we were to each other and how very bad that could be once the alcohol started to kick in. I wasn't known for subtlety once my inhibitions were down. Like at all.

He cleared his throat, releasing the tension that held his posture, his fists opening and closing twice. Quickly, I began to scan the club again, but I still didn't see any ethereal glowage going on. I told him as much. With one more intense look my way, he pushed himself off the bar and disappeared into the crowd. If it were anyone but Soren, I would guess he went to dance, but knowing him he went to sulk and question cagey looking people by the entrance. The guy was allergic to fun.

"Now that one, honey, is smoldering." I jumped and spun around at the bartender's voice. "Do yourself a favor and don't try to flirt with him, you'll have a better shot at bagging him if you don't."

"I'm not going to bag him. He's my best friend's brother. That's asking for a brand of trouble I have no interest in." I paused, forcing myself to remember other reasons for not jumping his bones. It took less than half of a second. "Plus, he's a jerk with the personality of a thimble."

"Ah, understood. If he's your best friend's blood, best to avoid any intimacy. I know his type, only good for a one-nighter. Super hot, sweaty, mind-blowing one-nighter, obviously—but if you'll have to encounter him again, potentially not worth it. At least probably not worth it. If it were me, I might take the risk. But good point, did seem like he had a stick up his ass." With one last wink, he turned around to a huddle of guys, ready to take their orders.

I might steal his number from Jax when I got the chance, the dude was seriously easy to talk to.

I finished the rest of my drink just in time for Jax to grab my arm and pull me towards El for some dancing. Any anxiety or unfamiliar feelings in my gut were long forgotten thanks to the tender caress of vodka.

Jax danced with us for a few songs before casually slipping away, no doubt sifting through all the sexual tension in the club for a little pick-me-up. Personally, I hoped he hit up the bartender—the guy definitely earned some of Jax's prime attention tonight. El and I danced together for half an hour, reproducing every dorky and awkward move we'd ever seen. Kay and Luis were gyrating a few feet away and I smiled at the tension in Luis's stance. The guy hated dancing. During a slower song, El started to waltz by herself, somehow making it look sexy and not depressing, until a cute black-haired girl asked her to dance. Smiling at how quickly a new partner had nabbed her, I looked up, my eyes meeting Soren's across the room. The intensity I found in them had me looking away only a moment later.

"I'm going to go grab a water, I'll find you guys in a few minutes." I whispered to El, smiling while she curled into the embrace of the girl. When I found my new best friend at the bar, he had a water iced and ready for me before I could even open my mouth. Taking long, steady sips I felt myself instantly cool down. I smacked my lips together—he even added in some fresh mint leaves. I shoved some cash at him for a tip, but he shook his head no and wandered back to some of his other demanding customers. As a server myself, I knew the value of a tip, so I slipped the cash under the coaster anyway, knowing he'd find it eventually and be pleased.

As the water successfully left me feeling refreshed, I placed the empty glass down, ready to return to the dance floor. And that's when I saw the glow on the other side of the bar. Bathed in gold was a beautiful woman with light brown skin and dark wavy hair. Her eyes were almond shaped and serious.

It was the fire-manipulator. She was standing next to a tall, stunning woman whose blond, bobbed hair hid her face. The blond was bathed in a similar golden aura. But even more shocking was the arm that she rested her demure hand on—

Michael's arm. His face was leaned in close to her neck, the two holding a conversation, as cozy as if they were in their own little world.

I froze, unable to quell the sinking feeling in my gut. It wasn't just that he was here with another girl. We hadn't defined our relationship or anything. No, even more than the twinge of jealousy was the disappointment that he'd lied about his study group tonight. And even more than that, he'd wound up catching the eyes of a supe. Which meant that on top of everything, I was afraid that the woman, or her friend, was going to turn him into a fireball. The fire-manipulator's eyes met mine, opened in surprise, and then she glanced back at her leggy friend and Michael. I watched as she whispered into the blond's ear, and as the blonde in turn whispered seductively into his, her lips pressed to the shell of his ear. Definitely not a study group.

"What's wrong?" Soren leaned next to me, confusion on his face as his eyes traced my features and the battle of jealousy, hurt, and fear that likely played out on them. He followed my gaze and stiffened as he recognized Michael. "Oh. Shit, that's your boyfriend." He paused, anger spreading across his features. "Sorry Black. The guy's clearly a dick." My shock gave me only a nanosecond to register the sincerity in his tone; strange since I'd only expected mockery from him.

"Not my boyfriend. She's a supe." My voice was so soft I almost wasn't sure if he heard it.

"You see the glow? Maybe she's a feeder, has him entranced?" The words were somehow both icy and gentle.

"Gold glow. Not just one supe. The woman standing next to her is the fire-manipulator." I looked up at him, sensing his desire to go over and eavesdrop, to pick up any information about the people after El. "Go," I nudged him forward, "you should go check her out. I think I'm going to head home. Can you let El know I left?"

Before he had a chance to raise the objection on his lips, I waved goodbye to the bartender and turned to leave. When Soren and I looked back across the bar, both manipulators were gone. His eyes met mine as I scanned every individual around, but there wasn't a single glow. Neither of them was anywhere to be found. Soren took off, likely in an attempt to catch them outside. And in the nanosecond it took for them to disappear and for Soren to disappear after them, Michael's eyes met mine. They were wide and surprised, and I backed into the crowd and made my own escape.

TEN

I was in a dark room with Ellie, the walls dripping with muddy water. She looked behind me and pointed to Michael as he stalked across the room. His black hair was uncharacteristically swept back and neat, the dark depths of his irises that were usually warm and inviting, unusually cold. He stooped over to pull me up and drew me into his arms. My eyes closed as he bent to kiss me; but instead of anticipation, I was filled with a sense of dread. Instead of his lips on mine, all I felt was the humid air of the room. When he pulled away from me, Michael was gone. In his place, Luis was looking down at me with blood pouring out of his mouth. He tried speaking, but I heard nothing but gurgling as ugly red bubbles escaped from his lips. His sad eyes met mine, and I felt the hard accusation there before he blinked it away and turned to leave. I reached for his arms to pull him back, but my hands were immobile and my arms fell to the floor in heavy shackles. Luis began laughing and shaking, transforming once again until a creature with no face stood in the spot he occupied moments ago. On top of its neck, where a head should be, there was nothing but a large mouth and rows of sharp, shark-like teeth. The monster pushed me aside and bent over El tearing her apart while I watched. It let out an earth-rattling shriek that rang through my ears, bits of her flesh stuck between its teeth like spinach. Her eyes were empty and lifeless, the rest of her lay on the ground in unrecognizable ribbons. I blinked and suddenly the monster was gone, and I was the one standing over El, ripping her into shreds. The monster's shriek grew louder, turning slowly into a cry of pain.

When a shove pushed me awake, I realized that the inhuman sound was coming from me. Sweat was dripping down my forehead and I couldn't catch my breath. I touched my face, my mouth, my teeth. I was not the monster. El was fine. My room was still bathed in the darkness of early dawn, so I couldn't have been asleep for more than a few hours.

I didn't need the fading moonlight to recognize Soren standing over me—the gold aura emanating from him highlighted all of his features. His hair was swept back like usual, so light it was practically glowing. The gray of his eyes swirled through different shades, as if deciding on which one to land; the scar near his left eye was made more visible in the soft pale light. He was striking.

"You were screaming. I could hear you through the wall."

"Bad dream, sorry. You can go back to bed." I fluffed my pillow, trying to cover the shaking in my voice, the trembling in my fingers. I turned away from him and closed my eyes, hoping that when sleep took me back under, it would be gentler with its dreams.

I felt him waiting next to my bed, neither of us fooled that I'd be getting any more sleep this morning.

"Too late, Black. I'm already up. Let's go." He ripped the covers off of me and I felt the cold sting of the morning air against my skin.

I shot up, standing on my mattress to put my glare in line with his. But I stood up too quickly, my body still not quite as awake as my brain, and rested my hand on his shoulder to steady myself. It was too early for this shit and I was in no mood. "Go where?"

His eyes weren't looking into mine, despite being level, but dropped down to my feet and slowly made their way back up. The familiar tick in his jaw returned and he took two large steps away from me, leaving my power-stance comically unbalanced.

"You woke me up, the least you can do is join me for a run. Besides, running will help you shake off the rest of that dream. I'll be outside when you're ready." He turned and left without another word.

I brushed my hair back after tackling the morning breath and threw on a pair of yoga pants with a sports bra and loose tank.

No voices trickled into my room, so I suspected no one else was pulled from sleep by my childish nightmares. I fell asleep long before the rest of the group made it back, giving me a blessed reprieve from having to talk to El about my Michael-related feelings in the middle of the night.

I closed my bedroom door quietly, prepared to tiptoe through the kitchen and outside. It was going really well too, the quiet graceful thing. Until I turned my head briefly and found myself slammed into a wall. Only the wall wasn't where the wall usually was.

My head travelled up the half a foot to reach Soren's eyes, while I forced my own to avoid paying attention to the very thin T-shirt separating us both.

"I lied—you didn't wake me up, so don't worry. I was on my way out for a jog anyway." His voice seemed louder than usual, surrounded by so much silence.

The tension from last night was so strong in my bones, that I was sure he could sense my discomfort.

"So, you'll join me?" His tone gentled, as if he could sense my not-so-put-together-state this morning. And I silently thanked him a thousand times for not mentioning Michael and the awkward shitshow that was last night. Or the fact that my desire to bail the club by myself, midway through the night, was far below playing it cool.

"Yeah, okay. But just so you know, you need to keep up. I'm not slowing down for you." I mustered a smile at my ability to be cheeky this early in the morning.

"Deal." He grinned, his lips pulling up into a barely noticeable, but super rare smirk that had my stomach flipping in a really annoying way.

In true Soren fashion, our run was carried out in silence. I found myself surprisingly grateful for his steady and strong presence, not laced with the usual animosity that radiated off of him. He was by no means a Care Bear all of a sudden, but he'd gentled towards me a bit this morning. With our feet padding along on concrete, our lungs filling with fresh morning air, we jogged our way into a temporary and easy companionship, neither of us naive enough to think it would last beyond this morning run.

Slowly, I felt the anxiety and frustration melt away from me. While I was still pissed Michael felt the need to lie about his plans, I decided to give him the benefit of the doubt. We never had the "exclusive" chat, and maybe he was uncomfortable telling me he had a date. With that decided, I tried to come to terms with how I felt about him seeing other people, with the slow and steady breaths of Soren acting as my own personal soundtrack while I sorted through my feelings. Jealous, a little, but I realized I didn't have hard feelings for Michael. This was more an insecure sort of jealousy, that he wanted to be with someone who wasn't me. Not the kind of jealousy that stemmed from me needing to be with him, that can't eat can't breathe kind of need.

The realization came with a deep breath of relief. Maybe this whole running thing wasn't as bad as I thought. Still devil's work, mind you. And I'd forever be leery of people who enjoyed running marathons when they could be marathoning Netflix, but it wasn't the pure form of torture I'd thought it was at the beginning of the week.

My mind comfortably settled on the happenings at Inferno last night, I found it wandering more and more in the direction of Soren. He'd pulled a few feet ahead of me half a mile ago, as if sensing I needed space to sort things out. Then again, maybe I was giving his empathy levels too much credit; maybe he just got sick of keeping perfect pace with me, but wasn't so much of an asshole as to leave me completely in the dust. Either way, trailing a few feet behind him left a pretty decent view on my horizon. His dark black shorts were baggy, but they still revealed the impressive push and pull of his muscles. And don't get me started on the muscles in his back, easily visible through the sweat-coated thin cotton shirt he wore. Not that I'd ever admit to perusing that view enthusiastically. Like ever.

After a couple of miles, I was starting to hate running with a fiery passion again—the tightness in my side making each drag of air painful and unfulfilling. Judging by Soren's steady breath and focus, the casual observer would think we'd done nothing but walk to the end of the driveway. Maybe it was a supe thing? Theoretically he could transform into a panther like El. And that girl had more energy than anyone I knew. Plus, there was the whole trained guard thing. He probably could have gone on for miles longer. In fact, he was probably one of those people who enjoyed running marathons, probably even placed first. Alrighty, back to hating him then—that temporary peace treaty deteriorated real quick.

When I thought my legs were going to collapse under me, I realized Soren had directed us back to my street. Maybe he was paying attention to my spiraling exhaustion and wasn't such an asshat after all. Not that I'd tell him; the dude's ego didn't need any favors.

As our jog slowed to a crawl, I noticed Charlotte standing outside on my lawn in front of the porch steps. Her back was to me as we approached, one of those spirally and stiff Santa hats perched strangely on her head. Seriously, I didn't know if I was dying to get a peek into her closet or avoiding that experience like my life depended on it. The look on Soren's face went from slightly amused to tense, angry even. When I looked back to Charlotte as we closed in on home, I realized why—Michael was sitting on the bottom porch step, fresh baked cookie in hand.

As soon as he saw me, he stood up quickly. "Odessa, hey." He threw a wary glance back at Soren who was standing a good five feet behind me. From the firm look on his face, I was guessing he wouldn't be giving us any privacy. Neither would Char for that matter. Once her hand was planted like that on her waist, the woman couldn't be persuaded to budge.

"Eat, eat, boy." She shoved the hand holding the cookie up towards his mouth, backing off only once he took a healthy bite.

"Michael, what are you doing here?" I asked, trying to move past Charlotte so I could operate under the illusion that just the two of us were having this conversation. While he was typically poised and polished, today he looked anything but. His usually neat button-down top was buttoned unevenly and the sweater sitting on top of it was snagged and lightly stained. He was wearing the same clothes he had on last night. I blinked my eyes hard, trying to erase the mental image of him spending all night with that beautiful blond supe I saw him with at the bar. The dark circles under his eyes made it obvious he hadn't slept well, if at all, and the rumpled nature of his usually smooth hair inspired a few guesses as to how he spent the evening if he wasn't sleeping. Still, I exhaled in relief that he was alive.

"I wanted to explain about last night, it wasn't what you think." He finished off the rest of his cookie at Char's insistence. If the woman ever decided to become a drug pusher, the neighborhood would be in real trouble.

"It's okay. We never had a conversation about being exclusive, I just would prefer it if you wouldn't lie to me. I wouldn't have been upset if you told me you were seeing someone else, but you shouldn't have told me you were going to a study group." I wanted to encourage him to pick better company than the two women he was with last night, but I couldn't voice that concern without giving him a valid reason why. Maybe I could spread a rumor that they had herpes? I reached for one of the cookies on Char's plate, hoping it might diffuse some of the awkward tension—when in doubt, stuff your face—but she shoved my hand away with more strength than I expected a small woman of her age to possess. I wracked my brain trying to remember what I could have done to piss her off. Maybe she was still punishing me for refusing to eat the eggplant she brought over last week. Blech. I'd do almost anything for Char, but I drew the line at eating eggplant. It was a texture thing.

"It wasn't a date. And you're right, I shouldn't have lied to you." He took a step towards me, his expression full of hesitation and longing. "Can we maybe go grab some breakfast or something somewhere—chat about this in a more," he glanced from Char to Soren, "private setting?"

I nodded my head and opened my mouth to respond, only to snap it closed again.

"Dessa, you okay?" He took another step towards me.

I grabbed Charlotte's arm and took two steps back, dragging her with me, neither of us concerned when the plate of cookies fell from her hand to the ground at my force. "You can't be. How?"

"Dess?" His head tilted in confusion, hurt skirting across his eyes.

"You're one of them. You're a manipulator. How are you a manipulator?" He was bathed in a strong gold glow, the aura popping up as if out of nowhere—a layer of white married into the strong golden hues like marble. Beyond the light, it was like Michael was coming into focus—as if any other version I'd seen of him had been flawed, watered down. His dark hair and eyes were somehow richer, the previously pale hue of his skin more golden. Even with the dark circles under his eyes, he looked like a photoshopped model.

"I've never manipulated you, what are you talking about?" His confused gaze traced the shock across my face. All of us jumped at the triumphant giggle that came out of Charlotte's mouth.

"Black, what are you talking about?" Soren took a step forward, aligning himself on the other side of Charlotte.

"I've never seen it before. How could I never have seen it before? The gold, it's so bright now." I pinched my arm, trying to ground myself into this weird version of reality in which Michael was a supe who had somehow managed to slip past my radar for months. He was my friend. And then he was something more than a friend. And now...he was this? I blinked my eyes, in case I was seeing things. Maybe I had more to drink last night than I realized, or maybe I was just super dehydrated from the run.

But no, no matter how many times I slammed my eyes closed and then opened again, this mirage wasn't going anywhere.

Michael looked back and forth between me and Charlotte, landing eventually on the plate of upturned cookies scattered across the lawn. He smiled softly, an angry amusement behind his eyes that made him look suddenly harder and stronger than he ever seemed before. "Well done, witch. What's in the cookies?"

My mouth dropped open, trying to process this nonsense. I knew my anger was really directed at him for being a supe, but I strangely found myself more than a little bit pissed he'd called an old lady a witch after she'd done nothing but bring him fresh-baked chocolate-chip cookies. I knew people who would all but kill for a plate of those. Myself included.

"Family recipe. I knew I had a bad feeling about you, but Dessa wouldn't listen. Couple bites of those," she slapped her hands together to make an impressive sound, "proves I was right, just enough to break that block of yours."

Soren stepped in front of us both, his body tense and intimidating. "You're from the Veil? Why are you here?"

Michael ignored him, his piercing dark eyes focusing on my face. "It's you." He paused, rubbing fiercely at his jaw. "My intel had me check into Ellie for a lead, but it's been you all along. Good show," his eyes travelled briefly to Charlotte, "you may have sped things along more than you realize." His lips turned down into the briefest of frowns.

Part of me thought that maybe his confusion was a good thing. He was clearly after Ellie, but if he thought it was me he was after instead, it could give us more time, prove a good diversion. Keep her safe.

Soren tensed, his hands pumping into tight fists. Michael looked away from my eyes long enough to notice Soren's violent edge. With a single raised eyebrow, he turned his head back to me. "We'll meet again very soon, Odessa Black. And we'll have a lot to discuss when we do."

Michael's hand reached in front of him, like he was pulling an invisible zipper, and then he disappeared, a moment before Soren's fist would have pummeled him in the face.

My mouth opened and closed several times, like a gaping fish. "Where did he go?" I asked no one in particular, without moving my eyes from the spot Michael stood only a moment ago.

"A space-manipulator?" Soren's hand ripped through his hair, upsetting the strands that were usually so neatly brushed back. "You've gotta be fucking kidding me."

I looked over at Charlotte. Though a minute ago she had been laughing with glee that I could see Michael's aura, her skin was now a strange hue of pale green.

"What's a space manipulator?" I asked. "And Char, how did you know he was a supernatural? And why weren't you surprised I could see him?" And more importantly, how had I dated a supe without noticing. What was going on with my senses? Did they have supernatural doctors who could check me out?

Charlotte turned back to me, grabbing one of my hands gently in her own. "A space-manipulator is a type of energy user that can literally manipulate themselves through space. They are quite rare." She spoke to me in a voice so quiet, so soft, like she was afraid I was too fragile—on the verge of breaking. Maybe I was.

Soren, not recognizing the softness of the moment, or perhaps not capable of prolonging it, looked over at us. "Not just rare. Extinct. There hasn't been one around in at least a century. Most people believe they are simply legends. Maybe he used some sort of spell or talisman?" The last part of his explanation was directed at Charlotte, respect lingering in his eyes, as if he was a soldier and she was his general.

"No boy, no talisman or spell. That was legitimate." Her head turned back to me. "Odessa, girl, what did you see when you looked at him? You are able to sense the energy, no?"

Figuring that we were going to be here for a while, and seeing as how my knees were beginning to shake, I plopped down on the grass to give myself a second to catch my breath. After a minute employing some of Jax's yoga breaths—which did absolutely nothing—I looked up at Charlotte only to find her seated across from me. "Yes, I can see auras, usually. But something must be wrong with that ability. I've known Michael for months and never once noticed anything before. Even today, he looked totally normal the first few minutes. It was just all of a sudden." I paused for a second and looked straight at the woman who'd been a strange fixture in my life for years. Somehow seeing her sprawled out on my lawn while wearing a Santa hat in the middle of spring was the normal part of this conversation. "How did you know I could see auras?"

It wasn't Charlotte that answered, but Soren. "What was in those cookies?"

At his question Charlotte beamed. A smile so big that the wrinkles in her face became more pronounced—etched deeper— making her somehow both older and younger at the same time. "Family secret. Knew my instinct wasn't off, there was something in his eyes. Gave him a taste of something to erase the block he had. It was a pretty strong block too, took longer than it should've to break. I was beginning to doubt myself for a minute." She shook her head ruefully. "Damn, glad I've still got my groove."

Soren's mouth was pushed up, in the closest thing to a smile I thought he was capable of producing. I emphatically ignored the butterflies that annoying almost-smile gave me.

Charlotte's pride was erased almost as soon as she stood up. "Still, he'll be back. You all need to leave." She directed her command at Soren, probably because she could tell I was still in a state of shock. "I'm going out of town for a while. Take the girls and get out. He'll come back for her and I don't know where his loyalties lie." She turned back to me, engulfing me in a hug filled with so much warmth it made my eyes water. "Farewell for now, girl. I'll be seeing you again. I can't help you now, but when the time is right, I'll find you." She whispered the last part softly in my ear so only I could hear it. When I opened my mouth to question what she meant, she added, "until then, be safe."

Shaking my head, I looked at her. "Char, where are you going, why don't you come with us?"

With a sad look in my direction she walked over to Soren. "Take care of her, boy." She patted him on his cheek softly, punctuating it with a hard tap at the end. "Or I'll come after you myself," she added. Then, she walked straight into her house, came back out with her small hands wheeling several suitcases that she'd apparently already packed, loaded them into her beat-up minivan, and left—one hand on the steering wheel, the other holding up her magnifying glass.

ELEVEN

Soren and I walked into the house without speaking another word. At least I was silent. And if he wasn't, the ringing in my head made it impossible to notice. Bypassing Jax and El in the kitchen, I made a beeline for the shower. The second the hard pounding of water hit my face, I exhaled. I washed the morning off of me, selfishly taking longer than I needed to in hope that Soren would explain the last half hour to the others, so I wouldn't have to do it. Maybe he was right all along, maybe I was the biggest danger to El. Not only had I dated the enemy, but I brought him into her life, into our home several times a week. And the supposed superpower that was supposed to be our first line of defense—my only way to help protect her—was faulty and easily tricked. Charlotte's damn cookies were better at parsing out the enemy than I was.

After soaking in the eucalyptus-scented steam I forced myself to push back into my room and face reality. I dressed quickly, brushed my hair roughly before throwing it in a braid to dry, and went out in the living room to join the discussion.

When I arrived, Sam was pacing—the usual picture of calm he presented to the world completely destroyed. El and Jax were sitting on the couch with expressions both serious and confused.

As soon as she saw me, El jumped to her feet and threw her arms around me. I wasn't much of a hugger, but it was nice to have her reassurance, the physical comfort to keep me calm.

"Well El, looks like I have even worse taste in guys than you do. That age-old question is finally solved, no?" My lips quirked up in a teasing question to try and alleviate the tension in the room.

Soren wasn't amused. "Really Black, take this seriously. This isn't a question of bad taste, this is a matter of literally sleeping with the enemy."

That stung, but I guess it only hurt because he was right.

I nodded my head, but El raised hers in defiance. "Hey, she didn't even sleep with him, just for the record."

Just when I thought my morning couldn't get any more embarrassing, I felt the blood rush into my cheeks. When I turned away to try to compose myself, Jax's shocked expression was captured in my peripheral.

"But. Months?" He asked.

"What do you mean months?" El squared off, ready to take on any battle for me. Her posture told me more than her words could that she was sorry for letting that factoid about my relationship slip.

"What do you mean what do I mean? Damn, Desi-girl. If you make me wait months, I'm going to go crazy." He punctuated the last sentence with a wink, a sure sign that he too was trying to lighten the mood. I exhaled, appreciating his weird Jax-like attempt.

"For the record, not my choice. He just...any time we got even a little intimate, he'd panic and put a stop to it. Maybe he was okay with using me to spy on El, but sex pushed it a bit too far past his moral compass?" I joined El and Jax on the couch, sinking into their comforting presence.

"Seriously, Desi, that should have been your first clue. I mean a guy who says no to you for months has to be either crazy or evil." Jax nudged my head playfully, messing up the neat braid I just fastened my hair into.

I don't know whose groan was louder, Soren's or Sam's. Either way, their discomfort selfishly made me feel better about my own.

"Jesus, can we seriously stop talking about my niece's sex life?" Sam grumbled through the hands that were covering his face, as if he could erase the whole conversation.

"Lack of sex life," El and I chimed in at the exact same time, causing our smiles to turn into full-on giggles.

"And just think," she added, "a week ago I was teasing you about ditching him because he was boring. Then he goes and turns into a freaking space-manipulator."

"Was his aura any different?" Soren asked, ignoring our frivolity and attempting to steer the conversation on to firmer ground.

"Very bright, kind of like yours." I looked up at him. "Honestly, before Michael, you had probably the strongest gold signature I've ever come across. His had some white braided into it, where yours bleeds into an almost silver shade sometimes. I'm not sure why or what that means, if anything. But it was crazy. I don't know if you could tell without seeing his glow, but he physically looked so much different."

"Yeah, I could tell." Soren nodded.

"Different how?" Sam asked. His hands had graduated from holding his face to scrubbing roughly through his hair.

"More powerful, stronger. He had more clarity, in comparison he almost looked sickly before the Charlotte cure." And he looked way hotter, something I knew El would appreciate hearing about later, just as much as the others would appreciate not hearing about now. There was a moment of silence, everyone's minds turning around the chaos of the morning. "Maybe this whole thing can work in our favor though?"

"How so, Dess?" El asked, biting her lip in confusion.

"I mean when he learned I could see he was a supe, he assumed I was one too. That I was the one he was after. When you think about it, it gives us at least a little advantage—he'll come after me, not you. Whenever he does come back. He can probably convince his friends from Inferno it's me too." Because I no longer had any doubt that he was in league with the fire-manipulator and her blond friend.

"That's not a good thing, Dess, just a different flavor of the same problem." El's eyes flared briefly, a rare view into the powerful shifter lurking beneath.

"Agreed," Jax added.

"I think you should all do what Char suggested—get out of town as soon as possible. Stay off the radar until we can figure things out. Who knows if he was really after El. Maybe he actually was looking for Dessa," Sam paused when I threw him a questioning glance. "We don't know anything about your ability to see auras. El's said for years she's never even heard of someone having that ability."

"And we know nothing about why you have a block that prevents us from feeding off your energy," Jax said.

"And we know almost nothing about your mother. Who knows, this could be a whole different kind of supernatural animal that's shown up on our lawn today." Sam's face was growing paler as his worry started to build up. "I mean think about it, Dess. I didn't even meet you, let alone know about you, until your father dropped you on my doorstep years after disappearing from my life. I have no idea how Charlotte knew about you, but she did. And I think we should listen to her. You should all leave. Today, as soon as you can."

My heart dropped through my stomach. "Sam you wouldn't come with us if we left?"

He shook his head. "I have The Tavern to run and I want to see what I can find out on my end. I'll just slow you guys down. But we'll find a way to check in. It's not going to be forever, just until we have some answers."

"But what if Michael comes back? If he's as dangerous as we think he might be, I doubt he's just going to willingly leave you alone. And running away, is that really what any of us should do? Running away never solves problems it just sounds like we are going to place a really weak band aid on a super big wound." Even though I tried to cover it up, the panic was clear in my voice.

"Yeah, Sam. Maybe we should all stay. I mean we did just buy all those groceries. Kind of a waste if we just peaced off." El was as uncomfortable with leaving Sam behind as I was. Even if she tried to cover it up with a poor attempt at humor—an attempt that only made her look more upset.

"I'll be fine. But I don't want you guys here. Not if Michael can just zip in and out whenever he wants. We know nothing of his power or his intentions." Sam's tone held a note of authority, one of the few times since I'd known him that he used the fatherly 'this is final' voice.

I could feel the water pooling in my eyes. The tightening feeling in my chest was growing exponentially, stifling my breath. How was this happening? Why didn't I just ditch Michael ages ago? Maybe he would have backed off after not learning anything. Why did we have to go to Inferno yesterday? He wouldn't have come here this morning to explain. We'd all be safe. Home. Together.

It was Soren who broke the tense silence.

"I have a couple of friends." He turned to Sam. "I trust them. They can be here by the end of the day. Help eat that food you're so worried about, El." He forced a gentle smile at El, her eyes were as full of unspilled tears as mine were. "They'll keep an eye on you and the house, Sam. They'll also provide a way to stay connected with us. Keep us updated." He paused, letting his words sink in. "But Sam and Charlotte are right. We need to leave now. I'm not keen on travelling around with a human, but maybe we can see what's up with your sight, Black. Visualizing supernaturals on contact can still be a useful frontline against anyone after El, if you can gain control of it."

I tried to ignore my instinct to glare at Soren for referring to me as a human; or at least for using the term human like it was an insult. Instead, I focused on the part of his speech that hit even deeper. "Today? You want us to pack up and leave by the end of the day? Leaving doesn't feel right. We need to do something, not just hide away forever. How does that solve anything?"

I found myself growing increasingly frustrated. In the movies, superheroes took action—they formulated plans. They did not run away and hide.

He turned back to me, eyes narrowing. "Not the end of the day. Ideally, the end of the hour. Feel free to stay here if you want, but El, Jax, and I are going. Obviously we can't run forever, but we need to pool our resources, get more information about what's going on, so we can handle it smartly. You don't run into battle without having as much information as possible, especially when fire- and space-manipulators are working together. That's stupidity, not courage."

Sam stepped up, squaring off with Soren. I knew that Soren had way more power than Sam in terms of manipulation and physique. Still, the intimidation and silent threat that laced his words as Sam looked at him were no party favor. His slanted almond eyes narrowed further. "She's going. And you will protect her and treat her with respect."

Sam wouldn't have been able to really do anything to Soren. At least I didn't think so anyway. It was still nice to hear him stand up for me, to know that he had my back. Even if his version of doing that was separating us for an indeterminate amount of time.

"Of course Dess is coming with us. Soren, stop being a jackass. And Sam, Soren wouldn't let anything happen to her. Plus, she's got me looking out for her, and I'm way more ferocious and reliable than my stupid brother anyway." El shoved her way between the two men, gaining their attention and somehow making them both flinch with her disapproving tone, despite the fact that they were both a foot taller than her. I needed to pay more attention to how she carried herself. I could learn something from El. "And we'll leave as soon as we are packed. But Dess and I are going to at least try to say goodbye to Luis first."

Luis.

My stomach tightened. In all the chaos of the morning I hadn't stopped to think. I'd be leaving Sam, yes. That alone was creating a deep chasm in my chest that I couldn't linger on for too long if I wanted to stay strong, or at least sane. But my brain and body hadn't had a chance to process the fact that we would also be leaving Luis behind. The other important figure in my ragtag family.

I left the others to continue bickering about the details and allowed myself a solid sixty seconds to break down a bit in the safety and isolation of my bedroom. Usually I was a major ugly crier. When I cried, you could see it on my face for days after, puffy and miserable. These tears were different somehow, silent and thick as they made their way down my cheeks. The evidence of their tracks would be easy to erase, but somehow this felt worse than sobbing outright.

Sixty seconds over, I pulled myself up, wiped my cheeks on the sleeve of my shirt and pulled out the black suitcase that was collecting dust in the back of my closet. What did one pack when they were running from a supernatural sort-of-not-really-ex-boyfriend? I doubted Google would have an answer for me, so I threw the regulars in: favorite jeans, favorite boots, clothes to train in, all the clean underwear and bras I had, which wasn't as many as I'd hoped—I wasn't great at many things but I was fantastic at procrastinating, especially when it came to laundry.

After collecting all of my skincare and makeup items, I grabbed the raggedy doll I kept underneath my bed. I ran my hands over the worn curves of the face, the matted nest that masqueraded as hair. It was the first thing Sam ever gave me. He had no idea how to handle his role as guardian and was clearly misinformed if he thought fifteen-year-olds still liked to play with dolls. Particularly dolls as deranged looking as this one. I didn't think it belonged in any well-balanced child's toy chest. Between the mismatched eyes that were slightly raised out of the plastic sockets, the slight tilt of the head, and the green-tinged skin tone, I was half convinced Sam bought it at an occult shop. Still, I could never bring myself to get rid of the creepy thing. Hell, the first year I lived with Sam, I secretly kept it under my pillow, an oddly warm presence that grounded me when it felt like my world was melting into chaos. So I smashed the doll under my clothes as I packed—that way it could comfort me without forcing me to look at it.

By the time I entered the kitchen with a collection of my belongings Soren was seated at the table, bag packed and ready to go at his feet. His fingers tapped on the wooden surface with a hurried, impatient rhythm. I could hear Jax trying to hurry El in the other room and I grinned. That explained Soren's impatience—at least he knew well enough that any attempt to hurry El's packing along was doomed to fail. Best to wait it out.

Leaving Soren with my bag, hoping he'd go load up the car, I found Sam sitting deep into the couch, his head tucked into his hands. Watching the clear sorrow in his posture, my breath hitched. When he noticed me in the room, he sat up taller—both of us trying to hide the burden of our sadness from the other.

"I have some contacts in the city, I'm going to see if I can find out anything about Michael, keep my ear to the ground. Sooner we figure out what's going on with the people threatening El, the faster we can put this all behind us and get back to our regularly-scheduled programming." He leaned his head back against the top of the couch and I hunched into the cushion next to him.

"Just be careful. I doubt Michael is still staying at his apartment. Now that the gig is up, he's probably off planning his next move." I paused, the image of Sam channeling his inner Batman or Sherlock Holmes filling me with a bubble of anxiety. He was powerful, but something told me that a guy like Michael was in a league of his own. And by something, I meant that sheer look of terror and surprise reflected on Soren and Char's faces when he disappeared into thin air. "I don't want you getting involved with any of this. Just try to lie low, keep one of Soren's bodyguard types near you at all times. I'm sure we'll have all this straightened out soon, now that the threat is a little more tangible, maybe it'll light a fire under everyone's ass."

"Soren's going to stop by Michael's place while you guys go say goodbye to Luis." When I sucked in a sharp breath at the last three words, Sam squeezed my shoulder. "Don't worry, kiddo. I'll keep an eye on him too."

"I just wanted to thank—" I started, choking on the emotion.

"None of that goodbye shit, Dess. This is just going to be a little extended vacation. If I don't see you within the next couple of weeks, I'm going to come hunt you down myself." I knew Sam well enough to read the anxiety layering his words:

"Soren and Jax know what they're doing."

I think.

"They'll figure this out fast."

I hope.

"Once you guys are safe and let things settle, they'll put out feelers for Michael."

Or I'll kick their asses.

"And I'll keep trying to track down Charlotte."

I'm going to stalk every supe I've ever encountered.

"It's clear she knows more of this jigsaw than she's ever let on before."

Holy shit, how did I not realize our crazy-but-lovable neighbor knew so much about this world?

I couldn't do anything but nod my head against the dip of his shoulder. If I tried to speak, I wasn't confident I'd be able to hold back the tears. And Sam, like most guys, was terrible at handling a situation when a girl started crying. We learned that the hard way when I first moved in and was trying to process being abandoned by my last parent and living in a new city. When I let out a long sigh, an attempt to temper my emotions enough to play it cool, he pulled me into a tight hug. After a quick kiss to my forehead and a ruffle of my hair, he got up to say a quick goodbye to El and left, without another look in my direction. Sam was as uncomfortable with my emotions as he was with his own. Soren grabbed the packed bags and went outside after him, likely to try and track down Michael with the address El had given him.

Five minutes later, El stumbled out of her room, a giant smile on her face that I knew was shielding her tears from saying goodbye to Sam. He'd been a part of her family almost as long as he'd been a part of mine. Jax followed behind with four giant purple bags, all filled to a bursting point.

"Good to see you can pack light when you need to make a quick run for it El," I smirked. "You are a masterful and inconspicuous runaway. Oh, spymaster, teach me your ways."

She walked up to me, leaving Jax to deal with loading the rest of the car up. "Hey, you never know what you're going to feel like wearing when someone's trying to kill you. And inconspicuous indeed, maybe we will have to dress up or something to hide our identities. You tease, but let's see who's laughing when I'm the only one prepared. I even found some fake moustaches from last Halloween. I have us covered."

I linked my arm through hers, both of us taking deep and steady breaths as we looked around the house one last time, each relying on the strength of the other as we closed and locked the door.

TWELVE

Our ride over to Luis's place was filled with silent tension. On the positive side, the tension was cut short since he lived so close; on the negative side, that left me practically no time to figure out how I was going to say goodbye to him for an indefinite amount of time. Especially since we couldn't exactly give him details. We had to say just enough to let him know we were leaving for a while, without giving him reason to suspect something was up. That was a tall order, especially since he knew I was a homebody.

I steadied my hands long enough to knock gently on his apartment door; then they went back to fidgeting and tugging on random parts of my shirtsleeves, my body carelessly looking for a way to release the anxiety and tension. It felt wrong leaving him behind—a different kind of wrong than it felt leaving Sam behind. Usually Luis answered the door immediately, so I was beginning to think he wasn't home as I reached up to knock a second time. Before my fist connected with the wood, the door swung open. Only instead of Luis, I was staring face-to-face with Kay. Her long red hair was tousled seductively, and her eyelashes were flaking with yesterday's mascara. As my eyes travelled down from her face, I noticed that she was dressed in the well-worn Ramones T-Shirt that I bought for Luis a few years ago; the shirt was baggy on her, but still revealed her very bare legs, making it painfully obvious that she was wearing nothing else beneath the familiar faded cotton.

"Hey Ellie, Odessa," her voice was cheery, but tinged with a layer of embarrassment at being caught half-dressed in Luis's apartment. And also a little bit of pride. If it were any other girl, any other situation, I'd be happy to see a girl owning her sexuality like that. I guess that made me a hypocrite.

I opened my mouth to respond, but the air had been knocked out of me while I tried to make the mental jump from saying goodbye to Luis to mocking last night's sexploits—the emotions weren't compatible, and they were throwing me for a loop.

Slamming my mouth closed, I made an awkward clicking noise with my tongue while I raised my arm for an awkward wave, not trusting my voice to sound normal. My eyes were focused on the faded letters dancing across her chest and I nudged my head up to make eye contact, figuring that several inches north would be a more natural place for me to focus my attention.

El cleared her throat and squeezed my hand. "Hey Kay, we were just stopping by to see Luis. We are unexpectedly taking a road trip and wanted to say goodbye before we left." I could hear the strange mixture of laughter and regret in her voice.

"Oh, that sounds fun. How long will you guys be gone?" Her fingers ran through her hair in an unsuccessful attempt to tame it down. Giving up, she began to tug lightly on the bottom of the top, willing it to cover more of her thighs.

"How long will who be gone?" Luis's voice carried over from the next room, the words were spoken in a flirtatious growl—a tenor I never heard Luis's voice reach before and my cheeks colored from the embarrassment of trespassing on such an intimate moment. I listened to the soft pad of his feet on the carpet as he walked towards the door. As he reached her, he laid a hand gently on the small of her back until he came into full view of El and me. His hand instantly dropped from her back as if it were on fire. Kay's lips pulled down into a slight frown. "Odie." He said my name so softly I almost couldn't hear him, or maybe that was just because of the ringing in my ears that only got louder until I reminded myself to breathe. "El. You guys are going somewhere?"

I was too much of a coward to look him in the face and my eyes bounced away from his chest as soon as I noticed it was bare. I spent all of my energy and focus on keeping my gaze safely leveled at the worn blue chair I could see beyond Kay's shoulder. That chair was disgusting and covered in stains, but it was familiar—cozy.

"Hey Luis," El started, but her voice momentarily trailed off. El wasn't usually one to get sidetracked by awkwardness. In fact, more often than not, she thrived in situations most people found uncomfortable. But even El seemed to be slightly taken aback by the sight of Luis and Kay post-hookup.

"You're leaving?" He asked again. I still couldn't bring myself to look at him, but from the soft tone of his voice I knew it would be filled with emotion—emotion I wouldn't know how to unpack or analyze. And honestly, it was safer and smarter to just not.

"Yeah," she replied. Her shoulder nudged mine, reminding me that I was supposed to be a part of this conversation too. "We are going to my family's place with Jax and Soren. I haven't seen them in a while and figured I might as well make the trip now. Dessa decided to come with me."

Hearing my name, I snapped my eyes back towards Luis, taking in the lines of his face, the deepening blue of his eyes, the warm brown hair. It felt wrong lying to him about something so huge. I kept my ability to see supe glows from him, but that seemed like such a small thing in light of everything else that'd happened the last week. The metaphorical separation between us, soon to become physical too, felt wrong and made my skin itch, like it was stretched too tight.

"You're leaving?" He repeated, his eyes on me, and while before I couldn't bring myself to look at him, now I couldn't bring myself to look away. "Why? When?"

"Road trip, babe." Kay chirped up, answering when I couldn't. She wrapped a possessive hand around his bicep, asserting her place back in the conversation. "Sounds super fun. How long will you guys be gone?"

Traitorous liquid was glassing over my vision and I sent a silent prayer to whoever was listening for me to keep it together until we were safely in the elevator. "We're leaving now. Not sure how long." My voice cracked, like I hadn't used it in weeks; I barely recognized it as my own.

"And you decided this when? You guys are in the middle of the semester." Luis took a step forward, reached his arm out like he was going to touch my cheek, but let it drop back down as he changed his mind, the familiar crease making itself known between his eyebrows.

"This morning, kind of a last minute spontaneous decision. Got a call from my dad, he's not feeling so great. Figured Dessa could come back and keep me company while he rests up. We can make up any assignments we miss remotely, won't be a big deal. Soren wants us on the road as soon as possible." El smiled sadly, and I silently thanked her for the sick dad bit. It would help to explain why we were both out of sorts about a road trip, which was supposed to be fun. Hopefully we weren't going to hell for the lie though.

"I can go with you guys, it'll take me two minutes to pack. I'll be happy to help you guys take care of him. Just give me a sec." Luis turned around as if he was going to do just that.

"No." The word came out of my mouth harsh, sharp. Shit, I was *so* not going to win any awards with my lying. "Please," I softened my tone. "Just keep an eye on Sam. He's going to need more help with The Tavern with us gone. It wouldn't be fair to take all of his reliable servers away from him in one go. I'm sure we'll be back before you even get a chance to miss us."

El scooped him into a tight hug, before looking over to Kay. "Take care of him for us, yeah?"

She nodded in response.

I tried to tell my feet to move towards Luis, so I could say goodbye properly, but I was stuck; both wanting to run towards him and away from him all at once. Without a second of hesitation, he closed the distance between us and pulled me to him, his arms somehow both gentle and firm. "I'll take care of Sam, Odie. You guys just be careful, let me know when you get...wherever you're going, and just come back soon. Seattle will be insufferable on my own."

Kay cleared her throat softly behind him. Luis was really great at sticking his foot in his mouth.

"Goodbye, Luis." It was all I could trust myself to say. His head leaned down, breathing into my hair. Something about the comforting weight of his arms hammered home how insane the morning had been. Everything was different, and I had a feeling it was going to get a lot worse before it recalibrated back to any semblance of normal. I mean hell, a week ago I was almost lit on fire and now absolutely everything was upside down and threatening the very fragile home I'd built for myself over the last few years. The realization pushed a traitorous tear down my cheek and I tried to swipe it away the second Luis pulled back. The arch of his dark brow painted confusion across his face. Before he could say another word, or cause another unexplainable, powerful emotion to rattle through my body, I turned and walked away.

I was vaguely aware of El's presence next to me in the elevator. Her hand snaked down my arm to find my own, offering her strength.

I looked up at her, no longer finding it possible to hide the tears carving trails down my face. "I know it's stupid." My whispers floated away into simply air and I traced circles on my chest as if that would somehow relieve the pressure building there. "This is all so much right now. Everything's changing. It feels wrong to leave him behind. To leave Sam? It's just a lot. Everything was so normal two weeks ago."

"I know," she said. "Things with Luis are complicated. Walking in on that plus having to say goodbye—you don't have to explain, you have every right to feel it, even if you don't understand what exactly it is you're feeling, Dessa."

A small bubble of laughter escaped from my lips. "And how ridiculous is this? Here we are going into the supe version of the Witness Protection Program, and now I'm choosing to breakdown? Not because we could've been killed in a fire or because the guy I was dating was using me for some sort of supernatural espionage. But because we are retreating into safety and leaving home for a bit? How does that make sense?" My laughter started to escalate.

In true best friend fashion, El embraced the macabre tennis match between tears and belly-deep laughter. By the time the elevator doors opened, both of us were cackling with damp eyes; tears that were filled with sadness or humor or fear. Or maybe all of those things at once. Either way, I felt lighter when we walked outside to meet Jax in the parking lot.

When we reached the car, Jax wasn't alone. Soren was lifting our bags from El's convertible and tossing them into a black minivan.

"What are you doing?" I could hear the panic elevate El's voice as she started to piece together his actions.

"Sorry Sis," Soren spared her a passing glance, "but a hot pink convertible isn't exactly the ideal getaway car. Not to mention that Michael's pretty familiar with your eyesore of a vehicle already."

"Eyesore? She's a classic, Soren. She makes a statement." El was practically fuming. That car was perhaps her most prized possession; people knew better than to insult it in front of her.

"Statement, classic, Barbie-mobile, call it what you like. Either way, Soren's right. Pink does not a getaway color make." Jax threw the final bag through the back door of the van.

"But really, a minivan?" I eyed the car, happy for the simple pragmatic discussion to take away the focus from my adolescent emotions. "Couldn't we have gone with something stealthier? This just screams soccer mom."

"Exactly." Soren was pleased, but I caught his brief longing look at the Porsche in the next aisle. "It's not flashy. It blends in. We can carry all four of us, plus whatever stuff we need for transport. And nobody is suspicious of a minivan. It's perfect. Sam did well."

"Sam?" I asked.

"Yeah, that's where he went off to before we left. He persuaded someone to indefinitely lend us the van. It's really too bad he insists on staying here. His manipulation could come in handy." Soren hopped on his bike. "I'm going to drop the keys to El's convertible back at the house and catch up with you guys in a few." He pushed the helmet down over his eyes.

"Wait, did you stop by Michael's house?" I asked as El reluctantly hopped into the minivan with one last wistful look back at her baby.

"Yeah, he wasn't there. Place looked kind of ransacked, like he blew in and out of there in a hurry. His roommate was clueless, just mentioned something about Michael leaving for a family visit or something." He paused and El and I looked at each other, the irony lost on neither of us that Michael used the same excuse we just did. "I didn't really expect him to stick around, but it was worth checking out anyway." Without waiting for another response or question, Soren took off out of the parking lot. With nothing else to do, I followed El and Jax into our new vehicle.

"So, what now?" I laughed as I buckled myself in. Now that I'd gotten a good cry out of my system, it felt like we were going on some sick and twisted family trip. Emotions were weird.

"We are going to head to Soren's place up north. It's relatively isolated and only a handful of people know about its existence." Jax's eyes bounced back and forth between the road and the rearview mirror. "All people he trusts, of course. So we'll go there to regroup. Then we can make plans and figure out what to do next."

"What do you mean make plans?" El was scrolling through the radio stations, never landing on a single one for more than a brief clip of a song.

"We can't just hide forever. This whole thing with Charlotte and Michael, it adds a new layer. There's some sources Soren and I will likely want to go through, see if we can get to the bottom of whoever went after your mom," he said, his eyes glancing at El. "It's entirely possible it's not even the same person or group after you. That's an assumption we've become too comfortable believing a fact. And there are some things going on Veil-side. Soren wants to stay reasonably close to the Pacific Northwest rift," he paused, nodding his head along to a catchy pop song. "Either way, we are shifting gears. Before, it was strictly surveillance. Soren suspected someone would come after you, but now he has proof. Which means Michael and the things going on in the Veil are potentially connected. That means we need to go play both offense and defense. Things are more complicated than we expected them to be."

Jax's words were met with silence, all of us letting them marinate. It was more than either he or Soren had been willing to reveal in my presence before. I was afraid to remind him of that by asking more questions. If the people after El were really the same people after her mom, they clearly didn't get bored easily. I didn't know what he meant by rifts or Veil problems, but from what I'd seen about serial killers on TV, it was unlikely that whoever was after El would move on now. Still, despite Jax suggesting they had sources and options to exploit, I couldn't help but fear that we were in way over heads with very few leads to go on. The chaos of the day had left me mentally, physically, and emotionally exhausted. Between sorting through my own thoughts and the gentle lull of the car as we drove, I fell into a dreamless sleep oddly comforted by El's tone-deaf humming.

As the car finally came to a stop, I woke up. It only felt like we'd been in the car for a few minutes, but a quick glance at the clock suggested I'd been out for a couple of hours. Jax and El were already exiting the car when Soren pulled up next to them on his bike. I was surprised he was able to catch up with us after stopping back at the house, especially since Jax drove like he was trying out for NASCAR.

I stretched my arms and legs after hopping out of the car, my muscles still tense and sore from the morning run and, let's be honest, pretty much every other morning workout this week. After giving my brain and body a second to wake up, I was able to take in our new temporary home.

It was beautiful.

The cabin itself was larger than I expected, it looked more like a rustic house than a simple campsite. The land surrounding it though was breathtaking. To the left was a large forest, so thick with trees I couldn't see where it ended. The rest of the perimeter was filled with more sparse vegetation, all opening into a giant lake and dock. From what I could tell, there was no one around for miles. Somehow, Soren had managed to find a house that existed in perfect isolation— almost like the rest of the world didn't exist. If I wasn't so amped to figure out what was going on, to do something, I could stay hidden away here forever. And if I closed my eyes, I turned off my brain for a bit, I could pretend this was a vacation, not a lesson in recon.

"How did you find this place? It's like a fairytale." I found myself voicing the childish thought out loud.

"I used to come out here a lot, so I built the house a couple years back." Soren scratched the back of his neck sheepishly, in an uncharacteristic moment of vulnerability.

"You built this?" I felt my jaw drop.

"Yeah, not too bad right?" His gray eyes latched onto mine, watching as I took in the cabin.

"Not bad? It's breathtaking." While I was the first to admit that Soren's ego could do with a few hits, I couldn't deny how beautiful his place was—to say anything else would have been nothing more than a badly disguised lie.

The left side of his mouth twitched up, in a shadow of a grin. For the first time, I could see the smile extend to his eyes, creating light wrinkles that made the scar running through his brow stand out—somehow both boyish and sexy.

The inside of the house was just as beautiful as the outside. The place opened into a giant open-concept living room. The walls were made of a dark brown wood with lighter exposed beams running across the ceiling. While the room had a very masculine feel to it, it was also very cozy—a giant black couch and matching chair were angled around a fireplace. The cushions were deep, the kind you could sink into, and after a day like today, I was tempted to forego the rest of the tour to curl up and nap on one. Above the fireplace was a giant TV decked out with several gaming systems. My eyes travelled across the room spotting several speakers. It was strange to see technology in a place that was designated "the cabin" out in the middle of nowhere. The house was filled with a rustic yet modern atmosphere. An odd mixture of two worlds.

Even the kitchen was filled with modern appliances. It was much smaller than the kitchen back home, and I knew I'd be missing Sam's cooking. Still it would suffice for a hideout—we'd be able to prepare meals comfortably. Beyond the connected kitchen and living room, the house opened into a hallway with four doors: two bedrooms, an office, and a bathroom. They were all simply but tastefully decorated. And Jax proudly announced that there was a small garage at the back which was used as a gym. The declaration had my stomach sinking in dread.

I soaked in the house, the scent of pine filled the rooms, and each had a large window making the woods and lake feel as if they were part of the house. My hand ran down the rich wood paneling on the walls. It wasn't like the fake stuff you found at the store, but was imperfect and full of naturally asymmetrical markings; the walls told a story and when I closed my eyes I could imagine Soren carefully pouring over every detail as he built his hideout. It felt almost like an adult treehouse. When I turned back around to face everyone else, I found his eyes on me. There was a softness there I hadn't seen before. He opened his mouth like he was going to say something to me but was disrupted by the slam of a car door.

"Ah, that'll be Sage and Dex then," Jax said while he walked over to the fireplace to get a fire started. "They have excellent timing."

THIRTEEN

When Soren opened the door, he enveloped a large man in a hug.

That was the first odd thing. Soren actually showing affection.

The second odd thing was the way that El blushed a deep red and took a step behind me, like she was hiding.

After pulling myself out of the shock of seeing El uncharacteristically sheepish, I focused on the newcomer. The golden glow let me know immediately that he was a manipulator, and a pretty powerful one. Then again, my spidey-sense was a bit off lately. For all I knew, he was a low-level boredom-feeder. His hair was an unusual red color that was somewhere between burgundy and black. The hair lining his jaw in a scruffy shadow was a few shades darker and matched the deep brown color of his eyes. He was dressed head-to-toe in black, but the simple clothing didn't disguise the fact that he was built with a lot of lean muscle; the kind of muscle you earned through work and constant physical activity, not the kind of muscle you built up casually in a gym.

Catching my stare, he side-stepped Soren and reached his large hand out towards me. "Hey, I'm Dex. You must be Odessa, Soren's told me all about you."

As a flirtatious grin split his face, I couldn't help the one mirroring it on my own. "Knowing Soren, I'm sure he's painted me in a lovely light. All the same, nice to meet you."

His smile faltered a bit as he caught El hiding behind me. "Elliana. It's been a long time."

I heard the sound of El's intake of breath and watched as she straightened up her spine and turned her head up. "Dex, good to see you." Cautiously, she walked over to him and they did an awkward dance trying to decide whether they should shake hands or hug. When he finally tricked her into a hug and pressed his nose into her hair to longingly take in the scent, it made perfect sense. While I didn't know much about El's past, I did know El. And there was some history between her and Dex, the kind that probably involved doing the horizontal dance. I'd have to get the story from her later, because she was usually one to kiss and forget, not one to get pulled into the awkwardness of an old conquest.

When I looked back at the door, Soren was embracing the single most beautiful female I'd ever seen. She was tall—at least six feet—and, unlike Dex, she appeared to be a feeder. Black hair fell in voluminous waves down her back, highlighted with streaks of purple and blue. Her skin was a rich caramel that made the golden color of her eyes stand out. She walked forward to shake my hand and I took in the deep cut of her leather jumpsuit that showed off her perfect figure. Was this chick even real? She looked like she belonged in an action-hero film.

"Hey, I'm Sage. Dex and I will be in charge of looking after your uncle." Her smile was warm and inviting, and I had no choice but to like her. After a quick shake of my hand, she practically jumped on top of El. "Ellie, gods it's been ages. I missed you girl. It's hell living without my best friend around."

El hugged her back just as emphatically, and I couldn't stop the petty feeling of jealousy that came over me. Of course El had other friends, even a best friend, before me. Still, I was possessive and too much of my life had been turned upside down in one day. El was the only anchor I had left. And it didn't help things that Sage was stunning and warm. Or that she kept sending hungry glances towards Soren as she plopped down next to him on the couch. Though I wasn't really sure why that bothered me so much. Maybe because I was the only one who didn't seem to fit in perfectly with this strange band of supes.

I walked over to Dex who was conveniently holding a six pack of beer. Grabbing one for myself, I popped the top off with my ring using a trick Luis taught me. The trick was that Luis gave me a ring that was specially designed to open bottles since I wasn't coordinated enough to learn the actual trick. Then I kicked back into the chair with a little too much force and took a long swig.

El took the remaining seat on the couch and Dex sat on the arm next to her, passing beers around to everyone else. Watching them, it was clear that they were close—all four of them had a deep history that I didn't know or understand. I was taken out of my mini pity party when Jax lifted me up to steal my seat and placed me down on his lap. When I jerked away to stand up, he roped his long arm around me, pulling me closer and deeper into the seat of the chair. His left hand started rubbing circles into my back and I relaxed into him, in spite of myself. I knew it was his weird, seduction-feeder way of making me feel less alienated. I could do worse than having someone like Jax as a friend.

Soren cleared his throat and tore his eyes away from me and Jax. "Thanks for coming over guys. You'll have to head down to Seattle in a bit, but I wanted you to fill us in on what's been happening while we try to fill you in on things here. Give you an idea of what exactly it is you've agreed to step into."

"Soren, relax. It's been ages since we've all been together. Give us a second to catch up with El." Sage swatted Soren playfully on the arm before turning her attention over to El. "So, what have you been up to? Soren tries to give us updates every few months, but it's usually nothing more than 'she's alive.' You know how he is, he never gives us any good dirt."

El grinned at Sage as she relaxed slightly into the couch, though I could tell from her side glances at Dex that she wasn't as relaxed as she was pretending to be. "Things have been good. I've been living with Dessa and Sam for a few years. We're finishing up college." She glanced over at me, and her smile turned down slightly. "Well, really, who knows now? I don't know when we'll get back, so I guess we'll have to worry about our degrees later. So much for two months left, right Dess?"

I nodded back to her with a wistful smile, Jax's featherlight circles were doing wonders to relieve my tension. If I didn't know that his feeding didn't affect me, I'd think the calming sensation running through me was a supe thing. Then again, maybe it was the beer that I'd drained in less than a minute kicking in.

"Oooh, human college? That sounds so fun! Any human boyfriends, or are you just playing the field?" Sage's tone was light and friendly, but Dex stiffened immediately, clenching the neck of his beer so tightly I was sure it would shatter in his hands.

"Catch up over, Sage. We need to know what's going on ASAP. Girl talk can wait for another time." Dex turned to me. "So, Odessa, Soren tells us that you can see energy registers?"

I wrinkled my nose slightly at the thought of Soren telling people about my weird little sense. Especially since El told me not to trust people with it for years. I didn't even know these people, yet I had to keep everything that happened in the last week from one of my best friends. "Yeah, I can sometimes see a faint glow. It's not very reliable though, so there's not much I can say about it."

"Like with your human boyfriend, right? He tricked you and somehow hid that he was from the Veil?" Sage's voice was friendly, but I felt like I'd been struck in the gut with the reminder that Michael was the reason we were all in this mess in the first place. That it was to some extent my fault.

I nodded, unable to say more about it and feeling more than a little useless that my one ability was so faulty and unreliable. As was my judge of character.

"And he's a space-manipulator? You're sure, Soren?" Dex asked.

"Yes. If I hadn't seen him disappear myself, I wouldn't have believed it. But it's true." Soren took a long drink of his beer. "He seemed under the impression that he was after Black instead of El. To be honest, the whole thing was a bit strange. If he really wanted to harm her, he could have just grabbed her then and there. Taken her with him." He scrubbed his hand through his hair, a gesture I was beginning to secretly dub the 'Soren's frustrated signal.'

I thought over his words, my own frustration beginning to grow. Why *didn't* Michael just take me with him then and there if he wanted to kill me? "Maybe he had to report back to someone first? Or maybe he can't bring people with him when he, you know...teleports? Can space-manipulators usually bring along other people for the ride?" I asked

Soren shook his head. "Honestly, we don't know. There hasn't been a space-manipulator on record in a very long time. And there's no reliable information on them as it is. Energy users are very secretive about their abilities. We have no way of knowing the extent of his power. It is possible, though, that he's reporting back to a larger group and needed to get the go ahead before doing anything permanent. Maybe he's working for Insurgenti?" He directed the question to Sage and Dex.

Sage shrugged. "It's possible. We don't know much about the rebels at the moment. Though it's hard to believe they'd be able to keep a space-manipulator quiet for so long. Especially as just an underling who'd need to report back. I'd imagine someone with that ability would be at the top of the totem pole."

"And it's hard to definitively know what's the work of Insurgenti anymore. Or if there is only one faction of people resisting your dad's rule," Dex added. "The guard managed to bring in a suspected rebel member a couple of days ago. Your father questioned him about your sister and mother, but he didn't get anywhere before he killed her."

Holy shit. I knew that we were dealing with some serious stuff, but the thought of El's dad killing and likely torturing someone sent cold shivers down my spine.

"I was there, during the examination." Sage pulled at her hair for nonexistent dead ends. "I really don't think the guy had any idea there was a hit out for Ellie. Plus Jacer was there and he's the most powerful truth-manipulator in recorded history. Between the two of us, it would've come out unless he was working with a pretty powerful blocking agent."

I wanted to ask Sage what kind of feeder she was, but I knew that was considered rude. So I settled for the second-best question. "Truth-manipulator?" I asked. I didn't want to halt their brainstorm, but I did want to follow along.

"They are able to manipulate people into telling the truth. It's not an exact science, and you have to nail the phrasing of the questions for it to be at all effective, but Jacer is known for being particularly proficient." Jax's words skated over the bare skin at my neck. He'd been so quiet during the conversation that I'd almost forgotten I was on top of him like an awkwardly large pet chihuahua.

"Maybe it wasn't the rebel forces then?" El stood up and began pacing; the effect was lost though since her height brought her to eye level when the rest of the group was sitting. "I mean do we have any proof they were the ones after my mom? It's not like we ever captured the murderer. Maybe it wasn't them, or maybe it was only a small faction of them. Or a different faction. Maybe it was one of the other leaders after my father. Or maybe it was even more personal than that. Someone Father pissed off. It's not like we have any fucking clue what's going on here. He's never been a fan of keeping us in the loop. Maybe whoever's threatening my life is a totally different person or group from whoever took hers." She was rambling, and I knew from the look of concern in Sage's eyes that, like me, she could tell that El was operating on unusually high wavelengths of sadness and anger.

Still, these were valid points she was raising, and I wanted to ask more questions. I wanted to hear more about the rebels, about El's mom and dad, but I could tell this wasn't the time for me to voice that desire. Everyone else in the room knew the history, knew life in the Veil. I'd just have to play catch up when we had more time and when El was less emotionally vulnerable.

"She has a point, Soren." Jax was tense against my body. "These are all avenues we are going to have to explore. And now with Michael and Desi in the mix, we are going to have to get more proactive in figuring this shit out. We can't just hide Ellie away for her entire life—and clearly living among humans hasn't kept her completely off the energy-user radar like we suspected it would."

Soren nodded his head in agreement, draining his beer in frustration. I could tell he felt helpless. And that was something that wouldn't sit well with a guy like Soren.

"So, what do we now?" Sage squeezed Soren's knee gently and the intimacy of the gesture sent a strange feeling through my body. I struggled to rip my eyes away from the point where her hand and his leg connected.

"Now? Now you keep my uncle safe. Michael knows where we live, he knows Sam. You stay in Seattle and you watch out for him." I was momentarily stunned by the iciness in my own voice. I leaned back into Jax, dipping my head down. "Sorry. I know you guys are here to help. It's been a really long, really screwed up day. I didn't mean to snap."

Sage looked at me with sympathy lining her beautiful face. "We'll do what we can, Odessa. I promise you that."

Ugh, did she have to be so genuinely nice? It made it impossible to dislike her. Or at least it made me feel really really guilty about it.

"Our best," Dex added, "might not be much against a space-manipulator, especially one who is likely working with a fire-manipulator and who knows who else. You have to understand that now. We can make no promises beyond watching out for him and keeping a line of communication open between everyone. To be honest, we have no clue what we are up against."

Dex's words hit me hard, but I decided immediately that I liked him—he was being honest with me and wasn't sugarcoating things for my naive human ears.

"You guys should head out now. It's been several hours since Michael disappeared, and I don't want Sam alone either. We'll check in with you every other day or so." El was fidgeting and I knew she was just as worried about Sam as I was. We were family, and it wouldn't rest easy with her that we were leaving part of that family behind to fend for itself. I was suddenly excessively happy that Luis had never met Michael—that could only make him safer at this point.

Sage nodded. "We brought some groceries to keep you all stocked up for a few days while you make plans for the next move, and we bought some throwaway phones. We'll change out every couple of days. I doubt anyone from the Veil would be checking that sort of tech, but it's best to be as prepared as possible since they found El once already. Especially if you insist on staying near the rift."

Soren's posture tensed at that and he stood up with Sage to grab the food from the car, his hand pressing into her lower back as he guided her through the door. I forced myself to swallow the little bubble of jealousy in my gut. Now was so not the time to worry about Soren's relationship with Sage. And never was the *only* time I would allow myself to think about Soren in that way, no matter how hot he was. Attractiveness did not cancel out assholeness.

As they brought the last of the groceries in, I said goodbye to Sage and Dex, thanking them both in earnest for keeping their eyes on Sam and making sure we would stay updated on everything going on in Seattle. When El asked that they also check in on Luis, some of the tension in my body seeped away. Luis likely wouldn't be as at risk as Sam, but I was happy to know that Sage and Dex would look out for him as well.

I moved to the kitchen to start putting the groceries away while El, Soren, and Jax said their goodbyes. There was so much affection between them all that I felt like I was intruding.

After they left, we heated up a frozen pizza. We mostly ate in silence, all of us lost in our thoughts from the chaos of the day. Even though it was early, El and I decided to go to bed, both of us drained. We were going to share the room Jax usually stayed in and Jax would take the ridiculously comfortable, oversized couch.

"So," I started, running a brush through my hair, "about Dex. Was I misreading the situation out there or was there some tension between you two?"

114

El's skin flushed, but she met my face with a reluctant smile. "Yeah I should've known that wouldn't slip past you, Sherlock."

"That wouldn't have slipped past Mr. Magoo, El."

"Fair enough. Dex was my first time, you know, makin' bacon." She winked at me while grabbing her pajamas out of one of her overstuffed bags.

"Ew. I'm so glad that I already hate bacon, because you would have just ruined it for me with that visual. Still, first time or not, it's unusual for sex to make you blush."

"Well, Dex and I are complicated. You see, he's a body-manipulator too." Her eyes bugged out at me like that should mean something to me.

"So? What, you guys learned the tricks of the trade together?"

"Remember when I said it's common for powerful supes in the Veil to try to generate the most powerful breeding line?" She paused, wiggling her eyebrows.

"Oh. Oooooooh. Your father wants you to marry him, doesn't he?" I tossed my brush on the ground and hopped on the bed, way too invested in the conversation to worry about untangling knots.

"Not just wants me to marry him, Dess. I'm betrothed to him now. My father tried to rush the match before I left, but Dex wanted to wait awhile and see if the mate bond would develop first. I think he felt bad that I'd been given no choice because of my father's stance on the issue and my position within the realm." She blew out a long puff of air, causing her hair to float away from her face.

"Mate bond? Are you shitting me? That sort of thing is real where you're from?" I'd heard about the stereotypical destined romance in books and shows, but it had always given me the creeps. Call it fate or whatever you wanted, but I was a fan of free will; anything that took away a girl's choice grossed me out.

"Not in the sense that you're thinking. So off of the soapbox, Dessa, before you get a chance to get comfortable. They exist but there isn't like a single soulmate situation in the Veil. From what I understand, the partners have a choice and can choose to break it or stop it once they begin to notice the connection forming if they want. And if you break one bond, you are potentially free to establish another. Which is really useful, because sometimes the bond is unrequited—" she paused, shaking her head at me. "Stop giving me that look. It's not that creepy, but it is sort of complicated. Anyway, it was actually really sweet of Dex to try to wait. He wanted to make me feel more comfortable about the whole domestic side of my role in the Veil."

"So, you wanted to settle down with him then? Start popping out little pink-haired shopaholics?" I had to admit, the girl could do way worse than Dex. Then again, I guess all supes were just on average ridiculously good looking.

"I always figured at the time I would. Eventually. Things back home are different than they are here, Dess. It's not exactly easy for me to go against my father's wishes." The sadness in her words cut me deep. El was typically so full of life, so happy, independent, and ambitious; it was strange to see how much power her father and her old life had over her.

"And now? Do you still want Dex?"

"No." The single word rang with a resounding clarity that seemed to even startle El as she spoke it. Her cheeks reddened, and I had a feeling she wasn't thinking about Muscles McGee. Maybe her tiny crush on Sam wasn't as tiny as I'd always thought.

I decided I'd pushed her on the subject enough. If she wanted to tell me more, eventually she would. And truthfully, keeping her alive was higher up on our list than dissecting the tangled webs of Veil politics and El's love-life. "We should get some sleep."

She nodded her head and we both got ready for bed. Luckily, Jax's room was outfitted with a giant king-sized bed, likely to fit his giant frame. We snuggled in and turned off the lights.

After a few moments, I could practically chew on the tension in the room, the heavy stakes of the day settling over us both. It was crazy to think that just yesterday we'd been working a typical shift at The Tavern and out for a night of dancing. Crazier even to think that two weeks ago, our lives were filled with nothing more than work, school, and hanging out with Luis. I turned towards her, a giant grin on my face. "Hey El, there is one good thing about all of this."

"Yeah, what's that?" Her words were unusually cynical, and I found myself missing the version of El that wasn't so bogged down by her past.

"We won't have to write that English paper now. In fact, presumably, we won't have to worry about homework for quite a while."

"Excellent point. How will Professor Sadjwick live without Jax's presence in class?"

We both broke out into a hard laughter, the kind that's so full that only breathy sounds came out. And then we slid off to sleep, smiles on our faces and tears in our eyes—somehow both conflicted and at peace with the day's turn of events.

FOURTEEN

I woke up with the sunrise. Apparently, my body had grown accustomed to its new sleep schedule. Ellie was spread out across the bed. Somehow during the night she'd wound up sleeping horizontally, the pink tips of her short hair hanging off the edge of the bed.

Quickly, I changed into a pair of yoga pants and a tank, tiptoeing down the hall to head to the bathroom. The house was quiet, and I could hear Jax's light snores echoing in the living room. After grabbing a bottle of water and tying my hair back, I left the house, careful not to let the door slam as it shut.

The landscape was only more beautiful than I'd remembered it the day before, the sunrise dancing lazily against the still water of the lake. It was peaceful here and, while I couldn't forget all that was happening in my world, it was nice to have a moment of serenity. I spread a blanket I found on the edge of the bed along the splintered wood of the dock. Taking a deep breath, I ran through the yoga poses Jax had taught me over the week, some of them leaving my limbs hanging precariously close to the water's edge. My body ached, but as I transitioned from position to position, I felt a beam of pride at how much easier it was to hit them, my muscles strengthening and stretching with each breath.

After an hour, sweat was dripping steadily down my back. When I paused for a sip of water, the skin on the back of my neck started to tingle as that feeling of being watched rushed over me. Had Michael found us already? Did he somehow stick a LoJack on me?

Turning slowly, I let out a quick breath of relief when I found Soren leaning against a post on the porch, his eyes steadily focused in my direction. The relief at finding Soren and not some serial supe-killer quickly trickled away, and my cheeks flushed at the intensity of his gaze. How long had he been there?

He walked slowly towards me, his expression unreadable; the glare from the sun made the features of his face indistinguishable.

"Odessa Black, awake early by choice? What dimension have I stumbled into?" His gaze travelled away from me, taking in the surroundings. "Your form looks pretty good. Jax said you were taking well to yoga." He paused when he was within a few feet, my eyes slowly adjusting to the balance of sun and shade on his face. "It's good for building up your strength, fluidity, and balance. All very necessary when it comes to fighting."

I opened and closed my mouth, not sure what to say. Soren and compliments mixed as commonly as oil and water. "Yeah, I guess," I said, too stunned to say anything else.

"Has he started to train you in fighting techniques?" His eyes traveled slowly down my body; not in a seductive way, but as if he were assessing the developing shape of my muscles. Clinical.

"Sort of. He's taught me a few punching combinations and worked with me a bit on my hitting form. Mostly we do yoga and run." I pulled the loose material of my tank, suddenly self-conscious of how the sweat made it cling like Saran Wrap to my body.

"I owe you an apology, Black." He rubbed the back of his neck, his gaze staring off into the lake.

"For what?"

"I didn't take you seriously when you said you wanted to train. That first day. I should have done things differently. I shouldn't have treated you the way that I did and then pawn you off on Jax when you asked me to teach you. It was clear you wanted to protect El, that you weren't going anywhere. I think I was trying to intimidate you into letting it, and her, alone." He paused, and I held my breath. This was the most he'd ever said to me, and I never imagined I would hear Soren utter an apology.

"Yeah, you were kind of an asshole." I smiled slightly, letting him know that I was both serious and trying to lighten the mood.

"Oh, I'm still an asshole. That's not what I'm apologizing for."

I crinkled my eyes in confusion. Surly Soren I could handle. But humble, teasing Soren? I didn't know what to make of him.

"Look my point is just that I should have taken training you seriously. I will now. Yesterday made it abundantly clear that El won't leave you behind and that we are up against more than we imagined. And I'll likely need your help as we track down our sources." He paused momentarily. "Assuming your aura vision isn't totally screwed up and useless, that is."

Ah, that sounded more like the Soren I knew and...tolerated. And also, aura vision? What the hell did he think I was? A knockoff, pervy superhero—seeing through walls, clothes, and fears?

Because I'd be fine with that.

"Okay, so when do we start?" Tension ran through my body, though whether it was because I was excited to take my training to the next level with Soren or dreading it, I wasn't sure.

"Now." The sunlight bounced off his wicked grin, making him look more sinister than usual. No wonder he let me finish all of my practice without interrupting. He knew I was already exhausted.

"Fine." And exhausted I most certainly was. But I wouldn't let him know that. "Where do we start?"

"Here. We're just going to jump right into it. I want you to try and block my attack when I move towards you. It'll give us a baseline." He smirked, a teasing glint in his eyes.

"What do you mean block you when you at—"

My words were cut off and I found myself uttering the last syllable over a mouthful of water. Icy waves cut into my skin and I pushed myself up towards the bright rays of light. Coughing, I broke the surface and grabbed onto the splintered wood of the dock. After heaving myself up, a workout in and of itself, I spit water onto the surface and caught my breath. When I stood to face him, there was no doubt in my mind there was a glare on my face.

"You pushed me into the water. What the hell is wrong with you? I liked you better when you were just being your usual version of asshole."

His eyes were glistening with amusement, but that changed as his gaze dropped lower. Inhaling hard, he turned away from me and walked towards the other side of the deck. "Yeah, well that was your first lesson."

"What? That you're an asshole? Trust me, I already knew that. I thought you were going to take the training thing seriously." I was fuming as I squeezed the smelly water from the top that was clinging to me like a second skin. It especially didn't help that it was white. Thank god I had a sports bra on. Though that was also white.

"I am." He turned back towards me, his gaze never dropping below my face. "If someone is going to attack, they aren't going to wait until you're ready and they sure as hell aren't going to fire off a warning. You won't forget that gem of advice anytime soon, I'm sure." He winked and spread his arms wide. "Now, again."

This time, I was prepared. If only because I knew I wouldn't be given the time to prepare or complain. Still, that preparation didn't do much. One second Soren was four feet in front of me, the next second I was making an embarrassingly large splash into the lake. This time I wasn't as angry. He was right, of course. I wouldn't be given the luxury of a warning when someone came after me or El. And I also appreciated that he wasn't going to go easy on me. Someone coming after El wouldn't either.

The third time, I braced myself. I meant to block or evade his attack—I just hadn't expected him to be so fast. I gripped the edges of the dock, ready for round four, the pain in my muscles from the morning workout long forgotten.

The fourth time Soren moved towards me, I took a long step to my left and attempted to trip him as he reached me. Didn't go as planned. Soren, being Soren, anticipated that move and rolled his eyes while he shoved me gently into the lake. When my head broke the surface, I smiled up at him. "Hey, at least I tried that time."

"Trying and failing is still failing, Black." His trademark smirk made itself visible as I pulled myself up. "But yes, it's a sign of improvement I suppose. And at the very least, you're getting a good upper body workout dragging yourself out of the lake like that every two seconds."

The next half hour was spent with me finding various ways for Soren to throw me into the lake. On the last try, I was able to hold him off for a few seconds—long enough to try some of the sparring techniques Jax taught me but not long enough to avoid the inevitable plunge into water. My smile when I came up for air was huge. That was an improvement. It wasn't much, but if I practiced every day, I'd get better. If this morning, hell this week, taught me anything it was that I was capable of learning and improving. Rome wasn't built in a day, and neither were kickass fighters. I'd be Buffy status by summer if I had anything to do with it. And, well, I did. What else was I going to do while I waited for Soren and Jax to mastermind some long-winded comic-book plan?

Soren peered down at me from the edge of the dock, his elbows resting on his knees as he hunched down. "That was better. Each attempt has been an improvement on the one before it. You're actually doing pretty well," he started, amusement shining in his gray eyes. "And let's face it, you can only do so much. It's not your fault my fighting technique is practically faultless."

He reached his hand down to help pull me up, his first offer of assistance. While I should have appreciated the gesture, I couldn't stop from grabbing his hand and pulling him into the water with me.

It was a cliché and cheap shot, but Soren fell for it. Literally.

When he resurfaced, I tried to ignore the way the sun danced off his blond hair, and the way the water made trails down his face. "What the hell, Black? I was being nice." He paused, considering. "Ish."

True. A grin stole over my face. "Lesson the first, Soren—" I paused dramatically, my voice deepening in a poor imitation of his. "An enemy will take advantage of any sign of weakness or vulnerability."

"Touché." A deep, rich laugh echoed around me. I could get lost in the sound of Soren's laughter and I tried to shove the electric tingles it inspired somewhere deep in my memory where I wouldn't find it. When Soren laughed, he was beautiful; his smile revealed perfectly white teeth and extended all the way to his eyes. I found myself mentally tracing the way his hair fell against the glistening white of his scar. He looked so carefree in that moment, so unburdened.

Uncomfortable with the intimacy of the moment, I moved back for a quick swim, deliberately splashing him as I kicked away. When I made it back to the dock, Soren was already perched on it, watching my less than graceful attempt to join him. With adrenaline disappearing from my body, I was beginning to feel exhaustion settle deep into my bones.

After two unsuccessful tries to lift myself up, Soren clasped my hands and pulled. I flew onto the dock, not expecting the strength and power behind his tug. As soon as I landed, he unclasped our hands and dropped back down to the ground. I joined him and laid back against the blanket I used as my makeshift yoga mat earlier. My eyes began wandering over the way his soaked shirt clung to the muscles of his torso; he was strong and lean, not bulky. The water made the material almost transparent and I saw that the tattoo on his arm extended across his chest. The swirls and shapes didn't seem to mean anything, but they were beautiful nonetheless.

When my eyes lifted towards his face, they were met with a cocky grin.

"Your tattoos," I started, trying to cover up the fact that I was blatantly checking him out. "What do they mean?"

The gray in his eyes shifted a few shades darker, the arrogance no longer present across his features. "Nothing. They don't mean anything, Black."

I pretended to believe him and closed my eyes, soaking up the sun as it slowly dried the cool water on my skin. My muscles trembled, and I was exhausted, but it was a good kind of exhaustion. Today's training wasn't a total failure and I was beginning to enjoy that ache in my body that came along with a good workout. I would never admit that to El, though. She'd have me institutionalized.

After a few minutes, I cracked open my eyes, uncomfortable with the silence. I half expected Soren had left, realizing that I'd be useless for any more training today. Instead, I found him watching me, his arms holding him up a few feet away. His eyes held a question, like he could figure out the answer, unravel my code, by staring at me long enough. When he caught me watching him back, I smirked—happy, for once, not to be the one caught gawking. He shook his head and turned around to watch the water. And I tried really hard to not stare at the muscles in his back. Really really hard.

"Soren?" My voice was softer than usual. I wasn't completely sure how to go about having a conversation with someone like him; he was all hard edges with mood swings I couldn't always follow or read.

"Hm?" He didn't turn back to face me, but he acknowledged me, and I was going to take that as the go ahead.

"Why do you spend so much time on this side of the Veil if you hate humans?" I bit my lip, frozen for a few moments while I waited to see if he'd ignore me or give me some non-answer.

"What makes you think I spend so much time on this side of the Veil?" He turned back towards me with a playful smirk.

"Gee, I don't know." I rolled my eyes. "Maybe it has something to do with the fact that you built this perfect house that, as far as I can tell, isn't in the Veil." I had no idea how to reach the Veil, or even where it was. Hell, maybe we were in the Veil and I just didn't realize it. Sage *did* mention that Soren insisted on staying near the rift.

Maybe we were closer than I realized? I wasn't going to press my luck and ask when getting even basic answers from him could be like pulling teeth. "Unless we passed through the Veil on the way here and I just missed it?"

"Perfect, huh?" He leaned forward, ignoring my question like I knew he would. "Yeah I guess it is." After a few more moments of silence, I was convinced he wasn't going to say any more. I opened my mouth to ask something else, something simpler, when his gravelly tone cut me off. "I don't hate humans, Black."

I scrunched up my eyebrows in confusion. "But you're always going on and on about how humans are in the way. You even make it sound like a swear word when you say it. Human." Then again, it wasn't just humans in general he seemed to have a problem with. He didn't appear to have any issues with humans we encountered at The Tavern, or Inferno, or even school. Come to think of it, he only infused the term human with disdain when he was using it in reference to me. "Oh," my voice came out in barely a whisper. "It's not humans then, I guess. It's me."

He dragged his hand through his wet hair, made several shades darker from the water, and bent his head down so I could no longer see his face. "I don't hate humans, Black. In fact, sometimes I think life would be a lot easier if I was human, simpler. The Veil is a complicated place." He paused for a second and scratched the back of his neck. "Then again, I guess the human realm is too. And I don't hate you. I just don't like that you got to grow up here, with El. In many ways, you and Sam have given her a family when she needed one the most. And I don't like that having you in the picture makes this all much more complicated than it should be." He grabbed a small stone off the dock and threw it into the lake. We both watched as it hopped across the water, the soft plopping sound the only thing breaking the silence for several seconds. "And sometimes...well, sometimes I worry that maybe El won't ever want to come back to the Veil. Even if I can keep her safe. Not if it means leaving you here. We were close growing up, I don't like that you've taken my place."

I blinked my eyes a few times, letting his words roll over me. Part of me was happy to hear that his indifference and aggression towards me wasn't actually directed at me. Part of me was too busy focusing on the fact that El would one day have to go home; that no matter how much we fooled ourselves, El wouldn't be able to be a part of my life forever. She had Dex and who knew what else. In fact, maybe the scariest thing I learned over the past week was that El's life here was never meant to be permanent. With her father's position it was entirely likely she'd end up ruling a group of people one day. I didn't have all the details on her role back home, but obviously she was important if she had a stalker threatening to kill her.

When I looked back at Soren, I found him studying me again. Curiosity and vulnerability possessed his features in equal parts. "I didn't replace you, Soren. And she'll go back." My voice cracked around the emotion lodging in the back of my throat. "When it's time, she'll go back." And hell, maybe she could visit me often when she did. Soren clearly spent a lot of his free time away from the Veil, maybe she could too.

He nodded his head and leaned towards me like he was going to say something else, but we were interrupted before he had the chance.

Jax plopped down next to me and raised an eyebrow when his eyes lingered over our lake-soaked clothes. "I was going to ask if you wanted to work out, but looks like Soren beat me to the punch."

"Beat and punch. Those are definitely two words that accurately describe this morning's training session." I nodded my head at Soren. "But don't worry, he got a few good hits in too."

"Oh, I'll bet." Jax grabbed my arms and lifted me up, not even trying to disguise the fact that he was checking me out as his eyes travelled slowly up and down my body. "I could get used to seeing you like this, Desi-girl."

"Like what?" I asked.

Soren stood up next to us, his body tenser than it had been a moment ago.

"Wet." He winked once at me before pinching Soren's cheek and turning back towards the house. "Come on Rocky, let's get some breakfast started. We've got a lot to figure out today," he called back towards me.

I turned to Soren as we made our way slowly behind Jax. "Is he always this insufferable?"

"Always? No. Lately? Yes." His jaw muscles tightened, and then Soren ran ahead to catch up to Jax, leaving me free to channel my inner sloth and drag my aching bones and muscles after them at a comfortable, snail-like pace.

FIFTEEN

After a long soak in the tub, I found myself exceedingly grateful that El was an over packer. There was an entire compartment in one of her many bags reserved for bath salts and bubbles. And right now, my aching muscles had me eating my words—I wouldn't make fun of her goo-hoarding anytime soon.

I dressed in what was quickly becoming my newest uniform: leggings and a black top. Despite how sore I was, I wasn't naive enough to think I could afford going without training this afternoon. Ideally, I'd have all the time in the world to slowly build my athleticism; our newfound roles on the run, however, made time a luxury.

El's sleepy form nudged me out of the bathroom, ready to claim the shower for herself. While she was more of a morning person than I was, I knew well enough to tread lightly until she was at least midway through her morning pampering ritual. With a quick smile, I left her to the bathroom and followed the enticing smells into the kitchen. Jax was lounging at the breakfast bar which separated the kitchen from the living room area, nursing a cup of coffee while he scanned through the paper. There was something so completely human and domestic about the scene that I couldn't hold in my laugh.

"Training to be a soccer Dad? Crossword's on page ten." I nudged his arm while I greedily stole a sip of his coffee.

"Hey, woman. Get your own caffeine, I made a whole pot." He gestured with his head into the kitchen, so I followed the promised trail towards coffee.

Soren was at the stove, four pans going at once. I cringed, knowing full well that if I were dealing with that much cutlery and that many burners, I'd be asking for a disaster. In true Soren fashion though, he handled it with ease. Ignoring my jealousy, I opened cabinets searching for a tall glass. After three failed attempts at locating the stash, Soren silently reached to his right and pulled a cup down for me. Without so much as looking in my direction, he handed it to me and added some chopped vegetables into a small pan already filled with yellow, eggy goodness.

I slammed an ice cube tray hard against the counter, piling my cup to the top with the blocks. As I poured the coffee over the ice, I smiled; I always loved the quiet hiss as cold met hot. A splash of milk later, and I settled against the counter for a few minutes of peace.

"Why do you have two pans of omelets going?" I leaned towards Soren, noticing a small and large pan, both filled with eggs and chopped up fillings.

He reached for a plate and dumped the contents of the smaller pan onto it before shoving the omelet in my direction. "You don't eat meat, right?"

My mouth dropped open, shocked not only that he would remember but that he would prepare a dish especially for me. "Thanks, you didn't have to do that."

"Why? Would you suddenly turn omnivorous if I didn't?" He arched his left brow and handed me a fork. "You need to eat if you plan on building any muscle."

The dish smelled amazing—the perfect combination of spices and a perfect mixture of cheese and egg. A girl could get used to this; might even make putting up with his typical asshole-ish side worth it. Maybe. "Well, I appreciate it is all. Thank you." Without another word, I sat next to Jax and dove in. When I came up for air, I found Jax smirking at me, the newspaper long forgotten. "Sorry, I should have waited for your food to be done. Morning workouts leave me too famished for my manners to keep up apparently."

I lifted the fork for another bite, unable to contain the small moan of pleasure. Food was great, as a general rule. Food after a workout was ten times better. And food you didn't have to buy or make? Well, that was downright orgasmic. When I opened my eyes, Jax and Soren were both staring at me, neither one blinking.

"What?" I asked. "Do I have something on my face." I reached over for a napkin and scrubbed lightly against my chin.

"Damn, Desi-girl. Remind me to cook for you next time." Jax laughed, grabbing the plate Soren extended to him. "But also, you know, breathe in between bites."

I could feel the heat pooling in my cheeks. "Shut up."

Jax ran his hand through my hair, shaking the wet strands everywhere. "Just teasing you, relax."

Soren cleared his throat and turned back towards the stove, readying his and El's plates. Both were piled absurdly high with bacon.

El walked out with her hair wrapped tight in a towel, wordlessly grabbed a plate from Soren, and sat down on my other side. "So, what's the plan for today?"

Her question pulled me from my embarrassment and I shoved my empty plate a few feet in front of me. "Have you guys heard from Sage or Dex this morning?" My workout, bath, and breakfast helped me feel less anxious about yesterday's turn of events, but nothing could make me stop worrying about Sam and Luis.

Jax shook his head, his mouth full.

I hopped off the stool and began washing some of the dishes Soren used.

"Hey, don't worry Dess. No news is good news. They've been in Seattle for less than a day and if something happened to Sam, we'd know about it by now." El's words calmed the bubble of fear that was brewing in my gut.

I nodded my head without looking at them and went back to cleaning while everyone ate their food. "Okay, so what do we do today then? I mean do we have a plan? We should have a plan, right? They always have a plan in novels and movies."

When I turned back around, Jax was watching me with amusement in his eyes. "The Nervous Desi Babble makes its first morning appearance. I'm growing quite fond of that coping mechanism, to be honest."

Soren's brows came together in thought. He looked over at Jax. "I've been thinking. We should try to find Raifus."

The humor melted off of Jax's face. "Raifus?" His voice was squeakier than usual. "Man, that guy gives me the creeps."

"He might be able to help us figure out how to track down Michael or Charlotte. Maybe even offer some insight on whatever it is Black can see and why it doesn't always work." Soren filled his mouth with bacon and scratched at his shadow of a beard, the hairs significantly darker than the ones on his head.

"Who's Raifus?" El asked the question I'd been thinking. It was nice to not be the only one in the dark, for once.

"Someone who is really good at energy-seeking. Sometimes, he's able to locate someone's signature." Jax paused and a dark look washed over his face. "Dude's completely crazy though. I met him once years ago and I have no desire to repeat the encounter."

Soren nodded towards the black ring on El's finger. "He's the one who made your jewelry set. The one that allowed me to track you. It works through his gift."

"Is he a feeder or a manipulator?" My eyes scrunched as I tried to think about how he might be able to locate someone's energy. It sounded more like witchcraft than a specific energy-focused ability.

"No one really has a clue. As far as I know, he's the only one of his kind. Most people in the Veil don't know about him and I only met him in a chance encounter years ago. He found me." Soren's words were quiet, like he was hesitant to voice them.

"Alright, when do we go? Do you know where he lives?" El hopped off the stool, ready to leave as soon as she uttered the sentence.

"Not we, El." Soren looked up at her, his fingers curling over the rim of the table. "I don't want you near Raifus. He's too much of a wild card and we have no idea where his loyalties are."

"But—"

"There's no wiggle room on this one, El. We go without you or we don't go at all. Those are the only two options." Soren met her glare for a moment but went back to eating as it fizzled out into compliance.

"Well, if this guy is as shifty as you say, I don't want you going alone either Soren. You're not completely invincible, you know. Take Jax at least." El picked at invisible threads in her shirt.

"Jax will stay with you, keep an eye on things. I don't want you left without one of us by your side at all times." Soren tilted his head in my direction without looking at me. "She can go with me."

"You think that's a good idea, Soren?" Jax's jaw tensed, his usually friendly demeanor suddenly harsh. "Raifus could eat her alive. And that's only if he's feeling nice."

Soren shrugged. *Shrugged.*

My stomach dropped down to my feet. If this guy scared even Jax, what chance would I have? Still, if this Raifus character gave us a clue to find Michael or Charlotte, I'd have to buck up. I wanted us safe and home with the whole family as soon as possible.

I cleared my throat in an attempt to rattle out any vestiges of fear. "I'll do it."

"Why do we even need to find Michael, aren't we currently running from him anyway?" El's eyes travelled between Soren and me, her face etched in worry. "On what planet is this a good idea?"

"Because we want to know where he is. Raifus might be able to lead us to whoever Michael is working with. At the very least, he could help us locate Charlotte and potentially shed some light on whatever the hell's going on. He's perceptive. He knows more about how our worlds work and weave together than anyone I've ever met, but he'll only tell us what he wants to tell us. If I've learned one thing from my dealings with him, it's that." Soren stood up and took his plate to the sink. After a quick look at me, he turned and walk towards his bedroom. "We'll leave in an hour."

One hour later, down to the minute, I found myself staring at the black curves of Soren's motorcycle. He was already straddling it, his hand impatiently wavering as he held out the second helmet.

"You're late, let's go Black."

"Do we really need to take this? Can't we take the van?" I took a step back, just to make it clear I was uncomfortable with the bike if it wasn't already glaringly obvious. It was one thing to take Michael's bike a couple of blocks, it was another thing altogether to travel on one for hours with someone who drove like a maniac. "I mean, I've broken a bone by simply walking before. On a flat surface. Let's not tempt the fates by putting me on one of these things."

The dark visor made it almost impossible to see his eyes, but somehow I knew they would be rolling. "Black, get on. Raifus lives far, it'll be easier and faster to get there on the bike in case there's traffic we need to weave through." He shoved the helmet into my stomach, not relenting until I grabbed it from him. "Plus, there's no way in hell I'm going to drive a mom van."

"Did you say weave through? We will not be weaving through cars like psychopaths, Soren Tesker." I said, my voice shrill even to my own ears. I pushed the helmet firmly on my head, aware that my hair would be a disaster when I finally lifted it back off. "I'm just warning you. I bring bad luck. So, don't blame me if something disastrous happens."

"Noted. Besides, I heal quickly so it won't really matter. Now get on and stop stalling." He patted the back half of the seat behind him.

I gulped. Like one of those can't-be-real, cartoon-style gulps. Soren made me uncomfortable when he was a room away—clutching onto him for dear life would no doubt give me an anxiety attack. "Are you sure? I mean I could drive the mom van if you don't want to."

"Black. On. Now." He revved the engine and faced forward, making it clear that I either hopped on now or I would be left out of the one opportunity I'd been given to do something that could be even mildly construed as helping.

"Fine." I mumbled a few creative curse words under my breath as I straddled the bike. Whether my stomach was flipping from my fear of the trip or from Soren's close presence, I wasn't sure.

"Hold on." The growl of his voice reached my ears, even with the loud sound of the engine trying to swallow it up. The thought of gripping onto Soren made me blush, so I lightly grabbed onto the extra material of his zip-up hoodie. As soon as he pulled away from the cabin though, the force of the acceleration drove away my inhibitions and I threw my arms around his torso, clinging desperately to him like a baby monkey. I pressed my face firmly into his back, trying to drown out the speeding landscapes and regain my equilibrium. The lilting chuckle spread from Soren's body and drummed into my own.

He was laughing at me. *Laughing.* I clenched my jaw and loosened my hold lightly, pulling my head to the side so that one of my eyes could slowly open and take in the ride. I refused to be the incompetent human Soren seemed eager to label me as.

My pulse was ringing in my ears and after several calming deep breaths, a skill I picked up thanks to Jax, my body started to relax and fold less desperately around Soren's. The ends of my braid slapped against my back as I greedily soaked in the beautiful trees surrounding us as we sped by. Soren's cabin was secluded enough that after several miles, we still hadn't encountered another soul on the road. I knew he was going way beyond any legal speed limit, but I crossed my fingers in hope that his supernatural abilities would give him enough balance to maneuver us safely around once we did begin to encounter traffic. Then again, maybe this was part of his elaborate plan to get me out of the picture permanently. It'd be pretty hard for El to keep me around if I was spread like a pancake against the pavement.

After two hours of riding, I was no longer afraid of the speed or the bike; instead I found myself noticing other things. Like how good the fresh scent of Soren smelled as the wind whipped it around my face. Or how hard his muscles were against my chest and fingers. At one point I found myself secretly hoping my fear would come back, if only to knock some sense into me.

Eventually, Soren pulled into a secluded, woody area and brought his bike to a stop. He parked it behind a tree, grabbed a bag from under the seat, and tossed some branches on top of it once I clumsily hopped off.

"What are you doing that for?" I tugged the helmet off and self-consciously patted down my hair. The smirk on Soren's face confirmed my suspicions that my attempts were useless.

"Hiding the bike. I doubt we'll encounter anyone out here, but it's best to be prepared anyway." He stretched his muscles out after the long trip and I had to turn away to stop myself from staring at the patch of skin that emerged between his jeans and shirt.

"Never would have pegged you as a boy scout, Soren." I turned around, taking in the tall trees surrounding us. We spent most of the trip driving southeast, so I knew we weren't anywhere close to Seattle. Still, I couldn't help but hope that Sam or Luis would casually drive by to greet us. And the fact that I was missing them both after a day did nothing but highlight my unhealthy dependency issues. "What do we do now? I don't see a house."

"You won't see a house unless Raifus wants you to." He turned away from me and started walking into the forest. "For now, we walk."

Soren spent the next twenty minutes in silence, casually sniffing and tracking as we made our way through the invisible paths. I wasn't sure what he was looking for, but his focus and concentration made it clear he didn't want to be interrupted with questions or conversation. Even though he was silent, he managed to stop me from falling twice without even casting a glance in my direction. I wasn't much of a hiker.

"You need to work on your balance, Black. No wonder it was so easy for me to continuously toss you into the lake." His fingers slid along some bark before he directed his strides a bit to the left.

I flipped him off from behind, his inability to see me infusing me with enough courage for that temporary rebellion. When I opened my mouth to respond, my face slammed into his back, the impact hard enough to land me on my ass. Whatever I was about to say was lost when I took in the open field in front of us. Too bad too, because it was totally going to be a witty and snarky comeback. Probably.

"Is this where Raifus lives?" I pushed myself up and walked into the beautiful field, the grass long and wild, but still flattened down like it had been tamed.

"No. This is where we wait." He rifled through the bag hanging off of his arm and tossed me a water bottle before taking one for himself.

"What do you mean wait? Is Raifus even here? How will he know we are waiting to see him?" I chugged down half the bottle, surprised by my own thirst.

"He won't be seen unless he wants to be seen. This was the last place I met him, and he told me to return here if I ever needed to get ahold of him again. It's entirely possible he won't meet us today." Soren dropped his bag on the ground and surveyed the land.

"So, what do we now then? Do we leave and come back?" The frustration in my voice was clear, but there was no hiding it. After speeding on a bike for two hours and trying to keep up with Soren's long legs as we hiked through a freaking forest, I was exhausted and ready for some answers.

"We train. We'll wait a few hours while we work on your combat skills." He paused, his gray eyes landing on me with a hint of amusement. "Don't whine, Black," he said, cutting me off before I had a chance to say anything. "You were the one who wanted to be included on the first stealth mission. Well, sometimes stealth is boring. And I would have made you train more this afternoon anyway, so it doesn't really matter where we do it."

I chugged the rest of my water and squared my shoulders. "Fine, but if you work me too hard, you're carrying me back."

SIXTEEN

The next two weeks continued in a similar fashion. I woke up early, trained, and traveled to the forest to wait out Raifus and train some more. And the only thing we really had to show for it was that my ass was slowly getting accustomed to riding on the back of a bike for extended periods of time. That, and I could sort of fend off an attacker, if he was having a really, really, *really* off day. My descents into the lake went from occurring every time I sparred with Soren, to occurring most of the time I sparred with Soren. Jax got in on the fun too, and between training with both of them, I had little to no time or energy to worry too much about Michael and whoever else might be after us. More importantly, we hadn't heard any bad news from Dex or Sage.

Preparing for another day of sore muscles and aches in places I didn't even know could ache, I woke up with the sunrise ready to start with some yoga. The stretching and morning meditation was becoming my favorite part of the day. After brushing my teeth and changing into some leggings, I made my way into the living room to find Soren and Jax propping up a very tired looking El.

"What's going on?" Usually, I was the first one up—which alone was a sign that the apocalypse was coming. I leaned against the couch and covered a laugh with a cough when I caught the glower El shot at her brother. That look was definitely genetic. Something about the identical anger in the blue and gray eyes had my lips twitching up—a rare feat this early, especially pre-coffee.

"Soren's making me workout too." She walked into the kitchen to start a fresh pot of coffee. "I'm not doing anything without some caffeine first though." El rarely needed coffee, so I could tell that the sleeping beauty was affected by her lack of purpose since leaving home. Soren was probably right, training would be good for her—I kind of missed the crazy, high energy El.

"Don't be mad, Ellie," Jax coaxed. "It'll be good for you to brush up on your moves. It's not like you've been practicing your fighting skills the last six years. And if you have, let's be honest, sparring with a human wouldn't be much practice for you." Jax turned to me with a silent apology and I tried not to take any offense. If there was a human out there who could take on an angry El, let alone a panther-shifted El, I wanted to meet them.

"I turn into a panther, Jax. Fighting skills are encoded in my DNA," she deadpanned.

"Still, it will be good for you to work out with us anyway. Plus, it will be helpful for Black to spar with a shifter to see how different abilities require different techniques." Soren opened the door and walked outside, ready to start even if we weren't.

"I could just spar with him though, right? I mean, El you could go back to bed if you want. Or at least give yourself some time to wake up." El was almost as allergic to exercising as I was. I reached for the cup as she poured herself one.

El and Jax looked at each other, their eyes speaking a language I wasn't picking up on. "Soren prefers not to shift around people, especially when it comes to training," she said, mumbling over the lip of her cup.

"Why? If I turned into a badass jungle cat, I'd be showing myself off at every opportunity. Unless, and please tell me this is it, Soren turns into an embarrassingly tiny panther? Like mouse-size? In which case, the ego hit could be good for him." I took a sip, happy that El remembered to add a ton of ice to mine. Even when she was tired, the girl nailed the friend thing.

El smiled at me before shaking her head softly and dropping eye contact. "Soren's just," she paused, blowing on her own coffee and taking a few cautious sips. "He's a bit different than me. When I shift, I'm usually still myself. With Soren, the animal kind of takes control. His instincts are hyper amplified. They're still his instincts, mind you, but if he's sparring with someone and suddenly drops on all fours, it's not always easy for the primitive side of his brain to distinguish between play fighting and real fighting. Rationality and empathy sort of disappear," she looked at me with a grin, "not that there's a whole lot of that when he's in human form."

"Trust me, Desi-girl, it's something more than one of us has learned the hard way over the years. He prefers to utilize the added strength, speed, and sense perception when he's in human form. The animal only comes out during the real 'oh shit' moments." Jax nodded his head and left to find Soren and prep for our training. "Meet us outside when you finish your coffee. I'll try to distract him long enough to give you a chance to take a few gulps."

"Well, that explains a lot." I smirked over at El.

"What?" One of her perfectly-groomed eyebrows arched up.

"Your obsession with meat. Soren's too. Plus, I always knew your balance was way too perfect. All this time, you've been making me feel like I'm clumsy, when really, you've had the balance of a cat the whole time. Even when you're in your pixie-person form."

"Trust me, you're still clumsy. Me having supe-amplified balance doesn't change that."

"And your sense of smell. Your hearing. You never talked about the supe stuff before, but now it makes sense. You are rarely in panther form, but you always experience some of the added benefits."

"Yup, which means I've always been able to hear you singing in the shower. Seriously, who sings commercial jingles instead of real songs? And not even the good commercial jingles, but the ones that make you cringe with their bad rhymes and puns." She threw me a wink, threaded her arm through mine, and dragged me towards the door. "Come on, today I get to join you in your misery. Part of it anyway, since Soren won't let me come on the super-secret stakeouts sniffing for Raifus."

"Such alliteration. Professor Sadjwick would be happy to know you aren't letting your extended vacation negate all your hard work in the English Department."

She rolled her eyes as we met the boys in the clearing. My eyes landed on Soren, who seemed more tense than usual. He turned slightly towards me. "So, today I want you to work with Ellie. It's one thing for you to learn how to fight, it's another for you to learn how to fight and defend yourself against someone with an energy ability. And, since Jax doesn't seem to affect you," his lips twerked up, his eyes mocking Jax, "Ellie is the best option we have today." He didn't give a reason for not participating, but now that I knew he also had superior hearing, he probably heard Ellie explaining his shift to me. I should probably be more aware of how close he was next time I wanted to complain about him.

Or not. I was only partially kidding when I said his ego could use some deflating.

"Got it, fighting Bagheera today." I winked at Ellie as she grinned at her old nickname.

"More like *trying* to fight Bagheera today." She hopped slightly from foot to foot, her arms in front of her like a boxer. "Beware though, Bagheera has some good moves."

Soren looked up towards the sky, in what was likely his version of an eye roll. "Ellie stop turning this into a joke. You need a refresher just as much as Black does. You've grown soft these last few years and need to re-train yourself to be vigilant."

Soren was always talking about the importance of vigilance. Sometimes I liked to close my eyes and pretend that I was being trained by Mad-Eye Moody. Of course, I'd never admit that to him, but I was sure El would get a kick out of it.

When I looked away from Soren with a small smirk on my face, I turned back towards El and Jax. Where my vertically-challenged, blond best friend stood moments before, was a giant black panther looking at me through familiar blue eyes. I went to take a step back and fell on my butt.

"Oh shit," I muttered, pulse hammering. "El, I know it's just you, but the prospect of fighting a jungle beast was way less terrifying in theory."

The panther lifted its top lips and made a strangled sound—it was an expression I've never seen on an animal before and if I had to guess, I'd say she was laughing at me.

"Okay, Black. Let's say you're facing a body-shifter who can shift into something predatory like a panther. What does your instinct tell you to do?" Soren paced beside us, calm and collected while I was sweating bullets.

"Honestly? Run," I answered.

"Right. That'll work if you see the energy aura long before the shifter sees you, but hopefully you've come to terms with the fact that you're not faster than a panther, Desi-girl." Jax was grinning ear-to-ear. "Not to mention that will just heighten the predatory instinct for the animal to chase its prey."

"Well I obviously can't fight an animal with her size and strength so what am I supposed to do? Throw some catnip at her and hope I can distract her long enough to get away? Carry a laser pointer at all times?" I was joking, but also kind of not. Cats were smart, but I'd yet to meet one who didn't succumb to the entertainment of a dancing red light.

"Think about the last thing Jax said." Soren's tone was even, in full coach mode.

"He mentioned her instincts." I took a casual step away from El. I knew she'd never hurt me and I was never afraid of her in this form before, but something about knowing I'd be fighting her in a moment had my nerves on edge.

"Yes. Shifters, when in their shifted form, tend to fight and think more through their instincts. El's still there, but her senses are heightened, and she'll fight using the panther's instincts. In human form, she'll be more likely to think about her strategy, and yours." Soren paused and looked at me, and I tried to ignore the little flip in my stomach when my eyes met his gray ones. "So, what do you think you should do?"

"Work against her instincts?" I paused for a moment, squinting against the sun. "Or at least anticipate them and move accordingly."

"Good, Desi!" Jax was bouncing on his feet like a proud parent in the stands.

Normally I'd find that sort of cheerleading patronizing, but I couldn't help beaming back at Jax. The smile on his face was so genuine.

Soren and Jax spent the next hour teaching me how to work with Ellie's weaknesses, to anticipate her moves and push against them. It was amazing to watch the three of them spar, each moving around the other in an elaborate and graceful dance. I messed up more times than I succeeded, but El never did more than lick my ticklish arms and legs to signal a bite. And of course, I could tell that she was holding back with me in comparison to when she went after Jax and Soren.

Even so, by lunchtime I was feeling more confident in my sparring. Realistically, I'd likely never stand a chance against a body-manipulator, but the exercise still improved my strategy and it was important for me to understand how different humans and supes were—and since we were being hunted by the latter, that meant I had a long way to go before I would be good for anything other than running away.

When Soren and Jax went inside to make lunch, Bagheera and I laid out near the pond, soaking in the afternoon sun. My hand absentmindedly scratched El behind the ear until I realized what I was doing and pulled it away. Our eyes met and I laughed, both of us remembering the day we met.

After a few more seconds of cooling down from the strange and intense workout, I moved back into the house, accompanied a few minutes later by a human El tugging down her shirt. I turned to her. "You know, I always wanted a pet, so it's nice that my roommate can fill that role for me."

She nudged me lightly before hopping off to the shower, singing an awful pop song at the top of her lungs.

I sat in silence for a moment, savoring the gooey grilled cheese. Jax added double cheese on mine—it was a work of art.

"So, back to waiting in the backyard of the elusive Raifus today?" I asked before taking another obscenely large and unflattering bite.

Soren nodded, looking over at Jax, the two of them lost in a silent conversation I couldn't follow.

"Have you heard from Sage or Dex?" I probed, panic suddenly dispensing along my spine.

Jax shook his head. "Not since yesterday. There was a little development." Jax paused and Soren tensed. "Sam's totally okay though," he added quickly.

"Why wouldn't he be totally okay? What development? You guys didn't mention anything last night." I stood up. And then I sat down again, unsure of what to do. If it was bad news, it would be best to sit. But I wanted good news, so I stood back up.

Soren pushed away from his chair, his hands clenching around the wooden lip of the table until I was certain it would splinter. "I'm going to go get ready for the day." He walked towards his bedroom, but at the last second turned back in my direction. "We'll leave in an hour."

"Sam walked into your room yesterday and Michael was standing there looking through your stuff," Jax said, careful and tentative.

"What?" My ears were ringing, and my hands gripped my sandwich until drops of melted cheese painted my plate like a high-calorie Jackson Pollock painting.

"As soon as Sam walked in, Michael disappeared. It didn't look like he took anything with him and he didn't attack." Jax's voice was gentle, like he was trying to calm an exotic animal. Suddenly I felt like

I was Bagheera and he was Mowgli.

The muscles in my body slowly released. If Michael didn't hurt Sam, then maybe he would permanently leave him alone. "What do you think he was looking for? And what do you think it means that he didn't attack?"

"I wish I had an idea, but honestly I don't know the answer to either of those questions." Jax's black eyebrows pulled together, carving an uncharacteristic line of tension between them.

A few days later, Soren and I were sparring in our usual clearing, waiting for Raifus or some sign of him. Honestly, I was beginning to think this whole Raifus thing was a dead end. That, or he was part of an elaborate plan for Soren to kill and bury me in the woods where I'd never be found.

"Are you sure," I swung a fist towards Soren, "this guy," I blocked his returning hit, "is ever gonna," I ducked to kick out his legs, "show up?" Soren leapt over my head, avoiding the kick altogether.

"No."

"That's it?" I asked the same question every day and always received the same answer. Didn't mean I was going to stop being frustrated or stop asking. I clutched my knees, panting. I appreciated the view in our clearing and, if I was being honest, the drive every day with Soren, but I was starting to get frustrated by this Raifus dude. "You don't know if he'll ever show up? Should we move on to a different source? We can't just wait here forever."

"I don't know what to tell you, Black. Jax is waiting to hear back from a few leads, but—" Soren's eyes grew wide when his head snapped in my direction.

"What?"

A second later, something pulled me back several feet by the hair. When I looked up, I was staring at the feeder girl from the night Kevin's band played. The fact that she was grabbing me by my ponytail made things worse.

Girls pulling hair just fed into all the awful clichés, especially when she was supposedly a badass supe. Not to mention, it hurt like a bitch and I'd be royally pissed if she damaged my roots.

She wasn't concerned with me though, her eyes taunting Soren as he stared at my throat.

And at the cold press of metal against my sensitive skin, I understood why.

I was *so* not okay with being bait, and this girl was about my size. Which meant I stood a chance. Maybe. Not to mention, she had the audacity to act like I wasn't a threat. At the same moment that I gripped the hand that held a knife against my neck, I elbowed her in the lady parts. Hard. She didn't have any junk down there, but Hollywood liked to pretend that kind of move only hurt guys. It didn't.

When she gasped in surprise, her hands loosened their grip around the handle and I was able to wrestle the knife from her. After a quick kick to her knees and a throat punch (I've always wanted to orchestrate a throat punch), I turned back to Soren with a huge smile on my face. While I expected him to look pleased that I defended myself from an actual baddie, his gaze hardened as he ran towards me.

About a second before he reached me, I was on my ass, trying to breathe oxygen back into my lungs.

I saw him tackle another huge supe. When my brain caught up to my surprise, I realized it was the blond guy who the female feeder was fawning over at Inferno. While the girl didn't look like she could handle herself in a fight, this guy definitely did. He had at least fifty pounds on Soren and I watched as the two met each other blow for blow.

His girlfriend rebounded from the attack way more quickly than I did, her hands clasping around my neck and pulling me towards her. She was wearing a deep-cut black leather dress that left little to the imagination and made it clear she probably wasn't expecting a fight today. That, or she was the most woefully unprepared shopper I knew.

My hands gripped hers as I momentarily forgot my training. Like absolutely all of it. It was hard to remember how to kick someone's ass when you were struggling to breathe. Her eyes squinted at me in concentration; a look that soon turned to frustration and confusion. That was a look I was used to with feeders, or at least all two I had encountered up close. I smiled tightly at the girl, probably making her think I was deranged. Good. That gave me an edge.

"What's wrong with you? What have you done to my ability you little bitch?" She shoved me back to the ground, focusing harder.

Ugh, did she really have to call me the b-word? I hated when girls didn't support girls. It was so not part of my life philosophy.

But not one to ignore a good opportunity, I kicked to my feet and punched her in the nose, pleased with the cracking sound it made on contact. Blood poured down her face, but somehow that only made her look more intimidating and motivated than I'd seen her look so far. She stood and squared off with her fists raised. I avoided the first punch, and blocked the second, landing my own hit on the edge of her shoulder far from where I'd aimed it.

The momentum from my thrust and her unexpected pivot had her behind me, allowing her the time and position to nail me in the kidneys. Pain erupted through my back and I found myself once again with my hands and face digging into the floor of the clearing. For the first time, I realized that Soren was really taking it easy on me when he landed hits during our sparring sessions—a thought that left me both grateful and annoyed.

When I leaned back up to try and kick her feet out from under her, a giant white animal leapt over me and landed on Gothic Barbie. A moment later, the pure white fur was covered with splatters of blood. At the same time that my eyes reached the feeder girl and realized she was now missing a throat, a deep and agonized moan echoed around me.

I looked back, expecting to find Soren still fighting her boyfriend, but lover boy was pressed against a tree, his shoulder impaled by a large branch. I turned back again, trying to find Soren, when my eyes locked onto the face of the large white—now, partially red—creature. Familiar gray eyes stared into mine, but the animal was unlike any I'd ever seen. Where El's panther was large and, well, sort of a normal panther, Soren's was easily twice as big. His fur was an ethereal silver-white that resembled an enhanced, more dramatic version of his usual hair color.

"Soren?" My voice was strangely calm, but impossibly quiet. And, try as I might I couldn't stop my hands from trembling—whether from the fight, the death, or the animal in front of me, I wasn't sure. It didn't help that El's words about her brother's panther form were bouncing around uncomfortably in my head. He shifted slowly towards me, a low growl reverberating from his body. The animal crouched down, it's limbs ready to pounce, and I closed my eyes tight. No matter how much I'd practiced with El, there was no way I stood a chance against Soren when I was in this position or condition. Not that I stood a chance against him even on my best day. I was nothing more than a sitting duck. Or a zebra. Or whatever the hell panthers ate.

A soft breeze kissed my face and I opened my eyes after the expected blow didn't come. When I turned around, amazed to still be breathing, Soren was pacing back and forth between me and the manipulator I recognized from the club. The final boss of the evil trio.

And by recognized, I mean he was wearing another ridiculous suit. Instead of the bright purple one he wore at Inferno, this one was a chartreuse green. I was beginning to think this guy got off on looking ridiculous. The manipulator ripped the branch from his companion, and I watched in horror as the feeder stood, prepared to fight. His aura might be weaker than the obnoxiously-dressed manipulator, but I had to remember that feeders still weren't human—they were faster, stronger, and healed more quickly.

The blond feeder was shaking with rage, his eyes following Soren's every step. "He killed Eileene."

"Yes, I see that Theonis," the glorified pimp said as he took a step forward. "You are an unusual looking panther-shifter, aren't you? You don't take on the animal's traditional coloring like most. I wonder why?" While Theonis was fuming, the manipulator merely looked amused, his intense golden glow enhancing his features.

"The girl. She's resistant to feeding, Ric. I saw Eileene try and fail, and I can't pull anything from her now either. It doesn't feel like a resistance buildup or a talisman." Theonis darted his eyes between me and Ric (seriously? Such a boring name for someone who looked so completely absurd), clearly hoping his words might convince his boss to quickly finish the fight.

"Well, that's certainly interesting isn't it?" Ric smiled, his uneven and yellowing teeth the most remarkable part of his face. "Tell you what, panther. You let us have the girl, we'll forgive the fact you killed Theonis's girl. He's only been screwing her for a year or so. It's not a totally catastrophic loss, all things considered."

Theonis narrowed his eyes in anger but didn't challenge the manipulator. Soren, however, emitted a bone-chilling growl, so low that I felt it more than I heard it.

"Too bad." Ric smiled again. "I guess we'll handle this the fun way then."

Both men focused their attention on Soren, deciding I wasn't enough of a threat. Soren flew through the air—

And then landed into a tree.

He hit hard, so I was surprised to see him get up so quickly and lunge at Theonis. Before Soren had a chance to make contact, Theonis flew above him. *Flew.*

Ric was an air-manipulator.

All three men were ignoring me, so I moved my fingers carefully along the grass until they met with the cool surface of Eileene's knife. Ric couldn't keep this level of energy use up forever and he definitely couldn't focus on both of us at the same time. That's what I hoped anyway.

Slowly, I stood, and edged the three feet towards Ric. Before he knew I was there, I kicked his knees out, using the move Soren taught me a week ago, the sound of a painful pop echoing around us. The manipulator hit the ground with an agonizing scream and I lifted the knife up, ready to finish the job.

Until, all of the sudden, I couldn't breathe. The knife dropped from my fingers and my hands reached to my neck as they reflexively and unsuccessfully tried to help the airflow. Lights danced before my eyes and my knees dropped to the ground, bringing me closer to the puke green suit. I was so not okay with this being the last thing I saw before I died.

I've never passed out from lack of oxygen before, but if I had to guess, I'd say I was nearly at that point. Luckily, with Ric focusing on me, Soren had enough time to do his whole gross panther thing and leave another supe without a throat. I wasn't a fan of death, and I had no doubt in my mind that I'd freak out about this whole thing later. But right now? I was just happy I could inhale oxygen again. Air-manipulation was a bitch. Who would've thought that air could be scarier than fire?

The air ricocheted with the sound of a twig snapping. With all the crazy running through my mind, I found myself grasping towards the sound, trying to find something normal and isolated to focus on. Theonis was moving away from us slowly, his arms held up in the universal sign of surrender. It was pretty clear that with Eileene and Ric out of the picture, he didn't stand much of a chance against us.

Well, against Soren anyway.

Soren growled, low and deep.

"Look dude, I'm just going to leave. I didn't want to attack you guys in the first place." Theonis dragged his feet back a few steps through the leaves, his hand now covering the bloody hole Soren ripped into his shoulder that hadn't yet healed. When neither of us made a move or sound of protest, Theonis turned his back and picked up his pace.

Two seconds later, he went from jogging into the horizon to dead.

Soren stood next to the final body, his gray eyes piercing into my own. I wondered what he saw in them. Fear? Shock? Disgust? Maybe when he shifted back he could let me know, because I sure as hell had no idea what emotions were running through my head. Or heart? Where did emotions hypothetically even run in the first place?

A low growl pulled me back to reality. Soren's large silver-white paws were drawing closer and closer. The look in his eyes was clear: he was still in attack mode.

"Soren calm down. The fight is over. It's me. Odessa. You can shift back now," I cooed like I was speaking to a puppy and not a giant, mythical man-cat.

I closed my eyes as he edged closer, another growl ripping dangerously from him.

When he reached me, he took several steps past me. I opened first one eye, then the second. His attention was directed towards a new presence at least twenty feet away.

This figure was tall, like most supes, with shoulder-length black hair and bright green eyes. More striking than his rugged good looks was the intense white glow bathing him in power, so bright I couldn't tell if he was a feeder or a manipulator. Or something else altogether.

Soren growled another warning. While I expected the man to cower in terror, his lips turned up into a smile instead, amusement dancing in his eyes.

"Chill out, old friend. I won't hurt her. No need to continue your unnecessary bloodbath." The stranger's voice was deep and smooth, not revealing any signs of fear or threat. If anything, he sounded legitimately intrigued. He cocked his head slightly to the side, not unlike a dog, and met my eyes.

When Soren growled in response, the stranger merely chuckled. Ignoring the giant panther, he walked over to the backpack Soren always brought on our trips. After a few seconds of digging through the contents, he pulled out a pair of gym shorts and tossed them in our direction. "Glad you came prepared, I have better things to do with my time than stare at your junk. Get changed and we'll talk."

I could feel the heat rising in my cheeks. I hadn't thought about the fact that when Soren shifted back, he'd be naked. Instead of taking the shorts and shifting behind a tree, Soren padded a few steps towards the clothing and kept the stranger in his line of sight. A few moments later, I was no longer staring at a beautiful, slightly terrifying panther, but a super naked backside. I covered my eyes to give him some privacy while he put on the gym shorts. Of course, I let myself take a nice long peek before my hands made their way over my face. I was after all, only human.

I had seen some dude butts in my day, but Soren's looked like it was carved from marble. And that wasn't the only aesthetically pleasing sight. His back muscles were tensed and shifted as he took the last couple of steps to meet his spare shorts. An intricate tattoo laced itself down part of his shoulder and spine, but my eyes were primarily drawn to a series of scars along his left shoulder blade. Did he get them the same time he got the scar near his eye? Or was he just frequently throwing himself in the way of danger?

While he was back to looking like Soren, he was also back to acting like him. Without even sparing me a word or a glance he dipped his head slightly to the stranger. "Raifus."

SEVENTEEN

"Soren," Raifus nodded, "I'd say it's good to see you, but really I was hoping you'd eventually get the message and stop showing up here every day."

"So, you sent those three?" The muscles in Soren's back were tight, his voice still laced with the remaining anger and growl that better suited his panther.

"Those three?" Raifus took several steps closer, a disappointed yet teasing gleam in his eye. "No, I've never seen the lot of them. Not enough power for me to find interesting or entertaining. I assumed they were after you. Then again," he paused, his gaze dancing towards the sky, "maybe they were stalking me like you have been. I guess we'll never know, since you had to go and murder them all."

"I had no choice." Soren's words were quiet but clipped.

"There's always a choice, as you are well aware. It's okay Soren, we all know you're bloodthirsty, but feel free to blame it on the panther instincts if it helps you sleep better at night." Raifus stepped around Soren, leaving him shaking in a barely contained rage. "Now, who do we have here?" Emerald green eyes met my own, the startling shade made even more stunning by the surrounding mass of black hair.

He was a striking sight from far away, but even more so up close. His face was angled and masculine, his square jaw was peppered with dark hair—more than a shadow, but less than a beard. His shoulders were wide and muscled, but he was lean. While his hair was down to his shoulders and slightly unkempt, it gave him the practiced look of danger, edge. He was dressed in dark jeans and a white button-up, the sleeves casually rolled to his elbows. The clothes fit his every curve so well that they had to be designer or custom made. He was older than Soren, probably closer to Sam's age. Catching my perusal, Raifus lifted one eyebrow and lowered his gaze. "You're wearing my necklace, I see. But you are most certainly not Elliana."

"I'm Odessa. Odessa Black." I wasn't comfortable on the ground before Raifus, so I pulled myself up with one too many grunts of discomfort to match his height. Sort of. The guy was just as tall as Soren. "If you knew we were here this whole time, why'd you wait so long? Kind of convenient to show up right after we'd been attacked, no?"

"Black," Soren's harsh whisper issued a warning. I knew that Jax was uneasy around Raifus, but it surprised me to hear the fear in Soren's voice.

Emerald eyes began their second appraisal, and I had the strange feeling that Raifus was peeling away layers of my mind to read my thoughts. After several tense moments, he barked out a loud, deep laugh. "I like her, Soren. If I had known your friend would so be entertaining, I'd have answered your desperate call days ago. Weeks maybe." He lifted a piece of hair off my shoulder, studying the dark strands between his thumb and finger.

I tried not to be overwhelmed by him, but Raifus had an undeniable presence. The white-gold glow was at least as intimidatingly powerful as Soren's was when I had first seen him, but somehow Raifus seemed like he was operating on a different plane. Almost as if we were all examining individual pieces and he alone was capable of looking at the entire puzzle.

"We need...we need your help. Soren mentioned you might be able to track someone for us." My voice was much shakier than I wanted it to be. If Soren's lessons with El taught me anything, it was that animals sense fear as a weakness, a vulnerability. Judging by the predatory amusement in Raifus's eyes, I was every bit playing the role of prey in this scenario.

"I told Soren many years ago that I couldn't afford to help him again. I stay out of Veil politics," Raifus said, his gaze steady and curious.

Frustration bubbled in my blood and pooled in my stomach. We had wasted so much time. This was our only lead.

"But," he started, letting my hair fall back along my shoulder. "I never told *you* I wouldn't help. So tell me, Ms. Black. Who is it you need tracked?"

"My old neighbor, Charlotte Veln. And...and an old friend, Michael Saber." I met his eyes briefly. "But that may not be his real name. He's a space-manipulator and he's after my friend. He's after El." I looked up at him. "Elliana, I mean."

Raifus smiled, finding a joke somewhere in my statement. After a moment, he tempered his facial expressions and snapped around to Soren. "Is this all you both seek?"

Soren nodded once, his jaw tight.

"Well, I can't give you the whereabouts of those two individuals. Usually, I require an object close to them in order to track their energy, something that's absorbed some of their energy if I don't already have a register on it. You've given me two names, one of which might not even be real. That's not a lot to go on." Raifus's amusement grew with each word. I found myself wanting to slap the smirk off his face. When he saw the anger lining my features, his smile only grew bigger. "I can tell you something more important, however. For a price, of course."

"What price?" Soren asked.

"Not something you can pay, Soren. This fee lies on Odessa's shoulders." He circled around me, assessing me from all angles. Not like a man checking out a woman, but like a collector who'd found a new piece to add to his storage room.

"What do you want from me? I don't have much money." I blinked my eyes against the sun and tried not to let on how badly my back was hurting from the fight. Kidney hits hurt like a mother.

"First, tell me. This space-manipulator, was he truly after Elliana?" Raifus leaned against a large tree, either oblivious or ambivalent to the bloody splatters surrounding him from where Soren had pinned the feeder. He crossed one leg casually across the other in a pose that belonged on a magazine cover, not amidst a slaughter.

"He thought he was after me, but really I think he wanted Elliana." I sat down on a rotted log. Not because I wanted to but because my body was screaming in anguish. The pain was no longer worth the power position of standing. I wasn't kidding anybody; we weren't on an equal playing field, pretending otherwise wouldn't make him weaker or me stronger.

"Actually," Soren started pacing between us, "he seemed pretty adamant that it was you, Black. Maybe we had it wrong."

"What would a supe want with me though? If not to use me to get to El?" I ripped long strands of grass into smaller pieces, eager for something simple to focus on and control. I couldn't intimidate someone like Raifus, but I could totally intimidate a lawn.

"Well, you have the sight, don't you?" Raifus was staring at me again, with that all-seeing, all-knowing power only he seemed capable of wielding. Soren stilled instantly. For several long moments, there was no sound, but for the soft noises of the clearing and surrounding forest.

"What sight?" My voice was hitched, tight. I was so not an actress.

"Don't play stupid, Ms. Black, it's below you. You can see the energy auras. I could tell as soon as I came close to you. The way you reacted to me. You could sense my power. While you disguise your fear well, micro expressions are more difficult to control."

"Fine. So what? I see energy clouds or auras or whatever. It's not a real power. I can't do anything with it except spot a supe. And honestly, even that is patchy sometimes. There's no reason Michael would be after me, my ability serves no purpose." I rubbed a knot out of my shoulder, my body aching from the training and fight. Movies always made fighting seem so glamorous. The heroes took a few hits but were always back up and running within a scene or two. They never highlighted the fatigue that comes after an adrenaline high; the kind of tired that seeps into your bones, deep and heavy.

Raifus's lips twitched and he arched a dark brow. "We'll talk another time about why he might have been after you. In the meantime, I'm willing to offer a trade. Information for a price."

"What price?" Soren's deep voice punctured the stillness of the clearing.

"I will help you obtain an energy neutralizer." Raifus plucked a loose thread off his shirt with a look of disgust. How he was upset about a single missed stitch when he was two inches away from lining his shirt in blood was beyond me.

"Those don't exist." It was a statement, but the slight inflection in Soren's voice told me he was willing to be persuaded otherwise. Soren was intrigued. And Soren was a hard man to intrigue.

"It will take work, but I can assure you that there is exactly one that exists. If you get it and bring it to me, it will ensure that no energy-user abilities will work against the person holding it. Give it to Elliana, and she will be protected from her kind. She will be hidden, her own energy disguised." He scratched the short scruff lining his jaw and shrugged. "Or don't, and move onto your next plan."

"And in return, for helping us find it?" Something told me as soon as I asked the question that I wouldn't like the answer.

"To be determined at a later date, Ms. Black." Raifus turned back towards me, ignoring Soren's scowl completely.

"Absolutely not, we can't just write you a blank check." Soren stepped towards Raifus, the muscles in his back tensing with each move.

"What other option do you have?" Raifus asked. "Tell me, Soren. Do you have a plan B? You've been out here waiting for the slim chance I'd answer your call every day for weeks. It's clear you need a lead. I'm offering you one. And *you* don't even have to pay the price for it. You should be thrilled. And who knows, if you prove useful and can actually bring me the neutralizer, I might even offer you some information you don't even know to look for yet."

"It's a deal." At my words, Soren's head whipped back at me. The glare on his face would have had me running away in fear a month ago. Now, coming from him, it was almost endearing. "I'll agree to a reasonable payment of your choice after you help us. By reasonable, I mean that the favor can't bring harm to anyone, human or supe...ernatural, and I won't do anything illegal." I paused, waiting for his nod of agreement. "Good, now where can we find the neutralizer?"

Raifus clapped his hands together once, a huge smile lighting up his face. The knowledge in that smile was somehow more frightening than the sheer power of his aura. What was I getting myself into? If it were for anyone other than El, I don't know if I'd have the courage to willingly partner with someone like Raifus. Or the death wish.

"Excellent. I knew I liked you, Odessa Black. This will mark the beginning of a very symbiotic relationship."

"Just tell us where to find it, Raifus." I was surprised by the conviction in my own voice. Soren moved to stand next to me, angling his body so that he was a few steps in front. I cleared my throat. "Um, please?"

Raifus chuckled, a deep throaty sound that was as appealing as it was terrifying. "You'll need to steal it from the pendant's current owner. He lives in San Francisco. There'll be a cocktail party this Saturday. He has them a couple of times a month, but this one will be a masquerade, in celebration of his birthday. I know, I know, it's all a bit cliché—relying on a fancy party to pull off a robbery. But that's your best chance to get in and grab it. The stones are black, three. They were set into a dangling necklace last I saw it. He'll keep it protected, but I can help you sense it out once you are in."

The timing was conspicuous, and I couldn't help but wonder if Raifus made us wait weeks for him to show up so that when he did, we wouldn't have much time to back down from the offer. Not when a masquerade offered such an opportune cover for theft.

"Why can't you just go there and steal it yourself then?" Soren asked.

I just kept thinking about how we were going after another magical necklace. These supes sure liked their jewelry. I was with Charlotte though, magical cookies seemed like the better way to go. I was hungry.

"Because I don't get involved with Veil politics. And I'm not interested in getting on the birthday boy's bad side at the moment. If I were so much as in the city at the time, Rennix would know it was me. You know him, always paranoid. A girl who, for all intents and purposes, appears human? And a rebellious shifter who's usually only interested in picking fights? He won't suspect you even know about the neutralizer, let alone are after it." Raifus stood straighter and took a step towards us.

"Rennix? You've got to be kidding me?" Soren's hand went through his hair and scratched the back of his neck. Never a good sign.

Great, Soren was nervous. Rennix sounded awesome. This didn't seem ominous at all.

"That's the deal, Soren." Raifus closed the distance between us and held his hand out to me after pulling a small blade along his palm. "Once you have it, I'll help activate the neutralizer. And then you can use it to help Elliana, and blah blah blah. Do we have a deal?"

I lifted my right hand, holding back a wince as Raifus sliced through my skin more gently than I thought he would. Then I latched my hand onto his, ignoring Soren's soft growl that punctured the truce. Gods, this couldn't be sanitary.

"Deal. Will we meet you back here when it's through? And if you aren't coming to the party, or even to the city that's housing the party, how can you help me sense this necklace? Also, what's with all the necklaces? Can't you supes come up with anything a little more superhero-ish? Like a warrior blade? Or a mystical chalice?" I snapped my lips shut after sensing Soren's annoyance and Raifus's barely-disguised amusement. I really needed to get a handle on this whole mental filter thing I heard so much about.

The corners of Raifus's lips twitched up and he took another two steps closer to me. Too close. I could feel the heat emanating off of him and if I breathed too deeply, our bodies would brush together. "Supes?" He said the word slowly, like he was familiarizing himself with the way his tongue formed around it. "I like it." His piercing eyes held my own and he reached a hand out towards my chest.

"Hey back off, perv." I took a quick step back from him, crossing my arms to cover my chest.

"The necklace, Odessa. My apologies, I wasn't trying to be forward." Raifus smiled, closing the distance between us again. He gripped the dark pendant that was the sister to El's ring. "I will be able to find you now. Your energy register is currently blocked, but I will be able to find you through the necklace. I will come to you for the next step, once you've tracked the neutralizer. Your necklace will guide you to it once you enter Rennix's house." Without breaking eye contact or letting go of his grasp on my pendant, he pulled a slip of paper out of his pocket with his free hand and handed it to Soren. "The address."

"You've had the address with you this whole time? This deal was always your plan?" My eyebrows drew together, and I sent my own version of a Soren-glare towards Raifus.

He only smiled again, a dangerous and twisted smirk. "We'll meet again soon, Ms. Black. I'm looking forward to it." His lips brushed my hand, which was suddenly encased in his own. "And be mindful. While your sight is useful, not all *supes* are what or as they seem. Your companion included." With a quick nod to Soren, he turned and walked away, quickly disappearing into the cage of trees.

Soren and I were silent for several very long minutes, until I became uncomfortably aware that we were still surrounded by three shredded bodies. And that I was staring at a very shirtless Soren. And really, I should be way less flustered by the latter than I was the former, but something in my brain was clearly very poorly wired. I was totally fine with blaming it on shock. For now.

I cleared my throat, willing myself to hold it together until we were back home. Between potentially signing my life away to Raifus and witnessing so much death, I wanted nothing more than to get drunk with El and forget about the entire day. "We should get home," I mumbled.

Soren nodded, grabbing the scraps of his clothes that had torn when he shifted. Luckily, he wasn't wearing his jacket at the time since we had been sparring, so he had something to cover up with. I couldn't quite reconcile the steamy thoughts I was having about a shirtless Soren with the bloodthirsty panther he'd been less than half an hour ago. He tossed me the bag of supplies he carried with him. "Drink some water and then start heading back to the bike. I'll take care of the—" he nodded his head towards the dissected supes. "Of, you know. Them. You can find the bike on your own?"

Shuddering at the thought, I sent Soren a silent agreement and set off on the twenty-minute hike back to where we parked. I took a few drags from the water bottle, allowing the liquid to act as a calming elixir, focusing on the sensation of it cooling my body. After a few minutes, I could no longer pretend that the scent of burning flesh was coming from some nearby campers having a barbeque. Somehow, I mustered up my remaining strength, like a mother lifting a car off her newborn, to sprint back to the car—needing to put as much distance between myself and that smell as I physically could.

Soren caught up with me just as I reached the bike, and he handed me a helmet before slamming his own on his head. He wordlessly climbing onto the bike and looked back expectantly at me. My mouth was dry, and I struggled to form the question I'd spent the last mile wanting to ask. "Soren?"

"Spit it out, Black. I want to get home. It's been a long day." He turned the bike on, warming up the engine while I tried to find the words and the courage.

"You killed them." I cleared my throat.

He lifted the helmet off his head and raised an eyebrow. "And?"

"Well, it's just. Raifus pointed out—you didn't have to kill them. Right? We could have just, like, seriously maimed them maybe? So, you know, we could question them and what not. It's just, did they *really* have to die?" My eyes were locked firmly on my feet. My courage quota for the day was evidently expired.

I waited over a minute for Soren to respond. And I knew it was this long because I focused on counting the seconds in order to take the nervous edge off my breathing.

"Yes, they could have survived, but they figured out too quickly that you weren't affected by the feeder pull. It wasn't worth the risk, seeing if they'd come after you or what they'd do with that information. We don't know enough about your ability as it is, we definitely don't need to leave room for fanfare. And I saw the look on Theonis's face, he'd be back for revenge if I'd let him escape. And men like that, well let's just say you don't want to deal with their version of revenge."

My stomach sank. His reasoning was sound, but that meant those three were dead because of me. I breathed in slowly, trying to tame the pounding of my heartbeat.

Soren shook his head. "Look, Black. Don't put the blame on yourself. To be honest, in that form I'm not known to really leave survivors. I can't turn off the predator instinct. Whether they figured out you could block them or not, they'd have ended up dead. The difference is just that the logical, non-panther, version of me agrees with their death knowing that they learned too much."

I pushed my helmet on and climbed onto the bike behind Soren. "I don't think you're as bad as you say you are. The panther—" I paused, wiping invisible dirt off my thigh, "I mean you. *You* didn't attack me." In fact, I was fairly certain that panther-Soren had actually been trying to protect me.

He grunted in response to end the conversation. And then he started the engine and drove us away from the unexpectedly bloody afternoon. For once, I didn't complain about him breaking the speed limit. Instead, I clutched onto his jacket, willing myself to hold it together until we were home.

In record time, we pulled up to the house. I closed my eyes in gratitude, not only for the comfort of home and El, but for the distraction. During the long drive, with nothing else to focus on, my mind kept torturing me with reruns of the fight, pointing out the things I did wrong and highlighting the gruesome killing blows. I'd never seen someone die before and today I not only witnessed, but participated in three deaths.

I stood as soon as the bike stilled. Weirdly, while I was still sore, my body didn't feel quite as destroyed as I thought it would after the beating I took. Maybe I really did have the iron constitution of an action hero. I tossed my helmet to Soren, staring at the sunset over the lake while taking deep breaths in and out, when I heard a deep growl emanate from him. "What?"

When my eyes found his, I realized that he was glaring at me. Well, not at me but past me. I turned back towards the house to see what had his knickers in a twist when a huge gust of air was pushed out of me as my body lifted off the ground and was swung in a circle. My heart stopped. Another air-manipulator?

"I missed you, Odie." The breath skated against my neck and the world stopped spinning when my feet were planted back on the ground.

"Luis?" My mouth dropped open and I returned his hug with just as much enthusiasm.

EIGHTEEN

"Luis, what are you doing here?" I asked, a smile uncomfortably stretching the skin around my mouth.

He was dressed in a white V-neck and black basketball shorts, the slight scent of sweat mixing in with the warm woodsy smell I usually associated with him.

"How did you find this place?" Soren's voice was low, ragged. I whipped my head back towards him, just to make sure he hadn't turned back into a panther.

"Honestly, I don't know." Luis ran his hands through his brown locks and I realized that it was longer than I'd ever seen him wear it. And judging by the dark beard that swept his face, he hadn't shaved in at least a week or two, which was very unusual for him. "I stopped by to see Sam this afternoon on my way home from the gym." When I opened my mouth to interrupt him he added, "don't worry, he's fine. But when I left your place, I started driving around, getting more and more frustrated that you hadn't returned. Sam had no clue where you were, and those other two assholes knew but wouldn't tell me. And I knew something weird was going on. Both your and Ellie's phones went straight to voicemail and Sam was obviously not telling me something." He paused, looking around at the cabin and surrounding land. "And then I just wound up here. It shocked the hell out of me when I knocked on the door and El answered."

"If they didn't tell you where to find us, why are you here?" Soren's voice was closer than it was before. Startled, I took a step back and found myself practically pressed against his chest. I quickly moved to the side, so that we were standing next to each other and looked back towards Luis, encouraging him to continue.

"I don't know how to explain it. I just kept thinking about how badly I needed to see Odie." Luis paused, a blush creeping up his cheeks. "I mean, El too. I just drove, not really thinking about

157

anything else." He shrugged. "A few hours later, I wound up here. That's really it. We've all been waiting for you to get back. El said you're usually home earlier than this." His eyes traveled from me to Soren, where they hardened. "Where were you guys anyway? Odie, what happened to you?" He pulled a twig from my hair before brushing some dried blood from my arm. "What the hell? Were you in an accident? I can't believe this tool got in an accident."

"Were you followed?" Soren took a step closer to Luis, the two of them squaring off and tensing up.

"No, of course not." Luis paused, looking away from Soren for a second. "At least, I don't think so anyway. Like I said, the whole thing was just weird. Why would anyone be following me?"

"It's okay, Luis. I'm glad you're here." I walked over to him and squeezed his hand. "We should go inside, we have a lot to talk about."

"Jax made dinner." Luis turned to follow me, but at his words I instantly stopped.

"Jax? Why?" I couldn't prevent the look of disgust that crossed my features. Jax was good at many things. Cooking, especially for a vegetarian, was definitely not one of them.

"Don't worry, Odie. I supervised." With a wink, he jogged past me and opened the door.

When I made it two feet in the house, El came running up to meet me with a huge hug. "Isn't it great? Luis finding us? It's totally destiny. Definitely didn't feel right not having the final leg of our group here with us. Well, not final leg. Sam still isn't here." She pushed back from me, giving her time to catch her breath, and then her brows scrunched together dangerously tight. "What the hell happened to you? Did Soren do this? He's pushing you way too hard."

"It wasn't me." Soren joined us in the house. He kicked his boots off and walked over to the table. "We'll talk about everything once we've eaten. I'm starving."

"Jeez, he's grumpy," El whispered before grabbing my hand and dragging me towards the table.

"Let me go wash up first. At least my hands and my face. I'll be back in a second. Feel free to start without me." Without waiting for an answer, I locked myself in the bathroom to furiously scrub the dirt and blood away from the visible parts of my body. I'd definitely be taking advantage of a shower or long, hot bath after dinner; but I needed to wash as much of the fight off of me first, if I had any chance of keeping food down.

When I made it back to the kitchen, everyone was staring off in an awkward silence while Soren shoveled mashed potatoes and turkey into his mouth, barely allowing himself to come up for air.

I cleared my throat and grabbed the only available seat, across from Luis and next to Soren. "Smells good, Jax. Color me impressed."

He beamed up at me, his happiness at the compliment shattering the tension. "You haven't even seen the best part, Desi-girl. I found a recipe for baked tofu and it actually looks edible." He hopped out of his seat and over to the stove, shoving something onto a plate before returning and placing it in front of me. The tofu looked and smelled great, which was actually pretty difficult to accomplish. I found myself chuckling, not only did he make tofu, he used a cookie cutter so the pieces looked like miniature turkeys.

"This looks amazing, Jax. Thank you." I piled mashed potatoes and salad onto my plate, suddenly hungrier than I'd been in a long time. I guess near-death experiences did that to a girl. Warm food, combined with the cozy feeling that Jax had gone to so much trouble for me, and with the fact that Luis was safe and here did wonders to thaw some of the ice running through my veins since the attack. And then it sunk in, Luis had somehow *found* us. What did that mean?

As if coming back to his senses at the same time, Soren pushed away his plate and looked up at Jax. "So, anyone want to fill me in on what the hell happened while we were gone. Why is he here?" Soren nodded at Luis, eyeing him like he was the chartreuse-wearing manipulator.

El exhaled and stood up, not that the gesture made her seem any more imposing. "Look, he doesn't know how he found us. He just did."

"Don't be naive El," Soren said, his jaw pulsing with tension.

"Soren, I need you to calm down for a second," her anger dissipated a bit as she turned towards her brother before continuing. "I've known Luis for six years, he's a terrible liar. He's not lying to us about this." She pressed her hands into the wood of the table, grounding herself, "and I've decided it's time he knows."

Soren stood, his arm sweeping his plate to the floor. I jumped as the crash of the plastic against the floor echoed throughout the room.

"It's final Soren, and it's my decision. I'm pulling rank here." Ellie's voice was low, softer than it had been moments before, but it held a quiet authority I wasn't used to.

"This is ridiculous," Soren looked between El and Jax. "You can't be serious? He shows up here, where we've been hiding for weeks, with absolutely no explanation, and *this* is how you want to handle it? Revealing everything to him?"

Jax turned away from Soren's accusing glare, suddenly finding his fingernails to be the most amusing thing in the room, while El stood firm.

"Fine. Rank pulled. Do what you want. I'll be in the shower." Without another look, Soren left. The bathroom door slammed so powerfully that I was shocked it was still attached to the hinges.

I sat back while Ellie and Jax took turns explaining the energy-using world to Luis and the truth behind why we left Seattle, or at least part of it anyway. They left out some of the finer details about the Veil and Ellie's situation, but they hit all of the major points. Their words filtered over me while I watched Luis's face turn from amusement, to confusion, to shock, to denial.

Eventually, Ellie took off her shoes, jacket, and undressed down to her underwear.

"El, what the hell are you doing?" Luis brought his hands quickly up to his eyes, a soft slap sounding as he blocked his vision a bit too enthusiastically.

"Luis, this is the kind of thing you just need to see. I need you to look at me." El was calm, like she was speaking to a child.

"Are you serious? Your brother already wants to kill me. Do you want to give him another reason?" Luis peeled one hand off of the other and finally opened his eyes when El pushed for him to look at her again.

One second, pixie-like El was standing before us, and then she was morphing and reshaping into a panther surrounded by scraps of what was likely a very expensive lingerie set. That was sacrifice.

Luis pushed back from the table, but he forgot to use his leg muscles and toppled over his chair. "Holy shit. How--how did you do that?"

Panther-El walked slowly up to Luis before plastering her tongue along his face and hopping around like a dog.

"This isn't real, this can't be real," Luis whispered, his hand tentatively reaching out towards El's velvety coat. "This isn't real, right?"

Jax glanced at me before looking back at Luis, a dangerous smile spreading across his face. "That's nothing, wait until you see what I can do."

I watched as Jax molded and pulled energy from Luis. And then I watched Luis blush fiercely as his eyes dilated in response to Jax, his breath coming quicker. My eyes caught the very visible evidence of Luis's arousal about a second before he became aware of the same thing. He grabbed Soren's discarded (and apparently unbreakable) plate to cover himself.

"Okay, I believe you. I believe you. Stop," his breaths were coming out as pants, "for fuck's sake—Jax, please—stop that. I get it. I believe you."

With a smirk, Jax relaxed his, er, gift and turned back to the table, shoveling more food into his face with a very satisfied smirk.

I rolled my eyes, while Ellie walked to our room to turn back to human-El and get dressed.

Figures, the guy literally watched a girl transform into a panther. But it still took another man challenging his sexuality for him to believe in the supernatural. Typical toxic masculinity.

After about an hour of Luis digesting the information and asking questions, Soren finally came out of his room. He kept throwing accusatory glances at Luis, but he knew he was outnumbered and that there was nothing to do about Luis learning the truth now. It was done.

I was amazed at how well Luis handled the information after his initial shock. When I first learned about supes, I wasn't nearly as calm or rational.

"How are you not freaking out right now?" I asked, slightly jealous of his collected questioning.

Luis tilted his head, squinting slightly, while he stared off at the wall. "Honestly, and I know this is going to sound crazy, but it feels like I always knew about the—" he looked up at Ellie while his brows pulled together, "the Veil, you called it?" When she nodded, he continued, "or maybe it just feels like I was always supposed to know? I mean, don't get me wrong, seeing you two use your powers was intense and took me off guard. But now—I don't really know how to explain it, it just feels right. Like I knew already but also didn't?"

Soren snorted, shaking his head in disbelief, until El shoved his shoulder.

I looked up at Luis. "So how long are you going to visit for?"

He looked back at me like I slapped him. "Um, I'm not visiting. I let you guys leave once before and was too in shock to chase after you in time. Not happening again. I'm in this for the long haul, so no trying to ditch me. Plus, not to get all googly-eyed like El with the we-all-belong-together bit, but I somehow found you guys and that's as close to destiny or fate or whatever that I think anyone can reasonably get. Plus, now that I know the big secret, there's no reason I can't stay. It's not like I can go back to Seattle knowing you two might be in danger. What kind of friend would I be then?"

"Doesn't matter. Let him stay here." Soren leaned back into his chair, distancing himself from his newly cleaned and now empty plate while he eyed the platter of turkey in front him, ready for another helping. With the excitement of Luis's arrival settling, I realized with a laugh that Jax had made a Thanksgiving dinner...in spring. "We're leaving tonight anyway."

"Leaving? What are you talking about Soren? Did Raifus finally show up?" Jax's tone slowly went from confused to horrified when he started cataloguing the splashes of blood and splotches of dirt still left on me since I had yet to shower. "Did he hurt you guys?" I couldn't blame Jax for the look of terror on his face—Raifus clearly had that sort of effect on people. Though with all the craziness, I'd sort of forgotten about the whole Raifus encounter.

"Raifus? Really? Who names their kid Raifus? That's just asking them to turn out a little wonky." Luis tried to lighten the somber mood that settled over the dinner table, but I didn't miss the look of concern on his face as his eyes traced my torn and dirty shirt.

"Raifus didn't hurt us. We were attacked by the three supes who were at Inferno the night Michael's roommate played," I said.

"What?" Jax asked, his scowl darkening in an expression of fury I'd never seen from him before.

I scooped up a heaping spoon of now-cold potatoes, hoping that a full mouth would give Soren the nudge to fill them in on the rest. He raised an eyebrow at me, the scar running through it emphasized by the arch. After a few agonizingly slow seconds during which Soren made it clear I'd have to continue, I swallowed my food, rolled my eyes, and did—apparently, he was still pouting about not getting his way with Luis. "They attacked while we were training, before Raifus showed up."

"What did they want? Were they after you guys, me, or Raifus?" El picked at invisible split ends, a nervous habit I'd long made fun of her for.

I offered Soren one more opportunity to finish the story, but he remained still and silent. Fine. If he wanted to throw me under the bus, it was my duty to reciprocate. "I don't know. Soren killed them all before we had a chance to interrogate them." I paused, turning to him with a tight smirk, arching my own eyebrow to mirror his. "Raifus showed up after the fight."

It was hard to tell who was fuming more—Luis or Jax. Both were now standing and pacing around the room, like mismatched shadows of each other. If the room wasn't filled with so much tension, I would've laughed.

"He murdered people?" Luis asked, and when his eyes found mine, they flashed a deep, dark blue. "Did he hurt you?"

"No. He saved me," I said reluctantly, my eyes finding Soren. He was studying me with an unreadable expression on his face.

"Did Raifus tell you where Charlotte and Michael are, at least?" El's eyes traced the distance between me and Soren, back and forth like a pendulum.

I shook my head, feeling an odd sort of shame, like Raifus's inability to trace them was my own fault. "No. He couldn't trace them, but he did help. We'll actually need to leave tomorrow most likely, to give us some time." I looked at Soren, to see if he agreed.

Soren had announced earlier that we were leaving tonight, but that seemed a bit unnecessary. It was Thursday night and the party was late Saturday night. It was probably best to drive to San Francisco early to give us time to prepare for the event, but I didn't think we needed to be there right away. And selfishly I wanted a long, luxurious sleep in my bed before we went all out for our superhero road trip.

"We're leaving tonight." Soren's tone was even, calm, his eyes following Luis's every move. "If the human was able to locate us here, there's no telling who else might be able to as well. He could've been followed for all we know. The sooner we leave, the better. He can keep an eye on the cabin or else circle back towards Seattle."

"No way. I'm not staying behind. If El and Odie are leaving tonight, I'm leaving with them. That's not open for discussion," Luis said. I wasn't used to him being so firm. He was always the one in our group to keep things light and funny, and the latter not always on purpose. I didn't know if it was being left behind that signaled this new change, or just the gravity of El's history and situation sinking in; but I knew him well enough to know he wouldn't be left behind again unless it was his idea.

"I think he should come, Soren. He can come to Rennix's party with me while you guys keep an eye on El." I nodded my head in Soren's direction. "Based on your reaction to Rennix's name when Raifus mentioned it, and based on Jax's now—" his face had paled several shades from its usually warm brown, "it seems pretty clear. El shouldn't be anywhere near that address on Saturday night. If you guys can keep her out of the city, that'd be even better. Maybe Luis and I can just drive down by ourselves while you and Jax take El to a new safehouse?"

The thought of walking into a lion's den without another supe present definitely terrified me, but I knew in my gut that the party wouldn't be a safe place for El.

El started picking up empty plates and walking them over to the kitchen. I let out a little whimper when she stole mine away when there was still a small lump of potatoes. Wasting mashed potatoes was a special kind of sin. "Serves you right for trying to place my safety above yours. I'm not letting you go off on some stealth mission while I sit in another cabin waiting for something exciting to happen. I have cabin fever, so I'm with Luis. Leaving me out of the recon is out of the discussion."

"Black is right."

My jaw fell open. Soren actually agreed with me?

"El, you definitely can't go to the party—" he held up a hand as soon as she opened her mouth to fight back. "Just hang on. I also agree with you that Black and the human shouldn't be left to fend for themselves. That doesn't sit right either. We'll all drive down to California tonight, then the night of the party, Black and I will grab the neutralizer while Jax and Luis drive you in the opposite direction. We'll meet up at a rendezvous after. That way, everyone is happy," he paused, his eyes finding mine, "well, happyish anyway."

Jax dropped his newly-opened bottle of beer on the table, probably more forcefully than he'd intended to. "Neutralizer? Are you barking mad? Those are from fairy tales. I don't know anyone who actually thinks that they are real. Or if they were real, no one that thinks they exist anymore."

"Raifus seemed sure and he seemed sure that Rennix had it. He made a deal with Black, so he had to at the very least believe he was telling the truth." Soren's voice grew increasingly gravelly.

"So what?" I didn't see the big deal. Yeah, Raifus and I had an agreement, but he could have been lying just to send us on a wild goose chase. The guy didn't seem to be completely all there in the head as it was, I wouldn't put it past him to get amusement from sending us on some ridiculous mission that'd likely get us killed.

"Supes don't enter into a deal on false pretenses, Dess." El's voice was quiet, with an edge of fear I hadn't heard in all the time she'd been literally running for her life. "Why did Raifus make a deal with Dess and not you, Soren?"

"Honestly, who knows? He isn't someone I can try to fully understand. His motivations are usually very much his own. He definitely seemed intrigued by her, and wasn't subtle about letting on that he knew more about her involvement in all of this than any of us do. Either way, she made the deal and it's done. He's delivered half of his deal by giving us the location of the neutralizer and our best chance at grabbing it. The second half will be activating it." Soren rubbed a hand over his face, the exhaustion from the day making itself known.

I didn't blame him. To be honest, I was surprised I was still functioning at all. It was so hard to believe that the fight, Raifus, and Luis had all happened within a few hours.

"Can one of you slow down and explain to me what the hell a neutralizer is and why it's so damn important that Odie is getting involved with supernaturals who sound like they bring more danger than they're worth?" Luis plopped back down into his seat, his eyes locked onto mine, even though he seemed to address the question to everyone but me. I was selfishly pleased that I was no longer the only one out of the loop during these discussions.

Before anyone could answer him, El slammed her hand against the table. "Hang on, someone tell me now—what the hell did Dess agree to? You were supposed to be keeping her safe on these trips, Soren. The way you talk about Raifus makes me think no one's safe around him. Going to him in the first place was a terrible idea. First, she's almost set on fire in a club, then she gets beat up by supes, and now she's entered into a deal with the devil."

"You guys can stop having a conversation like I'm not sitting right here in the room with you all." I let my frustration sink into my voice before I turned towards Luis. "A neutralizer can be used to prevent a supe from using their power. If El wears it, it means that whoever is after her will be in for a rude awakening when they try anything. Remember when we mentioned earlier that Michael is a supe and that he has the ability to basically transport himself wherever he wants?" I paused, waiting for Luis to nod in acknowledgement. "Well, if El has that on, it means that he can't just zip in and out to steal her from us. Having a neutralizer will give us an advantage we can't afford not to have. Especially since we have no idea what or who is even after her." I turned towards El. "And nobody *put* me in this situation. I *chose* to go with Soren and I *chose* to make a deal with Raifus. I'm willing to do whatever I can to help keep you safe. Not to mention that it'd be really nice to figure out what Charlotte and Michael have to do with all of this and why Raifus seemed to know more about my ability to sense supes than I do."

Luis and El both started to argue before I stood up and glared, my body tense and exhausted. "We aren't arguing over this. It's done. You've both pointed out that neither of you wants to be left behind or sheltered, well extend that desire to me as well. We're a group and it's clear our attempts to shelter each other are futile."

"Desi, what did you offer?" I turned and found Jax's calm, dark eyes focused on me.

"I don't know yet," I mumbled, fully expecting it was an answer nobody wanted to hear.

"You don't know? How do you make a deal with a supe without knowing what your end of the bargain is?" El glared daggers at her brother again. "Dess, you don't know how seriously deals and bargains are taken amongst supes, but you do Soren. How could you just let this happen? If it's an open-ended bargain, who knows what he's going to want from her and we'll all be practically powerless to stop it. Especially if he's as powerful as you say he is."

Jax, usually the one ready with a snarky comment to lighten the mood, seemed deflated when he walked over to El and grabbed her shoulder to offer some comfort. "It's alright El, as long as it wasn't a blood barg—"

"It was," Soren said, cutting him off crisply like he was ripping off a band aid.

"Jesus, Soren. The fuc—"

"What the hell—"

"Thinki—"

"How did you—"

"This happen?"

Jax and El's complaints battled each other until they morphed into one loud and confusing chorus.

Soren stood up and slammed his chair forcefully into the table. "I didn't let this happen. I tried to talk her out of it. She's her own person, I'm not her keeper. Black chose to make the bargain. And, honestly, it's the only break we have right now. Raifus is our only lead unless you want to just keep hiding out indefinitely? The bottom line is, it's done. We all need to pack the essentials and be prepared to leave within the next half hour. We've stayed too long as it is. Who knows how Luis found us or who's been tracking him? Black and I both need to clean ourselves up first. I've already showered once, but I can still smell the charred skin from the energy users. I'm sick of this stink and there's no way in hell I'm sitting in a car with it for hours."

He turned away from us and started to walk towards the bathroom. He paused briefly without looking back, his parting words so quiet I wasn't sure whether or not he intended us to hear them. "For what it's worth, Raifus seemed unusually interested in Black. I don't think he intends on causing her harm."

NINETEEN

I spent the next twenty minutes showering which left only ten for packing. Even though I'd have to rush through the cabin trying to find last minute things, it was worth it to spend time ridding myself of the dirt and blood from our fight. Not to mention that I still felt like I had been hit by a truck—literally and figuratively. While I watched the water droplets fall down the tiled walls I realized that while I was upset about seeing Soren kill those three supes, I wasn't as affected as I should've been. If anything, my reaction was an odd sort of apathetic numbness. And realistically, we didn't have time to dwell on that or on Raifus if we wanted to take action—we could sit here forever and wait for something to happen, or we could go make something happen.

I followed Luis into the mom van I was slowly growing attached to. Though I'd die before admitting that to anyone. Jax was driving for the first leg of the trip. Surprisingly, Soren followed me into the back of the car, leaving El in the passenger seat. I knew it was ridiculous to think he would drive his bike for the whole sixteen-hour trip, but I was still shocked he was willing to leave it behind. He was almost as attached to it as El was to her convertible. It must be in their blood. I reached for my seatbelt when strong fingers wrapped around my wrist and stopped me.

"Sit in the back, Black. You're exhausted, and I can share the middle row for now." Soren's gray eyes were locked on my own and I tried not to be affected by the way his wet hair dripped water droplets along his neck. I felt a momentary pang of regret, realizing that my long shower meant that Soren had practically no time to take his. Then again, it was his second since the bloodbath, so I didn't feel too bad.

I blinked my eyes, that thought leaving me with unwanted images of Soren in the shower. When I didn't move or respond, his thumb worked a small circle against the inside of my wrist.

"You need to sleep. Just lie down across the backseat and try to at least rest your eyes and your body. You took a few too many hits today."

I appreciated the gesture, and there was no denying that I was completely exhausted, but I took a fraction of the hits Soren did. The image of him being slammed by the air-manipulator had been replaying in my mind all evening. "You took way more hits than I did, Soren. Why don't you rest up the first few hours and then we can switch?"

The left side of his mouth twitched up, as if he found my reciprocated concern amusing. "I shift into a panther, Black. My body is way better equipped to handle intense physical altercations." The lifted brow and deep purr in his voice made his double meaning abundantly clear. Luis cleared his throat awkwardly, his leg tensing next to mine. I hopped over the seat and landed in the back, ungraceful but successful. If Soren wanted to give up the extra room I wouldn't fight him again on it.

I never fell asleep easily in moving vehicles, but I found myself drifting much more quickly than usual.

When I peeled back my eyelids, which felt heavier than they ever had, I couldn't see anything beyond my reflection against the darkness of the night. I cringed, realizing I slept much longer than I planned to. I moved to sit up, unable to stifle the groan as my muscles screamed.

"Worse after sleeping, isn't it?" Jax's light brown eyes were peering back at me from the middle seat. A quick glance around showed me that Luis was driving this shift and Soren was dozing softly with his head pressed against the window.

"I feel like I've been hit by a plane to be honest," I said. I fluffed the pillow a bit and nodded towards Soren. "Why don't you nudge him awake. He can take my spot and get a proper rest. After that fight, he definitely needs it, no matter how much he protests."

"I wouldn't bother with it, Dess." El's voice chimed softly from the front seat. I was surprised she was awake. Usually an hour or two in the passenger seat was enough to knock El out until the car stopped. "According to the map, we'll be on the southern edge of Oregon in half an hour. That's our halfway point. We'll stop at a small motel or hotel that's willing to take cash, so we aren't electronically tracked, and then we can grab some sleep." She craned her neck around the headrest, her blue eyes glistening with reflected moonlight. "Catch" She tossed back a small object, but Jax halted its progress."

"Really, El? You think she had a chance of catching that with anything other than her face? Have you met Desi?" Jax looked briefly back, assessing me with scrunched brows before turning back to Ellie and shaking his head. "I mean, honestly, you say she's your best friend." He chuckled and opened up the small pill bottle, rattling out two capsules. He passed them back to me with a soft smile. "We should have given you these before you slept, but take them now. They should help some with the muscle aches. Trust me, we've all been there," he winced.

"Thanks," I whispered, "at least my back doesn't hurt quite as badly as I thought it would. I was hit pretty hard."

"Oh yeah?" Jax paused, deliberating, "interesting." I watched him meet El's curious glance in the rearview mirror.

Soren shifted awake in front of me. When he turned back to check on me, my breath caught in my throat. His eyes blinked back sleep and his usually swept back hair was tousled in a disarray most guys would have to spend hours on to achieve. His mouth twitched slightly into a smirk and I found myself exceedingly grateful that the dark disguised the blush that most certainly covered my face.

"What about this place?" Luis's words carried back to us, disturbing the awkward moment.

"Too fancy," Soren said, his voice muffled into a yawn. "They likely will want a card on file if we grabbed a few rooms."

"Too bad I didn't inherit persuasion from Sam," I said. "We'd be staying at a five-star for the price of a soda." My amusement lasted only a moment, and I found myself swallowing back unexpected sadness. Sam and I hadn't gone this long without seeing each other since the day we met. Our family unit was a strange one, and I knew that he and my dad had a complicated history, but we quickly grew attached to each other nonetheless. I rubbed my hand against my chest, as if I could somehow rub out the ache—but this hurt went deeper than my bruised muscles and bones.

"There," Soren nodded his head to the right. "That place is perfect."

"Ugh, you've gotta be kidding me, Soren," Jax said. I couldn't see his face anymore, but I could hear the distaste in his voice. "That place is a total shit hole. We're probably going to pick up a disease just from driving by in close proximity."

Jax opened the window, like removing the glass barrier would somehow make the dingy building more inviting. I wasn't a hotel snob, but I didn't blame Jax for his open disdain of the place. The building was small, lined with the two floors of rooms joined by a fire escape. The electric sign out front that inspiringly labeled this place 'The Sleep' was falling apart and only illuminated the e's and p. There weren't any cars in the parking lot and I had a feeling this motel was the kind that only rented by the hour. I closed my eyes, trying not to imagine the kind of stains we'd find in our rooms. I briefly wondered if Soren and El would be able to see them without a blacklight when Luis parked the car.

"How should we do this? A room for the girls and a room for the guys?" Luis looked back at us through the rearview mirror.

Soren shook his head. "The whole point is keeping an eye on El. The girls shouldn't stay on their own." He slid open the van door. "I'll see if they'll give us two rooms with two beds. I can stay with El and Black."

"Shouldn't Jax go? I mean he's no persuasion-manipulator, but just in case they only take credit card, he might be able to use the whole sexy time aura-boost to get the desk manager to make an exception?" I asked.

Jax smiled and looked back at me. "Sexy time aura boost? Trust me, Desi-girl, a motel like this is not the kind of place I want to inspire any seduction if I can help it. All we need is some horny middle-aged man breaking into our rooms for a quickie."

My stomach churned at the thought. I guess there were negatives to Jax's ability I hadn't considered. At least I knew Jax could defend himself against unwanted advances. I wondered if they taught female seduction-feeders how to keep creeps away or it they had to deal with harassment on a whole other level. "Never mind then. Soren, go for it."

Ten minutes later, El, Soren, and I pushed our way into a small room. It was almost three in the morning. A month ago, I'd just be going to bed after dancing with El or watching a movie marathon with Sam and Luis. But with my new schedule, my body would likely wake me up in a few short hours.

The room had two full sized beds and I ripped the quilt away, straining to see if I found any unwelcome stains or bugs. Surprisingly, the room was cleaner than I'd imagined. Certainly much nicer than the exterior presentation made it seem. "Alright. El we should take the bed farthest from the door."

She threw down a small overnight bag and looked back at me. "Why?"

"Because your brother is going to make us anyway." I looked over at Soren and found him smirking as he dug through his own bag. "Plus, that way he gets murdered first if this place turns into the horror film it looks like."

"Fine. I call bathroom first. You both got to sleep in the car and I practically feel like a zombie as it is. I'm going to be out as soon as my head hits the pillow. Anyone wants to come in and try to steal me while I catch up on my beauty rest will have more than my angry brother to deal with. I can turn into a panther too, you know." El grabbed her pajamas and toiletries and made her way towards the bathroom. Before she closed the door, she looked back at me. "Oh, Dess, you didn't have time to pack a separate one-night bag since you insisted on an obscenely long shower, so I packed everything you'll need in with mine."

I smiled back at her before moving to rifle through her bag. My affection for El quickly soured when I pulled out the large black t-shirt she packed. It wasn't overly revealing, and it was my favorite thing to sleep in, but the thought of how it barely landed mid-thigh had my face burning. I was sure El didn't think we'd be sharing a room with Soren, but something about holding the thin fabric in my hands while I waited for El to finish in the bathroom had me hyper aware of the fact that I'd be sleeping a few feet away from him.

The door swung open a moment later and El walked out in a long T-shirt. On someone my height, it would be scandalously short, but El's stature made the pink top look like a comfy knee-length dress.

"Ready for bed in record time, bitches," El chirped. It was true. The girl was known to spend hours in the bathroom if you let her. "I'll shower in the morning before we leave. Dess, you're next."

Before I made it to the door, El was already tucked into her side of the bed, her eyes softly closed. She'd be asleep in seconds. I was always envious of that particular ability. El could sleep soundly anywhere and her body never took longer than a few minutes to drift off when she was tired. Me? I was known to twist and turn for hours. My body never seemed to get the memo it was bedtime. Instead, that's when my mind liked to wake up and torment me with ridiculous reminders and anxieties.

With a quick shake of my head, I brushed my teeth and washed my face. After a few breaths in and out to calm my nerves, I threw on the black shirt. A look in the mirror, mixed with an internal mantra reassuring me it wasn't too revealing, and I was ready for bed.

What I was so *not* ready for was being assaulted with a shirtless Soren sitting on the side of his bed. Thankfully, he was staring at the TV aimlessly scrolling through channels, so I was saved from the embarrassment of him witnessing my expression. I felt my chin discreetly to make sure my jaw hadn't dropped to the floor. Supes were built and just generally good looking. El, herself, had been warning me about it for years. I should be used to seeing them like this, especially since Soren had been practically naked when we met with Raifus. I wasn't.

He kicked off his shoes, leaving him in the black drawstring pants he had on for the trip, and looked in my direction. Without so much as glancing at him, I practically ran to my bed and dove under the covers.

"You can have the bathroom now," I said while staring at an infomercial like it was the most interesting thing I'd ever watched.

"I'm good. Brushed my teeth at the house before we left. And then again at the rest stop you slept through," he said, his voice gravellier than I was used to. I turned towards him, willing myself to stare at his eyes and not the muscles of his chest. He scratched his chin before continuing, "there's something about ripping someone's throat out with your mouth that makes it necessary to grab a tube of toothpaste as soon as you get the chance."

I found myself strangely thankful for the reminder of the afternoon's activities. Nothing like imagining the guy killing three people to douse whatever unwanted steamy fantasies were brewing in my mind. For the most part anyway. Who could completely resist a man with good oral hygiene?

"Are you hurt at all, from today I mean?" The steady breathing to my right told me El was fast asleep, so I kept my words to a whisper.

He shook his head. "A little sore, maybe, but fine for the most part."

"Not that you'd admit to being hurt even if you were though," I said, rolling my eyes. I breathed in slowly and exhaled. "Look, I didn't really get a chance to say it earlier. I guess from the shellshock of what happened or whatever." I paused, sliding my teeth lightly over my lip as I tried to muster the courage to continue. "But thank you. You saved my life today at the clearing. I'm uncomfortable with death, which is an okay thing to be, I think. And I'm trying to come to terms with what happened today. But I know I would probably be dead, or worse, if you didn't have my back today. You could have let me die. To be honest, it probably would have made things easier on you with keeping a watch over El." I smiled tightly, biting down harder on my lip. After a moment lost in my thoughts, I turned quickly towards Soren when I realized he hadn't responded or broken up my rambling.

His eyes met mine, darker than usual. I still hadn't figured out how or why the shades of gray changed with his moods, but I watched as their gaze fell to my mouth, a soft crease forcing its way between his brows. A second later, he turned away from me, back towards the infomercial. Neither of us were interested in purchasing the home gym equipment, but we sat in silence and watched with rapt attention as if we were.

When I was certain Soren wouldn't say anything more, I rested my head against my pillow and turned off the light. A few minutes later, he shut the TV off and turned away from me so that he was facing the door. "El would have killed me if I let you die. She would've been devastated." His voice carried quietly through the darkness. "And she wouldn't be the only one," he added, so soft that I wasn't sure whether I heard him say it or just imagined that he did.

TWENTY

The sun was just beginning to rise when I jolted upright in bed, panting. El was still sound asleep, though she'd moved closer to me throughout the night, clinging to my pillow like a koala. My body was somehow both cold and sweaty, so I threw the covers off of me, whichever covers El hadn't managed to already cocoon herself in like a burrito.

Over the last couple of weeks, I'd had a few bad dreams, almost all of them ending with El attacked by some faceless monster. Which made sense, it was what we were all terrified of and altering our lives to prevent. Tonight's was worse though, vivid somehow, as if the threat was looming closer. My eyes greedily inventoried that she was still there, sleeping safely and peacefully.

I slid off the bed as quietly as possible, managing to walk to the bathroom without tripping over anything. My reflection in the mirror was several shades lighter than the usual light brown I was used to seeing. With my dark hair plastered against the sides of my face, it looked like I'd just gone swimming. As my hands lapped up water, I winced. Each palm was lined with small cuts that perfectly matched up to my fingernails when I fisted my hand. I was known to move around a lot when I slept, but I'd never made myself bleed before. Throwing water on my face, I leaned against the countertop, applying just enough pressure on the tiny wounds to make me believe I wasn't dreaming. I wasn't sure if it was true what they said—that you can't feel pain in your dreams. That dream felt pretty damn painful, if not physically.

Satisfied that it was just a dream and that I was awake now, I walked back into the bedroom, stopping long enough to grab my leggings from yesterday and slide them on. I tiptoed to the door, hoping that the fresh morning air would calm me down and cool me off enough to catch a few more hours of sleep.

We were on the second floor, so I threaded my legs through the metal posts that held the fence up and sat down on the ground, my feet dangling in midair. I pressed my forehead against the railing, the metal cooling my skin where the cheap black paint was chipping off. The Sleep looked less ominous in the early sunlight. Sunrises had a way of doing that—of turning the most ordinary places into something quaint, peaceful even.

Or maybe the night just had a way of making everything look scarier than it really was. There was a reason horror films were always shot in the dark.

My head snapped back when I heard a door close behind me. Soren walked out, dressed in nothing but his black drawstring pants. They hung dangerously low on his hips. I tried not to stare at the way his abs edged into a deep V that disappeared below the sweatpants.

"I didn't wake you, did I? I tried to be as quiet as possible." I turned back, once again pressing my face into the metal of the railing, this time relying on it to cool my face down for other reasons.

He sat next to me, crossing his legs. His thighs were too muscular to fit through the openings in the railing. "I hear everything, it wasn't your fault. You were pretty quiet. For you anyway. I'm surprised you made it out here without falling over something."

I bit back a smile, hyper aware of the proximity of our bodies. "I couldn't sleep. I guess my body is just used to its new schedule of morning workouts."

His hand ran through his hair, scratching the back of his neck. I watched discreetly as his muscles rippled with every small movement he made. He was strong. Not gym strong, but useful strong. The kind of muscle build that was lean and earned.

"Is that why you were whimpering in your sleep?" he asked.

Whimpering? Well that was mortifying. "Just a bad dream. I'm sorry I woke you. I seem to unintentionally do that a lot."

"Do you have these dreams frequently?" He didn't look at me, but a small frown graced his face as he stared across the parking lot at the sunrise.

"Not as bad as this one. I've always had fairly intense dreams, but the bad ones are usually brought on by stress." Needing something to do, my fingernails peeled back small chips of paint from the railing.

"Yeah, well, I guess watching three guys get killed after being attacked and threatened is enough to make anyone stressed." He paused, shifting his weight slightly so that our legs were a breath away from touching. "I'd offer to take you on a run, but I can't leave El, and I'm not keen on letting you go off by yourself. That usually helps with nightmares."

"Do you have nightmares often?" His shoulders tensed at the question. I continued anyway. "It's just that you've mentioned that running helps with bad dreams before. I just figured you must know from experience?"

We sat in silence, and I tried to ignore how beautiful he looked in the soft rays of the morning. It was a strange kind of beauty, masculine with an edge of power and danger, but beauty nonetheless.

After a moment, he spoke again. "We all have nightmares from time to time, Black. No one is impervious to fear." He turned his head, his eyes piercing my own. My breath caught in my throat as he reached a calloused hand to my face, gently pushing my damp hair back behind my ear. The warmth of his hand lingered and after a brief second that seemed to last a lifetime, he dropped it away slowly, as if reluctant. The gentle light woven into his tattoos intensified. He cleared his throat, returning his gaze back to the almost empty parking lot, his jaw pumping softly with the clenching of his teeth.

"Odie?" Luis's familiar voice called from my left and I swung my head around as if I'd been caught doing something wrong. "Thought I heard voices out here. What're you doing up? You usually have to be dragged from bed before lunchtime."

"Bad dream. Needed some fresh air." My voice was lower than usual, my nerves rattled.

His eyes glanced over Soren, his brows arching when he took in his shirtless torso. "Him too?"

Soren stood up quickly and gracefully. "I should get back, I don't want to leave El alone in there for too long." Without looking in my direction, Soren walked past Luis, their gazes locked, neither of them blinking.

Luis walked over and settled himself into the spot Soren had just evacuated. "I had a bad dream too. Been having them a lot lately, ever since you guys left. Weirdly, I think I was dreaming about some of this supernatural stuff before I even knew it existed." He shook his head gently. "I know that sounds crazy."

I looked up at him, noticing that his hair was drenched and

pressing against his golden skin. I could practically see his pulse jumping out of his neck. His deep blue eyes that were usually filled with laughter were glazed over and distant.

"Shitty thing about nightmares, isn't it?" I asked. "They always seem to take place in creepy dungeons or forests. Just once, I want to have a relaxing bad dream that takes place on a beach," I said.

He smiled slightly which was my intent. "Kind of defeats the purpose of a bad dream, no?"

"Exactly. That's the point."

Both of us sat in a familiar and comfortable silence for a while. That was one of my favorite parts of our friendship, not that we could hang out and make each other laugh. That was important too. But mostly, it was nice to find someone you were comfortable just being with, not needing to do or say anything to fill the gaps. There was something refreshing about just existing together and being perfectly content with that.

"I need you to promise me something, Odie." Luis propped his elbows on his knees, his arms draped over them and his head ducked down so that I couldn't see his face. I stilled and remained quiet, an invitation for him to continue. "I need you to promise you won't leave me like that again. It was hard. Harder than I thought it would be when you and El left. It was the strangest, most uncomfortable feeling. I just—I can't—you can't do that again. Okay?"

His head tilted up, not making eye contact with me, but staring off at the parking lot and the sunrise, not unlike Soren had only moments ago.

"Luis, it wasn't easy for me either. But it was to keep you safe. There's no reason for you to be involved in all of this."

"There is every reason for me to be involved in this. You guys are my best friends, you're the only family I've got." His face turned in my direction, the glazed distance that coated his eyes when he first sat down was now replaced by a steely resolve.

I nodded in agreement, hoping sincerely that it was a promise I could keep. He was my family now too. "How's Sam?"

He had given me a cursory answer yesterday, but I needed to hear more about how he was handling things, needed to know that he was okay.

"Honestly, he was pretty miserable. As soon as you left, I think he changed his mind about not coming with you. He tried to give weird excuses for why you guys were gone and why I couldn't get in touch with you, but he's a lousy liar. And I could tell that those people staying at your place, Dex and Sage, were starting to get concerned about him. In retrospect, now that I know what I know, I think they were a little afraid Sam would come chasing after you as soon as he caught wind of where you all were. Honestly, I think he was waiting around for them to slip up and reveal a location. Sam even got Dex wasted a couple of times at The Tavern, but I don't think he got anywhere with it." Luis let out a soft chuckle. "I still can't believe Sam is one of these energy users. It's all so crazy. But also weirdly not."

"But he's safe?" At my question, Luis nodded his head. "Then that's what matters. It's all I wanted." I paused, staring at the tension in Luis's shoulders. His body seemed leaner and more muscular since I last saw him. "I still don't understand how you found us."

"Neither do I. I spent almost every minute at the house with Sam or at The Tavern. Even became sort of friends with Dex. He had Sam on this intense workout regimen. I think it helped to combat his stress and anxiety. And since I was around so much, Dex started training me too. He's arrogant, but more likable than Soren and Jax are."

I smiled, thinking of Luis training with a supe at the same time I was. I wondered if I looked different to him as well—harder, colder maybe.

"Then, yesterday I woke up from a really vivid nightmare," Luis said, leaning back on his elbows while he watched the sunrise. "Worst one I've ever had. Left me with a bad feeling. So, I got in the car to go for a drive and clear my head, thinking about how badly I needed to see you, and then suddenly I was driving for hours until I showed up on Soren's front lawn. Or, well, it's not really a lawn that he has, is it? More like a prairie or a forest." He frowned. "I know it doesn't make any sense, I've been thinking about it nonstop, but I honestly can't come up with a logical answer. Even with all this magical shit I've learned over the last twenty-four hours, it still sounds crazy."

"If there's one thing I've learned the last few weeks, logic doesn't seem to have much of a place when it comes to supes. And neither does coincidence. You finding us? It's just another question we have on our plate without an answer. Of course, it'd be really nice if we could stop racking up questions and start accumulating answers instead," I said.

It was amazing how much our lives changed over the course of a month or two. Everything seemed so different. *I* felt so different. I studied Luis, re-familiarizing myself with the soft waves of his brown hair and the peculiar purplish-blue of his eyes. I wanted him safe, without a doubt. But I couldn't deny the very large part of me that craved to have him next to me, like a limb—I could function without him, but my life was better and easier with him around. Especially now that things were changing so much.

Speaking of which, I thought about the last time I'd seen Luis before leaving. "What about Kay? Does she know you're staying with us?"

He tensed slightly and drew his brows together as if he was debating something, some mental argument or discussion he was having with himself. I wasn't used to him filtering his words with me, and I was surprised by the jolt of sadness that hit me at the thought. But I guess it was only fair. I'd been keeping loads of things from him. After a few seconds he relaxed, letting out a deep breath. He shook his head. "I haven't seen much of her since you guys left. After a day or two, I couldn't focus on much of anything else. She got the hint and left me alone after a little while. Maybe I'll call her when all of this is done," he paused and looked over at me. "Then again, maybe not."

We both sat in the pregnant silence for a few moments. I cleared my throat, aware of a tension around us that wasn't there before. "We should probably rally the troops," I said. "I know Soren wanted to get on the road early. Between sleeping almost the whole drive here and grabbing a few more hours last night, I'm more than rested enough to shoulder most of the drive."

Luis smiled. "It'll go faster if you let almost anyone else drive, grandma."

I shoved his shoulder, relieved at the familiar playful energy between us. "Hey, I drive the speed limit. You know, those super obvious signs every few blocks that tell you exactly how fast you should be going? That's not old-lady behavior, that's just following directions. And the law."

The deep timbre of Luis's laugh warmed me in a cheesy-gooey way. I missed that sound and I had only just realized how much.

"We'll agree to disagree then. How was bunking with El? She still sleep like a lunatic?"

I smiled and rubbed back and forth along the side of my stomach. "I have a bruise right here, fifty-fifty whether I got it from the fight yesterday or one of El's leg spasms."

"I'm betting on El being the culprit." With a soft chuckle and shake of his head, Luis stood up. He brushed his basketball shorts free of any invisible debris and pulled me off the ground with surprising force. As soon as I stabilized my footing, his arms crashed around me into one of his signature hugs. My body tensed until I relaxed into the familiar clean, spiced scent I unconsciously associated with Luis. My breath caught when he unexpectedly pushed his lips into my forehead—a soft kiss that lasted a hair of a second. "I'm glad I found you guys, Odie. Life wasn't the same with you both gone. I meant what I said. You're my family."

Before I came to my senses, Luis was already gone behind the door of his motel room.   I shook my head and went back to my own, wanting nothing more than to get ready and head back on the road. And I wouldn't say no to some food. Hopefully we could find a diner along the way that was willing to serve grilled cheese for breakfast. There was no doubt in my mind that we were driving into battle, and I wanted my comfort food if I was going to go through with it without kicking and screaming.

I was permitted to drive for the first few hours while everyone else had time to doze a bit more or wake up more fully. Once we finished breakfast though, Jax insisted on driving the rest of the way. He mumbled something about how getting me away from the front seat was the only way we were going to get to San Francisco by Rennix's party.

Usually, I'd fight him on such a catty remark, but I was happy just existing in my food coma for the rest of the day. The diner we stopped in was in fact very willing to make grilled cheese for me, and I unashamedly ate three. It might have been the first time I ever out-ate Soren and Jax. But the chef used five different cheeses, so I really wasn't to blame—it would take someone with far greater willpower than mine to resist that level of awesome. Diners sure knew what they were doing. Plus, I was still recovering from the whole almost-dying thing from yesterday, so I totally earned that breakfast of champions.

Around midafternoon El woke up from what she liked to call a power nap, but what was really four hours of El twisting, turning, and snoring in the back of the van. "So, what do we do when we get to San Fran?" she asked, the question filtering through a yawn. "It's Friday and the party isn't until Saturday. Does that mean we get to have some actual fun?"

I smiled, typical El. She was still half asleep, but already looking to get the party started.

Soren glanced at her through the rearview mirror while Jax silently wove effortlessly around drivers that drove a lot like me. "We aren't going to stay in San Francisco," he said. We're almost to Santa Rosa. About an hour out from where Rennix is. I want to keep you out of the city as long as possible, so that'll be our base for now. We'll find a decent motel and set a plan."

"And tell me dear brother, what are the odds of me convincing you to let me go to the party too?" El's left brow arched, a challenging glint mirrored in her bright blue eyes.

"Less than zero." Soren shot her a cold, tight smile. She wasn't looking at him, but judging by the slump of her shoulders, she felt the reproach in his words, if not in his facial expression.

The rest of us watched, half expecting a family argument to take place in the suddenly small confines of the mom-van.

Surprisingly, after a few tense moments, El flashed him a giant smile. "Fine. But I get to go shopping for yours and Dessa's masquerade outfits." The evil glint in her eye told me she was going to be ruthless. I wouldn't be surprised if she made Soren dress up in spandex. The uncharacteristically worried expression on his face told me his thoughts were along the same vein. "And, we are doing something fun tonight. We're planning, yes. But I've been cooped up in that cabin for weeks. I want to get out and get some fresh air."

I looked back at her. "I can't believe you aren't fighting him on this. I'm glad you agree, don't get me wrong. But you never let me win an argument so easily." Which was the truth. I'd learned over the years to pick my battles with El wisely, because the girl knew how to dig in. It was one of the reasons I didn't fight it when she decided to play dress up with me on Friday nights. Sometimes letting her win was the lesser evil.

"Usually I wouldn't let him win either. But I'm not stupid. I know you are all in this mess because of me—risking your necks because of me. I'm not going to do anything to put you all in any more danger than you are already in." Her eyes were watery blue, the color they became when El did everything in her power to hold her tears in against the rim. She hated crying, hated showing weakness. It was probably a body-manipulator thing because I gathered Soren was the same way.

Wanting to give her a second to compose herself, I nodded and turned back to the boys. "So, is it just Soren coming to the party then?"

"No way, I'm coming too." Luis tensed beside me. His blue eyes dark and set.

"You can't come, you're human and have no way to defend yourself. You shouldn't even be here in the first place." Soren's voice was even as it dismissed him, and he didn't bother looking at Luis in the rearview mirror. "Besides, it's bad enough taking Black to the party. But she's the one Raifus wants and who he is going to guide to the neutralizer."

"I'm not letting her go without me." Luis was fuming, and I heard El sigh in annoyance behind me.

"Honestly, Luis, she'll be safer if you stay with me and Jax. That way, Soren will only have to worry about getting her out of there safely. I'm not happy about being left behind from the party either, but Soren will make sure nothing happens to Dessa." El fluffed her pillow and closed her eyes. I knew she wasn't really going back to sleep, but her pretense doused the testosterone and gave everyone an excuse to sit the remainder of the trip in silence.

After a few minutes of quiet, Luis moved his hand discreetly to mine. After giving it a tight squeeze, he leaned over and whispered in my ear. "I'm sorry. I know you hate the whole male bravado thing, and I didn't mean to insinuate that you couldn't take care of yourself. Soren just brings out the worst in me. I know that he'll do everything in his power to keep El safe, I just don't trust that he's as concerned as he should be about your safety. He's a bit off an asshole, isn't he?"

His words were quiet, meant for only me to hear. If we'd been in the car with a bunch of humans, that would've been the case. As it was, I knew that Soren and El had supe-level hearing since they were shifters and, judging by the smirk on Jax's face in the rearview, he heard too. No one said anything, but Soren looked back at Luis with an odd expression on his face, but I couldn't tell whether it was amusement or annoyance.

Twenty minutes later, Soren pulled into a hotel parking lot. While I was expecting another shithole like The Sleep, this place was huge and inviting. When I looked at Soren questioningly, he shrugged as if to say, "it's worth a shot." We all shuffled out of the mom-van, collecting our various belongings since we would be staying here for the duration of our trip.

A petite blonde girl was working at the front desk, and she kept glancing demurely at Jax, her cheeks reddening with each stolen look. Soren dropped his bags and began to walk over to her, but I placed a hand on his chest, stopping him.

"Let Jax handle this one. I think he'll have a better chance getting us a decent set of rooms without a credit card." I nodded my head towards the girl and he turned back in agreement. The huge grin on Jax's face told me he was more than pleased with the girl's tentative perusal--and way more willing to have her as a midnight caller than anyone working on The Sleep's staff. Knowing him, he'd have her in his room with a sock on the door by dinner time. Actually, knowing him he'd probably nix the sock and leave the door open, more than willing to have an audience.

When he walked back over to us, I bit my tongue and made myself a promise not to insult his abilities again, even if it was only in my head. He managed to get a suite that had three connecting bedrooms and a lounge area, no card needed. While the price was obviously much steeper than the motel, I had the feeling Soren and Jax were just as ambivalent about money as El was. I made a mental note to force El to tell me more about her life in the Veil once all of this was over. Seeing as we were already in deep, I didn't think her usual refusal to talk about her old life would still hold.

We dropped off our bags and Jax charged in the bathroom to get ready for a date with the concierge downstairs. Apparently, she had an hour-long break and Jax was more than willing to fill that time.

I thought we'd spend the rest of the afternoon and evening making plans for Saturday night, but El had other plans.

"Alright, let's go shopping. I have two full outfits to get together and hardly any time to scope out the options." El collected her purse

from the pile of bags and stared Luis and Soren down as if asking them to challenge her.

They were both smart enough not to. Like me, they knew to pick their battles when it came to El and in this case, shopping was a relatively easy—and safe—way to placate her.

TWENTY-ONE

All things considered, the shopping trip was fairly quick compared to El's average. She managed to find me a dress and mask, as well as a suit for Soren. Not that she'd let us see what she bought. Which was fine with me. It meant I could fill up on soft pretzels and coffee in the cafeteria while she did her thing. I had a feeling that since she couldn't go to the masquerade cocktail party, keeping our outfits a secret was her way of joining in on the mystery of the evening. When we returned back to the hotel, Jax was alone and glowing. I tried to hide my blush when my traitorous mind started running through different scenarios that could add that refreshed glow to a seduction-feeder. If he noticed my embarrassment, he thankfully ignored it.

"Glad you guys are back. I'm starving." Jax grabbed the bags from Luis and tossed them halfheartedly into the room El and I would be staying in.

"Really? Because it kind of seems like you've had your fill." El's singsong voice danced through the room as she went to put her things away and get ready for dinner. Knowing her, that would involve a full ensemble change that would inevitably lead into an attempt to get Soren to agree to a night on the town.

Soren and Luis glanced at each other and then at Jax, all of them sharing a knowing chuckle. If they wanted to pretend like I didn't get the joke, that was fine by me. Mostly, I was just happy that Soren and Luis seemed to have come to a truce. They weren't at each other's throats the past few hours anyway, bonding over their shared misery of shopping. I was hoping that their tentative tolerance would last at least until Rennix's party, if not after.

While I fancied myself off the hook of changing from my dark jeans and baggy sweater, I realized that life on the run had not tarnished El's audacity when it came to taking charge of our outings. After showering and changing into a red dress that hugged her curves and somehow didn't clash with her pink-tipped hair, she charged into her shopping bags from the day. I watched her move gracefully around the room in a pair of black stilettos that gave me vertigo just from looking at them. While none of us were naive enough to think that she had only purchased evening wear for tomorrow night, we weren't expecting her to pull out three outfits for the guys and shove a boutique bag into my hands.

Soren opened his mouth to protest, but El clamped a hand over it, muting the words.

"Hey. No complaining. I've played nice, allowed you to run around all alpha-y while I played the damsel in distress locked away in a forest cottage. I don't get to go to the party tomorrow night and you're putting my best friend in danger. I get tonight. We are having a pre-masquerade ball. And you can just buck up and deal, buttercup." The four of us stared at her with open mouths. "Just because I like to play dress up, doesn't mean I can't still kick ass." When no one moved a muscle, she clapped her hands together once and yelled, "change."

My lips twitched as I waited for the boys to roll their eyes and camp out in front of the TV, until I noticed Jax and Luis scrambling over one another to follow her orders—a strange mixture of fear and amusement in their expressions. Soren looked stricken by the idea that he'd have to dress up two nights in a row, but he followed without a word, glaring half-heartedly at his sister.

"You too, missy." El grabbed my arm, guiding us to our shared room in the suite. "I'll do your hair." When I didn't respond, she chuckled. "Don't worry, your outfit is sublime. Outdone only by my dress tonight and tomorrow's gown."

While I suspected her words were meant to encourage me, they only solicited an agonized groan. Still, I followed and allowed her to have her way with me.

All complaining aside, I had to admire El's eye. She chose a burgundy dress that was tight up top but tapered out and was otherwise tasteful. While the right arm had a full sleeve, the left side of the dress was strapless—something I wasn't fond of until El overcame all odds and showed me a small lingerie bag containing the first comfortable strapless bra I'd ever encountered. To be honest, I didn't think a useful strapless bra existed, making El's find one of the greatest of the decade. Maybe even the greatest of the century.

She left my hair down in large, voluminous curls, before fastening her own up in a complicated bun. Under her instruction, I painted my lips with a deep burgundy stain, keeping my eyes simple with some winged liner and mascara. All things considered, I was done and decent-looking in a timelier manner than I'd anticipated.

Knowing that the odds of her being denied a fun night out after shopping and convincing us to change were slim, El shoved me out of our room, giddy from the anticipated release of her cabin fever.

When we entered the common area, Soren was the only one ready, most likely the first to snag the bathroom El delegated as belonging to the boys. He was lounging on a chair, his legs dangling over an arm while he sipped a glass filled with several fingers of a light brown liquid, likely whiskey, and rubbed a finger over the bridge of his nose as if wiping away a headache.

"This might be a record. You guys finished before the guys. Granted, they got caught up watching some sports game and spent ten minutes arguing over who had to shower first and miss the final ten minutes." His eyes remained closed while he spoke to us, as if he were recovering from one of the most difficult battles he'd faced. Then again, knowing Soren and his distaste of all things human and all things Luis, listening to him and Jax bicker over a game probably ranked pretty high.

While his eyes were closed, I allowed myself a second to admire his outfit—a tightly fitted burgundy button-up with thin black vertical stripes was already rolled up to his elbows and tucked haphazardly into a pair of fitted black pants. His hair was combed back in its usual style, but since he'd let his beard go a week without a trim, the combination added an enticing mix of debonair rebellion to the ensemble.

"I don't know, Sor, Sam has me almost liking basketball if I'm being honest. You scoff now, but a few more months in the human world and you'll be cheering in the other room along with them," El said. She grabbed the drink from his hands and took a sip before wrinkling her face in disgust. "Ugh. I can't even pretend to like the taste of whatever that is. It's like drinking rubbing alcohol." She made her way to the bar, clinking bottles aside as she scavenged. "Don't worry, Dess. I'll fix us up something decent."

I didn't have the heart to tell her that Soren was probably drinking bourbon, so I just laughed at the racket she was making and turned back to Soren just as he opened his eyes. The increasingly familiar gray hue deepened, and I thought I almost heard a low growl. My hand smoothed unconsciously over my bellybutton, and I sent a silent prayer that the noise I heard wasn't my own angry stomach.

He didn't say a word to me, but his body tensed as he stood up from his reclined position, took a step towards me, and sat back down, ramrod-straight. I blushed at his unblinking stare and tried unsuccessfully to break eye contact when I felt uncomfortable butterflies fluttering around in my midsection.

After a few long moments, I could feel the heat radiating off of my skin, heat that disappeared when El cleared her throat standing less than a foot away from me. Her eyes travelled between me and Soren several times with barely disguised intrigue while she arched a brow and handed me a cocktail. "Here."

I sipped the murky brown liquid. If El's proximity wasn't enough to disrupt the connection between Soren and me, her drink was. I spit my sip back into the glass, but not before the offensive drink had enough time to coat every single one of my taste buds. "Oh my god, El. This is the most disgusting thing I've ever put in my mouth."

"That's what she said." Jax stumbled out of the bedroom, smirking at his own joke. He glanced from me to El, his amusement growing into a more genuine smile. "Damn, ladies. Don't you both clean up nicely." He walked over to me, grabbed my glass and lined his own mouth to the stain left by my lipstick. Without breaking eye contact, he took a sip and winked. He must have missed the part where I spit back into it. The moment broke as soon as he started coughing and sputtering. He wiped his mouth on his shirt and shoved the glass into El's hands. "That was supposed to be way more seductive than it was. I don't know what you did to that drink, El, but there is some foul magic brewing in that glass."

Without a word, Soren surrendered his glass to Jax who gratefully took a generous sip.

"Better?" Soren asked, his voice low and more gravelly than usual.

Jax nodded his head. "Yo, Luis, let's hurry it up. I know you were last for the shower, but I need food. Like two hours ago."

Luis pushed into the common area doing up the last few buttons of his shirt. "You supes really grate on the nerves, don't you?" He came up short when I fell into his line of sight and I watched his eyes languidly devour me from top to bottom and back up again. I was unable to meet his stare, afraid that what I'd find there would cross the dangerous line between friend and something, well, else.

Instead, I took in his outfit, realizing that all three of them were dressed similarly but with differently colored shirts. Luis was in a deep purple and Jax in blue. After a quiet moment, while everyone awkwardly assessed each other, I burst out laughing, a laugh made more embarrassing by its punctuation with a snort.

A frown creased between El's eyes. "What? Do they not look okay?"

"They look great." I paused, trying to regulate my breathing through the laughter. "It's just they kind of look like an adult version of the Ninja Turtles."

Luis looked from himself to the other two before a huge smile broke out over his face. "You're right. We're just missing orange. Does this mean we get to go for pizza?"

Jax and Soren merely looked on in confusion and, eventually, in mortification when Luis, El, and I broke out in a poorly-tuned recitation of the TMNT theme song, complete with choppy dance moves.

There was something strangely exhilarating about stuffing your face with greasy pizza when you were wearing a fancy dress—like you were deliberately breaking the rules of polite society. While cheesy-goodness could never be bad, I'd be lying if I said that contrast didn't make the meal go down even more smoothly than usual. And when five people with appetites like ours were satisfied with a meal, plan making was a piece of cake. I was nervous, but ready for Rennix's gathering tomorrow.

Like expected, while we walked off our pizza and beer El managed to steer that walk into a night district that opened into a giant street fair. I let out a breath of relief, happy that she at least wasn't dragging us to a club tonight. We were absurdly overdressed compared to the rest of the fair's patrons, but that somehow added to the charm and theme of our night. My mouth watered at the smell of fair food, which was problematic seeing as my dress felt exponentially tighter with each piece of pizza I'd shoved into my mouth. When all this was over I needed to binge on some vegetables.

Luis and Jax raced to a water shooting game with their typical, competitive fervor, while Soren scanned the perimeter looking for threats. I rolled my eyes and grabbed his shirt, tugging him in the direction of bumper cars. "Come on, Soren. Don't be such a buzzkill. We aren't even in San Francisco. Try to have fun for one night."

He didn't say anything but raised a brow and allowed himself to be led into the line. El was practically hopping back and forth with excitement. I stared at her shoes, unable to figure out how she'd manage driving one of these rust buckets in her stilettos.

Which was a mistake, because El totally dominated both of us and spent most of our run blocking Soren into a corner while she repeatedly rammed into his car with infectious peals of laughter. She climbed out of her car gracefully and grabbed each of us by the hand. "Come on, let's do that janky rollercoaster ride next. I saw one in a Final Destination movie and I've wanted to ride one ever since."

Because who wouldn't want to be reminded of a freak death scene right before hopping on rusted metal? "You're kind of a lunatic, aren't you?" I whispered.

She stopped short, forcing me to awkwardly trip while trying to avoid running into her. "I'm perfectly sane, thank you very much."

"Oh, you're totally sane," I said through a smile. "You know, except for that whole completely crazy thing you have going on."

"And also, the insanity," Soren added.

With a roll of her eyes, she grabbed me by the arm and dragged me towards the death trap.

When we exited the rickety machine, luckily unscathed, my hands rested on my stomach, trying to gently calm the slush of beer and pizza the rollercoaster had me too aware of.

"Odie, I beat Jax. You can have this, I don't want it." Luis shoved a plush koala with a giant unicorn horn into my hands without looking at me. He pointed to the fun house for our next stop and tried not to draw attention to his gift, but I knew him well enough to catch the light blush flushing his cheeks. Luis hated calling attention to himself when he was being sweet.

Not wanting to embarrass him in front of the group, I nodded in agreement, whispered an awkward thanks, and directed our party to the fun house—even though the creepy mirrors had a tendency to make me nauseous. Which probably wasn't a good idea after already feeling gross from the food and rollercoaster.

I was at the end of the line, ready to follow Soren into the house of mirrors, when I caught sight of what looked to be a purple bird's nest on top of a short woman's head. At the push of excitement in my gut, I turned to follow the odd hat instead of Soren.

The woman walked deceptively fast and I found myself practically jogging to catch up to her as she wove through the maze of laughing teenagers and kids. When I reached the back exit of the fair, I lost track of her. As I strained my eyes, trying to spot the purple nest in the shadow of night, a wrinkled hand clasped over my lips.

I jumped and prepared to scream when Charlotte's familiar face appeared before me, a chubby finger pressed to her own mouth.

"Shh, girl. Don't scream, we need to talk." She turned away and began walking towards a small patch of trees until she noticed I hadn't followed. "Well, come on now. I don't have all night."

Unable to find words, I followed Charlotte silently until we reached a small, isolated park.

TWENTY-TWO

Charlotte sat down on a wooden bench and pet the space next to her. "Well, sit down girl. Let me get a good look at you."

I did as she asked, smiling at the warmth her presence provided. With everything going on the past few weeks, I hadn't realized how worried I was about Char. She was a steady fixture in my life since moving to Seattle, like the grandmother I never had growing up. I chuckled softly at her ridiculous hat—it was indeed a bird's nest. Instead of housing a few plastic birds, there was a small stuffed dragon perched on the side.

Her hands ran over my arms, until she pulled me to her in a fierce hug. "I've worried about you a great deal, Odessa Black. I'm glad to see you safe and in one piece." She drew her magnifying glass up and peered at the stuffed unicorn koala, examining it thoroughly and shushing me anytime I deigned to open my mouth. "That is a ridiculous talisman, girl. I don't understand youngsters these days."

"It's a stuffed animal. From Luis." I blinked, failing for the life of me to understand how anyone who dressed as Charlotte did could find something ridiculous or unusual about much of anything. "I'm happy to see you too, Char. But how are you here? And how did you know I'd be here? And why weren't you surprised when Michael turned out to be a supe back at the house?" Her wrinkled finger once again pressed softly into my lips, silencing my stampede of questions.

"We don't have time to discuss everything tonight, dear girl. One day, I promise we will. But at the moment, there are blocks on my memory that only allow me to know the bare essentials." She drew her finger away, confident now that I would shut up and let her speak. "I was a little overzealous to be completely honest, could've given myself a bit more to work with," she mumbled to herself.

Since she wouldn't have my words, I silently drank in the sight of her. While her outrageous hat and bright orange Halloween sweater fit well with her usual style, there was something slightly ragged in her expression. It was as if she had aged over the last few weeks and grown weary in her skin. For the first time since I'd met her, she looked old. But also, weirdly awake in a way she hadn't been before.

She rubbed absentmindedly at her knuckles and stared at our surroundings with a focus that suggested she was both appreciating the view and assessing the perimeter for eavesdroppers. But the park was quiet, and we were surrounded only by trees and a rusted swing set. Finally, with a long-exhaled breath, she turned back to me. Her deep, wise eyes stared into my own, calculating. "I'm not really sure where I want to start with all of this, girl. I need you to make me a promise before I do—" she paused, waiting for my nod. "You cannot interrupt. This situation is complicated enough, and I need to get this all out before I let you ask questions that will take us in unhelpful directions. My memory has been hindered, so the thoughts I want to give you are slippery and unsure." Her words were firm but not unfriendly.

I tried to silently rectify this version of Charlotte with the one I'd grown to love over the last few years. She wasn't aloof and grandmotherly tonight. No, she was powerful and infused with a quiet strength I hadn't noticed before. Her long, straight hair pulsed in the wind like she was summoning it around her, the power of a goddess.

"Agreed." I gestured with a nod for her to start.

"It was no accident that I became your neighbor, Odessa Black. I was a friend to your mother." She paused for a second at my gasp, blinking sternly when I opened my mouth to speak. Slamming my lips together, I begged her wordlessly to continue. "I was sent to find you if there arose a time when she was gone and you had left the protection of your father. You don't know the particulars of your mother's death, but she was hunted by those who would wish you a terrible fate. She died ensuring that your abilities would be blocked and make you invisible to the supernatural world. To protect you as much as she could. It was no easy feat, you see?"

"Abilities?" My mouth was dry, the word barely able to leave my lips. "You mean that I can see auras? It comes from my mother?" I knew Char asked me not to interrupt, but the compassion in her eyes told me that she understood how hard this would be for me to process. And it was. My mother was someone I thought about all the time and never—an idea I grasped onto, with no real way to possess.

"I don't think that is what she meant by your abilities being blocked. They are strong, girl, and couldn't be blocked in all capacities. It is perhaps even a built-in safety measure—that you can identify those who might wish you harm. I do not know. There are some elements of your story, and hers, hidden in my memory for safe keeping. You know of prophecies?"

The question in her voice alerted me to speak. "Yes, I've heard of them. But nobody really believes in them, right? El and the others seem to brush the idea of fortune telling off as a useless parlor trick." I stared at a lone swing a few feet away from us, it's brother long ripped from its chains, and found myself unsettled by an irrational need to hop on and kick away from the ground. A need to do something besides sit here as I processed her words and their implications. I dug my feet into the grass, to keep me planted next to Char. Why was it that we always wanted answers to our questions when we couldn't have them, but almost never when we could?

"They are complicated. There are some things that I, and you, can't know yet. That is why I made sure your mother told me the minimum I needed to know, and why I layered my own memories so that I would never know more than I should at any given moment. And, more importantly, so that *you* never know more than you should at any given moment. Knowledge is powerful, girl. And having too much of it can be a bad thing should one of us be compromised. Besides, I'm not meant to be a major figure in your story, girl. This journey is not mine to travel." At the question in my eyes she chuckled, a deep warm sound that reverberated in my bones. "I'm, as you and El would term, a supe. A memory-manipulator, to be specific. We are quite rare, not that I mean to brag." She winked and the wrinkles along her face deepened with her answering smile.

I bit nervously at my bottom lip. How had I spent so much time with this woman and never really known her? Never really seen her? "I've never seen an aura around you. Why did you hide your ability from me? Why tell me now?" Hearing the accusing tone in my words, I added a soft apology.

"You didn't need to know before now, and after my cookie experiment with that medical boy of yours, it should be obvious. I am able to disguise and reveal abilities. Energy can be manipulated beyond an energy user's individual ability." She paused, her eyes darting back and forth between mine, reading something on my face. "I didn't hide that boy's ability, Odessa. It is important that you know that. I am not the only one who is capable of infusing energy manipulation into objects or food." She chuckled softly to herself. "Though it is a rare gift and one of the reasons your mother wanted me to watch over you. To ensure you'd never be tracked through supernatural means. Something about the boy's energy rubbed me the wrong way. He was pretending to be human, but there was a power there, hidden beneath the surface. I could see it in the way he moved...in the way he studied you girls, so alert."

Kind of like how she pretended to be human, disguising her power? But I bit back my retort. "So why did you leave? Why not tell me this when Michael's aura revealed itself? And how did you find me now?" My fingers bit into the splintered wood of the bench. I was sure the others would be worried about me by now, but I couldn't leave without knowing more and I didn't have a way to contact them. "Please, just help me understand this."

"I left in search of something. I can't offer you more than that now, but rest assured it was to benefit you. The block that your mother placed on you—I cannot break it myself. Her hope was that you would never need to access your abilities, that for as long as the block remained, you'd be untraceable and safe." Her hat had slipped during her tale, so she paused to awkwardly right it. The small dragon bounced with each word she emphasized. "Clearly, that wasn't the case. I had a funny feeling about the boy. The block on him felt a lot like the one on Luis—different, but similar—so I knew how to break it. Then, I left to—"

"Luis? Luis has a block—" I felt air pull into my lungs, but I still felt like I was suffocating. I tried to duck my head between my legs to counteract the feeling of dizziness coming over me, but El's outfit choice made it almost impossible for me to do so without flashing Charlotte. I had a panic attack once before, and the familiar rushing sound of my blood and the tingly stiffness in my fingers pointed to the possibility of another. "Char, are you saying Luis is a supe?" I felt like the wind was knocked out of me. "And he's been lying to me all this time?"

"No girl. I mean, yes, he's got abilities. But, no, he's not lying to you. Like you, he has no awareness of his family's past. His mother was best friends with yours, and they died around the same time.

They agreed when you were both born to bind you together, a bind that would only enact in the event that your mother's wards were broken. It's why he felt unconsciously compelled to move to Seattle when you did. It's how he found you, wherever you were. He'll always be able to find you, and once he becomes aware of his abilities and his bond, that skill will come easier to him. Like all things, it takes practice and willpower." She paused, pulling an orange thread from her sweater. My eyes traced the exaggerated face of the pumpkin, and I breathed a small smile. Halloween was months away. Leave it to Char to celebrate when she chose to. The woman followed no one's calendar but her own. "And Luis, well, his story is complicated. There are some things he's been forced to forget. He likely doesn't tell you much about his life before Seattle."

Which was true. I'd always been so focused on how secretive El was about her childhood. My cheeks burned as I realized that I hadn't extended that same curiosity to Luis's past.

"You're *how* he forgot, aren't you?" I asked. At her guilty nod, my mind caught on the tails of another unexplained moment. I remembered Char, so frail the last time I'd seen her. "And Inferno," I continued, "you manipulated the memories of the bouncer and the people there the night of the fire, didn't you?"

"Yes, very good, Odessa. You've been paying attention," she grinned with approval. "I saw you come home that night, all in a tizzy. I took care of it. I went to the bar to find out what happened. Then, I had the bartender give me the cards of everyone there that night, who'd forgotten to close their tab. Of course, I couldn't get to everyone—but quelling the night down some did make the replacement story more believable. I saw a bartender light shots on fire in one of those late-night mystery shows I love to watch, always thought it looked coo—" I cleared my throat, trying to steer her back to the point. "Ahem, anyway—I didn't want any more energy users drawn to the event, not if there was a possibility they'd catch wind of you."

I nodded, digesting Char's story. I still couldn't wrap my mind around the fact that Luis was a supe. "But how did he find me? Luis, I mean. I thought you said I was magically untraceable?" My head was swimming, but I knew the only way to keep Charlotte talking was to approach the discussion logically. She was rushing through the story and her body was tense, like she was ready to run at the drop of a hat.

"The bond functions differently. I will explain more one day, but he will always be able to find you through it. Supernatural bonds cannot be deceived by blocks and wards. That's how I found you, eventually. I tracked Luis, knowing that he would eventually make his way to you. I've been searching for answers, biding my time until we could meet again."

"But his block is different than mine then? If you can track him?"

"Yes, girl. I could break it with slightly more effort than the disguise I broke from that boy. When he was young, I manipulated Luis's memories. He does not remember any part of his life that relates to the Veil. Like you, he was ideally going to live a normal, human life. But I think both of your mothers hoped you'd find your way to each other eventually." She scoffed. "That's changed, clearly."

"Why are people after me then? Why are Luis and I connected? And what does this have to do with our parents?" I tugged the hem of my dress down, suddenly uncomfortable with the judgmental way Charlotte was eyeing my outfit. Strange how I could be made to feel beautiful and trashy all in the same night and with the same cloth. Stranger that I found myself worried about what Charlotte thought about my fashion taste and style.

"That I don't know. As I said, I had my memories manipulated long ago, by a very *very* strong manipulator—me," she winked at me, "all so that I wouldn't know the specifics in case anyone tried to use me to get to you. My memories of your mother are all but gone."

Her large eyes suddenly filled with an empty sadness and I knew the same emotion was reflected in my own. When Charlotte told me she knew my mother, I felt a spark of excited longing. I'd finally have a connection to her, be able to know her through an old friend. That disappeared with Char's confession.

"I'm sorry girl. Maybe one day, I'll be able to tell you more. For now, I can only give you her name. It's all that I allowed myself to keep. That and the knowledge that she was like a daughter to me."

I perked up. "Her name?" My words croaked with excitement.

The lines of her face filled with pity. "Talia." She reached over and grabbed my hand, offering a squeeze of comfort, both of us rubbed raw with a loss neither of us remembered or understood.

"Thank you." I offered her a small smile. It was all I could muster at the moment. "Char?" I hesitated, the next question was probably the most difficult one for me to ask, "do you—do you know why my father left? Where he is?"

Her wrinkled lips tipped down in a pitying frown. "Not because he wanted to leave you, that's the only answer I can give right now."

I cleared my throat and nodded, as comfortable as I could be with the non-answer. "So, what now?"

"I'll keep looking for answers on my end. There are resources I left behind. A breadcrumb trail, in a way." She scratched her chin, laughing softly as her fingers trailed over a few stray whiskers. "The younger me was a bit in love with the idea of a scavenger hunt and I feel I can do little more now than humor her and follow the suggestions she left, until I can learn more when I need to learn it. But who knows...the younger me was also a bit of a trouble maker," she winked playfully at me, "it's entirely possible the breadcrumbs lead nowhere. And you, girl—eventually, you will need to go to the Veil. From what I've been able to track down from contacts I have here, your block can only be broken through time and work, away from the human realm. Though I don't have more for you beyond that." Her lips quivered slightly, and she coughed to cover her emotion. "This is where I must leave you for now. Stick with Luis, Odessa. Your mothers were wise in giving you each other's protection. You can trust him. And El, I believe, too. I'm not sure if the demons of her past are the same from yours, so keep a weather eye out." She stood, leaving me speechless as I tried to digest everything she'd told me. "If I learn of another way to protect you or break your block, I will find you through him. Until then, you should go back. They will be wondering where you are. Be selective with who you trust this information to, Odessa. Undoubtedly there are many other pieces to this puzzle I can but guess at."

Panicking, I pulled her sleeve, "Wait, Charlotte, don't go yet. Luis—how do I tell him—how does he even break his block?"

She chuckled, squeezing my hand between both of hers. It was odd how someone so small could infuse me with such strength. "Worry not, girl. You've already told him as much truth as you know, yes?"

I nodded.

"Continue to do that. He will come into his own as he processes. Like his connection to you, his ability will only grow in strength with the knowledge that he possesses it. Each block is different, his is merely buried in his memories. Finding you was the first small tug, he'll continue pulling on the loose thread until my manipulation unravels altogether."

Before she could turn to leave, I grabbed her in a firm hug, the dragon on her hat hitting my chin uncomfortably. She squeezed back, offering her comfort as my neighbor, my friend, my protector, and the link to my past.

"Thank you, Charlotte. Please be safe, wherever you are."

She nodded, her eyes glazed with tears, and backed away. I began the walk towards the fairgrounds, trying to will myself to move under the weight of what I'd learned, before her gravelly voice stopped me in my tracks. "And girl?"

I turned back to her. She'd all but caught up to me, with her large right eye magnified through the glass she wore around her neck. She looked me up and down, a tsking sound of disapproval coming from her lips.

"A ridiculous dress. That is no way to dress for a fair, Odessa Black. You'll give boys the wrong idea. Do better. Blend in." Without another word, she dropped the magnifying glass back against her chest, winked her left eye at me, and walked in the opposite direction of the fair with an impressive speed and grace.

Less than a minute later Luis came barreling into me. "Jesus, Odie. We've been looking everywhere for you. Where the hell have you been? I half thought some stupid supe came and kidnapped you." His words were mumbled against the layers of my hair as he squeezed me to him. I felt the steady thump of his heart, noticing that its beat matched mine, wild and erratic. Was this because of some weird, magical bond? Was our friendship completely fabricated? Planned?

I cleared my throat and saw El, Jax, and Soren trailing a few feet behind him. They all had matching looks of relief on their faces. Well, except for Soren. He mostly just looked pissed. I took a step back from Luis when I caught the intensity in Soren's gaze.

"Where have you been, Black?" His voice was tight, clipped.

I looked at the four of them as Charlotte's words about protecting our conversation ran through my mind. I looked at El, the steady blue of her eyes reading the confusion in my own. I'd tell her, of course. Even if I tried to conceal what Charlotte told me, El would drag it out of me eventually. I couldn't lie to her. We were bound together, with a tether likely stronger than any supernatural bond.

Luis would need to know as well, although I didn't fancy breaking the news that he was a supe and that we were forcefully linked by some creepy bond our dead mothers decided to force on us. I was obviously going to need an adjustment period while I digested that information.

And then my eyes trailed to Jax and Soren. Comparatively, I hardly knew them. They'd shown up in my life, my world, in a rampant storm of chaos and fear. But after the few weeks we'd spent together, we'd grown closer, developed a trust. My breath hitched at the gray swirls in Soren's eyes, at the steady pulsing of his jaw muscles.

Yes, I'd tell them all. I'd trust them all. "I'll explain everything. I promise. But not here." I pulled my dress down an inch or two, suddenly feeling uncomfortably exposed and started marching down the street. "Back at the hotel. Booze during the discussion would be good."

"Uh, Dessa?" El called to my back. "Hang on, wait a second, would you?"

I rolled my eyes and kept walking. "No, I told you I'll explain everything back at the hotel. I want to change and be less out in the open."

"That's fine. But, um, you're walking in the opposite direction of the hotel." El's tone was off and I knew she was struggling with deciding whether she should laugh at my mistake or grow more worried.

"Right." I paused and turned around, too lost in my thoughts to be embarrassed. "Other way then." I walked past them and led the way back to our temporary sanctuary.

TWENTY-THREE

I sat in the hotel bar by myself, nursing a bourbon with no pretense of enjoying it. After relaying Charlotte's revelations to the group, I found that I needed a few moments to myself to digest the information she'd given. More importantly, to avoid the shocked stares awaiting me in our suite.

Jax and Soren had worn identical expressions of surprise, and El clutched my arm in comfort during the entire retelling. It was mostly Luis I was avoiding, and I hoped that El would share some of that comfort and compassion with him. I blinked hard, trying to erase his reaction from my mind. He didn't yell or freak out; he just stared straight at me, his expression completely neutral. There was a puzzle, in his mind, that he was working out, and I couldn't help but feel a part of him hated me for Charlotte's story. He'd been pulled into this mess because of me; hell, he was in danger now because of me. I dragged him across the west coast like a dog wearing an invisible leash.

Was our friendship even real? Or was the connection and draw I felt with him just some hocus pocus the supernatural community cooked up? Did it matter?

I threw the rest of the bourbon back and signaled the bartender for another when I felt a presence on the stool next to mine.

"Doing okay there, Black?" Soren ordered a whisky and studied me quietly, his eyes dropping down to my oversized band t-shirt and baggy black sweatpants. "You changed."

I nodded, not sure which of his points I was answering in the affirmative. "How's Luis?"

Soren cleared his throat and drained his glass before signaling for another. "I think he's okay. In shock, of course, but then again I think we all are, more or less. El's talking with him now upstairs. You had some idea that you were different, you knew you could see auras.

For him? Well, I imagine that learning he has an ability and is tethered to you came out of nowhere. Especially since this whole world of energy users is completely new to him."

My vision blurred. And I sucked in a few breaths of air as I willed the tears not to fall. "He hates me."

"No, not at all."

"If he doesn't now, he will. He'll realize eventually, if he hasn't already, that he's literally been forced into my life. Our entire friendship is a fraud, a stupid supe magic trick." I took another sip, punishing myself with the taste.

"I don't think the human is capable of ever hating you, Black. It's not like this is all your fault. You're just as much a victim to the situation as he is." He chuckled softly. "I guess he's not really a human though, is he? I'll have to come up with some other derogatory term to call him."

I rolled my eyes and shoved Soren in the shoulder. His answering chuckle told me that was the exact reaction he wanted.

"I hate not knowing more. It's like Charlotte could tell me just enough to drive me crazy, but not enough to give me any real answers. I don't understand why people were after my mother, why they're after me. I don't know how to access these stupid abilities she was talking about." I ripped the small napkin under my glass into tiny shreds as my stomach sank. "You don't think Sam knows about this do you? That he knew about me, about Luis, the whole time?"

As soon as the questions were out of my mouth, I knew the answers. "No, never mind. Sam wouldn't lie about something like this. Plus, he's a terrible liar, I'd know. And he wouldn't willingly keep me in the dark about something this important. I wonder what my dad knew though. If that's why he never spoke about my mother. Did he know the real reason she died? And honestly, how do I act around Luis now? Michael was my sort of boyfriend, and bam, turns out he's a supe spying on me to get to El. Or maybe to get to me, I don't even know. Luis is one of my best friends, and bam, turns out he's been forced into that position against his will. It makes it hard to push past the bullshit to see the truth."

Soren's eyes darkened, and he reached a long finger up to my cheek, wiping away a tear I didn't even notice fall. He stared at the liquid, as if mesmerized, before closing his large, calloused hand around my own. "You get tonight to fall apart, Black. A lot was thrown at you today. But only tonight. Because tomorrow we have work to do and after the party, we need to learn more about this block you have and how to break it. I think it's the first step to figuring out how to protect you from whatever or whoever's after you."

"You're going to help me?" The words stuck in my throat when my eyes caught his intense gaze. "I mean, don't you think you have enough to figure out with El?"

Soren let out a short, dark laugh. "Yes, obviously I'm going to help you. We're all going to help you. We aren't just going to abandon you to figure this out on your own. El would likely castrate us if we even thought about it. Besides, it's entirely possible that whoever is after you is also after El. I don't think it's a coincidence that you two found each other." He paused, reaching his hand slowly up to my cheek, sliding it to the back of my neck so that I looked at him. "And Luis is your friend because you're you. The bond may have physically drawn him to you in Seattle, but you both chose to be friends. Supernatural bonds strengthen through free will. He wants to be near you, that's why he was able to track you like he did to the cabin. Trust me, he doesn't look at you the way he looks at you because someone's forced him to."

Soren's thumb drew unconscious circles near the base of my ear and my breath hitched at his closeness. I watched, fascinated by the slow tensing of the muscles in his jaw and tried to remind my brain that it needed oxygen, and my heart that it didn't need to pulse so rapidly.

His eyes travelled down to my mouth, where they lingered briefly, as if in a trance. "Being dragged to Seattle and along the west coast? Entering into some unknown battle with unknown supernatural forces? You're worth it, Black. If that idiot can't see that, then he isn't."

My body hummed with his closeness, with his words, and I swam in the milky gray swirls of his eyes. I could feel and hear my blood pulling through my veins, the energy in my body doing everything it could to get closer to him. "Soren—"

He swore softly and crashed his lips against mine. The kiss wasn't gentle, but hard and angry. After a moment of stillness, I heard a soft growl build in his chest and his tongue lightly parted my lips, infusing my mouth with the taste of whiskey. With the taste of him. I was dizzy with the feeling, needing more, all that he would give.

His hands fell from the back of my neck, down to my hips, until he lifted me off my stool and onto his lap. With our bodies glued together, he deepened the kiss, his lips softening against my own, his tongue slowly sweeping along mine, savoring.

I rocked my hips closer to him, the small movement enough to make him groan into my mouth and rake his teeth over my bottom lip. His fingers dug into my hips, rocking me across his lap where his arousal was glaringly evident.

"Hey, this is a hotel. You can go do this shit in your room. It's kind of the whole point of having one." The bartender's laughter pulled us out of the spell. Soren pulled away from me, depositing me back on my stool as quickly as he could.

"Fuck." He slammed his hand into the counter before draining the rest of his glass and mine.

Then he left the bar and went outside without another word or glance in my direction.

I ordered another drink, shooting it back the moment the bartender finished pouring. My body was tingling, my heart was pounding, and I felt practically dizzy with the feeling of Soren on my lips. No longer willing to put up with the bartender's knowing smile and raised eyebrow, I threw him some cash and forced my wobbly legs to make the short trek up to our suite.

The second I opened the door, Luis stood from the couch.

"There you are." He walked over to me and pulled me into a hug. My thoughts caught up to the action, and I puzzled over the fact that a single kiss could make me momentarily forget about everything I'd learned today.

"You don't hate me?" My voice was low and husky, whether from crying or from being mauled by Soren, I wasn't sure.

"Of course I don't hate you, Odie." He took a step back and brushed a hand through his hair. "I mean this was a lot to hit me with, don't get me wrong. But I don't blame you for it. How could you have known about all this shit?" Luis grabbed my hand and pulled me to the couch. "Look, I always knew that our friendship was close, that I was linked to you somehow, that I wanted to be around you as much as possible. I craved you when I'd go more than a couple of days without seeing you. Beyond what's normal. But part of that is because we became family—you, me, Sam, and Ellie. I mean, hell, my friends used to make fun of me for always hanging around a high schooler when we met, and for continuing to work at the bar after getting a degree." He winked and smiled; when his dimples showed up, I felt my shoulders sag with relief at the sight. He didn't hate me. We were just us. He was just Luis and I was just Odie.

"So you're not mad that you're basically tethered to a glorified leash?" I meant it as a joke, but I knew that he heard the note of insecurity in my tone.

He shook his head. "Look, I don't think this bond is exactly what you think it is. El and Jax explained a bit about supernatural bonds after you stormed out of here to drown yourself in a pity party." His knee knocked playfully into my thigh, and I found myself soothed by his familiar hand in mine, his familiar touch and comfort. "It's not like I'm literally bonded to you. We think it's just a sort of awareness that makes our paths in life intersect. To be honest, I think you and I have strengthened it."

"What do you mean?"

He pulled his hand from mine and ran it through his hair again—a move he must have made several times since I'd left, judging by how messy it was. His knees bounced with nerves. "I mean that the bond didn't force us to be friends. It forced us to be near each other. And lately, well, we've grown closer in some ways. Our friendship has changed somewhat. Those are our choices, that shifting. And I think it's only helped to solidify whatever the bond is." He paused, staring ahead, unwilling to meet my gaze. "Look, Odie. When you left, with Soren and Jax, it felt like a part of me was fused to you and I needed to be around you. My ability to find you? I think that's the bond. My desire to find you? I think that's just me." Bluish purple eyes locked into mine and I saw a vulnerability reflected there I hadn't seen before. "We'll figure this all out, okay. I promise. I mean am I rattled that my memories have been manipulated and that I don't remember my mother, father, or most of my childhood? Of course. But I'm in. Completely. I'm not running away from whatever the hell is after you, or us, or whatever. I'm not going home and pretending this never happened, that I'm just a human who works at a bar. We'll figure it out. But I'm not leaving you and I won't let you shut me out. That's not how we work. Okay?"

For the second time that night, my vision blurred with emotion. I nodded, not trusting myself with words. Luis wrapped me in his arms, drawing soft circles on my back while I cried with confusion, relief, love.

After a while I must have drifted off to sleep because I woke the next morning tucked into the bed I was sharing with El, her soft snores lulling me in and out of sleep while I tried to mentally prepare myself for the day. Soren was right. I had one night to lose my shit, but today was different. I needed to focus all of my energy on getting the neutralizer so that we could start fighting back against whichever bullies tried backing us into corners.

When I resurfaced from my shower, dressed in a ridiculously fluffy robe, Jax carried in a stack of takeout boxes, the contents of which made my mouth water.

He passed me a large cardboard box. "Here Desi-girl. Grilled cheese and steamed vegetables." I wrinkled my nose at the last part. "I don't want Sam complaining that you're vitamin deficient next time he sees you." He passed food over to El and Luis. "The dude can be seriously scary when he wants to be," he muttered.

"Thanks Jax, this is great," El said, beaming while she opened her own box.

"Soren, let's go. Come socialize. Food's here." Jax screamed into his bedroom before plopping down on the couch next to me. "I seriously don't know what crawled into him, but he's been a complete ass all morning." When El opened her mouth, Jax noticed his mistake. "More than usual, I mean."

"He's probably just nervous about the party tonight. You know him, some people get anxious, Soren just gets extra surly." El's words were punctuated around crunching mouthfuls of bacon. "Seriously though, Jax, well done. This is awesome prep food. I have my work cut out for me today."

"You? I thought you, Jax, and I were just hanging out here all night?" Luis leaned over and stole a piece of bacon from Soren's pile of boxes. A risky move.

"Yeah, but who do you think is getting Dessa ready? Me. Trust me, between Soren's bad attitude today and the vision I have for her, I'll be plenty busy."

Soren walked in, and I tried to ignore the way my stomach flipped at the sight of him. He avoided eye contact with me and took his food to the small breakfast bar on the other side of the room. The dark circles under his eyes and the uncharacteristically disheveled hair told me he didn't get much sleep last night. If any. He was always tense, but the muscles in his back seemed more rigid than usual, like he was forcing himself not to completely flee from the room. Or punch a wall. Or punch one of us.

Jax pointed at his back with a crispy piece of bacon. "See, what did I tell you? Cranky ass," he mouthed. His words were soft, but the low growl that emanated from Soren told me he heard him anyway. Jax's answering grin made it clear that he'd intended for him to.

I bit into my grilled cheese, feigning ignorance as to what could have Soren so riled up. I knew he regretted kissing me last night, so I focused hard on diffusing the weird mixture of hurt, anger, and embarrassment that was jittering around in my belly. I was more than willing to pretend that the nervous butterflies were completely due to anxiety over Rennix's party tonight.

After hours of curling, painting, and powdering, El helped me stuff myself into the long black dress and corset she picked out for the party. Aside from the difficulty I now had with breathing, I loved the dress. It was made of black silk and lace and covered with an asymmetrical shawl that hid the majority of the cleavage that the corset shoved up. While the dress was long and modest, the tight fit and slits up the legs revealed what the cloth covered.

For about five minutes, El tried forcing me into a pair of black stiletto boots, going so far as to walk me around the room in them like a show pony. After realizing how much weight I had to put on her to keep from falling, she let out a melodramatic sigh and threw a pair of strappy sandals at me. Maybe I'd get really lucky and my hidden supe ability would end up being the magic of balance.

"Really, it's my fault. I don't know why I even bothered to try." She grabbed the large floral and lace mask she purchased for the occasion and fastened it across my eyes before pinning it into my elaborate hairdo of braids, twists, and silver beads. "There. You're ready." She stepped back from me with a giant smile plastered across her face as she admired her many hours of work. And I do mean hours. I was already starving again. "Perfect. Rennix will be too stunned by your beauty to suspect you of any foul play. Sometimes the perfect combination of beauty and mystery is a girl's most deadly weapon."

I laughed at her enthusiasm, though I was impressed with the results. In general, I wasn't a fan of dresses, but this one was lovely. And El had done a miraculous job on my hair. Even my makeup looked phenomenal. Which was odd, considering half of my face was covered by a mask.

"Come on, Soren should be ready, so we can do one last runthrough of the plan before you both drive down to the city." My stomach dropped at the sound of his name. He'd refused to even acknowledge my presence all afternoon, remaining instead in his usual bubble of annoyed isolation.

Still, when we made our way to the common area, I couldn't stop my eyes from seeking him out. And when they did, I gasped. Soren was dressed in a slim-fitting tailored suit. Everything he wore was black as night, including the mask across his eyes that made his gray irises pop. His lips parted slightly when our eyes met, and I saw his quick perusal of El's work. However, just as quickly, he cleared his throat, closed his mouth, and turned his attention to El. "Good, you're finally done. We should head out now, to get this all over with."

"Aye Mr. Charming, give us a second to admire Desi, won't you?" Jax walked up to me, grabbing my hand in his before he brought it up to his lips. "You're stunning." He circled around me before adding, "absolutely stunning."

When I looked over at Luis, I found him watching me with an intensity I wasn't used to. He cleared his throat softly, scratched the back of his neck, and walked up to me. His indigo eyes pierced into mine, filled with emotion from our talk last night. He pulled me to him, my eyes connecting briefly with Soren's over his shoulder. "Be careful tonight, Odie. If anything suspicious happens, if you think for even a second you might be in danger or caught out, leave. Immediately. Even if you have to leave without the prick."

"You know that he can hear you, right? Hyper vigilant kitten senses and all," I whispered back.

"That's the point." Luis pulled back a bit, and his lips pressed gently to my cheek, against the corner of my mouth. "You're beautiful, Odessa."

I looked up at him, temporarily stunned by his use of my full name. I nodded and turned to El. "Right, well El wanted to do a quick rundown before we left. As far as I know, Raifus promised that I'd feel his guidance once we entered far enough into Rennix's house. I guess we just have to trust that he won't let us down." I nodded over to Soren. "He'll distract Rennix once I sense the neutralizer, and then I'll go all Catwoman with the stealth and stealing. The second I'm done, we haul ass back here in the inconspicuous mom-van. Missing anything?"

"Contingency plans?" Jax looked up. "What's the plan if things go to shit?"

"We gather as much information as we can, while being discreet, and leave the second things go south. At the very least, this party will be supe central, so there ought to be some conversations worth listening in on." I grabbed the small clutch El tossed in my direction, opening and closing the clasp. I never understood the point of clutches. They were awkward and so very easy to misplace. I'd rather stuff my burner phone and cash into my bra. The mere suggestion sent El into a complete fit earlier. I looked up at Jax, knowing that he was the one I'd have to trust for the next part of the plan. "And you guys? If we don't return here by the early morning?"

"We leave, and don't look back," he answered, a small frown pulling his eyes down. "Don't let that be an option, Desi."

Luis grumbled in agreement, though the tension he and El exuded told me that Jax would have to drag them both out of the hotel with nothing less than brute force and his ability. They would not leave us behind willingly. I knew Luis and El well enough to feel the confirmation in my bones.

"We'll do our best, but get them out if our best isn't good enough, Jax." I hugged them all goodbye before awkwardly making my way towards Soren. Something told me that getting captured by enemy supes would be less torturous than riding alone with Soren to San Francisco.

And I was right.

TWENTY-FOUR

We spent the majority of the trip in an awkward silence, punctuated only by the low hum of the radio station Soren finally settled on. I could actually feel him trying not to look in my direction, forcing himself not to acknowledge my presence at all.

So, I focused on the dull *thrum, thrum, thrum* of the rock song, humming along mindlessly and willing my thoughts to settle on the task at hand. I refused to be one of those girls who worried more about a kiss than about heading into a potentially deadly situation. Especially when that kiss involved Soren—asshat extraordinaire.

Finally, when we were winding through the streets of San Francisco, he pulled up to a residential side-street to park after circling the block several times in search of a spot. He turned the car off and began drumming a fast beat against the steering wheel while he opened and shut his mouth several times like a fish, trying to find words that wouldn't come.

I cleared my throat, staring at the tall and compact houses out the window, all in pale, pastel colors. "Are we here?"

"It's a short walk, ten minutes or so from this spot. Just didn't want to park too close to the party."

"Right. So, should we start then?" I dug through the useless clutch for the pale peach gloss El had thrown in there. Swiping it across my lips, not because I needed a touch up, but because I needed something normal to do to cut through the tension.

"Yeah, I just wanted to chat for a second." He paused, rubbing the back of his neck so roughly that the skin turned an angry red. "About last night."

"Look, Soren. We don't have to do this. We were drunk. I was emotional. It's not a big deal. It's clear from your reaction it was a mistake. So, can we just drop it and pretend it never happened? We have way more important issues at hand than a drunken make-out session."

I watched out of the corner of my eye as his jaw muscles clenched. The leather on the steering wheel creaked under his grip. With a quick nod, he opened his door. "Yes, I think that's best. That we forget it. It didn't mean anything. It was a stupid drunken mistake and we should try to pretend like nothing happened." He mirrored my words, almost more to himself than to me, stood up, and started walking at a slow pace down the street.

I followed, grinding my teeth, reminded by his brisk dismissal that Soren was an asshole. I'd make damn sure that I wouldn't kiss him again. Or entertain any PG-13 thoughts about him. Or think about the way the suit fit perfectly around his ass.

We spent the next ten minutes in an uncomfortable silence, the only sound my heavy breathing. Corsets freaking sucked. Thank the gods I wasn't born in another century. Wearing this thing for a few hours was bad enough—I couldn't imagine dealing with this every day. It seemed that women had spent forever finding ways to torture themselves for the sake of beauty. And how ridiculous, really, in the grand scheme of things. When we were done with this mess, I was *so* inventing a vain torture device for men, so they wouldn't feel left out.

"This is it." Soren stopped suddenly in front of a large house, causing me to crash into him. After rubbing my shoulder, where a bruise would likely appear tomorrow, I looked up. Actually, house might not be the best word. It looked more like a museum. Or a mansion. Or a small city entrapped in layers of paneling and concrete, or whatever the hell huge houses were made out of these days. He looked in my direction, waiting for my nod before he walked up to the door. "Just remember, in and out as soon as we can."

The door swung open, revealing a tall gray-haired man in a tuxedo. His eyes were covered by a teal mask that was somehow dull compared to the bright blue of his eyes. He was dressed like a Victorian butler, but he was equally terrifying and welcoming. I imagined Rennix hired him specifically with that combination in mind. When you were an influential supe, it was probably wise to layer your guests with a healthy dose of intimidation.

"Welcome." Teal Eyes blinked and bowed slightly, leading us from the foyer (at least I think that's what rich people called entryways) into a huge ballroom.

I swallowed my gasp. The room was filled with maybe two

hundred people, all lit up in varying degrees of silver and gold. I knew everyone here would be a supe, but still. Seeing so many in one place simultaneously filled me with fear and excitement. I had chills along my arms. Soren pressed his hand into the small of my back before nodding to the doorman and leading us into the masses. This wasn't a cocktail party. This was a full-on ball. El wasn't so far off in her costume choices.

"There're so many," I whispered, unable to keep the shock out of my voice.

Soren held a long finger up to his lips. "Be careful, Black. I'm not the only one in the room with excellent hearing." His words skirted along my neck and ear, sending chills down my spine for a completely different reason.

He was right though. If there were any other shifters in the room, we would be overheard. I'd need to keep my commentary to a minimum. I kept my thoughts to myself as I studied the decor. The room's walls were draped in expensive tapestries and fabrics, lit by hundreds of candles and an enormous chandelier. The guests were dressed elegantly in gowns and tuxedos, with most of the women's arms covered in elaborate gloves. The scene looked like it was stolen from an old storybook, crafted thoughtfully with an attention to detail that even El would be impressed by.

"Soren Tesker." A tall, deep-skinned man approached us from behind. "I'd recognize that white-blond head and arrogant strut anywhere." His words were laced with laughter.

Soren's hand dug into my back and I felt his posture stiffen. "Rennix. I was in the area, figured I'd stop by and catch a glimpse of one of your famous soirees."

Rennix smirked, his golden eyes the only clue that he didn't trust Soren. "Of course. Welcome. This is, perhaps, the most elaborate soiree, as you call it, yet." He turned to me, his face lighting up in a more genuine smile. I swallowed back the thrill of fear and excitement running through me. He was stunning, even with a mask covering part of his face. "And who is your guest?"

"I'm Od—"

Soren cleared his throat.

"Odette. Thank you for allowing me to be here. It's quite lovely." My cheeks reddened, not out of flirtation, but out of frustration with myself for almost revealing my name.

I was so not stealth.

Rennix bowed ever so slightly before grabbing my hand and pressing it to his lips, soft like velvet. "The pleasure is mine. I just ask that you save me a dance later. We can't leave you with this bore all night. It would be a disservice to such beauty."

I smiled demurely, taking in the gold aura bathing Rennix. He was a powerful manipulator, that much was clear. Soren had warned me that Rennix was a well-known lion-shifter. Probably the most powerful one alive. But no amount of preparation could prepare me for the predatory strength that practically oozed from his pores.

"Right, well. I better get Odette a drink then. Enjoy your evening, Rennix." Soren directed me towards the bar, his hand offering a comforting pressure against my lower back.

"Just a glass of red wine for me, please," I said, as soon as we made it to the marble counter. Really, my nerves wanted something stronger, but I imagined it wasn't a great idea to try to pull one on Rennix while totally hammered. I thumbed the lace detail along my bodice, hoping that having something to sip on would take the edge off. Pulling a heist in a building crowded with so many supes was a lot less intimidating when we were in a hotel room a whole city away. Now it just seemed like an absurdly naive idea.

"What about you, handsome?" The bartender turned her attention back to Soren, her green eyes unabashedly checking him out. I swallowed my retort but settled for rolling my eyes at her. It wasn't even like she could fully see his face. And I was right there. For all she knew, I was Soren's girlfriend.

"I'll take Balvenie. Neat." Soren flashed her a sexy smile, showing just enough of his perfectly straight, white teeth. I ground my own. It didn't help that the woman was gorgeous, curvy, and wearing a dress that revealed more than it covered.

"Ooh. I like a man with good taste." Her eyes slid over to me. "Mostly good taste anyway."

I drank the wine glass, turning away from them as I surveyed the room. I didn't have time to get in a catfight, though that was perhaps more appealing than stealing some ancient supe artifact.

People were dancing everywhere, but in no single style. There was a feeder couple dancing a slow waltz, and just next to them, a manipulator-feeder duo was grinding against each other like they were in a club. I placed all of my attention on the room's occupants, trying to ignore the jealousy and annoyance bubbling in my stomach. Soren was an asshole. One I had no interest in, as of twenty minutes ago. I just needed to remind my traitorous body of that fact. And to do that, I'd need to force myself to forget the feel of his lips, and that intense sensation of rightness when we were pressed together. Hormones told lies all the time, nothing to write home about.

My breath hitched as my eyes fell on a nose ring, piercing a familiar woman a few feet away. Her mask was just a thin, translucent piece of lace that disguised nothing but complemented her beautiful caramel skin. Still, the air of knowingness in her sharp eyes made her more mysterious than all the other guests I'd eye-stalked. I cleared my throat, elbowing Soren in the side.

He grunted. "Jesus, what?" He sent an apologetic smile to the bartender before turning back to me.

I pulled myself up on tiptoes, leaning into his ear and speaking as quietly as I possibly could— my words so soft that even I couldn't hear them. "That's the supe Michael was with at Inferno. The fire-manipulator." I nodded discreetly in her direction, disguising the moment as a neck roll. I could be stealth. It was a thing I could try.

He nodded, letting me know he'd keep an eye on her before getting back to the bartender.

I rolled my eyes and stormed off, with my almost-empty glass of wine. If Soren wanted to spend tonight flirting, fine. It wasn't like Raifus had given us much to go on for this party, plan-wise. We were mostly just winging it. I'd go mingle and see if I could overhear anything interesting while I waited for Raifus's mysterious clue to direct me to the neutralizer.

After a few feet, I managed to get in the way of four different couples. Which was a special sort of achievement.

"Watch it, girl," a red-haired feeder woman snarled at me. She yanked her dress out from underneath my shoe, causing me to lose my balance.

A large hand grasped my arm, stopping me before I ungracefully face-planted in the middle of a ball.

So not Cinderella. So not stealth.

"We meet again, Odette." Rennix's deep laughter washed over me. "And so soon. It must be fate."

I nodded, locking onto his golden eyes. "Or clumsiness—" I paused for a beat, considering. "I like the sound of fate better."

"How about that dance?" He looked back at the bar and tsked. "Since it seems your date is otherwise occupied."

I nodded, unable to think of a good excuse not to dance with the host. At the very least, it would be a good time to get more information. "I should warn you though. My dancing is no more graceful than my walking."

"I'm always up for a challenge, Odette." He wrapped one hand around mine, placing his other against my hip. I smiled softly at the distance he let remain between us. Guys in human clubs could totally learn about manners and personal space from supes. "And if it makes you feel better, I'm an excellent leader."

I calmed my pulse, moving my glance from the elaborate guests back to Rennix. "So, have you and Soren known each other long?" I asked.

"Since we were children."

"And judging from your affectionate greeting, I'm guessing you aren't close?"

He chuckled softly, turning me gently to the beat. I wasn't a great dancer, but he was—his leading enough to make me look almost coordinated. "You could definitely say that. We had a falling out many years ago, when we were young. That, coupled with the rivalry between our families? Well, I don't think our reactions will be affectionate anytime soon." He paused, looking down at me with a warm curiosity. "And how is it that you came to be close with Soren?"

There was friendliness in his voice and eyes, but there was also power and control, and that same kind of knowingness I'd seen in the mysterious friend of Michael. It was enough to keep me on edge, to keep me alert. I found myself wanting to know the history between Rennix and Soren, but also the history between Rennix and Raifus. Raifus made it clear that Rennix and he had a past, that Raifus wasn't welcome here. Why? I cleared my throat. "We haven't known each other long. My brother is an energy user and Soren knows him well. We were introduced through him."

When in doubt, lie your ass off.

His lips turned down slightly and I sent up a silent plea that he couldn't hear the pounding of my heartbeat. "I see. And would I know your brother?"

"I don't think so. He wasn't raised in the Veil. He was raised with me and my mom. Neither of us have abilities." There. Very inconspicuous. Vanilla.

A small wrinkle lined his forehead and I began to question whether he believed me. Could shifters sense lies? Did their super hearing and powerful sense of smell work like it did in the movies? From my experiences with El, it seemed unlikely, but I'd have to ask her or Soren about it sometime. Probably would have been smart to ask before tonight.

The teal-eyed butler and intimidator-extraordinaire walked up to Rennix, whispering in his ear. The slight arch of Rennix's eyebrow coupled with the dark expression washing over his face had me wishing that I didn't have boring human-level hearing.

Rennix nodded and watched the butler until he disappeared from the room. Then, he looked down at me with a sad smile. "Well, Odette. It seems that I am needed elsewhere. A host's duty is never done. I do hope that we will meet again, tonight or in the future." He bowed slightly, kissing my hand once again. "Thank you for the dance."

And then, like his butler, he left the room.

When I looked around to spot Soren, I found him chatting with the bartender, who was no longer anywhere near her bar, while standing covertly close to the mysterious fire-manipulator. Not wanting to disturb whatever mojo he was working in order to glean information, I walked along the perimeter of the ballroom until I reached the most glorious winding staircase I'd ever seen.

It was then, as I touched the bannister that I felt my necklace pulse. Gently, at first. In fact, I had to concentrate for a moment just to be sure I wasn't imagining things, that the wine hadn't gone to my head as they say. But it was there.

TWENTY-FIVE

A soft hum vibrated against my neck, pulling me forward with a quiet yearning.

After glancing around at the dancing, intoxicated guests, I was certain no one was paying me any attention. Soren scanned the crowd. He'd lost sight of me after Rennix left and was turning every which way trying to spot my trail again. Not wanting to call attention to myself by waving feverishly at him, and filled with a sense of fear that the thrum would leave if I walked towards him, I stepped onto the stairs. Because I was sure, beyond a shadow of a doubt, that this was where the necklace was leading me. I silently reminded myself to apologize to Raifus. I thought he was half mad when he told me a necklace could lead me to another necklace.

When I reached the top of the landing, the guests in the ballroom were no longer visible. Which was good, because it meant that I was no longer visible to them either. The pendant was pulsing more clearly now, I could no longer mistake it as my own heartbeat or fleeting fancies caused by too much to drink. I stepped to the right, walking a few feet before I noticed the pulsing grow more faint.

Wrong way then.

I turned back, going left instead and with the encouragement of the necklace walked down a long hallway filled with ugly, abstract paintings that were likely worth a fortune. It took everything I had to keep walking, to not give in to the insane urge to open a few doors and dig through Rennix's house. The desire to snoop was an insatiable itch. What else could a man like Rennix, with both social and political power, be hiding?

The hallway ended with a room, and when I put my hand against the door, the answering thrum of the necklace assured me this was the next stop on the scavenger hunt. I gripped the handle and turned, praying to the gods that Rennix left the door unlocked.

At the click, I knew that he did. And I understood why. The room was almost empty, just an unused guest room that had nothing but a bed and nightstand. The cobwebs along the posts made it clear the room hadn't been used in quite a while. It was a strange place to hide such a powerful artifact. Then again, no one who came looking for it would bother searching in such a nondescript room. They'd scavenge for a safe or look behind the paintings that lined the walls of the house. Raifus's parlor trick was a useful one; this was the most intense game of hot and cold I'd ever played.

I surveyed the room, trying to quickly catalog any hiding places. Gritting my teeth, I slid my hand underneath the mattress, searching for the neutralizer or holes in the padding to hide it, while fearfully trying to make sure that no spider or other unsightly critter surprised me by skittling across my hand.

Nothing.

I opened the drawer of the cherry-wood nightstand, pressing on all sides trying to find a trap door. There were old postcards and a couple of paperback books. I shook them loose, just in case Rennix went old-school prohibitionist and hid the necklace in a cutout.

Nothing.

There was a small door on the other side of the room that I assumed was a closet. The pulse from the pendant told me this was where I needed to go. When I pulled open the door, instead of finding a closet, I was faced with another staircase, this one much less grand and more worn than the first.

And so, I climbed.

And when I reached the top, I found another hallway, about half the length as the other and eerily quiet and abandoned. I couldn't even hear the loud hum of the party anymore.

It was when I pressed my fingers against the third door on the right that I knew I had found it. The necklace pulsed, a steady beat.

Thrum. Thrum. Thrum.

I couldn't ignore it now if I wanted to.

This door, unfortunately, was locked. I pulled two bobby pins from my hair, sending silent apologies to El for ruining her hard work. I unbent the metal. Using one as a tension wrench and the other as a pick, I worked the lock as Sam had taught me years ago. I was notorious for losing my keys and he wanted to be sure I'd never get stuck outside in the rain waiting for him. I silently thanked him for being such a badass and for turning my forgetfulness into a useful life skill. That's what good uncle-brother-friends were for. Still, with someone as rich as Rennix was, I expected a more high tech locking mechanism.

Click.

With a smile I pushed my way into the room, confronted with a wealth of objects, glass cases, and boxes. Knowing there was no way I could sort through all of these items in a few minutes, let alone a few hours, I closed my eyes, shutting off all sensation but the now ecstatic pulse against my chest—

Which wasn't the greatest idea because I tripped over a box and slammed my head into a shelf lined with pricey looking knick-knacks.

Eyes open then.

I followed the steady pulse until I reached a glass cabinet in the back. It was filled with the most beautiful jewelry I'd ever seen: diamonds the size of quarters, jewels as big as ping-pong balls, and ornate crowns that belonged on royalty.

None of this was what I was looking for though. I picked the small lock of the case, rifling gently through the contents and trying not to disturb anything from its original spot.

And then I saw it.

Tucked behind a beautiful tiara was a tarnished chain sporting a three-stone pendant. It was pushed in the back, as if it were there by mistake, seemingly junk compared to the other elaborately beautiful jewels the case housed. The second my finger touched it, my own pendant let out a final, pleased thrum, happy to be united with the object it was bonded to. The pendant hanging around my neck was now nothing more than a link to my best friend and my favorite accessory.

I tied the neutralizer around my neck, tucking it safely underneath layers of silk and lace. I needed to grab Soren and get the hell out of this house as soon as possible. I *so* mastered the whole stealth thing. Here less than an hour and I'd already found what we came for.

"An interesting choice, Odette."

I spun around to see Rennix leaning casually against the door frame.

"Now I wonder—why would you come all the way up here and grab that raggedy necklace when there are far more valuable and beautiful pieces within reach? Though I suppose since you clearly came here for it, you know that particular pendant's value, don't you? So tell me, Odette, who exactly are you and why, precisely, do you want that necklace?"

He smiled tightly, the predatory gleam I noticed in his eyes earlier far eclipsed any friendly pretense and had me shrinking back against the glass cabinet. What did you say to someone when you were caught stealing from them?

"Ummm—" I stalled, glancing around the room for an escape or a lie. Neither were blatantly obvious to me. "I just need to borrow this for a little bit. For a friend. If that's okay?" The truth then. I shrugged. Maybe he'd let me. It didn't hurt to ask.

Well, steal and *then* ask.

Rennix stepped forward, stalking me like the giant predator I knew he was. He growled softly, inching his way along the perimeter, never removing his eyes from my own. He was playing with me, like a cat with a mouse. And I was distinctly uncomfortable with being the mouse in this scenario.

Seeing an opening, I decided to run for the doorway. Stupid plan, but it was all I had. My first clue should have been the giant grin that spread across Rennix's face when he saw me sprint. The second clue should have been the fact that he didn't move an inch to pursue me. But it wasn't until my face collided with an invisible force field, landing me unceremoniously on my ass when I reached the doorway, that it became clear. I was trapped.

In this very small room.

With this very dangerous man.

Whom I'd just pissed off. Who? Or Whom? I guess it didn't really matter at a moment like this.

I cleared my throat, glancing at Rennix out of the corner of my eye while I pushed myself up from the ground. "Well, I wasn't expecting that."

"Come now, Odette. You didn't really think it would be that easy to steal from someone like me? You may have made your way up here, but I have cameras and guards everywhere. I was informed the second you left the ballroom and started roaming my halls. Halls which, by the way, are off limits to my guests." He picked up a random chalice along one of the room's many shelves and began tossing it back and forth between his hands. I followed the cup's movements hypnotically. "I decided to let you roam, to see what you were after. Imagine my surprise when you almost immediately entered the plainest room in the house and quickly found the second staircase. At first, I thought perhaps it was a coincidence. Or luck." Setting the chalice back down, he stalked closer to me, at ease and unconcerned. "Then, you made your way to this room. Fine, I thought, someone must have told her where I kept some of my more valuable possessions. I'd grill my staff later to find the mole. There aren't many who know of this room or its contents, so it wouldn't be hard to trace back to the informant...but then you swiftly made your way to that cabinet." He nodded quickly to the glass case that housed the neutralizer only moments ago. "And you didn't show any interest in anything that case contained. Finding instead, almost immediately, that pendant. Even though it was hidden behind several other items and appears far less extravagant than almost every other item in this room." He crouched down next to me, studying my face. When he tilted his head in a strange animalistic movement, I flinched.

"I...like simpler things is all."

A terrifying grin lit his features. "I think we both know that pendant is anything but simple, Odette. What I want to know, however, is how you found it and with such ease. I am the only one in the house who knew of its location. The only one, I had thought, who even knew I was the owner of that particular...investment."

"Luck?"

The smile disappeared almost instantly from his face. "I'll not play games, girl. Who are you and who are you working with?"

"I'm nobody, I'm not working with anybody. I'm here on my own." I infused my voice with a confidence I didn't feel. Hopefully it was convincing.

Rennix's answering growl suggested it wasn't.

"Fine. I have ways of making you talk, if you won't of your own volition. Though it would be a shame to ruin that pretty face." He lifted a single finger, and I watched, mesmerized, as he transformed his nail into a claw. I didn't realize a body-manipulator could shift in isolation like that. My heart pounded erratically as he lifted the long claw to my face, slicing gently through my mask until it fell away in pieces. "Ah see, lovely. Let's not mar it with scars, Odette. Just answer my questions. I don't enjoy torture."

Sick of being the prey, I squared off, lifting my fists in preparation for a fight I knew very well I couldn't win. But I couldn't leave through Rennix's magical barrier and I wasn't going to let him torture me without putting up a fight. "Let me leave. Now." I swung a fist at his face, catching only his ear as he dodged with ease. "Er, please?"

"The girl came prepared to play, did she? More fun for me, then." With a Cheshire grin he shook his head and I watched in amazement as he transformed into a fully-grown lion in front of my eyes. I turned to the door, and found a soundless Soren pounding furiously against the invisible barrier. He must have followed my scent or Rennix or something. I had almost forgotten he was downstairs flirting with the bartender and stalking the Inferno girl.

With a quick look his way, I screamed for him to run, tossing the necklace at the doorway—hoping the necklace might be able to reach him if I couldn't.

Wrong. The pendant bounced off the empty space before Soren's chest and landed on the ground. The lion and I watched as he bent to try and pick it up, his fingers grasping only air. Rennix let out a sound that I supposed would be the sound a lion made when it laughed—if lions did such things—while I raced forward and reattached the necklace around my neck. So much for trying to take one for the team.

Rennix stalked towards me, a low growl vibrating in the cage of his large chest. The moment he lunged for me, I dodged. I escaped his claws but fell against a wooden chest. Hard. I cringed, hoping my shoulder was only bruised, not injured worse. Then again, I was likely going to die in a moment, so I guess it didn't really matter. Soren taught me how to fight against a shifter predator, but that lesson mainly consisted of running away or playing against the animal's instincts. Neither of those options worked when I was prey trapped inside the caged walls of Rennix's trophy room.

Deciding to go on the offensive, since I doubted Rennix would expect that, I lunged for him, fists raised. And, honestly, punching a lion in the face was a lot like punching a human in the face. It hurt. A lot.

With an annoyed grumble, Rennix lifted a paw and sliced my side. I wasn't sure how deep it was, and the adrenaline running through my body prevented me from feeling the extent of it, but there was blood. Like a lot of blood. And my beautiful dress was torn and ruined. El would be so disappointed.

Desperate, I started picking up random objects along the shelves, bathing the room in dust as I whipped them at Rennix. He dodged most of my attempts, but I grinned with pained satisfaction when a particularly large stone ball hit him in the side, forcing out an annoyed grunt of discomfort. I was probably bleeding to death but basking in the enemy's pain dissipated some of my fear. It was the little things.

I looked back at Soren, watching as he ripped against the wall next to the barrier. He was in his panther form and, briefly, I looked at both of the beasts and found them beautiful. Not many humans could say that they died at the hands—er, paws?—of two predatory cats.

Not that anyone said anything after they were dead.

Pressing my hands against my side, I studied the bloody trail around the room, like I was painting a grotesque, abstract masterpiece with my body. Until I looked back up at Soren and found him no longer alone. There was a man, looking on as Soren dug his way slowly into the wall separating him from my invisible cage.

And then I blinked, and both the man and the panther were no longer there.

Good. Hopefully Soren got away. It was good that he wasn't here, wasn't around an angry Simba-supe who was about to eat me alive.

Safe. He was safe.

My fingers brushed against a long, old knife. It may have been old, but it was sharp and it looked deadly. Wrapping my fingers around the handle I braced myself to meet the lion's next lunge with a heady thirst for blood. I positioned my arm discreetly to slice his underbelly while he attacked. If I was lucky, maybe I could take him out with me.

I dodged at the right moment, slicing slightly off center along his ribcage. He let out a prominent growl that told me he was done playing with his prey. His next blow would be the killing one. I lifted the knife, staring at my blood-caked hand in a sort of horrified fascination, and bent my knees, ready for my final strike. I felt a rush of guilt run through me—I didn't want to hurt a beautiful lion and I didn't want to hurt Rennix either. I'd entered his home and stolen from him, knowing full well that he was a territorial jungle predator. Still, my hand raised, poised for attack as he lunged—because my survival instincts were stronger than my remorse.

Until I was blocked suddenly by a man's broad chest, with strong arms wrapped around me.

And as I fought to get loose, I felt my world go dizzy and clear all at the same time, while a profound sense of thereness and then not clouded my mind. No longer fighting to get free, I clung to the strong arms for stability, closing my eyes tight against the intense wave of nausea. I would not throw up. What an awful thing to do and feel right before you died. At least these arms smelled good, like the ocean and warmth. There were worse scents to die smelling.

My eyes opened, slow and sticky from being closed so tightly. Before getting my bearings, I leaned over and threw up, no longer able to hold power over the nausea.

A large hand rubbed circles along my back, silently providing comfort, and I was struck by an icy feeling of familiarity—comforting and terrifying. When I peered up, my throat burning and stomach still churning, I met a pair of concerned black eyes.

"Michael." The word was a croaky whisper that barely made it past my lips.

TWENTY-SIX

I stood up instantly, if not shakily. My hands balled into fists, my body rigid in a defensive posture. "What're you doing here?" I turned my head, taking in the serene desert landscape around us, not a soul in sight. For a brief moment, I allowed myself to appreciate the exquisite clarity of the moon and stars, so big and beautiful. Perhaps even more so moments after I was sure I'd taken my last breath. "Where are we?"

"Nevada. I wasn't sure where you and the others were staying in San Francisco and figured we'd need some time and space to chat first. You can't exactly get rid of me easily in the desert." He paused, scratching his head. "But I promise I'll take you to them soon."

"And Soren?" I scanned the horizon, trying to spot his familiar pale hair and striking eyes, but all I saw was dust and the sky and Michael.

"He's also in Nevada, about eighty miles north of us."

I tensed. "What? Why?" I inched a bit to the right, so that if I struck Michael in the face, the hit would land.

He smiled tightly, and I was momentarily struck by his harsh beauty. He was wearing a dark T-shirt, covered by a leather jacket. Dark hair stubbled his jaw and he looked so much more fierce and powerful than he'd ever seemed when we were dating, dangerous even. I wondered how much of the sweet, bookish persona that I knew was fabricated.

"I grabbed him in his panther form. The second we landed, he tried to rip my head off. I got away before he did any real damage." He nodded to his left arm where his jacket was sliced open and a deep-but-not-too-deep cut gleamed through underneath. He peeled the leather off, examining the cut on his arm with amused interest, his tattoos peeking out beneath his shirt, tracing his muscles in complex and interesting patterns. If anything, the claw mark almost

226

looked like it was at home on his arm, another fierce and striking battle scar. "To be honest I don't think he liked me much before he knew I was a space-manipulator, but his amplified hate and anger were more than I'd anticipated. I told him I'd go save you then be back when he was calm and in human form again." He looked up at me briefly, the hint of a sly smile battling the shyness in his dark eyes. "I wanted to get you out of there first, but I knew that once you were gone, Soren wouldn't stand a chance and then you'd hate me even more than you already do. They'd all be on him instantly. Rennix was toying with you. I'm not even sure if he really would have ended up killing you if given the chance. The look in his eye, he was almost intoxicated with intrigue. He may have just kept you." The angles of Michael's face hardened. He shivered slightly, his next words spoken so quietly I almost couldn't hear them. "Screw Soren's life. The guy's a dick anyway. I should've chanced the extra thirty seconds and taken you first."

"And how is it you knew where we were?"

He reached out a hand as if he were going to caress my arm and I took a step back. He flinched and ran a hand through his dark hair, slightly more wild and luminous than it was when I knew him. Or thought I knew him. Whoever Michael was, he wasn't the guy I befriended and dated.

"Odessa, there's a lot to tell you. But first you need to understand that I'm not going to hurt you. Gods, I would never hurt you." He paused, crouching down low to the ground with his elbows perched on his thighs and his face tilted up towards mine. I suspected he was trying to put me at ease, by taking away the intimidation of his height. It didn't work. "That day, you were so angry. And I wanted to explain everything, but I knew I needed to give you a beat to take it all in. Plus, your neighbor is absolutely terrifying." He paused a moment, a smirk briefly relieving the stoic expression on his face. "When I came back, you were gone."

"Michael, how did you know where I was tonight?"

"Raifus."

I felt like I'd been punched.

Stunned, I dropped to the ground, a large cloud of dust painting my now destroyed dress in a sandy ash. All this time, we'd planned on Raifus helping us. Instead, he was selling us out to Michael. The enemy. Would the neutralizer even work? Was any of tonight worth it? Where did we go from here? I felt my blood rush through my veins and my head filled with a dizzy mist.

"Before you panic, it's important for you to know that Raifus also doesn't intend to hurt you. He's a very complicated guy. And things, well, they are *very* complicated. And, honestly, if he didn't tell me you might need an extraction tonight, you'd very likely be dead." Michael dropped from his awkward squatting position onto his butt, the two of us sitting across from each other, covered in blood and dust and distrust. "I've known Raifus my whole life. He's a bit unusual at times, but he's not malicious. I trust him with my life."

"Well, that's great seeing as your word and trust mean so much to me right now. And anyway, if that's true, why didn't he just have you get the stupid necklace yourself? You could've just zipped in and out of that damn room. If he really means no harm, why did he have me do it?" I stared off at the infinite horizon, unable to bring myself to quite look Michael in the eyes.

I could feel him stalling, drawing lines with his finger in the ground. "Partially because I couldn't and partially because it was a test to see if you could."

My head snapped towards him. "What do you mean it was a fucking test? You need to be clearer than that, Michael."

"Only you could find the necklace so easily. I could get into the house, hell into any room in the house. But I never would have found the neutralizer. As it was, it took me a good fifteen minutes to find you in that room upstairs. I was going door-to-door upstairs straining to hear voices and the fight. It wasn't until I heard Soren screaming your name at the top of his lungs that I was able to find you."

"Why me? Why was I able to find it?" I fingered the pendant El had given me, layered underneath the neutralizer. "Because of this? Because Raifus made this?"

Michael rolled his neck, considering. "Partially."

"Couldn't he have just made you a pulsing trinket too?"

"No, it's more complicated than that. You see he was able to forge a connection with you through the pendant, he used that connection to help you find the neutralizer. All I can say now is that it wouldn't have worked if he tried to forge that connection with anyone else."

"So, he sent us in there like freaking guinea pigs? On some

ridiculous hunch that I might be able to locate the thing? With absolutely no advice on how to get out once I'd actually found it?" The nausea and confusion were quickly being overridden by a blanket of anger and pulsing rage.

"Perhaps, but he also sent me in after you. I was the fail-safe. The rest is for him to tell you. It might shock you, but Raifus isn't a big sharer." He chuckled softly, trying to lighten the mood. "He doesn't exactly divulge every detail of his plans with me. I didn't even know he'd met with you until tonight. Didn't even know about this particular mission until tonight." He looked down at his sand-coated fingers, considering. "In fact, that's probably why he didn't tell me. I would've stopped it. Would've stopped you from going. I wasn't supposed to get as close to you as I did. We were misinformed. We thought it was Ellie, that she was the one we were looking for."

I kept my hand pressed into my side, trying to stem the bleeding. With the adrenaline coursing through my body, I'd almost forgotten what my body had just been through. "Why Ellie?"

"Well, they've been keeping her hidden for six years, for one. That's not really a normal thing to do. And second—" he paused, looking around the barren, dark desert, stalling for the words to come. "Well, that's more complicated."

He broke off and I knew that he wasn't going to finish that thought, wasn't going to give me any answers I really needed. Why couldn't anyone just be straight with me? I was getting so sick of these half-truths. "Take me to Soren, we need to get him, and I don't feel so good." I pulled my hand away and it was covered with blood. My head spun.

Michael jumped to his feet and swore. "We need to get you to a hospital now, Dess. Jesus, why didn't you tell me it was so bad?"

I stood too, the sudden movement making me even more lightheaded. "Soren first. He'll maul some random Burning Man enthusiast if he's left alone. It's not that ba—"

Michael lurched towards me. The last thing I saw were his dark eyes full of concern.

TWENTY-SEVEN

I fell in and out of consciousness, vaguely aware of being passed from one strong set of arms to another, until finally landing in an uncomfortable and narrow bed where excruciating pain slipped into a quiet numbness and, finally, into a dull ache. Later, whether a moment or an hour or a day, I thought I felt a soft, warm pressure on my forehead and the whispered words "I'll be back for you" spoken softly into my ear, but the memory was fleeting and mixed with wild dreams and soft conversations filled with familiar and worried voices.

My head was pounding, and I wanted nothing more than to sleep for the next year. Or five. But I opened my eyes and had to blink twice in order to process the ridiculous scene surrounding me. Luis was seated next to me on a hospital bed, lost in his thoughts. Soren was on the opposite side of the room, his gray eyes dark and glued in my direction. A small pressure on my left hand confirmed that El was sitting on the other side of me, clasping my arm in her lap. She was tunelessly humming some odd pop song. Jax walked into the room carrying an abundance of water bottles and snacks in his arms.

"Ah, the lion tamer is awake, is she?" He went around the room handing everyone a bottle and a package of chemicals that masqueraded as food. "You gave us a bit of a scare there, Desi-girl."

El's head spun to meet me and verify with her own eyes that I was indeed awake. She let out a shaky sigh. "You're awake!" El wiped her cheeks. "I've never seen so much blood. Your dress, it was completely drenched."

"Seriously, Odie. It's a miracle the cuts were so superficial, you truly lucked out. Some of that blood had to have belonged to Rennix." Luis's eyes poured over my face, taking in every inch with an expression of pure relief.

"What?" I croaked, rubbing my hand along my side where Rennix's claws had ripped into my body. My fingers stilled. I could

230

feel the ridges of the cut through the bandages, but it was shallow and would heal quickly. I rolled my left shoulder, finding that though it was sore and stiff, it wasn't as damaged as I thought it'd be after falling into that heavy chest. My glance drifted to Soren, his eyes dropping as soon as he caught my silent question. He'd seen the blood in that room. That was more than just a superficial scratch. "I guess I wasn't hurt as badly as I thought?"

El cleared her throat and looked at Soren out of the corner of her eye, one brow arched in curiosity. "Yeah, maybe." She paused a beat, focusing her attention back on me. "Well, I guess we should just be happy that Michael showed up when he did, though I still don't trust the prick. And I still don't understand exactly how he's mixed up in all of this."

"Yeah, how convenient," Luis mumbled under his breath. "Couldn't have shown up well before she entered into a cage match with a lion."

Michael. I scanned the room, trying to see if I'd missed him in my preliminary tally.

No, he wasn't there. I didn't know why I was surprised. It wasn't like he could just stick around and join the party like he was one of us. Saving my neck didn't make up for basically being the cause of the wild goose chase to begin with. "Where is Michael?"

"We're not really sure." El looked down at me and I could see the conflicted emotions playing out across her features. "He transported you and Soren here, and then he showed up in our hotel room to tell us where you were and what happened." She paused, glancing over at Luis with a giant grin. "But not before Luis punched him in the jaw."

"I guess now I understand why you never let me meet any of the guys you date before." Luis moved to playfully nudge me in the shoulder but, after glancing down at the bandages, stopped before making contact.

"Well, what do we do with—" my fingers felt around my collarbone, but I only found one pendant tied around my neck. "Where is it?"

El's dainty hand pressed gently on my arm. "It's here, I have it, Dess. After Michael made sure we all got here, he took the necklace. We all freaked out at first, thinking he'd just come to steal it and nothing else. But I guess he took it to Raifus, because when he brought it back half an hour later, it had this energy to it."

I studied the three stones that seemed so large on El's small frame. "It works?"

She nodded. "As long as I wear it, I can shift, but no one else can access their abilities. We had a bit of fun getting Jax to try seducing Luis, but it didn't work. Same when he tried feeding off a couple of nurses. We still need to test distance and everything, it's not totally clear how far away you have to be from the neutralizer to access your powers, but it's a start."

My eyes traced her small frame as I tried searching out her now-familiar golden aura. It was gone. I smiled, happy that at least something went right during the shitshow that was Rennix's party. "And Michael just left?"

"We weren't in the room when he brought it back. There was like a two-minute window between when the doctor came in to check on you and when we came back into the room." Luis squeezed my free hand gently. "The necklace was clasped in your hands and the room was empty."

"So what do we do now?" Jax looked up at me, his face was tense with concentration. I could tell he was trying to get his ability to work. "Have to say, glad this thing works, but this is so weird. I'm going to have to get a date the normal way if I keep hanging around you, El." He winked at her, a sly grin taking over his face. "It's okay, I could use a challenge anyway."

"I guess now that we know Michael is working with Raifus and neither one of them seems to mean us harm, we can just go back to normal. The only reason Michael was able to find us in the first place was through the necklace and ring set." My fingers danced over the black pendant hanging loose against my chest. Strange how insanely powerful it had felt when it led me to the neutralizer. "Besides, Raifus can track and if he really wanted to find El, he would."

"Yeah," Jax added, "especially since Raifus was the one who helped hide her in the first place."

"So, we go home?" I tried not to get up too quickly, but the idea of sleeping in my own bed, seeing Sam every day, and even waiting tables at The Tavern had me nostalgic and excited. "Can we leave now? I don't need to stay here, do I?"

Jax looked over to Soren, waiting for him to answer. It seemed we all looked to him as the leader of the group. Probably because he was so bossy. Definitely not because of his winning personality.

His dark eyes glanced in my direction briefly, before he stared down at his hands clasped in his lap. He hadn't uttered a word since I'd opened my eyes. "You guys should all go back to Seattle. Get back into your regular schedule. Dex, Sage, and I will head back to the Veil, see what news we can find regarding the resistance." He looked over to Jax. "You'll stay here. Be my eyes and ears. You can fight hand-to-hand combat, so if someone tries to grab either of them, you can defend even without your ability."

Aw, he included me in Jax's protection detail.

Ew, actually, scratch that. I did not want to have those gooey damsel-in-distress feelings. That wasn't me. "Hey, I'm pretty decent at that stuff now too, you know. I mean hell, I did fight a giant freaking lion earlier and live to tell the tale."

Soren's lips twitched into that almost-grin of his that had my stomach flipping in uncomfortable, traitorous ways. "Well, this way Jax can keep training you." He paused, his face darkening as he stood and began pacing around the room. "Raifus will come calling eventually. You entered into a binding contract with him, Black. You're in his debt until that debt is paid. I don't think he wants to hurt you or Ellie, but we have no idea what his intentions are or how you play into them. You're safe for now, but don't get complacent or comfortable."

His words sent a chill down my spine. I'd forgotten about my promise to Raifus. Now that we knew that he was more or less behind Michael's undercover operation in the first place, he seemed much more nefarious. Which was saying something, because the guy was already an incredibly intimidating wild card.

"Right," I muttered.

"Well I don't trust this Raifus guy or Michael, but there's nothing we can do at the moment. We'll deal with trouble as it comes," Luis said, standing up. "The doctor said that your injuries were minor and there's no sign of a concussion. She said you could stay here overnight if you wanted, but that we had the option to take you home." My facial expression told him all he needed to know. "Right. I'll go handle the discharge paperwork. We didn't use your real name, so it's kind of pointless, but I'll see if there's anything you need or that we need to do before you leave."

Jax jumped up from the seat he'd stolen from Soren. "I'll get the car. We were parked illegally, and I had to move it kind of far to avoid getting the mom-van towed."

"And I'll grab you something to wear since you can't road trip in a hospital gown and that damn lion ruined your beautiful dress." El's grimace pulled a laugh from my lips. "I'm going to kill Rennix when I meet him. That was designer." She followed Luis and Jax out of the room. Leave it to El to combine her fierce supernatural strength with her love of fashion. And sprinkle them both with a psychopathic edge.

My gaze trailed around the room and suddenly caught on Soren when I realized we were alone.

He huffed out an angry breath and resumed his pacing. He'd been hopping in and out of the chair so much that I felt like I'd been watching a tennis match since I woke up. "You shouldn't have gone up there without me. What were you thinking, Black? That wasn't the plan." His words were short, but they were filled with a tense guilt.

I shrugged. Because, really, what else was there to do. At the time, I thought it was the best option. "Did you learn anything from the bartender or that girl we saw with Michael?"

"Only that Michael's mystery girl is named Serena. She was curiously evasive of my conversation. The bartender gossiped a lot, but not about anything helpful to us."

"Soren, you saw the fight, right? With Rennix?" My hand danced along the edge of the bandage under my shirt and I carefully peeled it back to examine the damage without revealing too much of my body to Soren.

"Of course I saw the fight." Long fingers swept through his hair and he flexed what looked like every muscle in his body.

I looked at the cut and it was practically already scabbed over. No stitches, just a series of shallow, dark lines from my ribs to my belly button. I rolled my shoulder again, barely feeling any pain. "Then you saw all of that blood. What the hell happened? I collapsed when I was with Michael. There was so much blood. This—" I gestured down to the cuts. "Well, this just looks like I got into a nasty fight with a house cat a few weeks ago."

"Let it alone, Black."

"Yeah, because that totally fits in with my personality. Soren, do you know what happened?" I pushed the bandage back down, tracing the tape softly with my finger until it stayed put.

"Odessa—" My head snapped up when he used my first name. "Please just leave it."

I shook my head. I was in the dark about too many things. If this was a mystery that could be solved, I wanted an answer. "No. What the hell happened between the desert and this hospital bed?"

Soren was silent for a few moments, his glare etching into the wall like it held the answers to the world's biggest mystery. Finally, he turned back to me and said, "okay."

"Okay?" That was a lot easier than I thought it'd be. Soren always made me fight him on everything. I sat back against the pillows, ready for his explanation. Maybe the damsel-in-distress thing had its perks.

Instead of words, he slowly lifted up his shirt.

My cheeks flushed, and I tried to stare up at his face. "What the hell are you do—" my words stuttered and died off as soon as my eyes travelled south of his neck. He had four matching claw marks from his ribs to his belly button, though they were slightly deeper than mine. "What? Why do you—how do—" I looked up at him, not quite sure what I was seeing or why his torso mirrored mine.

Pushing his shirt back down, he sat at the corner of my bed, carefully keeping a few inches of space between us. His long fingers scraped against the back of his neck and he swore softly before turning to me. "Look, you can't repeat what I'm about to tell you to anyone. Jax and Ellie are the only ones who know that I can use energy to heal...that I'm a panther-shifter but also a medica-feeder." He paused, studying the question written across my face. "It's a type of feeder, but extremely rare. I don't even know if there's another in existence. I'm assuming I inherited the ability from my mother."

"Do most supes with dual lineages inherit both of their parents' abilities?"

"No. That too is extremely rare, impossible usually. They usually just inherit the dominant ability."

"So, you can heal others by mirroring their injury or illness?"

He shook his head, standing up again. I watched as he paced back and forth a few times. Soren was always wound tightly, but seeing him so anxious and lost in this room had me on edge. He was usually the image of control. "It's a complicated sort of healing. It's a type of energy-feeding and, like all feeding, it works through give and take. If I feed off of someone else to heal myself, they experience part of the illness or injury I had, but to a lesser extent. It's a useful strategy in battle if I'm sure the opponent is going to die and not reveal my secret, but it's a selfish gift to have. Because medica-feeders can only heal themselves. At least I've only ever been able to heal myself, and I'm the only medica-feeder I've heard of outside of urban legends."

"But you healed me?" I looked down at my body as the evidence stared back at us "Almost completely."

He nodded, solemn. "I don't know how." His eyes met mine, worry filling their depths. "And I need you to not tell anyone that I did, not even Jax and Ellie. I need to figure out why and how it happened first."

I thought back to our meeting with Raifus, how quickly I shook off the injuries of fighting the supes. "That day, with the air-manipulator and the two feeders—" I looked up at him, questioning.

"Yes, then too," he sat in Ellie's vacated chair by my side. "You won't tell them?"

I wasn't comfortable with keeping anything from Ellie. Not with everything we'd been through. Or Jax. As insufferable as the guy was, he'd become a close friend. But Soren did sort of save my life, and he didn't have to tell me the truth about his ability. I couldn't exactly throw his honesty back in his face. I looked up at him, my stomach dancing as my eyes met his, my very blood thrumming with the presence of him. "Okay, I won't tell them. But figure it out soon, because I don't like lying to them."

"I'll do my best, Black." He smirked then, but his almost smile fell quickly into seriousness. "For what it's worth, I'm glad the healing worked, even if I don't know why it did. I'm glad you're okay. I don't know what I would've done if—"

His eyes shifted down as his words drifted away and I recalled the misery in his face when he couldn't reach me in the room, his fury as he watched me get attacked while he could do nothing but look on and paw uselessly at the wall like a declawed house-cat. The hospital room filled with that moment, that pain of uselessness and fear.

I smiled at him and threw my pillow softly at his face to bring us back to the present. "You're just happy because now we have matching friendship scars. Don't think I didn't notice how jealous you were of mine and Ellie's jewelry set." I winked at him with a smile, unable to hold back my teasing.

He rolled his eyes, stood up, and turned towards the door muttering something about friendship scars and ridiculous girls and checking on the car situation.

"Don't be bashful, Soren. It's okay to admit we're friends now," I called after him, in better spirits than I'd been in weeks. "I'll come up with a really cool handshake."

The door to the room closed with a soft thud, but I could've sworn I heard the hallway fill with a soft, deep, trailing laugh.

ACKNOWLEDGMENTS

This book started as an experiment and as a way to deal with stress, and it wouldn't have gone beyond that if my mom wasn't there as a constant cheerleader in my corner. Thanks for always pushing me outside of my comfort zone and for encouraging me in anything and everything I set my sights on.

To my family and friends—especially my brother (for real, I'm insanely lucky I got you as a sibling, even if you hate reading), aunt, and main squeeze—thank you for your constant love and support and for putting up with me even when I'm impossible.

A HUGE thank you to all of my wonderful beta readers, particularly Allie, Camilla, E.A. Lake, P, and Rachel. This book wouldn't be complete without your help and guidance. And an extra-special thanks to P for keeping me sane while listening to my daily rants about anything and everything—I almost feel bad that your favorite ship will never be realized.

It's an odd thing to thank a dog. But I'm going to anyway, because mine is the greatest and one of my very best friends. Riggs, thanks for keeping me company on late nights while I stressed and floundered. Your wagging tail never ceases to bring a smile to my face.

Finally, if you're reading this—thank you. It's a scary and crazy and wonderful thing to write words and have people read them. I hope you enjoyed the experience.

ABOUT THE AUTHOR

Gray Holborn is a student and teacher by day and a writer by night. She spends her time reading everything she possibly can, drinking way more coffee than any human should, watching Netflix when she is supposed to be doing other things, and hanging out with her hilariously cartoonish dog.

If you enjoyed this book (or if you didn't) please consider leaving an honest review and/or spreading the word. For all authors, and especially self-published and indie authors, reviews are super important. Not only do they provide more visibility for the book, but they also provide feedback for new authors who are eager to improve their craft.

Stay tuned for Odessa's next adventure!

Made in the USA
Coppell, TX
19 July 2020

30888873R00142